PURE

The Isle of Salvatorem Chronicles

K. Violette

DEDICATION

To everyone who has ever felt like their truth didn't matter.

It does.

SAND PARADISE
NORTHERN
PARADISE
CITADEL
WESTERN
PARADISE
UNWORTHY LANDS
SOUTHERN
PARADISE
ICE
PARADISE
ISLE OF SALVATOREM

PROLOGUE

Seven-hundred years ago, the world of man was destroyed by greed and sin. Overtaken by technology and power, the Last War pitted every man against themselves until there was nothing left but the dust and ashes of a fallen society. Cities crumbled beneath their feet. Forests burned themselves in shame as the earth wept for what had become of its rulers.

Discontented with the way his fellow men had treated the earth, one man fought to revive what once was. Climbing to the very corners of the earth, he searched for the ancient alchemy of the Gods we once knew – and at last he found them. Battered, decayed scriptures speaking of doorways to the soul and harnessed powers of the earth that no one but these Gods had ever been able to obtain. Determined, and desperate to save his fellow men, he cried out to the earth to let him through, to allow him to save it from damnation. All at once the grounds shook in answer, the seas swelling upwards towards the darkening clouds – roars of thunder echoing throughout the land. The ancient power of the earth swirled around him in a power so strong, he clung to the cliff in fear.

It accepted his cry for help.

He faces tests and trials so grueling and soul splintering – disintegrating everything he'd ever come to know, every false promise and sin ridden temptation disappeared before his eyes as he embraced everything the earth offered him return. Emerging from the final doorway, he noticed a change, not only in himself, but in the way he could *feel* the earth moving around him. He was a God. A man now forged of truth and clarity, of strong will and newfound purity. He became the *Saviour*.

He returned to his home and implored his peers to turn from their sins of the heart and follow his path of logic and righteousness – not only to save the earth he could hear crying out in pain and suffering for all that they had done, but also to save themselves. For he now understood that they would not survive this path much longer – but very few listened. They saw his new form as a weakness, their sins having grown too far to see him for what he was now. They sought to exploit him, to use his powers for their own malicious ways as they continued to best one another, but he was not like them – not anymore and he would not bend to their weakness any longer.

Stealing away the seven that were willing to follow him, he rose an island from the dark depths of the ocean, the earth's energy bending to his will as it sought to help him create a world that would save them all.

It is there that he created the Isle of Salvatorem, hidden from the rest of man as he watched them destroy whatever remained of their tainted world until there was nothing and no one left to destroy.

Years passed, and as the old world ended, the Isle of

Salvatorem was flourished. It had become a land of peace and humility; each person being judged purely on the sins they could not deny – on their base desires and the Saviour placed them accordingly within his newfound society so that they would not be tempted to sin further. Now, harsh judgement was reserved only for the few who could not hear the cries of their souls as they descended down the same path as the Last Men.

For centuries, the Saviour ruled over his land, with his Covenant – written law that guided his people to prosperity with kindness and freedom, the earth granting its new people longer lives so that they may learn its ways and save it from ruin, so that they may one day ascend alongside him.

Finally, the original seven that followed him were ready, all now terribly true in their own selves. It was with them he shared his knowledge of the God's Alchemic ways in order to purify their own souls as he split up his land into seven territories for them to rule over together. In his last act of servitude to the earth, he declared these people the Gods of the Seven Paradises. For one could not rule alone without the fear of corruption and sin.

When all was said and done and the Saviour was content with what he'd done, he grounded himself back into the earth in one final sacrifice so that we may continue prospering in his name.

But the Saviour was wrong.

One by one, his chosen God's died off as the Unworthy grew out of control. Armies were formed once again, and we learnt a crucial truth that the Saviour himself refused to see…

Man will never change his ways.

CHAPTER 1

I smiled as another silk merchant exited the family home, making him the sixth in as many days. All of them wishing that I would accept the honour of being dressed in their finest material for my Ceremony. A test, I am sure. One I am not sure I had any other choice but to refuse.

For accepting such niceties is gluttonous, and a sin.

"Surely the Saviour would permit you to accept one nice thing, even for the Ceremony." My sister said beside me as she twirled in her new silk gown, the palest of pink with the most delicate embroidery on the bodice, 'each flower representing the purity of the feminine' the merchant had told me as he flaunted his work at me. I had to smother the laugh that threatened to escape out at his words. Purity is not something that can be worn, though my sister had no problems accepting it on my behalf – or more accurately she accepted it as payment for being the sister of 'the Purest one'.

It did not bother me that she claimed these things. It was her body being marred as payment for further sins.

"I do not need such nice things, just for a day. I would rather accept something more beneficial than a dress that will tear the minute I take a step." I said as I watched her twirl through the lounge of our family home. The light seeming to capture her wherever she wandered, making her indeed look as pure as the merchant had envisioned. She stopped spinning a second to glare at my words, which were not a total lie. I was not the most gracious person.

"You look very pretty in it though." I added with a smile to soften what surely was an insult to Imogen's purity. She shrugged in acceptance of what she already knew and continued spinning her new skirts around.

"Pretty won't make you a worthy husband if you keep coveting after things, Imogen" Our father scolded – in his constantly disappointed tone that he only reserved for Imogen – as he walked into the room. As father always did, he seemed to instantly fill a room. When I was a child, I used to imagine that he was a giant, and I would pester him for rides on his shoulders so that I could be a giant too. As I grew, I realised that it wasn't that my father was tall and broad, but rather he commanded the air with a righteousness that made everything else in the room seem smaller in comparison. It was what made him the most renowned Judge across the Isle of Salvatorem and worthy of the Citadel Judge position he currently held.

It was that moment he turned to me, face instantly softening as if he were remembering those shoulder rides too.

"Another merchant and no dress for the Ceremony? It is getting too close for someone to make something as grand as you deserve, my dear." As father of someone about to receive her Ceremony markings, it is law that he does not intervene in anything related to choices of the heart. Least he directs his children into being purer than they deserve, and that was a mistake Judge Elijah Sandoval would not make twice.

The Ceremony in question, is a rite of adulthood — where the Sacred Servants of our Paradise would gather every sin, every bad deed that we had committed since our sixteenth year and create a final trial for us using whatever powerful alchemy the Saviour had bestowed upon them.

The trials were our final chance at redemption — of withholding ourselves from the darkest temptations of our hearts. Once our sins were tried and we were deemed impure of heart and soul, they would then mark us according to the sins that plagued us. Each mark corresponded to a specific place on the body — dark swirl like tattoos that wove along our limbs and stuck out so that everyone knew exactly where our weaknesses lay. Our sins would then determine where we deserved to fit inside our village hierarchy. Somehow, the noble society were made up of those who primarily lusted only after knowledge — greedy to climb closer to the Gods. While the working class were riddled with sins so basic, I often wondered how it was they were able to work with all their temptations plaguing them.

From that day forth, any sin that was brought against us in the yearly anniversary of our Ceremony, would bring upon more markings and a correction in our position if we had sinned enough to warrant such demotions in stature. Markings determined everything in our lives. We were not to bind ourselves to anyone whose markings were seen as more pure or impure than our own, and we were not to receive stations in the village that would either encourage our corruptive tendencies or falsify how impure we really were.

And those who were too impure to uphold the values

of the village? Well, we had more severe punishments for those people.

Imogen had undergone her Ceremony the year prior, and as shocking as it was to our mother and father that she received five marks, it was no shock to me. I had always known the things she got up to behind their eyes — we were sisters after all. Imogen had always had a problem with suppressing her greed for the finer things, and the attentions of men. Although, after her eighteenth Ceremony, the line of suitors we thought she'd have dwindled to nothing. Some of her past dalliances having received higher stations than she could achieve with her marks, and some of the others having been marked so much that they were sent to Sand Paradise to become part of the Radical army.

Despite the disappointment of binding prospects, Imogen was not worried. At the end of the day, she knew she would be paired with someone…it was the way of the world after all. Eligible women were bartered and sold by the men of their families like cattle, hoping the unions would bring stronger titles, stronger future bloodlines into their homes. Strengthening their positions in the world.

As a result of my sister's indecencies though, my parents had been watching me far more closely than they did her since the beginning of my sixteenth year. Just in case I decided to surprise them like she did — but I was not like Imogen. I did not care about how pretty a dress looked, or how much affection a boy could give me. No, in fact I cared so little about those tedious things that I barely interacted with anyone in the village. Much to the delight of my parents.

"It is not like I have many suitors to choose from father, or a choice in who I am bound to for that matter."

Imogen sang as she spun again, wholly entranced with the way the skirt flared as she did so.

"And who is to blame for that?" Father snapped as he stopped her spinning. His face was contorted in disapproval and anger, and I watched as his eyes oozed crushed hope and disappointment from their depths. He'd had so much hope for his eldest daughter... once upon a time.

"Come, we must get ready for the Commanding Lord's dinner. If you do not wish to be late, we should leave by the hour." He said, schooling his face before she saw just how disappointed he truly was in her, in himself. I did not blame him. The marks of one affect the whole family, and if there were ever a time one person were to be banished for their sins, the whole family would be looked upon closely — for they were the ones to guide that person into sin and depravity.

It was something that was drilled into us as children as much as the Covenant was — commandments our Saviour had left us to follow closer than any law. It was a way to scare us into making the right choices, so that as we grew, they would become the automatic choices.

Nurture all as Pures, and one shall arise from the ashes...

There was not much to be done now that Imogen was an adult. She was her own person, and in the eyes of the Saviour, she was subject to all her sins and choices. Father took one more look at Imogen before turning and leaving us as we were. Imogen looking after him for a second before resuming her assessment of her new dress. It was not like Imogen to dwell on the thoughts and feelings of others. She did as she wished, and sometimes I wished I had the courage to be more like my sister.

CHAPTER 2

Commanding Lord Orion Sandoval of the Citadel was decreed the youngest Commanding Lord in the all the history since our Saviour.

He was also our second eldest brother.

Our parents were so proud of him the day he was appointed successor of the previous Commanding Lord. I was still young when he left the house, but the memories I have of him are some of the happiest my family have been. He was always helping mother, always learning from father and the scholars of the village – and on the day of his Ceremony he only received three marks. One, for the gluttony of higher knowledge, and two, for his wife Alyssa. One mark for coveting her, as she was contracted to be bound to a blacksmith before Orion, and a second mark for defying the previous Commander's wishes to accept that she would not be his, and instead going over his head to the Sacred Servants. Before his trial had even begun, he begged the Servants to grant him Alyssa, and even though it earnt him one more marking of sin, they agreed – as his total sins still put him as a better match than the blacksmith who bore seven marks.

It was unheard of that anyone would dare ask for someone who was already contracted to another man – Orion already having his own line of females to choose from in the village with the knowledge that he would have been marked twice and immediately considered for Commanding Lord – but he did not care about any of that. Only Alyssa. They announced their acceptance of the Binding as reasoning for his third markings at his Ceremony. Orion and Alyssa married a month after and never looked back.

I had once asked him why he risked everything, his chance at purity and a higher station than Commanding Lord of the Citadel, just for Alyssa. He had just looked at me as if I were no wiser than an infant and told me that of all the things to be marked impure for, love was the only true thing in this world that was worth the sacrifice. His answer seemed silly to me back then – risking your entire future and status on one person? To this day, I am still not sure that I fully understand why he did it, though since the start of my sixteenth year, and every test I have faced – I think of Orion's words. I compare the worth of everything I do to the sacrifice I would have to endure to have it. And every time I choose, I choose that it is not worth it.

Nothing I have faced yet on this earth is worth the sin and markings of being impure.

Orion's estate stood high at the end of the village. As our carriage moved deeper down the drive, trees glittered with candle-filled jars like a fairy-tale. It was a celebration night to mark the tenth year of his rule as Commanding Lord of the Citadel, overseer of all the villages in our Paradise – and no expense had been spared to make this occasion as grand as it could be. Imogen had even worn her new silk gown, the pearlescent pink hugging every curve and limb, and not even the illusion of purity could mask the lustful looks she was practising in the window of the carriage as we rode to the estate. She had also piled her hair up on top of her head to showcase the jewels she had received as a gift from Alyssa and Orion the year before at the Saviour's Feast. She looked like an angel of sin in every way, enhancing the swirl of ink permanently marring her left temple as it scaled its way down to the corner of her lip.

The mark of Pride, or in her case, vanity.

I on the other hand, wore the same dress I'd worn to all events since my sixteenth year. A simple pale blue gown that may be growing too tight through the chest but was otherwise inconspicuous as it flowed down to my flat shoes. The sleeves were long and billowing, and constantly got in my way. It was not something I would have chosen for myself, but merely something I had in my wardrobe from one of mother's shopping trips years ago. Coveting new and pretty things was a sign of vanity after all – and vanity was not worth risking a mark for.

Orion and Alyssa were standing at the entrance to their home as we pulled up, welcoming everyone into their home personally. If it were anyone else, one would assume the hosts were there to gloat about the splendour of their home. But I knew my brother, and the intent was not to gloat at all – but rather to show that they were grateful of those who travelled the distance to make it to the celebration. And indeed, some had travelled far. As I peered through the window of our carriage – the horses waiting their turn to step up to the entrance of the house, I spied some Lords of nearby villages. All dressed up in gilded uniforms that came with the title, the golden embroidered swirls ranging from simple embellishments on their cuffs to swirls over their chests and shoulder, each swirl marking how high they ranked in society - how close to pure. Even their boots shone under the candlelight as more gold gleamed around the toes, curling up the sides to meet the perfectly pressed pant legs of the men who wore them. We were not a modest lot, that much was certain.

The Ladies of society were equally as dolled up in their silk gowns and jewels. Each wife more weighed down by gemstones and gold than the man she clung to. Somehow though, this was not seen as a show of vanity, but more of station. One cannot look lesser than they are, but one cannot also look *more*.

I always found it interesting that the higher you sat in the village, the less the sins seemed to look like sins — but rather an extension of the title you play.

I watched in horror as the carriage in front of us opened and the Lord of the Lake Village stepped out with what appeared to be his wife with the way she pawed at him with one hand and held up the scrap of blue cloth she passed off as a dress with the other. His wife looked thirty years his junior and surely not so long passed her Ceremony. *Lust and greed.* I thought as they neared my brother — all I see is the sin of lust and greed pouring off the pair of them like currents moving through that lake of theirs.

"Introducing the esteemed family of the twelfth Commanding Lord of the Citadel. The Sandoval family"

Orion's bellman proclaimed as we finally came to a stop, pulling me from my spying thoughts. I looked to my mother and father to see if they had noticed what I was doing, as some would surely tell me that ogling the higher-standing members of the Isle was a sure step closer to coveting — and well, coveting what one does not have is a

Sin.

A sin that I might add, was most definitely not worth the mark one would receive.

My father stepped out first and greeted Orion with a low bow. Forgetting formality, even if the greeting is towards one's own son, is strictly a no-no.

"Get up father, this is considered your home too, there is no need to bow to me." Orion laughed, as he picked our father up and clasped him on the back in greeting.

"On the contrary, Orion-dear, you never know who is watching and we must always present a respected front." My mother chided, as she was escorted from our carriage by the bellman – who for all intents and purposes was currently trying to do two things at once; help my mother out of the carriage with all her frilly skirts sticking to the door while simultaneously trying not to choke on his own tongue as his eyes landed on Imogen.

My sister, without shyness or shame did nothing to help him as she bent as far forward as she could on her way out of the carriage to give him the best display of herself without toppling headfirst onto the ground. I had to stifle my laugh as he finally swallowed his tongue and my mother looked back to glance at Imogen. No doubt disapproval leaking out of her as Imogen quickly straightened as she hit the ground – sheepishly smiling when the bellman launched into a coughing fit. By the time he'd noticed I was there behind my sister, I was already on the ground and without need of his assistance. A feeling I was thoroughly used to by now went through me as he spared a quick glance my way to make sure he was at least giving the illusion of doing his job before he went back to taking my sister in.

Too bad my sister would never be happy on a bellman's salary, or he might have stood a chance. As it were, she'd already forgotten he existed, and had instead begun scouting the actual guests of the celebration.

As I neared my brother and father, I could hear that the direction of their conversation had already turned to the main reason I was requested to be here tonight. Securing suitors for his *almost* Pure daughter, and since I didn't like venturing out to parties and gatherings of those in our class — I hadn't been properly introduced into society like my siblings before me. To rectify what my mother saw as a problem, this celebration was now meant to be my introduction into high-society, and a show and tell of the Sandoval family secret. The Pure one — that is, if I didn't sin in the next month.

I had already accepted the fate of being paraded around the village like a prized foul, the subject of my purity already garnering attention of people as they gathered around the carriage — everyone trying to spy the girl who had so far done no wrong.

This would be the perfect moment for me to trip on air and fall on my face I thought as I took the first step to the entrance of Orion's home, trying harder now to suppress the laughter off my face at my own thoughts. It would do no one any good to find that the purest of them all preferred talking to herself than others. Craziness, whilst not a Sin, was definitely *not* something people wanted in their lineage.

I heard the murmurs before I'd made it to the top of the staircase. Despite my rare ventures in public, I'd heard them all before — and they were just as tiring here, as they were whenever I ventured out into the town square, their whispers not as discrete as they perhaps thought, and their smirks equally as annoying. Normally I would hear the bulk of them through Imogen's late night gossip sessions. But now, now I could hear them as clearly as if they were speaking to me.

Some were not even hiding the fact that they were gossiping about me. Some claimed that despite the laws, my parents had barricaded me inside our home from my sixteenth birth year, ensuring that the family would prosper not just Orion, but also me. After the sins of our other siblings, we needed some nobility in our line to keep our position in society. Some claimed that I was grotesque, and that was why they kept me out of the villages eye. And some, rudely enough thought my greatest sin was the Sin of Ego. That I believed I was above all of them just because my brother was the Commanding Lord, and my lack of sin showed that I thought myself too good to be in their presence.

I guess come next month, those people would be standing in the front line, waiting for me to be marked by the Sacred Servant so they could confirm their theories.

"There she is…"

"I heard her Ceremony is but a month away…"

"…. They already have Binding prospects."

Well, that was news to me. But I did not pay much attention to the decisions of my life beyond the day.

"She cannot be a Pure… Orion is a darling, but the rest of that family…"

"… Not as beautiful as Imogen…"

Ouch, that one hurt a little. I looked down at my simple gown, long tendrils of dark hair obscuring my face in a blanket of dull soil-coloured strands. I had forgotten to pin it back like the rest of these Ladies and my mother had had wasted no time in scolding me on the carriage ride over here — but since we had no pins to fix the issue, she was forced to accept that I would look 'wild and unlady-like'. She knew that I did not care what society thought of my hair, nor did

I have the energy to sit in a stylist's chair like my mother and sister did, and she quickly ended the one-sided conversation with a loud sigh.

"Wynnie, if you don't smile, those gossips in the corner will confirm to everyone that you believe them nothing more than rodents." Orion whispered in my ear as I neared him. I felt the humour in my face as I looked up at him – not because of what he had said, but at the fact that he too had heard the rumours and the tone of his voice thought them as ridiculous as I did.

"When I pass my Ceremony, will you stop calling me that dreadful name?" I asked by way of greeting – bowing low and then moving on to hug Alyssa who was failing to hide her laughter at her husband's comment.

"Not a chance, now come inside before they tell me you aren't even my sister, but a witch sent to tempt them all into failure." He ushered us all in at that point, a clear sign to the partygoers that the time for ogling was over.

For now, at least.

The evening went along like it was tethered to a carefully designed string. It started with introductions and mingling – Imogen using this time to point out which Lords belonged to which villages, ranking them from most desirable to least as she went through the seven territories of the Paradise. She was also well aware of who was bound to who and who was 'free from restrictions' as she so eloquently called it – manoeuvring us away from the group of Ladies in the corner as she said this and laughing as they lifted their noses in distaste. Imogen caring even less in their opinions than I did. When we were far enough away, she whispered to me that she was not the most popular amongst the women, as she had provoked the lust of several of their husbands in celebrations prior. I should not have been surprised, but when I turned again to look at all the Lords in the ballroom, I could not help but wonder which of these men had risked marking themselves for a night with my sister.

After we made our rounds and gave our greetings to those who were not inclined to snub Imogen, I wandered over to a corner for a moment of peace. Watching as Imogen made her way over to a group of men who had been watching her movements since we entered. I shook my head slightly. I loved my sister dearly, but she did not understand the concept of propriety and decency. I only hoped none of those men were yet bound to another, least she wished to add another mark to her body.

"If you hide all night dear, they will never accept you as one of them." My mother stated by way of greeting. It was under her request that I attended tonight's celebration. Her final wish before I reach adulthood that I make some actual friends that would carry me and my supposed status in this village. I was not sure what friendship had to do with the status I'd be given, but I could guess it was just another way of her telling me that I spent too much time alone.

"I am merely taking a moment of rest. There are too many names, and my head is starting to ache." My mother looked less convinced at my answer than I sounded making it.

"You do not need to remember them, but you do need to be more friendly. I may not be young anymore, but even mothers hear the rumours they make – and I do not wish to let them affect your Binding prospects." She paused at this, watching my face, waiting for the reaction I usually gave at the sound of my impending Binding Ceremony. But I kept my face neutral, to her utmost pleasure.

"Do try to make an effort, dear. These are the people you will spend your life with. Act like you care, even if it is just for show. Now come, your father wishes to introduce you to some men we think you will get along with." With those sage words of advice, she took my arm and walked me around once more, creating more introductions on our way towards Orion and father — who were at the heart of the ballroom, surrounded by Lords I had never met.

"There you are little sister, come, I wish for you to meet Commanding Lord Grayson Westward. Lord of the Coastal village and Commanding Lord of the Western Paradise. His family produced the Pure Goddess that presides over the West. Grayson, meet Raewyn — my little sister and soon to be proclaimed the first Pure in all the Citadel." The man with the too long title for a name, watched me with interest and I noted how green his eyes were, how perfectly styled his golden hair was. If I had to guess his markings, vanity would be one of them. He was presented like my brother in every other aspect — swirls of embroidery marking his jacket in a way that spoke to the rest of society of his title, the gold on his boots polished like mirrors as they shone at his feet. He was a Commanding Lord all right, and he was proud of it.

He extended his hand to me, waiting and my mind wondered what my inevitable title would be. It all seemed like such a mouthful, and I was sure I would get tongue tied just trying to introduce myself. '*Raewyn Sandoval, sister of the twelfth, Commanding Lord of the Citadel, second daughter of the Noble Judge Sandoval,* and *first Pure in Citadel history.*'

I was not going to remember that.

Lord Westward cleared his throat as I just stood there

staring at his hand, clearly not even trying to pay attention to his introduction. Sheepishly I took his outstretched hand and watched as he lifted mine closer to his mouth by way of greeting. Panic raced through me at the thought of his lips on my skin and my hand shot out of his grasp so quickly, my mother did not even have time to gasp beside me. My eyes shot to Orion in a plea for him to fix my embarrassment — but he looked just as shocked as Lord Westward.

That was until Lord Westward straightened and let out a howl of laughter.

"I do apologise Lady Sandoval; I should have known better. My aunt threw a book at my poor uncle's head the first time he approached her. I should not have been so forward. But it is lovely indeed to meet you. Your brother and father have not done you justice." I blushed at his laughter towards me and his attempt at flattery, instantly wishing that I had hidden further into the corner my mother found me in, only to avoid being stared at by the whole room as people neared to see what was so incredibly funny to the Commanding Lord of the Western Paradise — their eyes piercing through my walls as heat seared my cheeks.

Out of the corner of my eye I saw my mother's shoulders relax, as if she considered this embarrassment a victory.

CHAPTER 3

After many more introductions to the other Lords that were surrounding us – none of them attempting to even shake my hand after the display of panic I'd shown with Lord Westward, Alyssa declared that it was time for the feast to begin and we all made our way to the dining hall.

Long tables had been set out, candelabras and bowls of golden fruit adorning each of them. I would have thought the decorum beautiful if I were not too busy realising that they had hired someone to painstakingly paint all those perfectly edible fruits and declared it all a waste of time and produce… Well, I declared it to myself, knowing it rude to speak such a thought out aloud.

Our family sat at the head of the dining hall, guests of Commanding Lord Orion, and I watched as all the other Lords and Ladies mingled some more on their way to their seats, as if there were some sort of seating chart I did not know existed. I waited for Imogen to take her seat next to me so she could gossip the dinner away, but as I watched her enter, I saw that she too must have seen this seating chart, for she made her way to the opposite side of the dinner table and sat next to Alyssa instead. Confused, I stared at the empty seat next to mine and silently went through everyone who would be considered honoured enough to sit up with us.

I did not have to wonder long though as a pair of gilded boots entered my vision. I looked up as Lord Westward sat down, smiling at me as if he were still humoured by my reaction to him earlier. It took all my lessons in dinner etiquette not to scoot my chair away from him.

"Your father and brother thought it might be a good idea for us to get to know one another over dinner, without everyone fighting for your attention." Lord Westward explained as he poured wine into two glasses, handing me one as if in peace offering.

"I assure you Lord Westward, no one is fighting for my attention." I stated, as I took a sip of the offered drink. I'd had wine before on a few occasions at home, though I found the taste bold and a little sickening. But if I was going to get through this arranged dinner, I would need all the help I could get.

"I disagree, I had to empty my vault to outbid the other Lords on who would be your dinner companion tonight." At his words, wine sputtered out of my mouth as I spit it onto the tabletop.

Surely not. Surely, they did not *bid* – And he is laughing at me again…

"I am joking, although if you always react so strongly, I may never say another serious thing in my life." He says through more laughter as I blot at the red stains blooming on the white linen, fighting the swirls of emotion in me to not scold him – and immediately losing that battle.

"That was not funny Lord Westward. I am not something that can be bought and sold. If you think Ladies little more than cattle, then we do not have anything further to discuss."

"I do apologise, I merely –"

"I do not need your apology; I just need you to not embarrass me for your own humour." At my tone, my mother turned towards us and kicked my foot under the table, clearly unimpressed that I was scolding a Lord.

"I am so sorry Lord Westward. Raewyn is not normally this blunt. She is just a little overwhelmed by all the festivities tonight. Aren't you Raewyn-dear?" My mother gave me another nudge on the foot, like a silent warning to behave.

"Sure, Mother. Overwhelmed is one word to describe tonight."

"It is quite alright. I do enjoy Miss Sandoval's spirit, and perhaps my jokes were not as funny as I had hoped. How about we start over? I am very honoured to be your dinner guest, and I hope we can use this time to get to know one another."

"It would be her pleasure to get to know you, Commanding Lord Westward." My mother answered for me, turning back to my father who was watching us from the corner of his eye. No doubt wondering if he would have not one, but two daughters worthy of receiving his disappointment by the end of tonight. I turned to the Lord beside me and smiled as kindly as I could manage as I brought the wine cup to my lips once more. I would indeed need all the help I could get tonight.

Dinner passed almost uneventfully after my initial embarrassment. Lord Westward attempted small talk, which I did not mind as most of them only required one-word replies, ones I answered around bites of food.

"Have you ever ventured out of the Citadel?"

"No."

"Where would you travel to if you could?"

"I do not know."

"What is your favourite part of the Citadel?"

"The woods."

"Do you have any questions for me?"

"Nope".

I was not trying to be rude, even as I could hear the silent scolding words of my mother as she glared at me from her seat during the dinner courses — I simply had nothing of worth to reply with, and no inclination to get to know the Commanding Lord of the Coastal Village and the Western Paradise any better. Especially when I was still getting over not one but two embarrassing moments that had all eyes staring at the two of us. Once I was thoroughly reprimanded for my poor dinner behaviour, my mother stalked away and Imogen appeared, having had enough of the men she had surrounded herself with before dinner.

"Have you ever realised that the higher you sit in society, the less the laws of the Saviour matter?" She stated, as we walked towards the drinks table — the wine I had consumed at dinner having little of the desired affect that I needed to get through the remainder of the celebrations.

"I mean, most of these men are bound, some with child even, and yet I have received cards and words of desire *only* from those that should not be speaking to me. I mean, I do not mind being coveted, but if they could do so in a more discrete manner that would be nice. The wives are starting to speak, and I stand no chance of becoming a Lady if they talk loud enough for the men to hear."

I did not feel a lot of empathy towards my sister's situation, but she was not wrong. Noble society was a sea of Sin, but because they all ranked so high, there was not much to do but hold any information you have until you can trade it to secure something greater or blackmail your way out of a problem. Both of which are falsities and sins might I add.

I had to move away from her after that, cheeks heating with the shame my sister has never felt as she rattled off about the nobility in this room who wanted her and how exactly she would manage to get away with a dalliance with each of them. *Maybe I am too much like father*, I thought sardonically as I made my way through the crowd. Not that I was disappointed in who Imogen was – it was just not the life I would choose and being openly unashamed of the sins she committed was something I could not come to terms with.

Now that I was unescorted, I took stock of the room and all its inhabitants. This was the part of the night where the Lords and Ladies began networking and discussing business. Or rather, the Lords talked business while the Ladies gossiped and traded information like it was gold – and at this present moment, all the Ladies were all looking towards me with curiosity and disdain. Imogen had warned me that they may feel threatened by me at first. I was new, and I was young, and above all I was about to be proclaimed better than them in every way when I had my Ceremony and announced *Pure*. It was something that I was quickly learning was not as favourable as if I had sinned along with the rest of them. Thankfully, not one of them approached me. All preferring to stand at a distance and speak of me as if I weren't an actual person. Contempt and anger rose in my blood as I walked through the crowd, through the chatter of my most embarrassing moments tonight mingling with rumours of what I assume is a chronologically inaccurate account of my life. Catching a waiter holding a tray of various drinks on my way through the crowd, I plucked the closest off and downed it in one go. The fire in my throat letting me know that I had just downed a glass full of whiskey — the bitterness settling rather nicely in my belly, matching the fire in my blood at these people.

I could not be here any longer.

I wound my way through the remainder of the crowd and slipped outside into the silence of the garden. Despite Orion's pleadings that someone could be paid to maintain the gardens surrounding their estate, Alyssa was a firm believer that nothing looked more beautiful than the labours that come out of oneself — meaning she was often found to be pruning and organising their gardens without aid. I had to say that on this, I did understand. Their gardens were beautiful during the day — but at night, with candles lining the walkways, and hanging from the trees, her garden was magnificent, and it was all thanks to Alyssa's ministrations.

I wandered down the walkway towards the hedges. I knew this place like the back of my hand, our family using any occasion to join our brother for dinners in his Commander's estate — that even in the darkness of the night, I knew the precise spot I coveted to be alone. *Not coveted, wished for. Coveting is a sin.* My thoughts admonished me as I stepped away from the light of the candles.

As I wove through the hedges, using only the pale light of the moon and muscle memory as a guide, my mind wandered to all those people inside my brother's estate. I could not fathom a time where I would become one of those cackling Ladies, could think of nothing worse in fact. But that was the way of our world. After my Ceremony, my father, as head of our household, would choose who I would be bound to and the marks I receive – or lack thereof seeing as I was nothing like those people inside – would be a societal guide used to match me with someone who was presumably my equal. Though since I was dubbed to be the first Pure in history of the Citadel, I am sure that my prospects for bindings had less to do with finding an equal for me and more to do with forming alliances between my family, the Citadel, and another paradise.

In any other Paradise, a Pure would be something to cherish and raise as the next God of their Paradise. As it was, Commanding Lord Westward's aunt was their current God – Chosen before her Ceremony if rumours were true. It made sense, since the Western Paradise went without a God for a decade before she came along.

But that would not be the case here. Here in the Citadel, this centre-hub capital of the world, we were graced with the only remaining Original God, chosen by the Saviour himself centuries ago. Although none of us had seen him in over a century, choosing instead to act through his Sacred Servants rather than interact with his people. It stood to reason that he was the most powerful man left in the world though, and with no way to resign from his duties except for in death – I would not be replacing him anytime soon. Saviour, even thinking of replacing a God was heresy. An absolute Sin of coveting much more than I deserved, and I was certainly not sure that I deserved the right to be a God to begin with. I knew nothing of how to run a Paradise and had very little desire to be at the helm of all the politics, gossip and sometimes outright war that came with running one.

Through all my thoughts, I found that I had reached my destination. In the middle of the hedge-like maze sat the fountain Orion had gifted Alyssa on their first year of being bound. Standing tall and wide, the fountain was shaped like one of the giant oak trees in the woods surrounding the village – its leaves solid and unmoving, pouring water from the tip of each branch as if it were eternally renewing its own life. It was a symbol of the strength they had had to face to be together, and a symbol of their undying love through it all. It had always been my favourite place on their estate since they moved into this home. It was close enough that I could hear the bells of the maid when dinner was being signalled, but far enough away that the water drowned out all other sounds of people and the surrounding village. It was a place to come and just be with oneself. It was something I was finding I needed more and more of as I neared my Ceremony, if only to escape the ever-present talk of my life after.

I moved towards the bench that was nestled into the side of the hedge, a place I had claimed as my own, when a sudden noise had me jumping out of my own skin and spinning to find its source.

Slumped casually against its base was what looked to be a man who had had a little too much to drink. Covered in shadows of the fountain, I could not see much of his face, but with the way his broad shoulders sat ready in his embroidered coat, and the gold glittering from his boots in the moonlight, I would hazard a guess that he was one of the Lords.

A Lord hiding from the world, just like me.

"*Saviour be*, I came out here to hide from the lot of

you. If you wish to coddle and corner me, could you please wait until I am at least ready to fake pleasantries again?" His rough voice came from the darkness. Loathing dripping from each word enough to raise my hackles and my defences went on attack.

Before I even had chance to reign in my reply, my mouth opened in retort. "I was not looking for you, though from your tone alone – I could not fathom the thought that anyone would ever willingly come to look for you. Though by all means, inflate your own ego. It is your sin and your skin to deal with, not mine."

To that, I received a quiet chuckle, followed by a hiccup as he took another swig from whatever bottle he had managed to smuggle from my brother's estate. *A brute and a thief then* I thought as the man turned himself to face me, still encased in the shadows of the fountain.

"Then why seek me out, if not to pester me with proposals?" At this it was my turn to laugh. The nerve of this man. Lord or not, this was no way to speak to anyone. Least of all the sister of his host.

"I did not seek you out at all. This is the spot I come when I wish to be alone. Had I known I'd be greeted by a denizen like you, I would have chosen otherwise."

"I see, so… no proposals?" He hiccupped once more, and I wondered how long this man had been here drinking himself into a stupor.

"None that I would even dare think to entertain with the likes of you." Silence ensued after that, and I was certain he had fallen asleep. After standing there for what felt like an awkward amount of time, I took in one last glance at the fountain that normally housed my thoughts and turned, ready to find another place in which to be alone and away from this wholly undignified Lord.

"Are you the generous Lady Alyssa then? Orion really should not let you wander alone in the dark."

"No."

"No, you are not the Lady of Sandoval house, or no you do not think Orion should leave you unescorted."

"No to both. I am more than capable of holding my own." I straightened my spine as I spoke, still facing away from him, but unable to continue walking away.

"But you know of these grounds, and you know of this fountain. Who are you if not the beautiful and poised Lady Alyssa of this estate?"

"I'm not sure that knowledge is any of your business."

"Uh, but that is where you are wrong. I was sitting here, minding my own business like I wished, when you rudely interrupted said business. If you are not the lady of this house, then you must be either a maid or someone who visits often. And since the maids should all be working to ensure the success of this celebration, my deductive skills reason to guess that you must also be a guest of this house. One of Orion's sisters perhaps?" Though his reasoning was spot on, I did not care to give him an answer, and used his ramblings as a chance to move further away.

"Now, Orion only has two sisters. Which would you be? The harlot, or the prude?"

I spun around, my anger flaring hotter, like no emotion I had ever felt before. "*Excuse me?*"

"I said," he spoke slower, as if the problem with his words were that he said them too fast for me to understand, and not that he dared to speak them at all. "Are you the *harlot*, or the *prude*. I do not mind either way, though if you are the harlot, I'm sure we could have some fun under the cover of this fountain."

"I am no *harlot* and I take offense to everything you have said so far." I could not help the bite in my tone, or the creasing of my brows as another chuckle exited the darkness from his direction, followed promptly by another hiccup. Drunken fool.

"Ah, the prude then."

"I am also not a prude!" I hissed as my anger burst into flames. The nerve of this man's egotistical ramblings causing my mind to swirl faster than I'd ever felt – emotions slamming inside me as they fought to break free of my walls and unleash themselves on him.

"But you are about to become the first Pure of the Citadel, is that correct?"

"That is up to the Sacred Servants to decide."

"And is the very definition of a *Pure*, not the same as a prude?" He said, with what sounded like humour in his voice. I am not sure what about this conversation he found humorous, but I was at my limit with this Lord. I had mind to find out his name and tell Orion of this. Surely, he would never let someone get away talking to me like this. Lord or not.

"The definition of a Pure is, someone who is without inclination to sin. Being a prude has nothing to do with it."

"Ah, but that is where you are wrong my little Pure. Sins are the very definition of free inhibitions, and what better way to suppress one's inhibitions than by being a prude."

"I do not know who you think you are to speak like this to me, but I have had quite enough of this conversation."

"Wait, don't go." He said, humour coating his tone as he hitched an arm over the fountain and dragged himself up to standing. "Now that I know who you are little Pure, I have questions." I knew the smart thing to do would be to walk away from this man and end this conversation, but deep down – past the swirling emotions that this man evicted from me, I could admit that I had never spoken so candidly to another person without recourse for speaking improperly or out of turn. And I was, surprisingly, enjoying such honesty.

"Tell me, are you really as pure as everyone believes you to be? Or are the rumours true, and you truly do believe yourself to be above everyone else and refuse to stoop down to our sinful level? Or..." He had risen to his full height now and was slightly swaying on his feet. But even when slumped over with liquor I could tell that at his full height, he would be over a head taller than Orion and just as broad – as it was, I was already in danger of looking like a small child next to my older brother. Standing next to this man would make me feel no bigger than an ant. "Or underneath all the falsities, are you hiding the most tempting sins of all?" His gaze raked down my body before slowly travelling back up to meet my gaze. Heat flushed throughout my body.

Heat and rage.

"I'm sure I do not know what it is you are implying, nor do I understand how it could be any of your business." My rage intensified my reply, fuelled by my thoughts of Orion's story and how measurable every action seemed to me. Surely, I was not the only person who weighed their actions to the consequences of the world. Surely even the Commanding Lords of the world had some measure of what was worth the risk of losing their position.

Though right now, the act of throttling this infuriating man was beginning to outweigh any risk of sin I would befall. My emotions thrashed in encouragement to this thought, and I had to grit my teeth in concentration as I leashed them behind my walls.

"It is my business, purely because I am curious." He spoke casually as he strode closer, his liquor bottle forgotten on the ground behind him. "But if you will not answer those — tell me then little Pure, why are you out here when this celebration is meant to also be your debut to our world? Should you not be securing prospects to bind yourself to like a good little Lady of society?"

"I came to be alone for a moment and gather my thoughts. Though this has not been the case — and as for my prospects, whether I am present or not does not change the fact that it is not my choice." Why was I being honest with this man? He did not deserve my truths, and yet I couldn't stop them from coming.

"Would you prefer that your heart chose for you?" He sounded like he meant it as a genuine question, the shock in his tone throwing me off guard for a moment.

"I… I-It is not something I have considered as that is no longer the way things are done."

"But if you could choose?" He prompted as he reached me. I had to tilt my head back to look up to meet his eyes, correct in my assumption that he was much, much taller than Orion.

"I cannot choose." The words tumbled out of me before I had time to stop them again. *Stop talking,* I scolded myself.

"Cannot choose because we are told not to follow the sins of the heart? Or you cannot choose what your heart wants?" He took another step towards me, and I noticed how the long, dark tendrils of his pure midnight hair hung over his too pale eyes as he searched my face. Watching for a reaction.

He was impossibly too close for comfort, and I was momentarily startled by how clear and wild his eyes were. It was as if I had been caught in a storm at sea and I could feel myself getting swept away, moving in time with his irises.

I watched as his brows drew together, head tilting to the side as if he were looking deeper inside me as the storm in his eyes raged on. Shaking my head, I averted my gaze from his, looking at the ground – breaking the spell. I needed to collect myself and walk away from this man. He was provoking me, and I was falling for all of it. There was no way I would answer his ridiculous question. There was no way I could without voicing how I really felt about the world around us – That I often thought of what life would be like before the Last War, where freedom meant being free to make your own choices based on your own wants and needs and not on what is considered worthy or not by the Saviour himself.

I would not tell him that I often wanted to speak to the Saviour. Ask him if he thought the world we lived in now, was indeed better than the one he came from. Was he proud of how well we held onto his teachings? Was he happy that we no longer fought in wars for only the trophy of being the strongest village? Or would he call us a failed experiment and wish he had never created this life for us.

I let my resolve sink in before I dared to look at this man again, readying myself to walk away and forget he even dared ask such things. But as I looked up into his eyes again, I could have sworn that I saw a deep longing and sadness and something in me twisted – though it was gone just as quick as he took a step back from me and smirked.

"Hmmm, maybe you are not too pure for me after all, little one. Now, if you'll excuse me, I may see if I can rummage up some propositions from those less...." He flourished his hand in my direction as he winked, and I knew he was insulting me again. Without another word he turned and walked out of the opposite entrance we were standing near, away from the party and away from me.

CHAPTER 4

Making my way back up to the house, I could see that people were beginning to take their leave. I had not realised I'd spent most of the night out in the gardens, but I was thankful nonetheless as I had too many emotions fighting for control inside me and I needed some time alone to compose myself.

"Raewyn! There you are, we have been looking for you for over half an hour. Where have you been?" My mother called from the porch. The light from the house hid her from me, and my mind snapped back to the candle lit face that taunted me not moments ago.

"I just needed some fresh air, Mother; this has all been so overwhelming." Not a complete lie, and half-truths were not sins.

"Well, next time, do tell someone where you are heading. Poor Lord Westward wished to speak with you some more and left early when he could not find you." She was still projecting her voice even as I started up the steps to the house, causing some stragglers to turn and look, no doubt taking in the new piece of gossip that I had upset Lord Westward and caused him to leave early.

"You will have to send him correspondence apologising and thanking him for taking time out of his duties to meet with you." Mother finished as I passed her. Heading inside, I let out an audible sigh and nodded my agreement at mother, knowing she would disapprove of the sound, but accept it as my agreement. I was nothing if not diligent in following orders from those above me.

In all honesty, I could not recall a single word spoken between Lord Westward and myself this evening. I could scarcely recall his face and only faintly recalled spilling my wine next to him at dinner. Maybe it was a sign that he just was not that memorable. Or maybe my mind was just too transfixed on a set of pale, storm ridden eyes that seemed to see directly into my soul – just to find me lacking and leave. If I were honest with myself, I could admit that I was a little hurt that he did not wait to hear my answer, though he seemed to know that I would not have given him an honest one. Who was I to question how we ought to act or feel? And who was he to demand that I do? What would be the benefit of sinning against the Saviour… it would change nothing and outrage everyone. No, there were no benefits to speaking one's mind when it goes against all our teachings. Voicing a thought was almost as powerful as committing the act itself; we were taught that all wars from *before* began with a single thought. A thought that one person shared because he believed he was right, and because it had been voiced to the people, they felt a resonating feeling deep within and divided themselves. Wars were just people trying to prove that their thoughts and feelings were the right ones.

I had no intention on voicing my thoughts and

feelings on important matters in our world. A thought like that was almost as bad as coveting because it meant that you wanted things to change, and in our world, change was not something that could be tolerated. With this, I was always careful of what came out of my mouth, for fear that someone would mistake it as intent to act and start change. And that was treason of the highest kind.

I found a quiet corner in the drawing room and sat away from the remaining Lords and Ladies, watching them as they spoke about the latest rulings from the Sacred Servants, on who was stepping down a rank due to the sin of adultery, those of who had shamed their families and ruined prospective Binding Ceremonies for their siblings. I wondered if any of these people had ever thought if they could live differently, if they ever thought about choosing their bonding partners – and if they might think we would all be happier that way…

Get it together, Raewyn. I silently chastised myself as I shook my head, but my mind was too wrapped up in the mysterious man by the fountain. If I had answered his question honestly, would he have pressed for more answers? Would I have given them to him? Would I even know how to answer them honestly? I had not even had my Ceremony yet, and I could admit that I have lived a very sheltered and small existence since coming of age two years ago. I did not have the experience to have an opinion on the world and how we should live. No, it is best that he left when he did for nothing good could have come out of speaking openly to someone like him.

It was a while later when my brother Orion found me in my

little corner of the drawing room. Only his close Lord friends and our family remained.

"I see our sister did not hesitate to be lead astray tonight." He said by way of greeting, pulling an armchair over towards me.

"I'm not sure it is them who is doing the leading, Orion." I said sardonically, as we watched a very intoxicated Imogen drag a Lord through the drawing room and up the stairs to the guest accommodations. I would wager that she would not be coming home until noon tomorrow. I looked to father who followed his daughters' movements with a scowl and then back to Orion who was just shaking his head as if in defeat. I smiled a little and added,

"Good luck with that in the morning." This earned another shake of the head as Orion lifted his whiskey glass in thanks.

"I am not entirely sure I know how to handle that to be honest. I am simply happy you do not take after our sister's influence."

"You most assuredly do not need to worry about that brother." I said with a laugh.

"We missed you after dinner, Wynnie."

"I needed some fresh air. No one told me I would have to talk to so many people tonight."

"Oh Wynnie, sometimes I do worry about you." He chuckled, as he finished his whiskey glass. My mind instantly flashed back to an hour ago by the fountain and that deep liquor filled chuckle in the darkness.

"Lord Westward was quite taken by you Wyn, he even implied that he would make an effort to be in town the week of your Ceremony and would love to see you after your markings."

"To see if I really am as pure as I am rumoured to be,

I am sure." I murmured, as I thought of the mysterious Lord's last words about me not being too pure for him.....

"I would not be so quick to dismiss him sis, I think he would be good for you, and you for him." At this I snapped out of my wandering mind and looked at my brother with a scowl.

"Brother, tell me you have not –"

"I have not solidified any contracts dear sister. I was merely stating an observation. I have known Lord Westward a while now and he is a good man, and I think he would like a wife who is not afraid to challenge him when he is wrong. Do not be so quick to judge people Wynnie, you will be living among us soon enough." With this he stood and walked over to where Alyssa was bidding farewell to the last of their guests.

Father shortly after announced our retirement for the night, calling the night a success as he clapped a hand on Orion's back. For posterity, I kept my mouth closed, knowing that in the eyes of society, this was not the successful introduction into the world of Ladies and parties that it should have been.

Though I found very little room inside me to care.

A week had passed since my brother's celebration, and all attention had now firmly centred around my upcoming Ceremony. My mother had decided that we would hold a party afterwards, something that was not common after one's Ceremony – and as much as I tried to tell her I did not need one, it was as if my pleas fell on deaf ears. The house was abuzz with planning and organising, and naturally I tried to stay well away from them at all times, but my mother was having none of it. Insisting that I need to take pride in myself and my accomplishment this far in life. Father and Orion on the other hand, were busy answering correspondence from all those they called 'undeserving men'. I guessed I made more of an impression at Orion's dinner than I thought. More than once my thoughts drifted back to the man by the fountain. I wished I had been collected enough to ask his name, at the very least so I could tell Orion about the man who had rummaged his cellar. But deep down I knew I had a curiosity about him. I wanted to know more about who he was and where he came from than was surely healthy. The man infuriated me, I shouldn't be this curious about him, yet here I was pretending to know the difference between apparently two different shades of white, as the silk merchant finalised dress details with mother and I.

"Surely the dove is more to your liking dear?"

"I honestly cannot tell the difference Mother, whichever one you think is best will be fine." I whispered, leaning closer to my mother so as to not upset the silk merchant with my lack of respect between two shades that I swear were cut from the same reel.

"The cream it will be Sir, thank you very much."

"Of course, beautiful choice for the Pure of the Citadel. If I could just have Miss stand now, I will get my final measurements and be on my way." The silk merchant replied, with a deep bow of respect towards the both of us. I guess that is something I will have to get used to, a lot more people will be doing it come the end of the month. I stepped onto the dais and lifted my arms as he secured tapes around me to take my measurements. To be completely honest I had no clue what design my dress was going to be, and I wasn't too concerned about it. My mother and

Imogen had made all the decisions while I sat behind them, mind wandering to keep me from screaming out how unimportant I thought all this to be.

"*Appease the masses,*" my father would always say as he headed out the door to work, and I couldn't think of a better motto to get me through the next few weeks.

After the merchant left, my mother had scheduled me some free time, and I was eternally grateful that she still understood my need to be alone. I laced up my shoes and headed out the door, calling out that I would be back in an hour or two.

Walking through the streets, I was always careful to avoid the most frequented places in the Citadel. I was not one for shopping, nor was I one to gather in the popular areas to discuss the most scandalous gossip rags. Rather, I walked with purpose to the edge of the Citadel where the city met the forests of the nomad's lands. Here the guards were scarce and the nobility non-existent, as they would rather be marked for a sin that they did not commit than be caught in the dirt and grime of the forest.

Which is why I find this the perfect place to be alone.

I wandered with precise steps. Knowing every root and twist in the forest as if it was an extension of myself by now, and perhaps it was just wishful thinking, but I felt like it was calling me home each time I entered. The first time I had entered the Wanderer's wood when I was younger, I was running from a group of my peers who were teasing me about my family, about our disgrace. I had run until I couldn't hear their voices anymore, until the sounds of the swaying bowed branches and animals had drowned them out. Tears streaming down my face, I didn't think to make note of the way I had come in. I got turned around in my ten-year-old panic and was lost. Back then I had stumbled for hours until I came upon the most beautiful thing I had ever seen. A clearing covered in wildflowers, shades of bluish purple that I had never seen before. The low hanging sun cradling them in hues of glittering gold. I felt as if it were calling me - it was the first time I knew what peace had felt like. As if the forest was saying, *welcome home.*

I had traced my hand through every flower in that clearing, brushing against the long grass that was almost as tall as my small self, registering the feelings within, calming the storm inside in a way I had never been able to before. That day I had decided to hide myself, much like this clearing. Only showing it to those who were worthy, those who fought and clawed their way to me. Inspired by the calm, I took each strand of sunlight from the petals, each sway of the wind and I made it my shield, my armour, my own inner forest.

It wasn't until the sun had set that I realised I still needed to make my way home. Turning back into the woods I wandered back, knowing that it would bring me back somehow. By luck, a guard was shirking his duties and brought his wife just outside of the clearing. Shock upon finding me there evident on their faces as little ten-year-old me began crying. They thought in relief – I felt as if I was mourning a loss of connection as that power that had calmed me left as soon as they spotted me.

It wasn't until I was questioned by my father when I arrived home that I learnt the man was meant to be patrolling the woods in aid of the search party my father had begun with the head guards – and that the woman he was with was not his wife, but his mistress.

Needless to say, he was punished and marked – and I learnt the value of truth in the hands of powerful men. Ensuring that I should never let myself be at the mercy of those men.

I walked far enough into the meadow, that if a guard were to pass by, they would not see me, and I lay down between the grass and flowers – each blade silently bowing beneath me as if they knew I needed the respite. I let go a deep sigh, thinking of how my life could play out from this very moment. Despite all the rumours and gossip columns about me, I'd never set much focus on how my actions may be perceived during my trial years. I certainly never expected to presume that I was the next Pure. Instead basing my actions on the notion that I would have to give up a part of myself, *show* everyone a part of myself if I ever dared want anything – and in that ruling, I found everything to be wholly unnecessary. But as always, the foundation of our lands and the society that had been built off it had other ideas. Other plans for me to follow. Ceremony, mark, bind, breed, death. That was the order my life would soon lead.

Simple.

Traditional.

Empty.

Even if I were to become the first Pure of the Citadel, my life would remain on par, on tradition of the high-ranking women in Paradise. The only thing that would change would be my title, one which may mean I have more say than my husband when it comes to diplomatic reasonings, but he would still rule the house, and I would still be his dutiful wife – bearing his heirs and obeying his commands. Slowly withering away, while he took all the glory he would no doubt get from a Binding with me. I wondered briefly if my father and brother would choose someone who would be good for me, not just on societal standing – but someone who I could grow to be fond of. Someone to break up the silence of my words and be happy with.

Instantly I dismissed the thought, knowing that I could not be happy with any of the Lords I had met so far. All too proud and wholly attached to the small stone of power they each held.

No, I would be lucky if they let me leave the house.

"Appease the masses…" I whispered onto the wind, as I watched the clouds go by. I had come to terms with the direction of my life long ago, but the one thing I couldn't shake was the immense sadness that always followed those thoughts. As if my soul was screaming at me, screaming for *more*. I had already come to terms with the fact that this feeling would never leave me — that this is how the world around us worked now. I would live and I would die with this hole inside me, and there was no use crying about it. It would never change.

I stayed in the clearing for as long as I dared to, knowing father would indeed send out another search party if mother came to him panicking that I was not back on time. But as I walked back into our home, I noticed a shift in energy. Everyone was gathered around the table, bursting with curiosity and excitement as all their attention fixed on me.

"There you are, Raewyn! I was just about to send out a search party for you, a letter arrived for you." My mother was practically jumping out of her seat to hand me the letter. I looked down at the elegantly messy scrawl on the front that made out my name and I looked back at my father in confusion. It was known in society that any and all correspondence to all eligible daughters must go through the father and head of the family, likewise, once bound to your husband, you held little to no power and all decisions went through him. Therefore, it was unheard of that I would ever directly receive any correspondence.

"It was delivered to my office with strict instructions that no one read this but you, Dear," My father explained. "Normally I would have ignored the messenger, but the letter has the stamp of a God, so not even societies rules can overrule that." At this my mother and Imogen squealed with excitement, both of them jumping up and down like small children.

"Maybe it is Lord Westwood sending his personal confession of love."

"Maybe they are formally inviting you to be a Pure."

They both squealed at the same time. I cringed at the noise and looked again to my father as he made the same face.

"Quiet! Whatever it is, it is no business of either of you! Now stop with those noises and leave Raewyn so she may read and respond, it is rude to keep anyone with the stamp of a God waiting in response." With that he sent me a wink, knowing his orders were for my benefit of peace and to keep these two from reading over my shoulder. Without another word, I walked up stairs to my bedroom and closed the door before even looking at the letter again. I was far too curious who it could be from, as I knew no one with the royal seal of a God, and if they'd used it, it would have to be for something important. The only person I could think of who would send me anything was Lord Westward, as he had yet to respond to the apology letter my mother made me write — and although he wasn't a God, his aunt was Pure Goddess of the Western Paradise. Surely that gave him some leeway.

With a deep breath I opened the letter and read:

My dearest Raewyn,
I cannot get you out of my thoughts, even though I have tried.
I even go as far as to write this in order to ascertain if you are in fact
real, or just a figment of my imagination.
As it seems that not only are you real, but you are also as Pure as
they come.
And it is because of this that I know I do not deserve to be anywhere
near you.
But I cannot help myself.
You have become my greed, the more I learn, the more I yearn to see
you again.
Your words pester my brain night and day, and I cannot lie and say
that I am not more than sinfully curious as to the answers you were
fighting to hide from me that night.
But all I wish to know is this.
Are you happy?
Truly?

I reread the letter over and over until the words imprinted themselves in my mind. How was I to respond to this? Lord Westward certainly has a way with words when he isn't in a social setting, and I found myself all too eager to respond to him. I walked to my writing desk and withdrew my pen from the ink before I paused. His letter suggested that he wanted to know the honesty behind my words, but does he truly? I know what is expected of me as a female of society, and yet my thoughts and feelings do not reflect it. They never have. Would Lord Westward be disappointed to learn this? Would I care if he disagreed with my thoughts and feelings? I guess there was only one way to find out, for at the end of the day if he did not then it would just be one less proposal my father and brother would have to deal with.

And so, I wrote:

Thank you for your letter,
Although I do not know what intrigued you so —
I can assure you that I am in fact real, flaws and all.
Though maybe not as many as the rags suggest I have.
I was not aware anyone other than the bored wives of society read
those, but I guess if you need information, they are a good way to get
it.
Those Ladies know everything.
As for being pure, I have not yet had my Ceremony, so until then I
will just be plain old me. Raewyn.
I do apologise again if I said anything that may have upset you that
night, it was a first for me to be so out in society that I am afraid I
said a lot of things that I did not mean.
As for your question, how does one define true happiness?
I may need clarification in order to answer you more honestly, as I
have happiness in my life and I am granted the opportunity of
happiness by many things, but true happiness?
I am not certain that I have experienced anything I would define in
that light.
Sincerely,
Raewyn Sandoval.

I sealed the letter and handed it to my father. He had instructions from the messenger to call on him and he would hand deliver it back to the owner of my letter. That way we didn't have to wait on the mailman next week to send it.

The next morning at breakfast, there was a knock on the door. Father was preparing for a day of duties in his home office when it sounded – coffee still in his hand as he opened the door to the world outside. I watched from my seat at the dining table as he greeted the messenger, collecting the mail addressed to him with his free hand as he closed the door with the toe of his shoe. His brows rose in question as he turned the singular envelope over, and a humming shot through me. It was identical to the one I'd received yesterday.

"I think you made an impression my dear." Was all he said as he ruffled my hair on his way to kiss my mother good morning. Imogen walked in at the same time spying the address to me and snorted her thoughts as she sat.

"Maybe my little sister is not as innocent as we all thought." This earned her a reprimand from not only my father but mother as well, who was usually good at turning a blind eye to her eldest daughter's antics.

"That is no way to speak, Imogen. Moreover, I need to speak with you later today, I have some potential husbands for you."

That shut Imogen up fast as I watched her shrink back with the knowledge that she would soon be bound to a stranger. Father went back to grabbing his morning coffee and sitting down with his papers, as if he hadn't just dropped news of that magnitude, while mother looked between her husband and child, worry creasing her brow as she tried to mentally rearrange her day to support either one of them. It would not be a pretty meeting. I only hoped that it was during my allotted 'free time', so I did not have to bear witness.

I made it all through breakfast and today's schedule of

organising and colour choosing for my Ceremony celebration before I let myself think of the contents of today's letter. Which was easier said than done when it stayed in my line of sight the entire time. I noticed more than once my mother and Imogen leaning closer to it, as if being in its orbit would let them absorb what was inside without being seen as too curious. Once we were done, I made to excuse myself, and both Mother and Imogen gave me knowing looks as I held the letter in both hands like it was a precious gem. I made my way past them and up into my bedroom before they could say anything. I am sure they have deduced that these letters are from Lord Westward as well as I have, and I am certain that if I gave even the slightest permission, they would be analysing every single detail of the letters and giving me advice on how to secure him as a husband. That is something I did not want. Not only because I did not care about securing myself a husband, but also because part of me felt oddly protective about our letters and that is not something I was willing to share with anyone.

I sat at my writing desk and began to read, a feeling of anticipation and nervousness thrumming through my body.

Rae,
It is I who should be thanking you for being undoubtedly the most interesting person I have met so far in my long life.
And I disagree on your assessment of yourself.
While I would call you many things, plain is the furthest word from my mind when it comes to you.
Although I am surprised at your apology as I was under the impression that your candour was an honest interpretation of your feelings towards me.

You should never apologise for being honest.
If someone cannot handle it, then that is on them and not on you.
As for my previous question, I am impressed by the depth of your
thought and the separation between happiness and true happiness,
and so I pose the question back to you — what is it you believe true
happiness to be?

I felt my skin heating at the words on the page. At his casual shortening of my name, which I admit I liked a lot more than the nickname my family used against me. This man spoke so much more elegantly than I could have ever thought he would from our small conversations at Orion's dinner. His words were so carefully put together like poetry that was written just for me, just to tease my mind into thinking of things no one had ever asked of me. Smiling, I immediately grabbed my writing tools and responded:

While I am humbled by your words of flattery towards me,
I cannot help but think they would have more effect on a lady less
inclined to see through them.
I too believe that one should never apologise for the truth — but I have
come to learn that sometimes, the truth is better left unsaid when it
could affect the livelihood of another, although I am glad that my
candour did not affect you too much.
As for my definition of true happiness, it is something I have thought
a lot on.
I find happiness in many things, a field of flowers for instance brings
me happiness because I know I can be myself in private and without
judgement there.
But is it absolute true happiness?
No, I do not believe so.

I would believe it to be intangible.
Something that cannot be taken away from you by any means, and
no matter how hard people try.
True happiness to me would be an inner feeling of utmost peace and
contentment that cannot be defined at all with such simple words, but
it is all we have to describe it.
Sincerely,
Raewyn.

The letters stopped arriving after that.

CHAPTER 5

"Has the dress arrived yet, Imogen? He is running it a bit close if we need any alterations made." My mother commented, as she ran through the dining area of our home, swatches of cloth and sketches of bouquets drowning her hands as she chose which ones would better present our home.

"No, I shall go check in on him later today. I will also pick up the bouquets if you have them chosen before then." After Imogen's meeting with father the other day, she has acted like the perfect daughter they had always wanted. She would not divulge what happened in their talk, but it seems that Imogen is under the idea that she would not be contracted off so soon if she turned a new leaf in front of them. Though I still watched her climb out her window and down the trellis we shared every other night, returning just before daylight when she knew our parents would rise. It seems that she did not care that much for fathers' consequences, and despite all his grumblings, neither he nor mother wanted her to overshadow my big day.

I would have preferred it, the thought of everyone's attention on me sent nausea to my gut more than I would like this past week.

"Have we any word from the Sacred Servants yet? Surely, they would speak to us before Raewyn's Ceremony if they knew something grand were to happen?" Imogen carried on, as she finished up her breakfast of berries and oats.

"No, it does not work like that dear. All will be revealed at Raewyn's Ceremony, but we can surely ascertain a high ranking. I mean what possibly could our dear Raewyn have done to scorn any mark of sinners?" Mother replied, causing Imogen to look at me with nothing akin to sisterly love. Despite Imogen being my sister and only friend, I knew it hurt her to have our parents dote so much on me because of my actions, and scorn her for hers.

"Absolutely nothing, isn't that right, Wynnie?" My brother answered for me, as he strolled into the dining room.

"Brother! What brings you here?" I squealed, running, and jumping in his arms like when I was a little girl. He let out a deep chuckle and caught me mid leap.

"I stopped by to see if my little sister was free, there are some things that I wanted your input on before the Ceremony."

"What kind of things?"

"It's a surprise, but if you are too busy planning your Ceremonial celebration then it can wait." He said as he released me.

"Mother? Surely you do not need me, I have not been a single use to you these past weeks!" I bounced as I turned towards our mother who was looking at me with a glint in her eyes. Did she know something that I did not? Either way, a day out with Orion sounds a million times better than planning tapestries and floral arrangements knowing that the ever-present shadow of my Ceremony was approaching.

"I am sure one morning off would not hurt. Just remember that we have to finalise the guest list this afternoon for the caterers." She said more to Orion than me, as I'm sure they both knew I would forget on purpose.

"Then it is settled. Get your coat little one, we have a way to travel."

A squeal left my throat as I ran from the dining room to retrieve my coat and shoes. If anyone could take my mind off everything happening, it was surely Orion. He had always been the gentle and carefree brother when I was younger, patiently waiting for me as I used to follow him like a shadow, especially once he became the Commanding Lord. Alyssa had all but adopted me with the number of times I would show up at their house expecting to trail behind Orion, but he'd been out on important business.

After buttoning up my coat, I slipped on a pair of simple gloves and gathered myself in the mirror to make sure I looked presentable enough for wherever we were going. I didn't put a lot of effort in to how I looked, but I at least liked to look like I hadn't just rolled out of bed. Satisfied, I moved from my room and towards the parlour as I overheard my father speaking to my brother.

"Raewyn has been receiving quite a few letters this past week, am I to assume the young Commanding Lord Westward is the reason?"

"I do not know what the good Lord does outside of business father, but if he were to write Wynnie a letter, is that so bad?"

"Of course not, I have not seen her face light up so

much since she was a young thing picking wildflowers. I merely wish for him to write to me his intentions so we can make things official. Anyone who can make my Raewyn smile over parchment is fit to bind himself to my daughter."

"I will let him know of your desires Father, but I am sure all of this is as good a sign as we will get."

With that, I stepped around the pillar to let myself be known. I wasn't about to let them know that I had been eavesdropping, but the blush that crept onto my face at the mention of the letters I'd been receiving could not be helped. I plastered a smile on my face and breathed a little deeper as to give the impression that I'd just run from my bedroom so as to not give myself away. The responding smiles from both father and Orion at my excitement showed that they believed the ruse.

"Ready Wynnie?" My brother asked, holding his arm out for me to take. I placed one hand in the crook of his elbow, while the other playfully slapped him for the use of his nickname towards me.

"I do hope that wherever we are going, you won't be calling me that in public. As much as I love you dear brother, if the rags start printing my nickname, I may have to commit the sin of murder on you."

"Oh, I do not doubt you would, my dear Wynnie." he replied, laughing through his words as he led us outside to his carriage. As Commanding Lord of the Citadel, Orion was entitled to only the best carriages and horses, and while our family was not by any means modest in their standing of society, I could not help but be careful of where I put myself for fear of dirtying the spotless cream upholstery or tearing the delicate lace that surrounded the windows as if the highest ranking members of society were afraid of a little sun.

As we waived farewell to our family, Orion thumped twice on the roof of his carriage, and we were off. I watched out the window as the horses trotted us along the roads and society flitted around in their everyday lives. It was not often that I was able to observe them objectively – usually if I absolutely had to head into town, it was with my head down at a fast pace, so I did not gain any attention. Almost always I had my sister with me so she could take most of the spotlight, which we all knew she loved, despite our parents' wishes.

While in the capital, I liked to remain a shadow, but with the with lace netting covering me, I could see them without fear of being detected. I watched briefly as we passed popular spots the Ladies liked to frequent to share their 'knowledge' over tea and biscuits, each of them gaggling over which Lord had recently shamed his wife with adultery, which Lady they now had to shun in shame of being the one to draw such lust over their husband's eyes. I spied my favourite bakery along the edge of the town square, and blacksmith next to it as he hammered away with his tools in the cooling breeze of the day. The town square was where all the workers made and sold their goods, as well as maintaining all the weapons and carriages for the Citadel's use. Only the best of the best blacksmiths and carpenters were invited to work in the Citadel, the Paradise having been named the capital of the Isle long before I was born, and it often showed in the way the nobility here saw themselves when compared to other Lords and Ladies of the neighbouring Paradises. We, supposedly, were better than all of them, and so we only held the best inside our walls.

I could never see myself as one of these people of nobility, wasting their lives away in society, making sure that people saw them in order to validate their standings. But as my Ceremony came closer and closer – I was well aware that I would soon indeed be one of those wives, one of these people who had to validate their lives with clothes and parties. With luncheons and tea meetings filling my calendar as my heart blackened a little more each time with gossip and covetous behaviour.

Each time I thought of my future, I felt a sickness inside my soul.

I turned my head away from them as we left the centre of the Citadel, towards the more rural parts of our Paradise. In total, we had seven villages inside our boarders, the farming villages filling up the edges as they raised and maintained livestock or crops that would eventually be bought and sold to the other Paradises. As we passed through the villages on the western side of our Paradise, the houses grew more and more sparce – trees and wild grass inhabiting the spaces between. The Wooded Village was the Capital of the Citadel, and anyone who was worth anything lived there – cramming themselves and their homes in wherever they could fit. Even the maids and shop keepers were seen as better off than those who lived in the farming villages, as they lived in filth and dirt as opposed to the opulence of our Capital.

I wondered, not for the first time, if I would have been happier living amongst these people. Granted they were not as upstanding and noble as the family I was born into, but I did not hold that as high a regard as others may. I watched as we continued down the road as a father taught his boy how to rope the cattle into the pen and stifled a laugh as the boy toppled backwards with the incoming herd.

Had I been born in this level of society; I would be in the house cleaning and cutting the vegetables and preparing meals for the hard workers surrounding the ranch. No, I do not think I could have lived out here. But it appealed to me, nonetheless.

As we drew closer to the road leading out of the Citadel's boundaries, I began to wonder exactly where my brother was taking me. I had never left the Citadel, for I never had a reason to and could not think of why I would need to venture outside of it now. We approached the west exit route out of town, a well-maintained cobblestone road that led right through the forest and into the space between Paradises. Only noble society could freely move between Paradises – and merchants, with the express permission of the Gods, of course – so it was only natural that the roads be maintained to become as comfortable a ride as any road around the towns.

Nobility weren't known for suffering, after all.

What I wasn't expecting though, were the dozen guards that stood blocking the entrance. I watched as our carriage slowly came to a stop as the head guard approached the window, choosing to speak directly to Orion as our driver would have less authority than the guards themselves.

"I am sorry for the inconvenience, Commanding Lord Sandoval, but we are under strict orders to not let anyone in or out of the Citadel." The head guard spoke only with his eyes to the ground, never once looking at my brother. I found it odd the level of respect and dignity Orion had, as I often forgot his standing in society. Choosing instead to remember the boy who used to push me into fountains when I would complain the day too hot. Glancing at my brother, I could see that he was wearing the mask of a Lord too. Stoic face, no emotions, and even less impressed given the news the guard was bringing him.

"And why, pray tell am I not permitted to leave? I

have important business to attend, and it is not wise to keep your Commanding Lord waiting." His tone too had gone from light and brotherly, to the sort of tone I always associated with my father in his study or the courthouse. Cold and unfeeling.

"U-un-unless you have express permission, I am afraid that I cannot let you –"

"I am Commanding Lord Sandoval; I am the one who gives permission!" My brother suddenly roared making me jump, fighting everything in me to not shrink back in fear as I watched the guard do, his head bowing impossibly lower. "Now I demand that you let me through, this is absolutely unacceptable. I will be taking your name to the Lieutenant for him to have your hide." I watched the guards' eyes as they popped out of his skull as he rounded to the front of the carriage, shouting at his men to move aside, and let us through. Orion sat back in his seat as we began moving forward, adjusting his coat buttons as if nothing had just taken place.

"Where are we going, Brother? Surely business cannot be *that* important if I am with you today."

"Dear Sister, everything with you is of my utmost importance. Now get comfy, we still have a way to go." He said, leaning his head back and closing his eyes.

"But they were under orders to keep everyone in, surely there would be a good reason for that to happen. It is not normal for this number of guards to be stationed Orion, what if the journey is unsafe?" This caused him to open one eye with which to look at me, and I must have appeared more shaken than I thought as he let loose a sigh and sat up straighter, taking my gloved hands in one of his.

"Sister, there is nothing dangerous out here in the forest. It is the Wanderer's Wood. No one comes here because no one can find their way out. As for the guards, the God of the Citadel is a cautious man, and it is often that he guards the exits more closely. Likely he saw a bump in the road and took offense…"

"But they were orders nonetheless Orion, maybe we should turn back…"

"Nonsense, if the order were serious, the Lieutenants would be out, and I would not have so easily gotten through the barriers with my voice alone. Now hush little one, I have many a thing to think and you need to enjoy your first outing out of the Citadel." With that he lay his head once again and I knew I would get no more out of him.

The journey through the Wanderer's Wood was quiet after that, and as I looked out the window, all I could see were the guard towers stationed at various points throughout the trees. Nothing else moved, birds did not dare to make a sound for fear that we humans would deem them a threat and eradicate them. From the history books, I remembered reading about a time before us where creatures used to roam free through forests, this was their domain and we respected and cherished the places they lived. Deeming some of the forests sacred enough that we were not permitted to move through for fear of bringing disease through their land. I imagined what it would be like to watch deer and elk roam through the gaps in the trees peacefully as we made our way through, squirrels perched on trees here and there. It made me feel even more alone knowing that we were the reason these animals only existed in history books now. Rare, restricted ones at that too.

After about an hour, I felt my eyes grow heavy as I continued to watch the trees whip past.

***

My eyes opened slowly, and I realised I was no longer

in the carriage with Orion. Instead, I was laying in my meadow, the wildflowers hiding me from the view of everyone who would dare venture this far out into the Wanderer's Wood. I felt an inner peace surround me that I had never known and as I breathed in deep, and the most beautiful and calming scent entered me. It smelt like burnt parchment and fresh rain. It made me smile, knowing that this smell meant he was close, although I couldn't tell who *he* was. Sitting up, I looked around the meadow trying to pinpoint the direction he was coming from, but the soft wind that blew made it feel like he was all around me, consuming every part of me.

It took everything I had not to get up and run to him, but I also knew that he would find me here in our spot regardless, so I lay back down and soaked in the sun that was beaming down on me.

Seconds later I was covered in shadow as a deep chuckle filled the clearing.

"How did I know you would be here." The voice said in amusement. I didn't even bother opening my eyes as a smile filled my face.

"Because you know every single thing about me"

"That I do, my love. Now come home, everyone is about to arrive."

"Must I? I would much rather just spend the night here, lying next to you." I sighed. I knew in the back of my mind that something important was happening tonight, but for the moment I just wanted to revel in the peace that I was feeling, for I knew that it would be some time before I felt it again.

In an instant, I felt shivers as pressure was laid on top of me. I squirmed as a warm breath tickled my ear as he whispered, "And I would much rather be laying on top of you all night, love." His voice was deep and raspy, the kind I couldn't resist, and it caused me to suck in a breath in anticipation. "But we cannot keep everyone waiting my dear, no matter how much you tempt me." I sighed in disappointment at that, and he chuckled in response, his breathe tickling my cheek as I pouted like a child who'd been denied another sweet. Sooner than I would have liked, I felt the pressure of his body lift off me as he moved to stand again.

"Come now my love, we really should get going." Breathing out another sigh, I opened one eye to see the shadow of this man standing over me and for a second, I thought him an angel with the way the sun shone around him like an ethereal aura of grace and peace. He extended his hand for me, but as I went to take it, I heard someone calling my name on the wind, causing me to whip my head to the side to see who the voice belonged to. Seeing no one was there, I turned back to my mystery man, only to find that he had disappeared. Confusion furrowed my brow as I looked around the clearing for him, knowing he was right in front of me a second ago.

"Where did you go?"

"Wynnie,"

"Wyn, it's time to wake up"

CHAPTER 6

I awoke with a shock as Orion's hand gently shook my knee. Heart racing, I leaned my head back and tried to steady my thoughts. What kind of dream was that? Never had I dreamt in such vivid feeling and colours, and here I was dreaming of a man I could not even see but felt in my soul like I had known him my entire existence.

How could a dream feel so real? How could a dream make me feel *so* much? I felt so free and liberated in the dream, but not once in my waking life had I ever felt that way. I almost wanted to cry out in sadness at having it taken away from me, and then I froze. Would coveting the feeling of a dream still be classed as a sin? Would I really want to risk myself just to lay back down and have that again? Or worse, would I begin to covet those feelings of contentment? I ran through the rules that were constantly running through my brain and to my knowledge no one had been marked for the sin of coveting peace, but then people who covet such things become desperate in their attempts to achieve such things. I shuddered. No, I would not be willing to risk everything in desperation to feel that again.

"Wynnie? Are you awake?" Orion's voice penetrated my thoughts once again, startling me. I should not be thinking about this in such public spaces. I should *not* have been dreaming of such things in Orion's carriage.

"Yes Brother, I apologise, I did not mean to fall asleep."

"Don't worry about it Wyn, it was quite a journey with nothing to do. I should have thought to bring you a book or two, but we are here now." At his words I opened my eyes again and peered out the window. 'Here' was at the entrance of a big estate. Much grander in size and décor than Orion's and I knew instantly that I was not going to enjoy where we were. "Don't look so worried Wynnie, it is just a simple lunch with a friend of mine that I thought you would enjoy getting to know. You will be in this life soon enough and it is time you started making connections." I turned my stare on Orion. Did he not know me at all? There is no way I would have agreed to this if he had told me, but as I watched him put his gloves on, I knew that he hadn't disclosed where we were going for this very reason.

"Whose house are we at Brother?" I asked, with a tone steadier than I felt. I wondered if he'd just let me sit in the carriage while he conducted his business by himself.

"I have brought you here to meet with Her Pure Highness Patricia Westward. Goddess of the Western Paradise. She is currently in the Citadel on business, and this is where she resides when she comes to visit."

"We are still in the Citadel?" I asked recalling the long journey we took to get here. We had to have been riding in the carriage for close to two hours.

"Technically no, but his Highness, God of the Citadel owns land all over the Wanderers Wood and some house important guests who do not wish to stay in the city. Do not fear, they are all well-guarded when he has visitors.

"Will the God of the Citadel be here as well?"

"No, he just owns this home Raewyn. Now come, we must not be late for lunch with a God, she could have our heads for rudeness." He chuckled at the last bit as I froze in fear. I did not want to meet a God, nor did I understand why my brother thought this would be a good idea. I would have to maintain the highest etiquette I had ever been taught if I was not to offend her highness. Though considering I always made myself scarce if I was made to attend an event, I was not sure my best would be good enough for someone like her. The carriage opened then, and I was ushered out with the help of a nearby guard. His eyes quickly roamed over me before they landed on the ground and even though I had caught him assessing me, I ignored him. I had more pressing matters to worry about.

Orion left instructions for his carriage driver and then guided me inside the expansive estate. The inside was a sea of marbled floors, gleaming in the natural light of the open planned foyer – the only decoration in an otherwise empty entrance was the wide gilded staircase in the middle of the room. Gold bannisters slithered like branches of a tree along either side of the plush gold carpeted steps – the over-the-top design leaving no question that this house belonged to someone at the top of the elitist ladder. Nothing but the absolute best for the God and his guests, of course. The estate did look spacious though, I would give him that, but it also seemed so impersonal and emotionless that I couldn't help but wonder if the God had ever stepped foot in this place. Or maybe that is how he liked it, who was I to judge – all I knew was that it was a stark contract to the warmth and homeliness I felt whenever I entered Orion's estate, or my family's home for that matter.

We walked through without directions from any of the staff milling about, my eyes dancing over every filigreed gold doorframe, we passed through, the only decoration in an otherwise typical hallway – causing me to become less and less impressed by it all until I realised something my brother had omitted to tell me.

"You have met her highness before, haven't you Orion?"

He smiled down at me as his eyes sparkled with pride, "Nothing gets past you, does it Wynnie? Yes, I have met her highness plenty of times. Perks of being friends with her nephew, I guess. Or it could have something to do with the fact that she took a liking to the story of my Ceremony and invited myself and Alyssa for tea once to tell her our story in person."

"Well, you do tell a good story my dear boy, and as far as stories go – it would have to be my favourite." A voice said as we entered the courtyard in the back of the house. Sitting under an alcove of trees that had been carefully crafted in a half circle to provide the perfect spot to sit outside, sat a woman with the most vibrant shade of red hair that I had ever seen. In the sun I am certain it would have looked like flames, her eyes dancing as though she held the power of fire within herself. It was hard to believe that she had been the Goddess of the Western Paradise for over twenty years now, as she looked younger in years than my brother – though despite her young appearance, she looked fierce and strong as she looked me over, assessing me for all I was worth.

This time I felt something – fear.

As she stood and moved towards us, I felt myself stepping behind Orion – using my older brother as a shield from the outside world like I was a child again. From this positioning I could just make out the sway of her crushed velvet dress as it swayed around bare feet, the colour a pale sort of teal I had never seen in the silk merchants stores before. As tall as she was, inches off the height of my brother, the dress still draped in the grass around her. It was a stark contrast against the curves of her tanned skin and brightening fiery hair, that I wondered for a moment if it suited her at all. But as she met us at the base of the estate, a small smile playing on her lips as she eyed me with those swirling irises, I decided that nothing this Goddess wore would ever look bad.

"I see you brought me another interesting story, Orion. I cannot tell you how much I have come to enjoy your visits." She motioned towards me, and Orion stepped aside so that she might take in all of me. I cursed my brother in the recesses of my mind for ever thinking that I would be happy with this arrangement — but in my head is where it stayed, as my mother's sterner voice drowned out any improper thoughts I might have voiced.

"The joy and honour have always been mine your highness, thank you for gracing us with your presence." Orion replied as I watched his body lower in a bow of respect. I was too busy being frozen under this woman's stare that I completely forgot everything I was taught and so was left standing straight as a rod. In the back of my head my mother was screaming at me to bow, but my body would not co-operate. Orion saw I had not moved and shook his head slightly.

"You'll have to excuse my younger sister, this is the first time she has ever met somebody with a higher status than I, and I would say you have scared her speechless. Something I might add is not often done." This caused them both to laugh and my face to heat with embarrassment.

"It is quite alright my dear, I am not as scary as my title. Please, come sit with me and we shall have some tea. I know my Gray is around here somewhere, he will be joining us for lunch if that is okay with the little lady?"

"W-wh-who is Gray?" I asked, as I cringed inwardly at the high tone of my voice. If I didn't look nervous beforehand, I definitely did now. Goddess Patricia just laughed at my response and moved back towards the tables, waiting until we were all fully seated to answer me.

"I believe you know him as Commanding Lord Westward, my dear. I have to say he has not been this excited about another woman since he first learnt of their existence. You must have made quite the impression on him." Lord Westward was here as well? My nerves went up a notch as I thought of the letters we had exchanged over the last week. Although he had never explicitly stated that the letters were from him, there could only be one person from the night of Orion's celebrations that I had spoken to at length enough to warrant correspondence afterwards.

Well, there was him…

I shook my head as I refused to think of the other man that I had met that night. It had taken everything in me not to find out who he was and track him down afterwards, if only to give him a piece of my mind for the things he had said to me that night. But I still couldn't shake the way I had felt when I was speaking to him. Almost as if I could state my mind and not have it marked on me that I was not who everyone thought I was.

Turning my mind back to the people present at the table, I had noticed that they had carried on the conversation without me.

"…. His highness is being paranoid again, I had a dreadful time getting out of the Citadel this morning. What could possibly be out there that could harm us, we are the only threats left." Orion's voice scoffed through my thoughts, bringing me back to the present and the company we were in. I'd always thought my mother's teachings would snap into place when I finally entered society, but I guess that was not the case as I would surely be scolded for zoning out in front of such an important person. I watched as the Pure Goddess of the Western Paradise smirked in response to my brother, her eyes seeming to hold a lot more than she would ever dare admit in our presence. She lifted her tea to her lips before she deigned to respond, keeping Orion in waiting suspense the whole time. Only I seemed to notice that this was a stall, as if she were mulling over how much truth she should put into her next words.

"There are many things out there that threaten us young Commander. Things only the God's know about. You would be wise to head the warnings of yours, especially as he has been here longer than any of us."

"His Highness never leaves his palace; how would he know of the threats that surround us though? The last time any Lord saw him was years before my time! Surely his years must be catching up to him."

"Are you implying that his highness, God of the Citadel and the last of the Original Gods, is past his prime Commanding Lord Sandoval? For such words could be considered a great sin, if not a challenge." Goddess Patricia stated, lowering her tea as she raised an impeccable eyebrow. I turned to Orion, who's face had gone red in embarrassment as he stuttered for the right words.

"I – I – I would not dare imply such things, your Highness! I was merely making an observation, as all Lords have recently in the Citadel. We only worry of his health but would never dare challenge our God." The table went silent, as Orion's chest heaved with fear. I knew little of the politics world, but I knew enough to know that his words were as close to sin – and possibly even treason – as you could get. Challenging a God meant that you coveted his position. Which was a breaking of the Covenant. Greed like that could not go unchecked, especially in this world. If anyone were to hear this out of the confines of the garden, Orion could be punished and stripped of his title. And that would be best case scenario. Growing up, children all over the Seven Paradises heard tales of the great and wise God of the Citadel. He was as cruel as he was powerful, and no one got away with disrespecting him. The fact that he had not been seen in the last hundred years did nothing to diminish the fear he instilled in society. To children, he was a bedtime story, but to the marked members of society he was the very meaning of justice and breath. Breath that was precious if you were caught speaking out of turn.

As it were, speaking like this in front of the God of the Western Paradise was a terrible crime. She could punish Orion for his words on behalf of our God, and no one would be able to do anything about it. I glanced at the Goddess, to try and gauge her reaction, but her face was passive, and I feared that would mean my brother's demise. Something I couldn't let happen.

"Goddess Patricia, please don't take my brother's words to heart. For all that he has said, he is a good and noble man and has never coveted anything but his wife. I know his words are punishable, and treasonous but I beg of you, please leave him be. He would never have acted on them and by the sounds of things they weren't even his own words, but the other Lords in the Citadel. If anything, you should be filing an investigation on the rest of the Lords and not just Orion himself –"

"Hush child, for all your ramblings you have much to learn on the art of begging for someone's life." The Goddess spoke in a soft laugh, dismissing my words with a wave of her hand. "I am not going to punish your brother for his thoughts, or thoughts on behalf of the other Lords, though I would have every right to. What I do admire though is that you would rather defend him and face the wrath of a God, than sit quiet and save yourself as many others would do – but this was not even a thought for you, and I am curious. Why would you do such a thing?" She asked, directing her amused gaze onto me, her too green eyes swirling slightly.

I let loose a breath I didn't know I was holding and answered her without thinking. "I judge everything I do on what I would care to lose. Stature, wealth, materials, I couldn't care less about those things. The people I care about however, they are the only thing I could not bear to lose. Therefore, I would do anything, say anything, risk any markings or sin or even the anger of a God to ensure that I tried everything I could to keep them safe. Maybe this makes me naive in the ways of society, but that is not something I am accustomed to care deeply about. While I do apologise for speaking out of turn – or for upsetting you, your Highness, I could never sit in silence while knowing I had not tried to save my brother from himself."

"Spoken like a true Pure. Did you hear that nephew? I can see why you are so infatuated with this girl, she definitely has the heart of a God, if not the gall of one." The goddess laughed as footsteps sounded behind me.

CHAPTER 7

Whipping my head around, I saw Lord Westward approaching the garden we were seated – and from the look of amusement on his face, he had also heard my speech. My cheeks flamed red in embarrassment as I quickly looked back to the table, only to see the Goddess' head tilted slightly as she looked at me, her gaze curious and far too penetrating. Smiling softly at her I looked at my untouched tea and became enamoured in it.

"I certainly did aunt, and I cannot wait to see what more is hidden in that beautiful head of hers but let us not embarrass the poor girl or she may never return to me." He said, as he approached the table, amusement still clear in his voice, "Thank you, friend, for accepting my invitation. Although I do apologise to being late to my own luncheon. It seems business does not end just because I have guests attend. I trust you have been well since the last I saw you, Lady Sandoval?" He inquired to me at last, as he settled into the only available seat left on my right.

"I have nothing of note to write about, Lord

Westward, but am pleasantly surprised to see you today." I said politely, finally lifting my head from my still untouched tea. My mother was screaming in the back of my mind that it was rude to leave tea untouched when invited into someone's home, even if I despised the watery taste.

I watched Lord Westward carefully to see if he would give anything away — but whether he got my hint of writing to me or not, he did not show. As if he could sense me watching him, his eyes locked onto mine, those spring green eyes giving away his lineage as they looked almost identical to his aunts. He was dressed more casually than he had been at my brothers' celebrations — his Commanders jacket now laying open in the front, the top few buttons of his pristine white tunic undone as though he were lunching with family and not another member of nobility, though his golden hair was still perfectly styled back away from his face. His trousers today were a woodsy dark tan, and I had to say that I much preferred the colour to the lifeless black men often wore. He watched me watch him for a few moments more, before turning his look to Orion, a smirk gracing his lips.

"You did not tell Lady Sandoval that I invited her to lunch?"

"I know my sister, and I feared she would have denied us both the pleasure of her company today." My brother chuckled, causing my cheeks to redden again as Lord Westward looked at me, amusement glistening in his eyes.

"You do not wish to have lunch with me?" He inquired, tilting his head and I felt everyone's eyes zero in on me. I felt nervous as I picked up my tea and took a sip, using Goddess' Patricia's move of stalling for time as I gathered my thoughts, so as not to offend anyone.

"It is not that I did not want to have lunch with *you*."

I began as my mind scrambled to find the most dignified way to put how I felt about such things, but I was coming up with nothing other than how I truly felt. "It is more than I do not wish to have lunch with anyone."

"You do not like lunch?" Lord Westward inquired further, his mouth stretching into a grin as he made fun of me.

Something I did not appreciate.

"I like lunch just fine."

"Just not with me…"

"Not what I meant, Lord Westward." I replied through gritted teeth, as I felt he was making a fool of me for his own amusement once gain. I looked to Orion for help only to see that he was silently laughing at this exchange, he would be no help to me. I glanced to Goddess Patricia only to find her swirling gaze assessing me once more, and I feared that I had also offended her.

"I do not like luncheons, or galas, or spectacles that require me to be out in the middle of society for everyone to stare at and make a mockery of me, my Lord. Much like what you are doing now." I finished as I glared at him, now fed up with being the centre of attention at this table. His eyes widened in shock at my candour, for surely, he was not expecting a Lady of society to speak so freely.

"Gall of a God indeed," Goddess Patricia chuckled, and my eyes flitted back to her as she laughed. I sighed a breath I didn't know I was holding. "Tell me something child, how certain are you that you will be the first Pure of the Citadel? Surely you know that others have tried to claim this title before you. Yet your family seem so adamant that your Ceremony will not be the disappointment that others have faced before." She asked with a raised brow, assessing me as I thought how best to answer.

Indeed, she was right. I had read of others in the past claiming that they were to be the first Pure of the Citadel. They told tales of their selflessness and generosity - of their strength and determination to do good - but in the end, most of them were hiding things deep within themselves, that when it came time for their trials, they fell short. Some failed purely on the sin of coveting such a position in the Citadel.

When it came to marking someone, the Sacred Servants had ways of finding even the tiniest thread of sin and pulling it out of you.

"I do not claim to be anything, your Highness. People's assumptions are not my own, and if it were up to me, I would ask to not be labelled as such. For now, I do not claim any such title as we will not know until my Ceremony – where I am sure the Sacred Servants will do everything in their powers to make sure my markings are true. That is all I ask for." I looked around the table once I was done and noticed my brother and Lord Westward were staring at me in astonishment, and I wondered if I had spoken too much.

I knew the Goddess would appreciate nothing short of honesty, and if I were honest with myself, being labelled as a Pure terrified me to the core. It was not something I had ever wanted to aim for, in fact it was the complete opposite. Being a Pure meant that I would be in the spotlight of society more than my family already were, being a Pure meant that I would never get a moment to myself ever again. I would be in a position of power, and the Lords and Ladies of society would constantly want to befriend me for their own selfish gain – even thinking about a life like that exhausted me. I glanced back at Goddess Patricia to see if she too was shocked at my honesty, but all I saw was a small smile, her eyes telling me that she knew exactly what I was thinking now.

"I commend you, Lady Sandoval. Not many people in this world would wish to *not* be crowned with the highest honour of our world – aside from ascending to a God that is. You truly have an interesting mind. I cannot wait to see where that takes you." And with that she raised her hand and the maids all appeared, all carrying trays of assorted foods and drinks.

Lunch was a lavish affair, which was to be expected since we were in the presence of a God. We were served everything from simple sandwiches to exquisite dishes you would only find at a banquet. Is this how the God's lived every day? There was simply so much food here that we would never be able to finish it all in one sitting, though this seemed to bother no one else as they all took what they wanted from the passing maids and shooed away the rest, trays still full. I grabbed some sandwiches and grapes, knowing that my hunger had disappeared the moment we stepped foot in this mansion, and that I would not take something just to let it go to waste. I briefly wondered if I should ask what happened to the rest of the food but thought that to be rude and resisted the curiosity. Throughout lunch the Goddess made sure to steer any topic away from me, and for that I was thankful. She was somehow aware of how much my honesty had taken a toll on me, and so the conversation steered more to the politics and nobles lives that I had no opinion or interest on.

I let my mind wander. My Ceremony was to be in a few weeks' time and then I would officially be a part of society. Regardless of what the Sacred Servants decided, I would become a Lady of the Citadel. Truth be told I was more nervous about becoming a member of society, than I was about the gruelling tests the Sacred Servants would place upon me before my judgement. I'd heard tales from Imogen, of how they tested your weaknesses, to see if you would break under the pressure of knowing you were being judged for the wants in your heart while in the same heartbeat having them thrust in your face, testing you. Taunting the sliver of sin as it crept up your spine until you inevitably cracked. She would not tell me what was shown to her, only that she had failed and caved and yet they had still taken it away. It would be different for me, I knew, as I had not the same sins and greed's that my sister possessed, but I was wary, nonetheless.

The rest of lunch was uneventful as I concentrated on making it look as though I was eating, although no food touched my lips. I could not eat with the wild thoughts coursing through my mind like a dull thrum — and though I noticed from the corner of my eye Lord Westwards circling back towards me and my uneaten plate, I could not fathom the energy to converse with him either. Just as they all set down their napkins, the maids came bustling back, all without prompt. I had just about had enough of his gazes and was about to say as much when the Goddess Patricia suddenly stood, her chair scratching back the dirt and stones loud enough that I finally looked up.

"Orion darling, walk off this lunch with me and tell me once more how you fought for your beloved's hand." She requested, already turning towards the gardens at the other end of the estate. Orion had no choice to abandon me, although I looked at him with pleading eyes not to leave me, he bowed toward Lord Westward and shot me a look as if to say *behave*.

Silence finally befell the courtyard and our table instantly felt too small, far too small for two people sitting alone as if this were entirely planned. We sat there as our silence became awkward and stifling and though I refused to be the first to speak, I had almost convinced myself to get up and leave when he finally spoke.

"You did not like the luncheon?"

"The luncheon was plenty pleasant." I could not tell him that my mind was humming with the truths I'd spoken in the open, the consequences of them and the feeling of freedom of them finally being uncaged. I could not tell him that I thought only of the letters we sent each other, of the feelings they expelled of me, of the *want* I have to continue speaking so freely and openly and unashamedly me. That my stomach was waging war with my mind, and I could do fathom to eat a thing while this turmoil raged inside me like my own personal fire.

"Forgive me if I am mistaken, but I do not think I saw you eat a thing on your plate. Are you unwell?"

No, no I could not tell him a thing.

"Perhaps by the journey, it is the farthest I have been out of the city and being it unexpected, had not prepared for it." I replied instead.

"I fear that may be my fault. When I caught up with your brother the other day, I suggested a meeting of this nature and he, well, here we are." He sounded nervous. I could feel my veins pulsing in the same rhythm of his nervous heart. But his words also seemed too simple to the ones I had become accustomed by.

"And what would be the nature of this visit?" I shot back, looking the Lord in his spring green eyes. Warmth poured from them. Like summer, like the dewy blades of grass I found in the meadow when I dare trek out early enough to catch it before the sun dried the glistening beads away.

"I wish to get to know you, Lady Sandoval. You made quite an impression on me at the celebration. One that has intrigued me, however short the meet was." He was talking about my disappearing after the dinner – of my running into the gardens for peace and quiet, away from him and towards……

"What would you like to know?" I said instead, distracting my own thoughts as I forced them back down and away from their path. The question seemed to please him as I watched his lips curve upwards in what I am sure was meant to be a smile to charm any lady he wished. It had caused me to smile in return, but in politeness only.

"Tell me something no one knows about you?" he asked assessing. I felt my cheeks burning under his stare and noted the change in his eyes as he appreciated the colour coming to them. This, this had the power to be dangerous, but I did not think the tone of his voice called for a thoughtful answer, and so I spoke to the same tune.

"No one knows a thing about me, you will have to be more specific, Lord Westward." This earned a chuckle of amusement from him as his eyes warmed with mischief.

"And why is that? Surely all the boys in the village want to know the Pure of the Citadel?"

"I am not a Pure." Was my only response

"A woman of your beauty, then. I am sure you will have many suitors when the time comes. But my question remains, why do you not let people know you?"

"I am not interesting enough to know" I replied with a kernel of honesty, and then added "People do not wish to know someone who they perceive as *above*. Rather they care to judge from the shadows and whisper in corners as if I do not have eyes and ears. As if I am not a living, breathing being."

"And you believe everyone to be like this?" He questioned, looking at me as if he were trying to figure out if I truly thought that much of myself or if I was being genuine. Pride and Ego were sins after all, I would expect nothing less from a Lord.

"I have no evidence to suggest otherwise." Was my only reply. Knowing he would get no answer on my thoughts. Had he pressed deeper, he would have seen that my words were a statement of observation, not egomania. I did not think so much of myself to believe everyone below me, in reality it was exhausting ignoring the whispers and judgements of others. I didn't crave much, but I often craved silence from it all. From all the watching and wondering if I would show any hint of sin for them to exploit. If he had probed deeper, he would have seen the craving for silence and something more than what we were given.

But he didn't. No one ever did.

We fell into another silence as I watched the gardens for a sign of Orion's return. I felt more than saw Lord Westwards gaze on me permanently, I felt like a puzzle he was trying to solve and failing. I sighed, ignoring him completely. He was not what I thought, that is for sure. From his letters, I had thought that I finally may have someone who thought like me, who challenged everything in the darkness of their mind. Someone who was as afraid as I to speak their words for fear of misinterpretation. Perhaps it was just the luncheon, or the fact that there was a Goddess in earshot, but I was left wondering if it were him at all who had written such powerful letters.

I tried one more time to gain something, anything *more* from him than flirtatious attempts and gazes.

"How would you define true happiness?" I asked into

the light breeze that had crested under the tree we sat beneath, knowing it would have carried my words with it even though I was facing away from him. I didn't dare look at him yet, didn't dare see whether the recognition of my words would spark in those too green eyes.

"That is a mighty question, Miss Sandoval. One I had not thought on in a very long time. Though I suppose my answer has not changed. Happiness to me is the status of my position, all the guidance and good I can do in my Paradise because of it, and all the people I see that I am taking care of. Though I also hope that one day my happiness can include that of a family nature, I would not be a wise Lord if I wished for things that I did not yet have…" His words held a glimmer of hope anyways, as if his heart had already decided this were something he had. It was a noble thing to find happiness in, I could not deny him that. Seeking happiness in one's title and position was self-centred in nature, but he made it sound as if he were as selfless as a Sacred Servant. Giving up everything to provide for the people he governed – and maybe he did, maybe he was a selfless leader. I have not seen the Western Paradise to make any comment on the generosity of his command. But his words were surface level, fickle and exactly what I would expect from any Lord worth anything. They were not the words of the man I had been writing with and thoughts swirled with the realisation that it was not Lord Westward that I was corresponding with.

If not him then……I halted my train of thoughts before I could think of the only other person it could be. The man who, without trying, made my heart race, and blood boil with his insinuating gaze and anger inducing voice. The man who I refused to think about for fear of craving the chance to finish our conversation by the fountain, for me to open my mouth and answer with the truth for once in my life. For me to speak and act how I truly believed myself to be and not just how my mother taught me. I thought of the dream I had in the carriage ride here, and the freeing feeling of knowing that one person, just one, knew me enough that I could be myself – and be loved for it. I wondered if I had let myself dream some more, if it could have been his face I would have seen beneath the shadows... No, he could not be thought of for those very reasons – and yet the thought of him writing to me thrilled me more than I should ever admit.

I was so caught up in my own mind, in every word ever written in those letters, deciphering, marking them as so obvious that I should have thought of them before that I almost missed Lord Westward's words when he asked me "How would you define happiness, Lady Sandoval?"

Lie. *Lie,* my mind urged of me. I could not repeat what I had written in those letters, not if he was not the author on the other side. No, I would have to lie and pretend that my soul wasn't craving release from this. Instead, I told him what he wanted to hear, turning back to face him so that I may convince him fully – not of my heart, but of my intent to keep my heart hidden. His eyes flickered from my eyes to my mouth in anticipation, as I spoke the words I knew he would approve of.

"Happiness to me is my family."

And I knew I had sinned before I even spoke the words.

Orion and the Goddess appeared shortly after, followed by my brother's announcement that he should be getting me home before our mother hunted through the Citadel for us. We bade goodbye to our Western Paradise hosts, after the Goddess made me promise to come visit her after my Ceremony so I could tell her my story. Reluctantly I agreed, though I was not sure I was in any position to say no.

Lord Westward watched me closely as walked through the manor and into the carriage, and I felt a pit of guilt well in me for lying to him – for the selfish sin I was sure I had committed in telling such a lie. I loved my family, yes, but I could not tell you that they were where my happiness laid. My family were a part of society after all – and with that came all the drama and ridicule, rules, and structures that I did not care to understand.

No, not because I did not care, but rather because deep down I knew that I disagreed with the way things were done - the way the Saviour had created this world.

I knew from schooling that things were far, far worse before he ascended, but in my mind this world – made in his image as it was, was just another cage for humanity to wander through until they reached the invisible bars. Until someone tugged hard enough that the walls would come crumbling down, and I knew for certain that was the inevitability.

CHAPTER 8

Days passed and my mother pressed me more and more to make decisions on my upcoming ceremonial celebration. Caterers were hired, flowers picked, my dress was finalised after many hours of my standing still while the silk merchant poked and prodded and measured. I was thoroughly over my Ceremony, and I had not even begun it yet.

With just over a week left before my Ceremony – I wandered through the Citadel's main streets with Imogen as she dragged me through shops, helping me pick out the final pieces of what would be my Ceremony ensemble. Shopping with Imogen was always my favourite time with her; she knew more about fashion than I did – often letting her use me as her own life-size doll – and so she relaxed more and viewed me as I should be. Her sister, and not her rival. It was also the worst time as the women who ran the gossip rags seemed to trail behind Imogen wherever she went - commenting on her style, grace, and charisma, and in turn, I heard more whispers about myself than I ever wanted to. To be fair, they were not terrible people. The

Ladies in the village were born and bred to do two things; be judged and bare offspring to those that judged them.

My perceived Pure ascension it seems, was not as holy a rite as the Sacred Servants made it out to be. The women trailed behind us all afternoon and pestered me with questions about how I defy the temptation of sin with men on every corner looking, and I quote 'a delicious feast', or how could I *not* covet the latest fashion as they all looked me up and down in judgement of the simple dress I wore.

I answered each of them the same: "They simply do not matter more to me than the marking I shall receive for wanting such things."

I thought this answer would appease them, let them know that I was not in the market for stealing the eligible men they so clearly love to ogle more than their husbands, or the fashions that I would not dare attempt to outshine them in. But I was wrong. This seemed to fuel their attempts at making me admit to a sin, any sin, so that they could feel better about themselves. I wished – if only for the sake that they would stop talking – that I had a sin worth admitting.

I followed Imogen into our last shop of the day: a jewel craftsman and stepped away from them under the pretence of looking at the necklaces in the far cabinet. They were giving me a headache and I was not sure how much more I could endure before I snapped at them.

As I looked through all the beautifully crafted pendants of diamond, rubies, and sapphires, I noted that I felt nothing towards them. Yes, they were absolutely beautiful. Delicately crafted and held by the smallest of metal bindings…but they were just rocks, and within them they held nothing more special than the person who wore it.

"Your sister is a bore; does she ever do anything fun?" I heard one of the Ladies hiss at Imogen. I pretended not to hear, although I was sure everyone in the store could. She had not learnt the art of whispering, it seemed.

"Hush!" My sister's voice quickly cut through the air. "And no, Raewyn is not known for fun. Seriousness, yes. Crudeness, yes. But no, in the notion of fun, I believe I took the last of it from the womb." She added with a breathy laugh. The Ladies all followed suit and I had to swallow hard to stop the anger at my sister's words from rising to the surface.

"Why does she act like this, though? Surely, she is no better than us. She is *your* sister after all, and we all know how you are." Another lady added with a giggle.

"I can assure you; she is not. In fact, she has been receiving mysterious letters from a certain Commanding Lord, and refuses any of us to see their contents. My guess is that her sins are written in those pages, and she is too invested in her purity and devotion to make our parents proud that she would rather act better than us, than admit that she is just like us." Hurt lodged in my throat at the knowledge that my sister thought as little of me as the rest of society, but she was not done. "You know how it goes Ladies, they all say they are Pure until their tests, and then we all find out they've been coveting the worst of sins and that throne they're sitting on crumbles to dust. Mark my words, my little sister is a heathen underneath those simple frocks, and I will not be surprised when the Sacred Servants declare her so." More giggling ensued after that, and I felt all their eyes on me as I made myself invested in the jewels below the glass. I knew my sister disliked the attention I was receiving from our parents surrounding my supposed purity, and the pressure Father put on her to act *more* like me…but I never thought that she would think so low of me. To think that she was banking on the failure of my Ceremony hurt me, and I was not sure how to handle that in present company. So, I pretended that I did not hear, and they pretended that I did not know they were talking about me as they wandered over to my side of the store as one, as if they could not function without the others moving in sync with them.

"Oh, that is a beautiful sapphire you've found, don't you just love it?" One crooned, as they crowded around me all too-closely.

"Oh yes, and it would go perfect with your colouring Raewyn, you simply *must* have it!" another one added.

"And it would go perfectly with your ceremonial dress that Imogen was telling us about." The third finished. Move as one, speak as one it seemed.

"What do you think, Sister? You are the one in charge of my outfit, after all." I said, taking a step away from the trio – ignoring their obvious gawking as I spoke directly to my sister. Any trace of guilt for speaking about me seconds ago were washed from her face, *if* she felt any guilt at all that is.

"Mmm it is a beautiful sapphire, but I do not think it is the one for you. I did find this though." She spoke as she lifted her hand. A thick necklace, wound with big stones of garnet and onyx intertwined between thin gold strands, dangled from between her fingers. I was not versed in what was pretty by society standards, and although the piece was not ugly, I knew it was not selected out of kindness. More hurt clawed its way up my throat as I saw a spark of defiance in her eyes.

"Oh, that is marvellous! So fashionable," Lady One instantly crooned.

"So chic, it is perfect!" The other added.

"Aren't you lucky Imogen is here to help you, Raewyn?" Lady Three finished. I should have remembered their names, but they all looked so like Imogen with their long, chemically altered blonde hair that I seriously could not tell the difference.

"I am very grateful my sister is willing to help me." I managed out. I could not tell whether Imogen had picked the necklace because she genuinely thought it would go with the outfit she had put together, or if she was trying to make a point to her friends – but as I watched her, I couldn't help but detect a glimmer of cunning in her eyes as she waited for me to object to such a hideous piece. As much as I did not find the piece appealing, the part of me that should want to object, was silent. I could not care less what necklace I wore to the Ceremony – it did not matter to me if it was the wrong shading for me or the dress that was being made. At the end of the day, they were all things that I would never wear again. Impractical, material things. So instead of telling them that I did not care, instead of fuelling the ammo of rumours I knew they would spread after today, I gave them what they thought I was. Simple, doe-eyed, innocent, and above all, Pure.

"If you think that one is best, then I shall get that one. After all, I have no clue about these things and could not have done any of it without the help of you and your friends." I turned to the shop merchant, plucking the necklace from my sister's fingertips as I walked over to where he was waiting.

The man looked me over as I placed the necklace on the counter, his face telling me he knew exactly why I was here.

"You are Miss Sandoval, first Pure of the Citadel - are

you not?" He inquired, as he moved his gaze to look at the piece I'd placed before him.

"I am just Miss Sandoval, Sir. I have been crowned no such title as of yet." I replied, honestly. I'd found that people had begun addressing me as a Pure when I came into town these days — now that they knew who I was. Thanks to my appearance at Orion's celebrations, I'd given people a face to put behind the rumour of the mysterious girl who had not sinned. It made me wish that I had not attended the gala; made me wish that I was just a normal girl who liked normal things so that I would not have so much attention on me whenever I felt like leaving the house. As it was, the ceremonial celebrations my mother was planning did not help keep me out of the spotlight. If anything, people were now using it to spy on the next Pure more closely to see if I would fail in the last days of my trial.

"Well, I am honoured you chose my little store to purchase from, Milady. Although if I may, I could recommend you something much more suitable than this old thing? I'm not certain people even wear this style anymore." The merchant replied, confirming my suspicions that my sister was not thinking of me, but instead of how she could once again one-up her sister in front of her gaggle of followers. I let loose a sigh as my eyes darted to the group, still standing in the corner cackling like I was falling for their little trickery.

"Thank you, Sir, but there will be no need for that. My sister picked this one out for me, and I shall like to wear it for my Ceremony." I added, raising my voice at the end to ensure they'd heard me. When the cackling turned to snorts, I knew they had. The merchant looked from his piece, to me, to the group of girls in the corner barely containing their delight at fooling me and then back to me again. I gave him my most innocent smile as he packed the piece away in a soft lined pouch and slid it across the counter back to me.

"In that case, I require no payment." He said, smiling back at me. The instant silence behind me, and his knowing smile, let me know that he was aware of the audience and the test.

"That is not necessary, Sir. I am just a customer, and I will pay like everyone else." I said, as I placed my money on the counter towards him - but he wasn't having it.

"No need, it is payment enough that the Pure of the Citadel wears *my* piece to her Ceremony." He replied, pushing the money back towards me. It was then that my sister and her group found their feet and rushed towards me, realising they had something to gain from being with me.

"If she does not wish to bear your charity, I am happy to." My sister crooned, as they closed in. "After all, I am the sister to the soon-to-be Pure of the Citadel, and it is only fitting that I should have to dress for the occasion too." The shop keeper eyed my sister with nothing short of irritation that she would abuse his gesture of kindness. I on the other hand was not surprised.

Rolling my eyes, I stepped closer to the counter, picking up the bag containing the necklace and slid the money back towards him a final time. "I will pay as everyone else does. It is only fair to recognise your hard work, Sir. No one will be taking anything for free today."

Turning on my heel, I walked out of the store as my sister and her cronies were trying to convince the poor shopkeeper that despite my words, they still deserved free merchandise. I would wager that he'd kick them out soon enough. If my words were not final enough for them, the look he gave Imogen when she suggested she take advantage of his kindness, was. For all she knew, he would be reporting this back to the Sacred Servants as soon as they were gone. Greed is a sin after all, and they all but yelled to the town how much greed was in their hearts. No, I would not be surprised if my dear sister earned a few more markings this year. Clearly, she had not learnt from her original sins.

Walking through town, finally on my own for the first time in days, I could not help but enjoy the peace and beauty that was around me. It was close enough to the end of the day that there were not many people about - most having shopped when the sun was higher, and the people more abundant. More gossip to hear and spread then.

Without them surrounding me, the city was beautiful. Forestry outlined the Citadel's town square, with tiny one-roomed shops made of wood and stones, and anything else they could cultivate from the earth around us, nestled themselves between the trees. Selling goods of every kind, from butchers bringing in the cattle from neighbouring villages; to the fashion boutiques, silk merchants and jewellers — creating day and night for the latest trends the Ladies had decided to pay attention to. We catered to everything you could possibly think of, we were the capital after all — prominent members of other Paradises opting to make the long journey here in order to do their shopping.

The Citadel set precedent to what was and was not in season for style, beauty, and all manners of other things the wives of Lords cared about. Most of the time I ignored this part of our village, knowing that once I stepped foot in it, I would be watched and judged. Walking to the centre, I turned in a slow circle, breathing deep – listening to the night life of the forest that was creeping its way into my ears, having been drowned out by the bustling people for most of the day. I imagined what the old villages would look like. Enough time would have passed that the ruins would have turned back to nature, vines and shrubs claiming back what was once theirs. I imagine it would be beautiful now. Serene. *Cities,* that is what they used to be called. Glassy, giant, sky-reaching buildings towering over each other with businesses, housing and carriages that poisoned the world as they sped through it. That is what I'd read in the history books. I would like to have seen what it was like, in all its glory; but I do not think I would have liked it there. Noise, people, they were the things I could do without. Of course, the sins there would be greater, too. It is why they fell after all. They were all too consumed in being better, smarter, prettier than those around them that they forgot that it only mattered what was inside of them. *Just as poisoned as the earth became,* I thought as I turned away from the town and towards the only building here that dared to rise above the others, and with reason.

The Citadel Palace. Raised above the rest of the town – the Citadel was a feat of glory and power: a sprawling palace of smooth stoned towers and iron gates. It is where all important business took place in the capital, and where our God resided. Not that anyone had seen him - his closest generals and men doing his bidding for him in his stead.

I wondered briefly what he would look like. I knew the basics, of course: that he did not age, that he was the original God of the Citadel. The first God anointed by the Saviour to be exact. But even with that knowledge, no one truly knew how old he was as the history books were written well after the ascension of the Gods – and since centuries had passed since the Saviour had disappeared, it was hard to ascertain a number. The Alchemic powers he'd acquired on his ascension were wrought with purity and honed with a skill only centuries of life could acquire. This, spoke enough about his age. He was undoubtedly the most powerful person left in the world - something we all knew without question. But I wondered idly if his ascension meant he was happy? If ascension was truly something we should all be aiming for as if it fixed every problem we still had as a species. I wondered if the reason he'd holed himself away in his kingdom had more to do with the exhaustion of life and less to do with the paranoia and masochism that surrounded his rumours. I'd be foolish to believe in those, as I knew what surrounded my own.

"Those thoughts could get you into trouble." A voice sprung out of the silence, startling me enough that I visibly jumped out of my own skin – all thoughts crashing back down, as if they knew to scatter in the presence of another person. I whirled around to the direction of the voice and locked eyes with the last person I'd expect to see again.

"*You!*" My voice came out breathy as I tried to reign in my fear at being caught, at seeing *him* again as I recalled our last encounter. The realisation that all memories of him in the darkness, could not come close to the reality of him standing before me now. In the light of candles and darkness, I remembered him looking handsome but rakish. Something I would never dare to wonder about in the nights where sleep evaded me. But this man, here, in the evening light with the sun sinking behind him – this man I would dream about.

He was *beautiful* - if a man would ever dare to be called such a thing.

He was not wearing his Lords uniform now, no, now he looked like lust personified. So much so that I was certain Imogen would sneak out from between the buildings and sniff him out as she always seemed to do with handsome-looking men. But as I took him in, I noticed the sleeves of his pristine white tunic were rolled up his arms and I saw no markings of the sin – or at the base of his neck, where the buttons were undone slightly, showing more skin that was decent, as though he were relaxing in his home and not out in the middle of town.

He was unmarked there too.

I gulped in a breath as I realised, I was staring far too much at this man. But for the life of me, I couldn't look away.

His answering smirk told me he knew exactly what was going through my mind.

"Me." He grinned, flashing me his teeth as he bowed slightly in greeting, though more in mockery than of respect, that mop of dark hair falling into a disarray as he did. "It is a pleasure to see you again little Pure, though if I knew I would have this effect on you, I would have sought you out sooner."

"And for what reason would we ever seek one another out, may I ask? If memory serves me, our last encounter was less than pleasant." I replied, finally having settled my racing emotions.

"On the contrary, that was the highlight of my night."

"What a low bar you set for your evenings, then." This earned me a chuckle, as he stuffed his hands into the pockets of his black pants - so casual and yet every move he seemed to make engrained itself into my bones. Especially as he strolled towards me like a predator, and I resisted the urge to take a step back as he settled in front of me.

"What were you thinking about?" He inquired, as he lifted his own head to look at the Citadel, which was now behind me. I tore my eyes away from him and turned back towards it, using it as an excuse to stop looking at this man who had invaded my thoughts far too easily.

"Nothing. I was just enjoying the peace of the evening, until you once again came and ruined it." I lied.

"If I remember correctly, it was *you* who interrupted *my* night."

"Then you remember wrongly."

"For someone so innocent, you certainly have a strong mind, little Pure. One I am sure you are determined to hide from others." I felt him turn towards me as he spoke, felt his gaze assessing me. As if I would give away who and what I truly was with a look alone.

"I have nothing to hide from others. I am who I am, and I never asked to be anything more."

"Why not?" He pressed. I let the silence hang for a moment. I had answered something similar at the luncheon with Goddess Patricia and Lord Westward — and while I had been uncomfortable to answer the question, it was missing an essence of truth that I was uncomfortable in revealing. Yet, the way he looked at me now, I felt as though he would sense the missing piece of my answer. This made him far more dangerous than the Goddess.

"I have never aspired to be anything more. I think it foolish to do so." His mouth twisted into a frown at this, and I knew he felt the underlying words that I left unsaid.

"And I think aspiring for nothing is a choice only fools make."

"Did you just call me a fool?"

"Did you not just answer like one?" He retorted. I snorted in indignation, turning to him as he continued to watch me.

"You have no right. You do not know me."

"Don't I?" He smirked, something like a challenge shining in those bottomless swirling grey irises of his. I refused to look at them, instead noting on how low the sun was getting the sky.

I needed to leave.

"No. You don't. Now if you'll excuse me, I must be heading home before my father wonders where I am." With that I gathered myself, necklace crushed in my now clenched hand as I calmed my emotions enough to remain polite. Turning away from him, I started towards the road that would lead me back to society's quarter. I had only taken a few steps when suddenly he was in front of me again. So fast I had not even heard him move. How did he do that?

"I am sorry for offending you, little Pure. But I can hear the lie in your soul, it is all but shouting at me to let it out." *What?*

"I do not know what you are talking about." I said instead, heart pounding faster than I had ever felt before. Surely, *surely*, he could not sense the words I hide beneath my skin like an armour. Quickly, I peered inside and made sure they were still locked down, just in case he could see them breaking through my defences. No, it was not possible. Though looking at him, as his face twisted into a scowl at my words, I was starting to think that he may be telling the truth.

"*Stop doing that*" He growled in a low voice. Stunned, I just stood there and watched as his eyes swirled like a storm – magnetic and powerful. I was being pulled into their depths again.

"I was wondering if the God was happy." I blurted

without thinking – answering his original question instead of the one that seemed to invoke such emotion in this man. Emotions that turned to shock at my statement.

"Why would you wonder such a thing? He is a God! He has everything he could ever want." He scoffed.

"You asked what I was thinking, before. I was wondering if he was happy up there all alone all the time, if ascending meant that he was above all the emotions that plague everyone down here. If he was content in his life after all this time."

I felt as though a wall inside of me had cracked for this man, letting out thoughts that I would never willingly share with another – but that I seemed to *want* to share with him. That realisation scared me more than anything. Without waiting for his answer, I stepped away from him and continued on my way home. My own mind racing in time with my heart at what I had just shared.

If this were a test, I had surely failed.

And yet, for the first time since my trial began, I could not find it in myself to measure if it was worth it.

CHAPTER 9

Imogen was to be bound.

Much to her misery, father had finalised a contract for her binding on our return from the shops that day. She was to be bound to Lord Ruskin from the Northern Paradise - Lord and Lieutenant of the Radical Army. It was as prosperous as she would get with the sins against her name. In fact, if she had any more sins against her, she would be worth nothing to the men of this society — birth right or no.

My only hope for her now, was that she completed her Binding Ceremony before her next marking — before they found out that she had not changed her ways. Once she was bound to Lord Ruskin, he would have no choice but to accept her. Going back on something as sacred as a binding was a Covenant breaker.

She refused to speak to any of us for days. Wishing to drown her sorrows the only way she knew how: sneaking and sinning around. I watched her duck out, night after night — as day by day she skulked in corners, barely uttering a word of help for my Ceremony. I had to admit, I felt for my sister. Despite her sins and mistreatments, she was still the closest person in my life, and I couldn't bear to see her sold like cattle to the highest bidder.

On her third day of now-unbearable silence, I attempted to snap her out of it.

"You don't have to go through with the Binding Ceremony if you do not wish it, Sister."

Her head snapped towards me from across the room. As usual these days, she was sat in the corner of the parlour where we laid out everything that was to be done for my Ceremonial celebration. Mother had just walked out to finalise some details with the caterers, and I'd suggested keeping an eye on Imogen. Her eyes were rimmed with red as if she had been crying non-stop for the last three days. She looked barren and unkempt, something completely at odds with the person she always presented as she snuck out each night.

"You speak as if I have a choice in the matter, Sister. Not all of us are like you — respectable prospects lining the streets, days before your Ceremony. Father and Orion have been searching to find *anyone* who will take me, no matter the person." She sneered at me, baring her teeth like a caged animal.

"After my Ceremony, *if* I am crowned a Pure — I will have more authority than Orion and father. If this is not what you want, I can see to it that you are not bound to Lord Ruskin. He may be a Lord, but even I have read enough about him and his armies to know that he is a brute."

At this, she stopped her snarls and blinked as if she were just waking up from a nightmare. "You would do that, for me?"

"Of course, I would. You are my sister, Imogen.

Despite our differences, I only want you to be happy." I replied, as I inched closer to her. She looked at me with nothing short of hope in her eyes. I felt the weight of my promise in her gaze, heavy with the knowledge that if I did not become the Pure of the Citadel, I now had something to lose.

"But I have to say — if this is something that I can do, then you need to help yourself too. No more sneaking off, no more sins. If I am able to break this contract with Lord Ruskin, I cannot save you from the Sacred Servants if you do not find another suitor before your next marking day." I added, as I crouched down to meet her eyes, taking her hands in mine so that she would understand how much this would cost her.

The choice was now hers.

I knew she would not be able to stop her ways, it was who she was. She craved attention and affection from everyone, no matter the price. Not even the vanity marking she received at her Ceremony stopped her. I knew that if she were to agree to this, it would be at the cost of suppressing her base urges — and that was something I was not sure she could do.

We stayed in that position for a while, silently communicating with our gazes as all siblings do when they are close enough. I could feel the war inside of her soul, and I soothed it as best I could with my own. Eventually she let out a long breath, breaking all contact with me. She shrank back into her chair, making herself as small as she could as she whispered so quietly, I had to strain to hear her, defeat flooding her tone.

"I guess binding myself to Lord Ruskin is not the worst thing that could happen to me."

It was the morning before my Ceremony, and although I could hear the bustling of the staff and my mother's commands downstairs, I found that I did not yet wish to leave the confines of my bedroom.

Tomorrow would change everything. Tomorrow they would take the culmination of everything they had learnt about me and create my final trial based on any weaknesses they saw. I was more worried about the final trial than I was being marked for sinning. Marks may indicate that I am not as pure as everyone supposed I would be, but that would mean I was just like everyone else — and so I would be able to fade into the background again.

No, I was not worried about that. What kept me up these past nights were the contents of the final trials — not that there were any grievous sins that they could test me on, but rather I was afraid the Sacred Servants would be able to see what was *really* inside of me. The discomfort of society, the endless questions about the world we live in — and that they would judge me for it.

Sacred Servants held a power similar to the Gods, and they used that to concoct a specified trial for each and every person. I had heard rumours that they also had the ability to completely overwhelm the senses until you forgot you were even on trial in the first place.

Something I should do well not to forget, least my mind opens fully for them to peer inside and see the truth.

That I was broken.

I always had been.

A knock woke me from my thoughts and as the door crept open, I knew who it would be before they appeared.

"Morning sweetie, we have your final fitting this

morning for your gown; followed by a tasting of the menu from the caterers, a practice run for hair and makeup, and then your father would like some time with you to go over potential binding prospects before tomorrow." My mother listed, as she pulled back my curtains, momentarily blinding me as the sun poured in. And here I was hoping for a little more solitude.

"Mother, I care for none of those things. I do not need my hair, or my makeup done, and I am sure Imogen will be more help with the caterers. Can I just attend the fitting and fathers' study and then spend my final day preparing myself?"

"What do you think all this is?" She scoffed, throwing my safety of blankets back. Staying in bed longer was clearly not an option. "This is all in preparation for tomorrow, there are a lot of Lords who have agreed to attend your ceremonial party, and you need to be presentable to them, to everyone. This is your official debut into society as a woman and *it will count for everything.*"

She emphasised the last words as if that would make it sink in further. I knew that from my mother's point, this is everything she'd been working me towards my entire life. All the lessons, time spent preparing for both my Ceremony and my debut. The reaction of the other mothers as I was brought into society. It would dictate not only my life in society but cement hers in the prominent eyes of the mothers. My success was my family's success, and we needed this to go well – especially after the shame my sister had brought upon our family, not to mention the brother I barely remembered.

The one we never spoke of.
Sebastian was the eldest of the four of us, a few years older than Orion. I was too young to remember him well, but

what I do remember were the tears on my mother's face as he was exiled from the Citadel, my father's roar of rage as he discovered the atrocious acts his son had brought down on his family. I still had no clue what he did that was so wrong, but from what I was able to wring out of Orion when I was old enough to ask questions, was enough to make me never ask about him again.

My brother was a *Covenant Breaker.*

It took years for my family to recover socially, most of their friends having deemed the entire family Unworthy of our status after the actions of my brother. It wasn't until Orion was named Commanding Lord of the Citadel that people started engaging with us so openly again.

"Okay Mother, I promise to make the most of today."

"I knew you would, Raewyn. Now I'll have Analise bring up your breakfast in a moment, so why don't you bathe and freshen up and I will come and get you when the merchant arrives?" It was her peace offering, always making sure that I got what I needed. I smiled in return and headed to my adjoining bathing room.

I wrapped myself in my dressing robe once I was done, and sat at my dresser, brushing my hair as I waited for Analise, our head lady's maid, to arrive. As much as I did not worry with my looks, I couldn't help but wonder briefly what people saw when they looked at me; at my lifeless hair that often looked more like dirt than silken sheets. I wondered if my Sandoval blue eyes were as innocent and doe eyed as they all claimed me to be, instead of cold and bored like I always felt myself to be. My mouth too small, as it rarely spoke to people for fear that I would say something that I did not mean.

All the things I knew men liked to look at — from Imogen's late night gossip sessions — were all things that I found rather boring about myself. Sighing, I turned away from my small mirror and dressed for the day.

Analise arrived just as I was finishing up, smiling as always when she entered the room. Alongside my mother, this woman helped raise all children of the Sandoval family, and I was eternally grateful for her presence and wisdom in our lives.

"Good morning sweetie, I have breakfast and a written itinerary here for you, least you forget where to be today." She finished with a wink, knowing full well that if given the chance I would run off into the woods to be alone. The first time she saw me enter our estate from the Wanderers' Woods, she'd almost had a heart attack. I'd never seen her growl once at any of my siblings, but I caught her anger as she dragged me back inside and made me promise never to go in there again. After the third time, she had changed her promise to make sure I was being careful. She would never tell me what was out there to make everyone so worried, but I assured her that the only thing I encountered on my excursions were rabbits and birds that occasionally liked to follow me because they were curious, not because they were ravenous. As she placed the tray down on my table, I noticed something that I had not seen in over a week.

"Is that a letter for me?" I inquired, reaching for it before she could move the itinerary, causing it to drop to the ground. Forgotten completely.

"It is indeed Miss, though I rather thought you were done with those after your luncheon with Lord Westward."

"As did I." I murmured, turning it over in my hands. It was indeed from the man I was writing with weeks ago, though I hadn't told Analise that I'd discovered the man I was writing too was in fact *not* Lord Westward. As much as

I loved her like my mother, I knew that she also reported on the coming and goings of the children, and that was knowledge that I couldn't let slip to anyone.

"Now, your mother told me to fetch you in thirty minutes. The merchant shall be here by then, so drink your coffee and I will be back shortly." With that she left me alone, still looking over the letter, not even having opened it. I was not sure that I wanted to, not now that I didn't know who I was speaking with.

It could be a test, something the Sacred Servants dreamed up to test how pure and respected I really was before the Ceremony. Although as far as tests go, this one would be rather dull in nature.

No, this could not be a test – but then that left only one other option…

Without thinking further, I tore the letter open and read:

My Dearest Rae,
Despite the womanising cretin you have painted me out to be,
I only wish to know you – Your thoughts, your dreams, your secrets.
These have intrigued me like no one else before.
I read your letter a dozen times when I first received it and a hundred times since.
How does one provoke such thought and feeling inside me?
I am pleased that you also aspire for something intangible in true happiness.
Pleased because I could not stand simpler words from you than the ones you wrote to me, and I am honoured by the honesty in them.
Though I still believe that it should be spoken at all turns, no matter the cost.
For the cost can sometimes be greater to oneself than it is to those we speak it to.

Tell me Rae, when was the last time a lie affected you so?

I read the letter, and then I read it again. His words evoking in me the same thoughts and feelings he had described on the page. *I* also wanted to know *him*. All of him, his thoughts and feelings. I felt as if there were no limits we could not cross, a secret that I would not bare in these pages to him. If he asked, I would tell him, and I would not regret it. His eloquent script, his thoughtful words and flattery made me believe that he only yearned to know me, or that he already did and was just waiting for me to catch up to him.

Suddenly I could not stand the thought of not knowing who this man was. I could feel my heart pounding against my skin as I grabbed a blank piece of paper and wrote three words that I needed an answer to more than anything else in my life.

Who are you?

I sealed it as I ran from my room, down the stairs as I hoped the messenger would still be waiting nearby for my response as he always was. I heard Analise shout in surprise as I bounded down the stairs past her, arms filled with laundry for the bedrooms. I called my apologies without stopping and knew I would receive an earful later about the proper way a Lady was to walk down staircases. My father called a hello as I ran past his study and to the front door, throwing it open and stopping as the light of day once again blinded my eyes. Searching around for any messengers in sight, I was about to walk back into the house when a noise to my left caught my attention.

The source of the noise came from a man, standing in the shadows to the side of our estate, leaning against a tree as if he had all the time in the world to wait. As far as messengers went, he was not at all what I had imagined. Tall, and broader than the trunk that he was leaned against, he looked more like a radical solider than a messenger, and I was apprehensive about approaching him. His arms were crossed over his chest as he glared down at me and what I could see of his folded forearms and hands were covered wholly in the markings of sin. Whorls of ink telling the tale of his inner most demons – *Lust and Greed.*

Beneath his folded arms, his torso was only covered in a vest, one that showcased exactly how defined and chiselled the rest of his tanned body was, all the way down to his leather pants and scuffed boots. Not the boots of a Lord, of that I was certain.

The man before me snorted and I raised my eyes to his face again, blush creeping up my face as I realised, I'd been caught looking him over. The wide-toothed grin he gave let me know that he thought I was looking at him for reasons that went far beyond assessing a potential threat. Though even I could admit that grin was the reason for his blackened arms. Women would fall at his feet happily in lustful sin just at the barest mention of that grin.

I on the other hand, only felt wearier of him.

"Is that a letter for me?" His gravelly voice spoke out into the silence between us as he pushed off from the tree, his shoulder-length hair billowing away from his face in tendrils of dark brown and red. Like a smouldering flame in the woods. That is what he reminded me of. Calm and lethal grace, ready to burn the world down and laugh as we ignited.

"That depends, are you the one who delivered this?" I replied.

"I am."

"But you are not the one who wrote it?"

"No, milady, I am not the one who wrote you those letters." He said, with a laugh in his voice. *Of course not*, I scolded myself internally. I would have definitely remembered meeting this man.

"But you know who did?" I questioned further. This caused his eyebrows to raise before he let out the fullest laugh I had heard come out of a person. Genuine laughter, full bellied and loud – not polite chuckling as we are taught to do in society, least of all we offend someone with the sound. I watched him with irritation as he doubled over in his fit, waiting patiently for him to finish.

Offended I am indeed.

"You do not?" He asked, looking up at me from his position halfway to the ground. When I shook my head at him, his laughter started up again, and it almost looked as if it pained him – his hand coming up to wipe tears from his face. "Oh, this is golden…. I will never …. *Never* let him live this down." He said between breaths as he finally regained some sense of self, standing up straight and taking in the anger that was surely taking over my features.

"I do apologise, Miss. I am not laughing at you. But to answer your question, yes, I do know the man who is writing these letters to you."

"Obviously." Was all I could manage to say through my gritted teeth. I hated being made fun of almost as much as I hated people gossiping about me. At least he had the decency to look apologetic as he grinned at me sheepishly.

"Well, if you just hand it over, I can be on my way to delivering it back to him. I know he is waiting for your response." He stated, taking a step closer to me. I matched him and took one step back.

"I want to know who he is." I stated, standing my

ground as he took another step towards me, palms up as if he thought I were afraid of him.

"I'm afraid I cannot do that miss."

"Why not?" I inquired again, as he took the final step towards me.

"My only orders were to deliver the letter and wait for a response. If he did not tell you in those letters, then I suggest asking him in your next one." He replied with another chuckle, as if he were not over his previous bout of laughter.

"You are taking this straight to him?" I asked instead.

"Yes, those are my orders." He replied, holding his hand out expectantly. I handed the letter over, thinking through my options as he made his way back down the stairs, readying himself to leave.

I had to know, and I couldn't wait for his reply to find out.

"I could just follow you, then I would find out who was writing these letters to me." I called to him as he made his way to the street.

I heard him laugh loud as he kept walking, followed by a snort. "You could, but your sister requires you." He didn't turn around once, throwing his hand up in a wave as he moved down the street.

I didn't have time to think through what he said as the door opened further, and I realised what he meant. Imogen had been watching our exchange and her face was formed in a way I'd never seen before.

Shock.

CHAPTER 10

"Who was that man?" She asked in a hushed tone, closing the door to the house, leaving us outside on the porch. The last place I wanted to have this conversation. I grabbed her arm and moved her over towards the tree he had been leaning on moments before.

"He was just a messenger." I answered as soon as we were far enough around to be partially hidden from the street.

"*That* was no messenger, Raewyn. I know you do not care for things, but even you cannot deny the God-like man who stood not three-feet from you!" I couldn't deny it. Even I could understand the pull women would have towards him, even if I did not feel it myself.

"That is not important, nor is it the reason for his being here. He was simply waiting for me to respond to the letter he was charged to deliver."

"I heard you tell him that you would follow him sister. Are those letters not from Lord Westward?" *Shit.* I hadn't realised she'd heard. If this got back to father, he would be furious.

"I am going to tell you something, Sister. And like all those times I neglected to tell Father your whereabouts, I need you to swear to me that you will not tell a soul."

"I swear." She said immediately, her eyes lighting up for the first time since she had been told about her impending Binding Ceremony.

I suppose to her, I was about to reveal my deepest sin, a day before my Ceremony. An admittance that her Pure sister was not as pure as she claimed. If only it were as exciting as that.

"No, the person I have been corresponding with is *not* Lord Westward. At first, I thought it was, because he referenced the night at Orion's estate. But after the luncheon I realised that it wasn't him." I confessed, thinking that Imogen would lose interest when she discovered I wasn't as conniving and secretive as she was when it came to me. But the glint never left her eyes.

"So? Who is it?"

"I do not know." I whispered, embarrassed that I would be conversing with a stranger like that.

"You don't – you don't know? How do you not know?" she asked furrowing her brows in confusion.

"Just that. He does not sign his letters."

"And you are certain it is not the Commander?"

"Yes. At the luncheon, I gave hints to the letters – clues that only the author would understand. But he did not acknowledge a single one of them." *Though even if he did, the answer he gave me when I asked him what he thought happiness was – was answer enough.* I added to myself. While I was confessing the letters to my sister, I was not ready to share what was in them. I looked back at my sister to see what she was thinking, to see if she thought this to be as bad as how it sounded now that I was saying it out loud, how *foolish* it had been of me to write this man back.

But what came out of Imogen was the opposite of my thoughts.

"*That is so romantic.*" she swooned, leaning back on the tree, and fanning herself as if she may faint. It was enough to break my morose thoughts and laugh at her reaction.

"Really?"

"How much more romantic can you get than a secret admirer?" She stated, as if it were meant to be obvious to me. "Now, we must figure out *who* your admirer could be. Who else did you speak to at Orion's?" She asked, settling down in the grass, leaning against the trunk. I sat beside her, noting that this was the first time in a while that my sister and I had been like this. Just two sisters hanging out, and I would miss these rare moments when she left.

"I barely spoke to anyone that night. A few Lords attempted to make pleasantries, most just spoke to Father or Orion."

"Well, it had to be someone that spoke to you at length. We know it was not Westward, although anyone competing with him will have their work cut out for them. The West do *not* engage with other Paradises often, it would be an honour for him to propose a Binding to you."

"I'm sure if I am made Pure, it will be *them* honoured to have me." I remarked snidely. I was aware of how uncommon it was for the West to engage with other Paradises, especially when it came to Binding yourself to someone. Orion often had to travel to the Western Paradise to do business with Lord Westward as it was — though I am sure Orion and Father saw this as the honour it was intended to be seen as. Regardless, I am certain I would feel the same with whoever I was destined to be bound to.

My sister just scoffed, as if my comment was a sign of my arrogance — not indifference and went to say as much when the hobbling figure of the silk merchant climbed our front doorsteps, ending our conversation completely. We followed in after him into the parlour where Mother was already waiting, dais set up for me to climb upon.

For the next hour I was poked and pushed around, ensuring every angle of the gown was perfect and nothing else needed altering. Aside from the look of boredom on my face, my mother deemed the dress perfect and sent him on his way with our gratitude. Imogen went back to her quiet self in the corner, answering only when mother called for her opinion — but I could tell, deep within she was still pondering the mystery of my letters, as I was.

She was correct in assuming that anyone who wanted to pledge themselves to me, would have to battle with the advantageous Binding I could have with Lord Westward. He was Commanding Lord of the Western Paradise, and it was not often that they ventured out to acquire new blood into their closed off lands. The West were a quiet Paradise, often wishing to be left well alone when it came to diplomatic matters, pushing more and more to be independent from the rest of the Isle: a fact their Goddess made clear whenever she travelled outside of her home. The only time they really congregated to the Citadel was by order of the God — and well a calling of all the Gods had not happened in centuries.

For Lord Westward to come to the Citadel not once, but *twice* spoke volumes about his intentions for me.

I opted to have lunch in my own room after finalising the caterer's menu — not that I was any help to my mother on those matters. Truth be told, my mind was further away from my Ceremony than it should be. Instead, it was planted firmly in the letter I received this morning and the abnormal messenger that came with it.

Although the author made no move to speak of Binding contracts and courting, I could not help but wish that he did. He captivated my mind like no one else before, and though we had shared very little, I could tell that he thought like me, *was* like me and I was more and more intrigued to find out who this man was — least of all a name and face to put on the other end of the paper.

Immediately I dismissed the man by the fountain, the one that had snuck up on me in the square a few days ago. If it were him, he would be arrogant enough to admit it without my asking. Proud that he managed to sneak in a few words to the *Pure of the Citadel.* No, it could not be him. Besides, I am sure he has easier women to prey upon than the one that didn't want anything to do with him.

Then why do you keep thinking of him? My mind crooned, betraying me as I picked at my simple lunch of greens and vegetables. I groaned into my plate. I do *not* think of him. In fact, I make a conscious effort to make sure he is nowhere near my mind at all times, for fear that he would raise my fury from mere thought alone — and I couldn't have that.

Not when I was being made to venture out in the public more and more, people watching me closer and closer as the day of my Ceremony dawned nearer. No, I forbade myself from thinking of him, not because he attracted me, but because he infuriated me, and I couldn't be sure that people would mistake it for the former.

Maybe if the messenger came back with a reply, I could follow him then. I had been serious in my threat — if they would not tell me, I would figure it out for myself. I was not a helpless woman who would fall for anyone's kind words. I needed a face to see the truth in their intentions. Yes, that is what I would do.

By the time my father called me down to his study, I had devised a plan to unmask my secret letter-writer. Wait for a response, hand mine to the messenger and wait long enough for him to move down the street, making sure that I would not be noticed if he were to turn back.

Orion was standing in my fathers' office when I arrived, him and Father behind the desk as they looked up and smiled at my entrance. Despite my wandering mind, I did feel a sorrow at thinking that soon I would not be around them. Having been contracted off to another and shipped to wherever my husband lived. *If it were Lord Westward, I would be even further*, I lamented internally.

They of course, would think it a natural progression – like when Alyssa moved villages to be with Orion, very rarely travelling back to her family as it was a journey – and they still lived within the Citadel. Moving further would ensure that I never saw my family again, and that thought made me frown.

"Whatever could be the matter, my angel? We have a Ceremony to celebrate tomorrow! You should be a bundle of nerves and joy, not looking like I'm about to ship off your favourite diamonds." My father commented, as he came towards me at the sight of my frown. He wrapped me in his arms like I was still his little child, and I knew without a doubt that this would be the thing I missed most. Despite the contact that I often avoided with others – I always craved my father's warm embraces. He had always been a net of safety and encouragement for his children to be themselves, ignoring the societal pressures and shame that our family has gone through over the years. My father was always the one that made us feel like we mattered — that whatever they said about us was nothing next to the love he felt for us. His values were what ignited the values Orion had stood by in his markings, and through the years they had also been passed down to me.

"I am just realising how much I may miss you after I am bound to my husband." I replied carefully. The words *after you sell me to my husband* an acrid taste on my tongue that I swallowed down. My father knows only that I find the Bonding Ceremony uninteresting, and not the internal war inside that I could never love someone I was sold to via a contract. No matter how much it may benefit family.

But it is because it would benefit them that I would do it.

"I am sure whoever we deem worthy of you will still let you visit, dear sister. If not, then we can come to you. I am sure Alyssa would love a reason to buy a new gown." Orion added in joke, and I forced a smile to my face so that they would believe it made all the difference in the world. It seemed to work as they ushered me into a chair in front of father's desk and laid out their options for me. No, not options for me to choose from — more an awareness that tomorrow these men would want time with me in order to discern their liking towards me and their willingness to compete for my contract.

My father added as he lifted the list of names I was to memorise "Being crowned the Pure of the Citadel will be advantageous to any family who ties their name to yours, and the men all know it. What we want to know is if they are *worthy* of it, of you." And so, I spent the next two hours memorising the names of every man who had put forth interest to my brother and father, and where their titles lay. They had set the process up like small interviews. Tomorrow I would be escorted by Orion around the room where I was meant to greet the eight eligible men and make small talk – while Orion judged their character by standing beside me. It would not be until they came back with their final offers of a Binding contract that we would worry about who was more worthy of my hand. The whole process was starting to make me feel ill.

"…Lord Carron is from the village of steel, where Alyssa came from. He is most respected there as an archivist. He is also council to the Lord of that village and together they have prospered the village from what it once was before they took over… Then there is Lord Morozov. He is Commanding Lord of the Southern Paradise. He has been married once before, but she passed away a year ago. He is a hard man, but he runs all three villages in the south alone and has power behind his title and is in need of an heir…"

"I heard that man is ruthless and unfeeling." I threw in, dismissing him immediately from the rumours Imogen had brought back whenever he visited. She had tried to seduce him once and he just laughed and pushed her away. She was not pleased her advances had failed – and though I was pleased I was not being put near a man who had touched my sister, I did not like the air he created around himself from sheer ruthlessness. I wondered briefly how his wife had perished and a shudder ran through me.

"He oversees multiple villages – and as the God of the southern paradise wishes to drink and frolic his way through life instead of leading – I would say Morozov has done the best to lead that Paradise than some others would in his place." Father replied, dismissing my comments as if they weren't important traits to consider when bartering your daughter to a man. I agreed with his comment that it took a certain type of man to run three villages without the aid of their God or another Lord in sight. A strong, resilient man – unafraid of the things he may have to do or see considering the long battles the South has had with the Unworthy. But that was not a man I would particularly want to be attached to, could not see *him* being able to attach himself to someone. I would be a breeding machine for him if I survived longer than his previous wife. "And finally, the man you already met, Lord Westward. I must say he does have his work cut out for him regardless of his heritage." My father finished while I was brooding over Lord Morozov.

"Yes, but you forget Father – the connections he has with the Goddess, his aunt. Imagine the stature our family would rise to if we were to be associated with not one, but *two* Pures. Not to mention, the likelihood of their children being a Pure rises if it is both sides of the gene." Orion finished, neither looking at me. By the time he was done speaking, my body was thrumming with energy, face flushed with the effort it took to keep quiet.

"You have a good point there, Son. We must not forget the lineage options. Grayson received only two markings at his Ceremony and is yet to receive further. That speaks to his testament, and from knowledge none in that family have fallen to the Unworthy. This could be the beginning of an exceptional bloodline..."

"Not to mention, the Lord of the South had his own twin brother defect to the Unworthy just by choice alone, their mother was a servant too..."

"Mmm, it is only by the blessing of our Saviour that Morozov has risen as high as he has. Perhaps luck is not what we need."

On and on they went, as if I weren't there. Leafing through the men and their achievements, through their family histories and potential downfalls in genetic coding. As if that mattered more to them than my own opinion on these men I did not know. As if my progeny were more important than my own life, my own wellbeing. As if lineage determined how pure a soul would turn out and not the temptations that lined a person as they grew.

I felt the thrumming seep into my bones, electrifying every nerve, every atom of my body until I tasted blood on my tongue from holding myself back. *Appease…..Appease the masses.* I tried whispering in my mind, trying to calm the flames shooting through me. I went through every argument in my mind, trying to ascertain exactly how much my future was worth to me – how much it mattered who I bound my life to – how much Sin I would willingly commit to risk my happiness and if that outweighed being bound to a man, one I knew I couldn't love – even for the sake of my future children in this world.

In this world that I despise – it was worth every Sin in the world. That fire inside me hissed.

"*Enough.*" I forced through my teeth, with enough volume that my brother and father both snapped their eyes to me at once, like they were remembering I was there. I breathed in deep, calming the flames that poured up my throat, threatening to expose themselves. I couldn't, I couldn't unleash this on them. They would assume I had a preference. They would see my anger not as the riotous pleading to keep myself whole, but as a child throwing a tantrum.

They would see a girl infatuated and unable to see anyone else but the man they thought was sending me letters. No, I had to reign this in, act as if I was done with this conversation because I didn't care, and not because I cared entirely *too much*.

"I would like to retire to my room now, if that is okay." I said instead, schooling my face into the impassive mask that I had protected all too well. "You both seem to know far more about these men than I do, I am sure you don't need me to weigh in at this point." They both looked at me for a second longer than I found comfortable, like they saw the fire leaking out of my teeth before I could catch it. I would have to gain control of it before tomorrow night if I had a chance at surviving the party. Once they were both satisfied that my words were indeed that of a woman bored with matters of men, they nodded their dismissal. I rose from the chair as calmly as I could and walked out of my father's study, right through the house until I reached the garden doors.

Calmly I strolled as if I needed air, a feeling of being watched looming over me, prickling my spine until I reached the woods at the edge of our property.

And then I ran.

CHAPTER 11

My Ceremony Day had arrived.

As much as I did not let things influence me, I was nervous. This day was taught to us from the moment we were able to understand the difference between right and wrong. Grace and sin. It was the defining moment in a person's life, and no matter what you had done before hand — this would shout to the Paradise who you truly were.

I wasn't ready for them to know the truth.

My mother for once, left me in peace this morning. Choosing instead to have Analise bring my breakfast tray to my rooms. I knew they were watching me closely, hearing me move about but choosing to give me my space. I was thankful for it.

I tried not to think about what my final trial might look like, too afraid that if I thought too much, I would send a beacon to the Sacred Servants. That they would find a way to see my inner most thoughts and turn it all back on me. Imogen had told me her trial was the worst thing she could ever imagine, and she had failed instantly. Others, those who had claimed to be Pure had also failed.

I might fail.

No, I scolded myself as I started to feel my walls shaking in fear. I had committed no sin, found none as worthy as giving away that piece of me it would require. I would be fine. They could not search deeper than my own desires, and of those I had none.

Dressing in my same simple gown, I opted to leave my hair down and neck bare, as I would just have to take it all off again once I arrived home. Mother had insisted on the stylists coming to prepare me for tonight, even if I did miss their rehearsal yesterday. After my meeting with Father and Orion, I had run off into the Wanderers wood to my meadow. Feeling myself implode more and more the closer I got - I stayed there until I had rebuilt every wall around myself, every piece of armour back in place ready to face the world again. Until I was me again in every way that did not matter – and on my return, my mother had been furious that I had shirked my duties as a Lady in training. Scolding me for hours on the proper way one must deal with appointments, even if they did not want to attend them. Father had tried at one point to console her, to lessen the sting as no doubt he felt bad for making me sit there for hours while they poured over my binding prospects, but she would not have a bar of it. According to my mother, I would have to face many more days sitting in rooms I did not want to be in. I just sat there and accepted it all, head bowed as she went over every etiquette and Ladies teachings that I had forgotten in my running off.

She was right of course - soon I would not be able to run off whenever I wanted. Once my Ceremony was complete, and I was bound to another as his wife, I would be confined to the rules of society and would have to act like it. That did not help the concept of the Binding Ceremony sit any better than it did before.

Once I was presentable, my walls firmly in place, emotions locked in tighter than I had ever had them, I left my room in search of my parents. They would be the ones to escort me to the Citadel's palace where the Sacred Servants were waiting.

Everyone who was born this day would be there to receive their trials – though mine would be the only one anyone would be watching out for. Entering the dining room, I watched as one by one my family turned towards me, Orion and Alyssa present in support. Their nerves thrumming through the air, stifling it to the point that I had to check my walls were still in place.

"There she is - the Lady of the hour!" My father said by way of greeting, raising his cup to me.

"There is no need to be so nervous, dear, you will pass with flying colours." My mother added, as though I was the one feeling nervous and not her, as I watched her tea slosh in her cup as she raised it to her mouth.

"And even if you do fail, we will still love you little sister." Orion threw in at the end with a wink. Alyssa beside him gave me a small smile, as if he spoke for the both of them. He probably did. There was a moment where I watched them all contemplate exactly what would happen if I were to fail my final trial. I would be like every other self-proclaimed Pure to go for their Ceremony. I would be ridiculed as a liar and my family would be disgraced in the eyes of society. This path is not one any of them had dared give much thought on, for fear that it would become reality.

"Where was this encouragement when I went through my Ceremony last year?" Imogen butted in, breaking the morose spell Orion had cast on everyone. I was once again thankful for her self-absorbed nature. "If I remember correctly father, your words to me were 'let's get this over with'."

Orion was the one to answer her, a laugh evident in his tone. "That is because we all know who *you* are, dear sister." This caused a scowl to fill Imogen's face, making everyone else laugh and her to stomp off in anger. We all heard her door slam closed before they all turned back to me, as if expecting me to have some last words I wanted to speak before everything changed.

"I do not wish to be late." I said instead, my mask of indifference stronger than ever – signalling to my mother and father that it was time to leave. They nodded their farewells to my brother and his wife before leading me out the dining room towards the carriage that awaited us at the front of the house.

The carriage ride was uneventful, neither of my parents deigning to fill the silence. I could still feel their nerves for me, as if I was feeding off them – inhaling the spicy scent it left and exhaling my own stone-walled coolness. I focused on releasing it all, I could not afford to get nervous. The Sacred Servants would surely sense it.

As we passed through the streets, I watched as people's heads swivelled to watch us, their mouths moving as this morning's gossip was uncovered. They all knew who the carriage belonged to – our family crest was laid firmly on the doors, and all of them knew exactly where we were heading.

The capital of our world.

The mighty Citadel Palace.

We quickly pulled up outside the gates, waiting for the guards to admit our entrance, and I briefly thought back to my last carriage ride, when they had tried to stop Orion and I from riding into the Wanderer's Wood towards their master's estate. I wondered if they would try to stop me again today — if they could somehow feel that I had raised my shields higher today, hiding the emotions swirling beneath it as they fought to be released into the world. I wondered if the guards could sense that I was a danger and deny my entry into the sacred palace of the Original God.

But the gates swung open without effort and the carriage pressed forward up the steep drive towards the looming building that held my final judgement.

We slowed as we reached the front doors of the palace, guards instantly stepping forward to let us out like they had done to thousands before me. Though as I stepped out, each one of them looked me up and down, assessing this supposed Pure. Their gazes seared me to the bone with judgement, as though they too could see what was truly inside me.

"Good morning, Sandoval family and welcome to your trial, Miss Raewyn Sandoval." A monotoned voice called out from the steps above me. Three men stood in a row above me, all in long floating robes with hoods that obscured their faces completely — the colour pale and earthy, like seeds waiting to be planted in the spring. I guess for all intense and purposes the Sacred Servants were the seeds to our society. Planting us exactly where they deemed the best place for us to flourish.

"Only Miss Sandoval is allowed past this point." The second one called in the same tone, the sound echoing through the wind as if there were more than just the three of them — as if a symphony of Sacred Servants were speaking through them. I shuddered slightly, as my parents turned towards me. Since they had three children who had undergone trials before me, they knew that was coming. My father patted me on the back as my mother leaned in and kissed the side of my cheek. That would be all the encouragement I would get at this point. I turned and watched them as they strolled towards the gardens to the side of the building.

I guess that is where they wait. I thought to myself as I watched them disappear between the hedges. I was alone from this point onwards – something that normally would have brought me peace, though turning back to the three hooded men above me, I knew that isolation would bring me no solace this time.

"Come, we have much to learn of you." The final Servant called, as I began the climb towards them; towards the place that would endeavour to strip me down to my bones and rebuild me in the eyes of the Saviour. Whether I was worthy of the name *Pure* or not, I would not come out until I had been tested thoroughly and marked accordingly.

They walked on ahead as I neared them, as if they were too important to wait on someone like me. I felt it in the air of superiority and power that swirled around each of their cloaks, and I gulped in air as I reached the top of the stairs, fear lodging itself in my throat as I followed them inside.

As we entered the grand foyer of the Palace, I did not have time to marvel at the cool tones of the room – though a quick glance at the way the stone seemed to bend around the aged wood, creating intricated marble like patterns as they climbed the walls around us. The ground was a smoothed stone, as if it had been raised from the ground and worn down over centuries of footprints – and I wondered what stories this building would be able to tell me if it spoke. Would they be happy tales of a newly built world? One that was filled with so much hope and promise that one could not help but feel at peace and content within themselves. Or would it tell one of blood and death — of a world that tried so very hard to be what it should have been, that the blood of its people soaked the soil in sacrifice.

Or maybe it would just tell me of the isolated God of the Citadel, and why he chose to spend the rest of eternity hiding away from the Paradise he helped build.

I heard the heavy gold encrusted doors close behind me with a loud thud, closing me off from the world outside, and I was suddenly aware of how quiet it was — as though even the walls truly were holding their breaths, waiting for me. I raced to catch up with the Sacred Servants, who had continued walking through the halls without looking back to see if I was following — not that I had any other choice. To refuse your Ceremony or your marks was as treasonous as breaking one of the Covenants.

Making sure to keep the Sacred Servants in sight so that I would not lose them, I focused only on the swish of their cloaks and not on the direction they were leading me in as I double checked the strength of my walls.

It was this unawareness that caused me to miss the shadow of bulking mass before me until they stepped directly into my path.

"Miss Sandoval, we meet again." The messenger of my letters smirked as he blocked the corridor I was heading down. I watched as the Sacred Servants continued walking — unconcerned that I had been stopped.

"Messenger," I said by way of greeting, for I did not know his name. *I need to start asking for people's names!* I thought inwardly as I watched his smirk grow at my name for him. Clearly, he was not used to being someone's messenger.

"I have a letter for you." He stated as he held another

letter in front of himself, identical to all the others. My heart pounded at the sight of it, at the thought that this letter might contain the answers I so desperately needed.

"Now is not the time, nor the place." The words were directed at him, but they were aimed at the pounding inside me, the storm the parchment had incited in my blood.

"Now is most definitely the time, I was specifically ordered to deliver it before your trial."

"Why?" I breathed, the air around me hotter, breaths coming in shorter. I couldn't let this affect me; I would *not* let this affect me here.

"I do not ask why – it is not my job to." Was his only reply, thrusting the letter forward so that I had to take it.

Once it was safely in my hands he bowed once and strode past me, back the way I had just come without another word. I stared at the closed letter, feeling the weight of it in my hands. I did not have to open it here. I did not need to. I did not need to know his name right now.

I breathed in once, taming my pounding emotions that were threatening to be let loose, but they only beat harder, demanding I feel them.

On my exhale I tried to convince myself that I could wait to open it, I could wait until after the trail.

I breathed in again, reinforcing my armour, tightening the reigns on my emotions, on the pounding that seemed to echo in my ears, the thoughts that wouldn't stop swirling in anticipation.

Inhale…

Exhale…

Inhale… I need to know…

Exhale…

Now.

Glancing up I saw the Sacred Servants walking

through an open door – I only had seconds to read the letter, if that.

Ripping open the seal, I unfurled the letter and glanced at the elegant script that wrote only one sentence.

You are not ready for the answer to that question,
my little Pure.

No.

How…. *Shit.*

My walls shattered as I exploded internally – my armour trembling under the weight. I stared at the open door where the Sacred Servants were waiting for me to begin my final trial.

That selfish, rakish, *prick!*

How dare he order his man to deliver this to me right before my Ceremony, how dare he do so right before I was to be subjected to someone pulling at every thought, every temptation and desire I'd ever dared to have.

Right before I needed to *not* think about him.

Somewhere inside of me, beneath my armour and walls, I always knew it was him. The man from the fountain. I knew it could only have been him. The one man to evoke anything out me that mattered, without effort – as if every thought, every feeling that I ever had was waiting only for him. I didn't like that, didn't like that I had no control what came out of my mouth when I was around him. Although I still didn't know his name, I knew who I was speaking to now, and I couldn't tell if the tremor that ran through me was from anger or excitement.

I felt the paper crumble as my fists clenched tight, the tremor rumbling through my veins, under my skin as I felt cracks forming all along my armour. I couldn't do this now.

I couldn't think about this now. I needed to focus, I needed to not be a mess when I walked through those doors. Already too much time had passed since the Sacred Servants went into the room. They would come looking for me soon, and any time they spent waiting was another second they had to plan my trial, to notice that I was not what everyone claimed.

They would delve deeper because of it.

I couldn't have that.

Breathing deep again, I imagined the corridor was the clearing in the Wanderers woods. That every door I passed was the dense forest that surrounded it. That once I cleared through the door my armour would be remade, rebuilt and at peace once again as if I were laying between the wildflowers again. I felt the trembling climb back through my arms, fingers unclenching as the paper fell to the ground, discarded from body and mind. I did not have room for him now.

After, I would analyse every stroke of pen on page – but right now they did not exist. My heart beat a steadier rhythm as each step I took echoed through the walls, the sound strengthening my own walls, my resolve; my emotions disappearing with the steadiness now thrumming within me.

As I passed through the open door, my face as stoned as the walls now tightly binding my thoughts – I watched as the Sacred Servants assessed me. Any trace of why I was held back left tin the corridor.

I was now Raewyn Sandoval, of the Citadel. Appeasing the masses with what will soon be true. I am without sin, without temptation. *Pure.*

"Are you ready for your final trial, my child?" One of the Servants asked. I looked each of them in their faceless hoods, but it was as if the voice came out of all of them at once, echoing through the room in voices that sounded too many.

"I am." I replied, voice like granite, strong as the walls that now stood tall in my mind.

They each nodded, parting so that I could see the rest of the room. It was an empty room – four barren walls staring back at me, small and sterile as if we were in an infirmary and not the very place my life would change forever.

The only thing that seemed to inhabit the space was a simple weathered chair that looked as if it had been borrowed from a school room. They stood parted and expectant, and I knew they were waiting for me to take my place on that chair. Slowly, I moved towards it, keeping my mind clear of everything that did not have to do with this moment, with these men who were no longer men as they watched me from behind their cloaks. As soon as I walked past them, I felt them closing the gap, the door closing with them as if pushed by the wind. I sat as the quiet thud of the door hit my ears, and I somehow knew that door would not open until they were satisfied.

"We have watched you for two years Miss Sandoval, and from that we have gathered many a thing about you. We will now use that knowledge to test your faith, your loyalty to the Saviour and lastly your temptation to sin. Once we have seen what is in your mind, we will decide on your markings. Our judgement is final as are the markings we place upon you. Are you ready?" The words seemed to echo through each Servant as if they were all speaking at once, my body seeming to relax more and more as their words seeped into my mind. I guess this was the beginning of the trial, to lull me into a stupor so that I was more willing, my mind more malleable to pry open and see into.

My eyes began to droop as heaviness enveloped them and it was all I could do to nod in their direction, fuzziness clouding my vision tunnelling the world only as far as the three men in front of me. I felt a sudden silence in every fibre of my bones as I felt more than saw as they moved closer, gliding silently on whatever powers they held within themselves – until there was nothing left between us but the slow breaths coming from my lungs. I watched dazedly as the Servant in the middle of the trio reached one cloaked hand towards me, pointer finger spindly and elongated, aimed directly at me – and although I felt a surge of panic rise behind my shields, it did not make it further than that.

The spell I had been cast under seeming to have a double effect in keeping me placid and my walls intact.

As soon as his finger made contact with my skin I was gone.

CHAPTER 12

The first thing I registered was muffled voices. Fast and filled with emotion – as if they thought speaking over top of one another would help them get their point across.

The next was the feeling of something hard yet soft beneath me, tiny fissures woven throughout its sturdy exterior giving it a worn and comfortable feel…. Could it be leather?

One by one my senses returned to me until I could smell my father's distinct scent – coffee and ink. I felt the coolness of the room that I knew was caused by a little window in the upper corner of the bay window that was always slightly ajar. I heard bustling in the distance, the sounds of a house running efficiently without order.

Light softly filtered the room as my eyes opened, I was in my father's office. *What was I doing here?* I wondered, as I moved to a sitting position. My head felt heavy and strange – and for the life of me I could not remember how I came to fall asleep in here, or what I was doing before I awoke.

The muffled voices grew heated and clearer as their voices rose to an octave I could no longer ignore, and I looked up to seek out their owners.

"*I will not bind myself to that heathen!*" Imogen screeched, and I flinched as the sound pierced through my still fragile senses.

"You do not have a choice daughter. Your sins have made you unsuitable for every Lord in every Paradise. Thank the Saviour that God Morozov is in need of another wife and took a liking to you. This is far better than I could acquire for you, and frankly far more than you deserve." My father screamed back, red-faced and heaving – as if he had been repeating himself for a while now. Father was never a cruel man, but he was loyal to his position in society and devout to the whims of Gods.

"And what about you, Sister? Do you agree with Father? Will you allow me to be bound to Morozov and be slaughtered like the last three of his wives?" Imogen whirled on me, noticing that I was finally awake. How I managed to sleep through all their bickering was beyond me. Clearly, I had missed something important here.

"That is speculation and gossip Imogen, have some faith in your husband-to-be, he would not bind himself to you if he did not want to."

"But I do not wish to be with *him*, Father." she sneered back at him. "It is not fair that he gets to choose and yet I have absolutely no say in the matter. I will *not* walk down the aisle for that man. I would rather become Unworthy than be his new brooding mare."

"That is enough, Imogen! The contracts are completed, he will be your husband and I will hear no more words on this matter." With that my father stormed out of his own study, washing his hands of his daughter. Sold and bought without a mere glance at her feelings. I watched as Imogen's eyes followed him out of the room, her breathing uneven, hair askew. I had not seen her this passionate about anything before. Not even when she was contracted to be with Lord Ruskin. Him she had accepted when the alternative was lowering her station in society. What had changed?

"Will you not say a word, Sister? You once offered me a way out, why will you not speak now that you have the power to do something?" Imogen's words baffled me enough that my words could not form around the thoughts swirling in my mind. "God Morozov has been through *three* wives, and no heirs. He does not want me because he finds me beautiful, he wants me because he thinks me desperate enough to bend to him. But I will not bend. I may not have much left, but I have my spirit, and I will never give that away." As she finished speaking, she turned fully to me, and I let go a startled breath. The left side of her face was hidden in blackened whorls, her arms *covered* in markings, reaching down through to her fingertips.

Vanity. Lust. Greed.

She had sinned too much, done so much that by all rights she should not be living in this house anymore. Father was right, no Lord would want her now.

"Well?" She prompted again when she noticed me staring at her.

"The *God* Morozov… he has only had one wife." Was all my voice would allow me to speak, my heart still crying for my sister and her refusal to be better, to *do* better. But despite my sorrows I wracked my brain for any memory of Morozov becoming a God. Last I recalled he was a Commanding Lord in running for my hand. When had that changed?

"Where have you been living, Sister? You know as well as I that he has had two more since Lady Mara. After your Ceremony, when you refused his proposal of Binding — he overthrew the old God of the South in a fit of rage that you would deny him and took Lady Daphne instead. She lasted about a year before he tired of her and her inability to bear him an heir. Then he took Lady Grea — Daphne's body not even cold in the ground and though she lasted twice as long as Daphne, she too could not bear him any children.

Three years. It had been *three years* since my Ceremony. Where I was in fact crowned Pure of the Citadel and Morozov had risen to that of God, something that was not heard of considering his sins…

Something did not feel right here, but my still foggy mind could not tell me what it was, so I stuck to the facts my sister presented, clinging to it like it would pull me from the sensation of all this being a dream.

"Imogen, Morozov is a God. Even if I wanted to do something about it, I could not."

"But you are the *Pure of the Citadel.*" She spoke my title like it was a curse, her lip curling in disgust that she had to remind me of the spatial difference that now resided between us. We were no longer just the Sandoval sisters. No, I was now titled and powerful in my own right — seated at the helm of society next to all the Gods, and she was… Imogen. Consumed by her temptations; wild, sin ridden, and proud to be who she was.

While I could envy the confidence and freedom with which she had always roamed, I could not deny that I no longer wished to be her.

"It does not matter my title, Sister. Even I do not have the power to go against the Gods. No matter how damning his rumours."

"So that is it then, is it? Your promises mean nothing to you now that you are better than me, than everyone?"

Again, something inside me fought to get out, something didn't feel right. I had never thought myself better than anyone else, and I had always assumed that my Ceremony would not change that. But three years had passed, and I had done, what? What had I done in the last three years? Imogen says I refused a proposal from Morozov — but then what?

Why could I not remember?

"Sister, what happened to Lord Ruskin? Why are you not bound to him?" I asked as I fought to recall everything I knew for certain, attempting to piece it to the present. This apparently though, was a sore spot for Imogen.

"What happened? What happened was that Lord Ruskin attended your celebration, intending it to be our first formal gathering together — and realised that he was getting the scraps of the Sandoval family. Once he saw how wonderful the Pure of the Citadel was, he did not want me. He called off our contract the next day."

"Did he propose to me?" I prodded, rubbing my temples as a pain shot behind my eyelids, muffled screams shouting in my ears.

"Did you hit your precious head on the sofa, Raewyn? Why are you asking me these questions? You know damn well he took Stacia for his bride. You went to their Binding Ceremony." Stacia was one of the girls from Imogen's gaggle of followers, and I could feel the pain in her voice at the mention of her former friend.

"I am just trying to make sense of all this," I replied by way of explanation, the screams now echoing through a cavern of space inside me — one that I knew was once filled with…. *Something.*

Damnit what is happening to me?

"Well, if you will not help me, then I will have to take measures into my own hands. Farewell Raewyn, I'd say this is last we will ever be seeing of each other." My head snapped up at her words, forgetting the screams, the cavern, and meeting her steely blue eyes — so much like my own, though one almost drowning in the shadows of her markings.

"Sister, you *cannot*. It is treason to go against the wishes of the Gods, and Morozov's is to have you. It does not matter how much truth there is to those rumours. If you do not go ahead with the Binding Ceremony, the God of the Citadel will have your head."

"And Morozov will have mine regardless. I do not see any other choice."

"There is always a choice sister. Morozov can give you everything you have ever wanted. You just have to bear him a son and he will leave you alone. In all that you have done with the men of this village, surely you can do that for your husband?" I pleaded, as she began to walk to the door.

"You still know nothing Raewyn, I may have been marked as a whore — but I have not been with anyone but my beloved for the last two years. If you had deigned to visit you would have known, would have met him. But you never did, and Father never allowed his blessing. From now on, when I am marked — I am marked because of my love *not* because of my sin. I tolerate the shame and the stares for him, because for the first time someone has seen me." With those final words piercing through the fog in my mind, she walked out the door.

The screams inside echoed everywhere until it was all I could hear.

THIS IS NOT REAL! They screamed at me through the noise. I was not *here*, not really going through this heartbreak on behalf of my sister as she was thrown to the wolf of the South. This was just a test to see how I would react, to see if I would choose blood over God, sister over Covenant.

Those sneaky bastards.

Had Imogen stayed any longer, I would have caved. I would have led her to the Eastern Paradise border with her beloved and given everything inside of me to ensure their safety. If she is truly loved, truly happy then there is nothing I wouldn't give to see that she remains so.

My mind pounded against my skull, as waves of envy, sorrow and anger washed over me, overpowering everything else in me until all I could see was the injustice of society – the injustice that would have befallen my sister had this been real.

One could only be bound for station, sanctioned and approved by the head of each family. Officiated by the Sacred Servants, in the eyes of our God, so that it became as binding as the law. True love never had anything to do with it. Love encouraged sins after all.

The screams grew louder as my emotions raged freely within me, for the first time in years – and I realised in a cornered part of my mind that the screams were no longer *inside* of me. They echoed through the room until it was all I could hear; all I could see above the storm raging inside.

"Raewyn, what did she do to you? I swear I will throw her on the Unworthy border and leave her to her fate if she has done you any harm." My father shouted above my screams as he ran into his study, winding his arms around me as he found me curled up on his couch that had begun my journey into this mess.

I couldn't reign in my emotions as they pummelled me from the inside fighting to be freed from my skin – ready to be heard, to be felt, to be *feared*. I couldn't speak for fear that they would escape me, couldn't move in case they took over my body without my consent. I was a slave to my emotions for the first time in my life.

I finally understood why Imogen was the way she was.

If this is the power of grief, the power of love, of happiness, of being your true self – it would be worth every sin in the world, every broken Covenant, every denial of the Gods. But I couldn't be that person. Not now, in this false vision of my life, not here in this trial where I was being judged on my actions.

I had to control them.

Brick by brick I built my walls back up, limbs trembling, head pounding as the screams became internal once more – begging me to let them out, to let them *see*. Once my walls were secure, I placed the thickest armour I had ever conjured in front of them, willing it in place, protecting me from my emotions and preventing them from entering my mind once more. I had been caught unaware once, I would not allow it again. This time I was ready, this time I would not let them fall.

Slowly I came up to sitting once more, tears streaming down my face as my father clung to me throughout it all. Softly rubbing circles on my back as only he can, slow comforting breaths giving me a guide on how I was meant to be.

Once I was back under control, I lifted my head to him and said "Imogen is breaking the Covenant. She is defecting to the Unworthy with her lover so that they may be together, so that she can deny a God his bride."

And just like that, it was over.

Opening my eyes again was the most terrifying thing I had ever done. I was still reeling from my first trial, my body trembling with the remnants of the emotions that briefly tasted freedom and sought it again — I was not sure I could handle any more.

"Raewyn Sandoval, you were tested on your faith in the Sacred Covenant written by the Saviour himself." The Servant who had placed his finger on me spoke, bringing me back to the present, back to the men standing in front of me. He was retracting his hand from me as he spoke, as if mere seconds had passed from the beginning of my first trial. It had felt like an eternity.

"In this, we used the knowledge we learnt that you would do anything for your family — the only thing worth sinning for in your eyes. The test was designed merely to see how far we would have to push you before you defied even the Gods." The Servant on the left added. I had said those words before, to the Goddess Patricia. Had they been watching, or had she been another test to wring information out of me to use for my Ceremony?

"We almost thought we had you, at the end. The notion of love is something every human craves — it is always their downfall. You surprised us at the last second — showing us who you really are. Something that does not happen often." The third servant finished, as if they were sharing one mind — and perhaps their powers extended to even that.

I sucked in a breath at the accuracy of his statement. I was not above the rest of the humans they had tested before me. Love *had* been my downfall in the end, my mind broke with the heartache of losing my sister to the Unworthy, of denying her the love and acceptance that she so clearly craved in her life. Of the bravery it took for her sacrifice her standing in society, her skin in order to keep that love.

I could never be her.

I watched them as they readied to deliver their verdict of my first test – knowing that I had failed in the end – in the moments where I had let my emotions run rampant and my scream ring through me.

As one they spoke. "You have passed the first trial."

A breath I didn't know I was holding loosed itself at their words, my body sagging with relief. I had passed, I had kept myself hidden enough for them to believe that I would not have burnt the Citadel to the ground with the emotions raging through me like an inferno.

"It was your steadfast dedication to the Covenant, throughout it all – even in the end when we believed that love would have won out, you reported your sister so she could be punished for even considering abandoning a God. That is what won you this trial. Well done." The middle servant said by way of explanation. I still felt the guilt of my final words, damning my sister to death – whether she was real or not – did not sit well with me.

But I knew it was the only way to win.

"It is now time for your second Trial." The Servant on the left declared, stepping towards me, and breaking through my thoughts just as the fog descended on my mind again. I would not let it take over me completely this time. Grabbing hold of the fogginess in my mind, I held it like a thread – well away from the walls it had destroyed in seconds before, and I felt its energy pulsing, moving through the space between them and the doorway they'd found in my mind.

As his finger came towards me, I felt his foggy power push harder against me, forcing me to submit to its trials. But I would not. Gripping that thread of power, I tugged, watching it reverberate right through to the essence of the Sacred Servant before me. Keeping a hold of it, I let the world fade around me as I willed his power to heel.

This time I was in control.

CHAPTER 13

I was aware of my surroundings all at once, my senses slamming into me like a brick wall that disorientated me more than I was prepared for. But I was still aware of where I was, and why I was here.

This was still a trial, and I was in control this time. Opening my eyes I blinked rapidly against the bright light of the large room, beige and dull like the room my body was sitting in with the Sacred Servants. I heard the people rumbling in hushes and accusations in front of me — watching as they filed themselves down the aisle, making their way to their seats. It took me a moment to figure out where I was. I was sitting on a dais in the Citadel's courthouse, a place my father had taken me once to show me where he made his living.

I had not been here in years, albeit I had never seen it from this angle. This was a place I had never wanted to return to for all I found in its walls was a coldness that seeped into my bones. Clinical and unfeeling.

"We call you all here today to bear witness to the

rulings of those who have failed this society – a showing that those who sin shall never go unpunished, as is the will of the Saviour and the God's he bestowed upon us." A voice called out to the people who were anxiously gathered before me. I watched as they sat in their pews, readying themselves for this judgement – stealing glances towards me in excitement and in dread.

Why was I sat facing them all instead of in the pews next to them? Perhaps the test was my own trial, perhaps they had indeed seen my slip in the last test and were showing me what was now to become of me, now that they knew my entire being was not set towards the ways of the Saviour, but to the will of my own heart.

My heart froze at the idea that they had been able to see inside me in that second of freefall, while emotions beat against my walls inside me at the same time – fighting their way free again so that they may go down with a fight and part of me thrilled at the idea. Surely, they would have mentioned the slip up if they saw it. They would not have passed the trial if they had, would they? My mind raced as my heart pounded so loud, I was sure the crowd could hear it, hear the deception inside me.

As I struggled against the thought of my impending judgement, I felt the fogginess untangle itself from my grip, slowly making its way over me, the panic inside me overriding the need to stay in control. Slowly I felt myself become groggy and pliant once again and my head dipped as the fogginess seeped its way through my armour. Soon I would forget why I was truly here, believing once again that this was happening to me and not for the enjoyment of the Sacred Servants.

My eyes slowly blinked as my mind muddied. Why was I here again? I shook my head to try and wake myself as I looked upon the crowd once more. Were they here for me? I wasn't sure, but if they were then I must have done something terrible — and if that were the case then I deserved this, whatever it was. People looked at me as they sat, readying themselves for the beginnings of a trial as I tried to gain my senses.

I sat up straighter as they all gazed towards me, resigned to the knowledge that I would be the entertainment. But what had I done? I dove through my mind as memories of my life played, nothing of note standing out. Could it be that I did not remember committing a sin atrocious enough to warrant judgement?

Next, I looked at my hands, my arms, any piece of visible skin that would tell me of the sins I had committed, for they would have to be high enough to be cast out of society. Again, there were none.

Panic rose in me as I tried to figure out why I was sitting up here and not down there with the people. *None of this made sense!* I screamed internally as I felt something pummelling me from the inside. I should not be put on trial if I did not deserve it, I should not be condemned for something I did not do.

The pounding inside me continued and two words slithered out of a crack in the wall I found it coming from. *not real, not real, NOT REAL!*

It was if I had doused myself in freezing water, my senses all slamming back into me once more. I was in my trial. This was *not* real — but merely a conjuring of the Servants will inside my mind.

I could not lose control — I could not lose, period.

Slowing my racing heart, I breathed deep as I curled my mental fingers around the fog again, weaving it through me so that it was almost a part of me, throwing more shields up to keep it from seeping its way into me again – ensuring that even if it freed itself, it could not influence me. Once I was certain it was not escaping anytime soon, I turned my focus back to the people who were settled down now, hushed and awaiting like I was to hear the judgement.

Whether I was under control or not, did not change the situation I was in. My trial was to be about my own impending trial – and in every scenario I would lose, regardless of how I held my mind now. I would not be here if they had decided otherwise. Steeling myself with the knowledge that this would be the end of me, I sat back and accepted my fate – a small smile now playing on my lips, my mind now relinquishing wholly to that part of me that craved for people to know who I truly was.

If they wanted this trial to be about my own impending doom, then I would make it one worth remembering. If this were to be a confession to my outburst before, then I would show them exactly what they would have found if they had delved deeper into my mind – knowing that once I did so, I would not get the chance to stand a real trial. My heart and mind seemed to quiet in sync as they accepted my new plan, my blood thrumming with what was soon to come. The thought of showing society who I finally was, flawed and emoted and against everything this court stood for brought a wave of tranquillity over me that I had never experienced before.

I breathed deep, readying to lower my amour in permission to those raging feelings, but the voice spoke out once again before I could do so.

"As she is protégé to our God of the Citadel, Pure Sandoval shall reign judgement on these cretins as her words are as pure and just as the God himself."

Well, I was not expecting that.

They all looked towards me expectantly, as if I were to impart some sort of wisdom from the Gods on them, but all I could manage was a nod towards them as I sat there, stunned – my emotions halting in their quest for freedom with the new knowledge that this was no longer my downfall.

I was not the sinner.

I was the Judge.

Shit.

This was worse.

I schooled my face into one of boredom and indifference, as I had done many times, and I watched the guards signal for the sinners to be bought forward. Bracing myself for this twist in my trial – I would be judged on how I judged these people. These people would not be beggars and thieves. They would not be denizens of society, those people are imprisoned and marked – but released back into the world, the consequences being no more than some land or title taken away from them if the cause was severe. They would not even be the murderers or Covenant Breakers – they were executed on sight without trial, as their crimes were greater than life itself.

No, these people I am to judge are normal, worthy of breathing just as I am. Their only downfall was trying to be themselves, no matter what the Covenant or Gods had ruled was the right way to live. Damning themselves to the consequences.

It was something I had just resigned myself to do. Something that was still screaming inside me *to* do now that it had a taste of attention. My breathing became shaky as I watched the five on trial be led towards the front of the courtroom, directly separating me from the rest of society, just as my status should.

The motion as well as the raised dais in which I sat showed that I was above all these people, that my title afforded me more than them – and in title, they were right. But the more I watched them approach – sacks covering their heads so that we may judge the sins and not the person, chains rattling around the ground as they were all joined together with shackles that bound them to this society, dirt covering every inch of them as if they were no longer good enough for water and dignity – and slowly come to a stop, I knew that in every fundamental way that mattered that they were wrong.

That this was so very wrong.

And I could not be a part of this.

The guards arranged them in a neat line before me, as if presenting a show before bowing low towards me and turning to walk back to their posts on either side of the stone walls.

The coldness that I had noted when I was younger seeped into my bones at the thought of what I was about to do. I needed to condemn these people to the judgement of a God – to the harsh and cruel punishments that came with going against the Citadel and all that this new world stood for.

I braced myself as the speaker walked forward, I had met him before. He had attended many of my fathers' parties in the past, though the look of cold distain he now held in his face was never present at any of them. How could my father do this so calmly? Or did his blood boil as mine did now whenever he had to bear judgements of people he may know. I wondered how he slept, if his job haunted him at all, for I was sure that even though my mind told me this was a test – that I would dream of these people, of these judgements for the rest of my life and die knowing that I chose to punish these people under the will of a God and Saviour that I did not know.

"Our first sinner has earned a total of 15 sins this year, bringing his total to 30 markings. He has performed every sin since his last markings – from Greed to Wrath and some with such atrocity that it warranted two markings for the one deed. He has raped a Lady of nobility, challenged a Lord for his title and accosted a Scared Servant. These deeds cannot and will not go unpunished. What say your ruling Judge Sandoval, Pure of the Citadel and Protégé to our God?"

He looked up from his scroll then, directly at me. But I was too focused on the man in question, on the way his tattered and torn clothes showed that indeed almost every part of him was blackened with the markings of sin, of his atrocities. I could not deny that he was not a good person, for any man that takes what is not his without asking is surely the lowest form of a man that there could ever be – and yet I could not help but feel for this man. For the fact that had our world been equal in every way, that there would not be the need for him to claw at what he so clearly wanted. Yes, this man's choices were his own, but this society had deemed him Unworthy from the beginning, setting him up for failure in the eyes of society and causing him to fight back for what he wanted. The silence in the room was deafening as I looked up from the man towards the people, each one of their eyes trained on me as they awaited me verdict. I could do this. I could judge him, I *had* to judge him.

But as I opened my mouth, no words came out, my throat constricting as the moisture left my tongue completely. *This isn't real, this is just a test.* I tried to remind myself as I looked at this man again, sack covering his features — awaiting my verdict so that we may look upon him once his sins have been judged.

"Unworthy" I whispered out. Quiet enough that for a second, I thought no one had heard me. But the speaker nodded his head and moved on as a guard stepped forward and removed the sack from his head. I did not know this man, but I could not deny my sorrow for him all the same. My heart broke as his green eyes glistened with tears as he registered my words. Under the right circumstances he would have been a handsome Lord, tall and lithe albeit I could see that he had starved multiple times in his life.

"Our next sinner was caught harbouring unapproved technology from the Old Times. He claims restoring the automatic carriage is a scientific hobby of his — but the Covenant is the law, and it is not to be broken. What is your ruling on this sinner, Judge Sandoval, Pure of the Citadel and Protégé to our God?" The speaker had moved on before my mind had time to come to terms with the first ruling and I scrambled to piece together what he'd said.

Using forbidden technology was against the Covenant, but I always thought it was an odd law to decree. Yes, the world before us used it to benefit their greed and wrath but harbouring a transportation carriage hardly seemed like it would cause a war. I needed more information, who this man was, why was he hiding it and where he got it from. But I could ask none of those, I was to judge this man on the breaking of the Covenant and punish him accordingly.

"How many marks did this man have before he broke the Covenant?" I tried instead. If I could not judge him on his person, I would judge him on all his sins. Unlike the man before him, this man was more finely dressed — even if they too were torn to tatters, I could still see what used to be a well-made embroidered Lords jacket. That meant he had to be a somewhat upstanding member of society, perhaps he simply found the technology and needed to know more about it. Committing the sin of Greed, while not good, was a much better punishment than any you'd get from breaking the Covenant.

"That does not matter, Judge Sandoval, Pure of the Citadel and Protégé to our God – all that matters is that he broke the Covenant by coveting the monstrosity in the first place." The speaker replied. I had to stifle a laugh every time he referred to me with my *entire* title. If this is how people would have to speak to me once I was crowned Pure, then I'd rather people save their breath.

I thought momentarily on the worst things that he could have achieved with an automatic carriage and could come up with nothing other than using it to show off his wealth and skill – not that he would even be able to since it was forbidden technology. Maybe he was simply fascinated by it and wanted to restore it in order to gain knowledge on it. Though if he had none of the means to restore it or document it then he would not have done so, and so I came up with my punishment.

"He is to be stripped of all titles and land and banished from the Citadel. He can live the rest of his days as a Radical." I spoke a little more loudly this time, knowing that if I was going to get through the next three sinners, I needed to have some semblance of belonging in this chair.

The speaker nodded in agreement and moved down the line, the guard once again stepping forward and ripping the sack off the sinner's face.

I gasped as he came into view, the crowd behind him following suit as I am sure many of them recognised him as a prominent member of society. He was indeed a Lord. One that lived a few doors down from my family. I had grown up next to his children, and though I wasn't particularly fond of them or him — my heart still broke a little more at knowing that I had broken up his family. His punishment would have a rolling effect on them, and they would practically be shunned from society.

"This sinner's punishment shall be a lot easier to decide, Your Pureness." The speaker said with a kind smile as he unfurled his next scroll. As if he could see that this was taking a toll on my soul. "This man defied and slandered his God, *your* God. One of these infractions is punishable by death, but to have committed *two* — there will be no saving you, Sir." The speaker finished with a sneer as he ripped the hood of the man before him, not waiting for me to decide on my verdict.

The crowd behind him shouted words of outrage that he could defy our God and called to me for his head. The chants filled the room, spearing through me like a pulse until the speaker stepped away from the man and he came into my view.

Immediately the breath left my body as I stared at the man I most certainly did know. His hair looked a muddier brown than the smouldering flames that I saw before walking into my trial, and he was still wearing that same vest I had seen him in. To his credit he did not look as worn and haggard as the other sinners, and he still held himself with lethal grace — constantly ready to rescue himself if given the chance.

His eyes said as much as they stared up at me with the same hint of defiance I always saw in those green orbs of his. I watched as his mouth quirked up at one side, as if daring me to deliver my verdict and sentence him to death. He knew this was coming — there was no other way than for him to die.

I was surprised he was here as the God's usually exacted justice immediately on any of those who were caught defying them. But I guess this was part of the test I was facing. I had to judge not just the people of this society, but the people that I knew – and no matter how personally I knew them, I had to do so according to the wills and laws of the Saviour and Gods.

I held my head a little higher, using the chants of the courtroom witness to stoke the fire coursing through my veins. I took the challenge in my messengers' eyes and the anger at the Sacred Servants for putting me through this test to begin with and fanned those flames. I would not fail now. No matter who it was.

Steeling myself, I uttered one word.

"Death."

The crowd roared in praise at my verdict, but I drowned them out as I looked at my messenger for the last time. He nodded his head once at me, as if I had made the right decision on his behalf – and for this test I knew I had. But that did not stop the flames of my emotions from burning through me.

I was done with this trial, and I needed it to be over. I only had two more to go. I could do this.

"The last two Your Pureness committed the sin as one, and so you we will trial them as one. These two conspired against the wishes of a God, slandering said God *and* one is Unworthy scum no less. His life was forfeited the day he stepped over the borders." He hissed the words towards the taller hooded figure before turning back to me

"What is your ruling on these sinners, Lady Sandoval, Pure of the Citadel and Protégé to our God?" The speaker looked at me expectantly, already knowing my answer as the crowd once again rose up at the absurdity of these two.

My answer would have to be the same as my messengers. If he was not able to save his life after two acts of breaking the Covenant, then these two deserved the same fate.

"Death as well for these two. No one is above the Covenant." My verdict earned another roar of cheers and blessings from the crowd, and I finally looked towards them – I was done.

This was the end of my second trial, and I had passed.

CHAPTER 14

I leaned back in my chair and sighed. Even if I was declared a Pure after these tests, I was not sure I wanted any part of the political world of society. I could not do this in the real world, could not weigh people and decide their fates for the good of the Gods. It was cruel and barbaric and spoke nothing of the trials each of them had to face in order to get to where they now stood.

Though in the eyes of the powerful, ascended beings I guess none of that mattered anyways. All that mattered in this world was how pure your soul was and how high you sat on the ladder of society. None of those things factored in the pain and suffering people had to go through on a daily basis – on the inner turmoil of finding oneself versus the good of the Saviour.

Our world may claim it was a better one than the old, but it was just as fractured at the heart.

I waited for the moment it would all end, and I would be taken back to the enclosed room with the Sacred Servants – but when it didn't come, when the people turned their shouts from joy at me, to hatred and obscenities at the two I had just condemned – I realised it must not be over.

Looking back to the two sinners, sacks now pulled completely off their face; one weeping inconsolably as she hid in the arms of her friend, I didn't immediately recognise them. It wasn't until the man holding her – manacles on his wrists encircling the girl in more chains – turned towards me with hatred in his eyes that my heart stopped in its tracks.

Those were my eyes, my families' eyes.

And although the hair had grown long and shaggy and he had aged considerably from the small number of memories I had of him – I would know who he was anywhere.

He was the shame of the Sandoval family.

The one we never spoke of.

The one deemed Unworthy and cast out of the Paradises, never to be seen or heard of again.

Until now.

My eldest brother, Sebastian Sandoval.

My breathing followed my heart as I struggled to draw in a breath. As I tried to make sense of what I was seeing before me.

I tried to remind myself that this was just a test; that it was not real, and he was not truly here, risking his life by entering the Citadel once more. But the more he looked at me, the more panic set in – and when he mouthed the word *traitor* at me with his lips pulled back in a sneer, I stopped breathing completely.

I looked down to the girl in his arms and begged her to turn towards me, for her to show me that she was not who I thought she was – that I was not betraying my family. In my last test Imogen had threatened to leave the Citadel, to run away from the God of the South and become an Unworthy with her love. Could it be her? Could they have used that implanted thought in my mind to conjure her here, to make me deliver judgement on her, when I knew I would rather gouge my own eyes out than declare my own sister's death?

The one person I considered myself close with.

My brother unhooked himself from her as he whispered in her ear, her once blonde matted hair bobbing as she rose off him and turned back towards me, wiping her face with her dirt covered hands. She titled her head towards me, and I leaned forward in my seat, praying that I was wrong — that they would not do this to me.

Praying that the Sacred Servants were just but not cruel.

The fire inside me sputtered and left as Imogen gazed up at me with tears still filling her eyes, though defiance now shone in them. As if she did not regret a single thing that had led her to this moment — to her death.

No, *no, no, no.*

I had just sentenced my best friend to death.

My own *sister.*

It did not matter to me at that moment that this was just a trial - that none of this was real. That the theoretical outcome did not matter once I awoke from this. I couldn't breathe and I couldn't be here any longer waiting for them to pull me out.

So, I did the only thing I knew — I ran.

Leaping off the dais and straight through the crowds of people who were now standing to congratulate me on my serving of justice, all attempting to touch and speak to me, but I pushed and weaved my way through them — ignoring their attempts to ensnare me in their trap as I dove towards the exit. I wheezed in as much oxygen as I could, my lungs constricting as they refused to inhale a thing – my heart jumping from not beating at all, to thudding so hard I thought it would burst through my chest; the fire that had sputtered out moments ago, blazing through my veins consuming me whole.

I couldn't do this. I couldn't be here.

Faceless limbs reached for me through the masses, grabbing at every piece of me as they turned frenzied – halting my progress as if the Sacred Servants themselves were trying to keep me from leaving the room. I flung my limbs whenever they tried and shoved through the throngs of people in front of me, more and more of them compacting the way ahead – the thread of fog that I still grasped on to slithered itself up to my walls, trying to find an opening to stop me from within at the same time.

Sluggishness descended on me as the fog moved in me, taking all my concentration to keep it from entering my amour and pulling me back under. They were trying to control me again, trying to monitor the situation inside of me and I could not have that. I just needed a moment away from it all – and I could not wake up yet, I was set to explode, and it did not matter where it was.

This fire demanded release.

"Raewyn."

A familiar voice called from behind me, and I spun towards it on instinct.

Sitting front row with tears streaking down her face, unmoving despite the throngs of people moving around her, was my mother. My steps faltered and changed course without hesitation, the fog urging me to move back towards her as it sensed my conflict. My mind was on overdrive as I tried to process everything around me, everything that I had done – everything she had seen.

Had she witnessed one daughter condemn her other two children?

Were those tears because she sensed my heart breaking with the knowledge of what I'd done or were they anger at the verdict I had bought down on her elder children.

Cautiously I started making my way towards her, the fog growing and caressing my mind, crooning in my ear that this was where I was meant to be going. That my mother needed me.

The people parted easier now that I was going in the direction of their choosing, all having decided to leave me be for the moment.

"Mother, I – I had no choice. I am so, so s-s-sorry." I stammered as I made my way towards her. My words were barely above a whisper, but I knew she had heard them as she called my name once more. I'd made my way back to the front of the courtroom now as I stood before my weeping mother, my own eyes stinging as unshed tears threatened to fall.

"I am what you wanted me to be mother. I am a Pure, and this – this is what I must do. Had I known, I would have tried to save them. But I did not. I swear it Mother, I did not know who I was condemning until those hoods came off." The words fell out of my mouth before I could stop them, the fog seeking entrance to every corner of my armour.

I couldn't hold out for much longer.

"It is okay sweetheart. You can change your mind. You can still save them." She smiled through her tears, her hand raising to wipe away my own fallen tears.

Could I change my mind? Was it that simple? Go

back up there and declare them saved — but for what reason? The sacks covering their faces provided impartial judgement on the sins and not the person, it was why they were not revealed until after the sentencing. Ensuring that they got what they deserved and not what the Judge wanted to give that person.

No, even if this was real and not some messed up conjuring of a trial the Sacred Servants were putting me through, I would not be able to change the outcome of this — and even if I did so, this was not real, and I would fail.

No, I had to stay with my decision.

"I am sorry Mother, I cannot. Their sins are theirs to bear, as are the consequences."

Although I knew they were the right words to speak, watching my mother's face turn to stone made me question it all.

"We always knew you were the Pure of the Citadel, Raewyn — though back then we thought it meant that you had *too* much heart. Now we know it meant you had none." She hissed back at me, turning her back and walking away from me in a fit of rage.

Was this part of the trial? Was I to run after her and convince her that sentencing two of her children was the right call? Was I meant to change my mind and rescind my punishment on Imogen and Sebastian?

My mind was on the brink of collapse at the state this trial had turned into — the fire bursting at the seams inside me causing my skin to tremble in both fear and anticipation.

If they wanted a Pure; someone next in line to claim this throne of God, ruler of their precious Citadel — then I would show them exactly who that person was.

I tugged hard on the threads of fog attempting to breech my defences and checked to make sure they were still intact. Happy that they hadn't yet broken through I wove mental fingers all through the fog inside me and leashed it, pulling it away from my mind, my armour and drawing it into its own corner, controlling them completely.

I would not be tortured with my family any longer.

This may be a trial created by the Sacred Servants, but this was *my* mind – and I was the one in control.

Turning back into the crowd of people that blocked my exit, I willed them to part for me, to let me pass without acknowledging me. I dug those mental fingers into the fog and told it my will, shaped the world to my own bidding and prayed that it would work.

At first nothing happened, and I thought that the fog was not the connection to this world they had created that I thought it was. But after a moment, people started shuffling to the side, parting a way out for me like long grass bending under my might in a field. I didn't spare them another thought as the fog writhed in my claws, fighting to gain control again.

I ran through the opening and threw my hand towards the door, willing that to swing open and clear the path for me once more. It complied silently and I passed through them without looking back, the room having grown eerily silent under my control. I flew down the steps of the courthouse breathing deep as the cool air of the morning hit my face.

The fire inside me exploded at the contact and I screamed all my fury, all my heartache into the wind. The burning coursed through every inch of me, consuming me completely until all my walls had crumbled away to ash and every emotion I had ever felt, ever suppressed used itself as fuel to the flames.

My screams turned into cries of outrage as I

condemned this whole damn world for ever thinking that someone should have to live like this. That I had to suffer like this.

I burned so hot that my tears dried as they hit my flesh, my bones strengthening into the strongest steel a forge could ever create, my blood like lava as it coursed through me.

I felt the fog tremble under the leash in my mind, as if afraid. I watched internally as the flames licked at the edges, approaching the fog like a predator, testing it for weaknesses and then pouncing – devouring it whole and burning any trace of it from my body.

I felt a change in the air around me as the fog disappeared, a quietness.

Peace descended on me, silencing my screams, and coaxing my fire back within its walls – still present, but now contained. I looked at my surroundings and realised I'd run right into the Wanderers Wood, my soul craving the tranquillity of my meadow and directing me there without conscious thought. I looked around for signs of someone, some indication that I was still in my trial – body coiled tight and ready to face whatever they threw at me. But there was nothing. Relief flooded through me as my knees buckled, slamming me into the grassy floor below – extinguishing any rage I had left.

I was free for the moment.

CHAPTER 15

I spent my time alone breathing in my meadow and rebuilding my walls. Strengthening every mental shield I had ever built.

I knew they would come for me again – this was their conjured world after all. The only question was when.

I pushed back all my thoughts and emotions, caging them once again behind my walls – refusing to acknowledge the fact that in this world that I was stuck in, I had condemned two of my family members.

That my mother had called me *heartless*.

That one hurt more than it should. If my family knew the real me, they would see that I am anything but the bland and heartless girl they had pushed into becoming a Pure. That I was more than my inability to find things tempting. They would know that despite all the tests and trials, the one thing that could make me fall to my knees and beg to sin was the knowledge that in doing so, I would save them – for they were the only thing I loved, and though this society did not believe in such matters of the heart… I did.

And I would fight with everything in me to keep the things that I loved.

What I did not know though, was if I would have done things differently in the real world — and that is what scared me most. As a Pure, I would be watched more closely than the rest of noble society and *any* infraction of the law would be seen as a breaking of the Covenant.

Thou shalt not bear false witness to the Saviour, was Covenant law number seven after all. If I was crowned Pure of the Citadel after this, I would have to maintain this ruse of perfection for the rest of my existence, longer even if I were next in line to become a God.

It was something I wasn't sure I could handle — a lifetime of pretending to be something I knew I was not. A lifetime of keeping my emotions behind a wall so strong that eventually I would not feel them at all. Fear that I would become the very thing my mother thought I was. Heartless, indifferent, cold seeped its way through my heart at the thought.

I shuddered as more emotions washed through me in encouragement. No, those were not things we were thinking about now, for I would not be able to build my walls if I was dwelling in the sea of my emotions. Giving them one final shove, I encased them in the corner of my mind I had carved out for them and placed my armour in front.

A shield to protect them from others and myself from the impending breakage.

As I scanned my mind for anything else out of order, I noticed that the flames that had freed me from the Sacred Servants were still inside me. Having carved out their own spot next to my wall of emotions, simmering away — ready and waiting to be unleashed again.

I probed them gently, assessing them, and gasped as a shock of power ran through me, heating my skin, strengthening me for battle as the flames ignited – and then calmed once they realised the threat was me. Then they caressed me gently, inside my mind. A humming filled the meadow as a calmness washed over me. I could feel it like whispers in my mind, begging me to let them out again, to show them who we were and what we were capable of – and some parts of me wanted that too much.

To be able to freely be myself in a world that would otherwise crush me without this power.

*We can crush them first…*The flames whispered, and I felt oddly comforted at the notion that I could be powerful enough to do it, powerful enough to carve out not only my mind, but the world and rebuild it brick by brick with my own happiness in mind.

Flames licked at my fingertips as I let them wrap around my mind, too enamoured by their warmth and protectiveness. I let it pool in my palm as a ball swirled, dancing through my arm and feeding itself, growing bigger as I watched it – and when it had grown too big for my hand, I let it fall from my fingers and singe the meadow below me, before billowing out in a cloud of smoke. Though where I had expected dirt and ash, I instead only saw darkness.

A hole forming in this world they'd created for me.

I could escape.

The thought excited and terrified me. If I did manage to escape this place, I would only wake to the beige room where the Servants no doubt waiting for me. No, I couldn't do that, they'd surely realise that I was not what I seemed and kill me on the spot. No, I needed them to believe that I did not know anything, that perhaps I was Pure enough to still pass this mess of a trial and then they'd leave me be. I would figure the rest out once this was all over.

With that in mind, I pushed the flames back into their corner again, their hissing and whispers letting me know that they were not too happy at being caged – but it was a risk I would have to take for now.

Slowly, I built more walls, surrounding my flames as I made sure they could not escape unless I willed them too, and hoped that this new cavern inside me would not be discovered once the Sacred Servants came to collect me.

I knew it would be a bad thing if they discovered my new talent for fire – as it was, I was not certain I would be able to explain *how* they had freed me from the grasp of the Servant's trial, only that they had.

To my knowledge the Sacred Servants were meant to be in complete control of your trials from start to finish, and you were certainly not meant to know that you were in one. There was not meant to be room for me to move freely inside of it, or to rid them from my mind completely – and yet I had done it all and they would want answers.

Though, aside from the flames brewing inside me – I had no answer for them. Yes, I had things I needed to keep from them; thoughts and emotions that would be shunned upon in the eyes of the Sacred Servants – but they were things I would *never* act on, most being a curiosity of why things had gone the way they had and if this really was the best solution for us all.

But this *fire* that had erupted in me… they would have all the cause they needed to fail me and banish me on the spot. Or worse, kill me in the name of the Saviour.

I would be seen as a threat they would need to snuff out before I grew any stronger, no matter how I tried to convince them that I never wanted this. That my only want was to be left alone in this world.

Even if that small taste of fire had made me believe that I could burn it all… if I wanted to.

I was not sure how much time passed, the sun refusing to move across the sky the only reminder that this place was indeed *not real* – but I started to wonder if they would come after me at all. If they *could* come after me since I'd all but shoved them out of it.

But as I sat up from the spot I'd lain down on – next to the hole in the world I had created, I noticed that the meadow was the only thing surrounded in the light of the sun. Behind the trees of the wood, I saw only darkness, as if night had descended on it and a spotlight had been placed solely on me. Maybe they had found me and were just watching me, seeing what it was that I would do next. I stood and peered into the darkness, trying to sense if I could find the fog in the world again – but there was nothing, they weren't here.

Maybe if I walked back to the courtroom where I was meant to be, then they would come for me, and we could get on with the last trial – *or they'll punish me on the spot for pulling myself out of their grip.* My thoughts added morbidly. Either way I would have to make them come to me if I had any hopes of surviving this day.

Making my way to the edge of the forest, I caught movement in the darkness – though as I looked closer, I noticed the darkness itself was *moving*. Shock coursed through me as I realised that what I thought was darkness, was in fact such dense, dark smoke that light failed to penetrate it. Silently, as if it were trying to go unnoticed, it writhed between the trees, watching, waiting, trapping me in this false meadow of my mind.

They're here.

Or rather, some*thing* was here — seeing as it wasn't the same weightless fog that I had captured from the Sacred Servants before. No, this smoke felt infinitely more powerful than them, the fire inside me thrumming at the knowledge, begging to be let out and show them my own powers.

Ignoring the pleas in my mind I took another step towards the smoke, thinking that they would guide me back into my trial, but it did not budge as I approached. If anything, I felt it tighten its hold on the world, swirling faster as if it did not want me to leave.

The fire behind my walls ignited as my panic grew.

I watched as the smoke formed a shape inside itself, directly in front of me — swirling so fast that it began to look like night again and I would have missed the movement had I blinked.

One second there was nothing, and the next stood a man, face still covered in smoke, but I instantly recognised the shape of him.

It was the man from the fountain.

The man who had been writing me letters.

The only man to entice my mind enough that I had *wanted* his company.

My final trial was here.

Breathing deep, I thought of every possible sin they would want to test me on, every temptation that I could possibly give in to, and swallowed them all.

If they were continuing with the trial, then I would not fail it because of one man. I could control myself around him.

No matter how badly I wanted to throttle him.

He casually strolled out of the woods, lazily, as if he had all the time in the world – and I guess in this place we did, but that did not mean I wanted to spend it all with this man who seemed to infuriate me with a look.

Though that was before I found out about the letters. My traitorous mind added as he strolled towards me, eyes watching me carefully for my reaction. Though I hadn't had time to process that bit of information, I was not going to let it slip if they did not know about those letters.

I would deal with my own thoughts later once I was done with this.

"I do apologise for intruding on your alone time again." He said by way of greeting, coming to a stop a few feet from me. The sunlight finally hitting him and showing me his face…not that I needed reminding.

It was one I forced myself not to think of often.

He was dressed as he was by the fountain a few days before. His white tunic billowing slightly in the breeze of the conjured meadow, his stance was casual, relaxed, unburdened.

And yet everything in me coiled tighter in response.

"And yet here you are, intruding again." I replied, schooling my features as my own heart betrayed me, beating faster at the sound of his voice, at the memories of his words on paper.

"Yes, well, it would seem that your hiding spots are not as hidden as you would think." He replied, grinning wider, his eyes swirling in time with the smoke that had remained behind him. I scoffed in reply. This meadow was far enough away from the Citadel that even the guards did not patrol here. I hadn't been caught here in the eight years that I'd been coming here.

If this was real, he would not have found me so easily.

"If all you wanted was a sparring match, you can go. I am in no mood." I said, hoping that if I denied them everything then the trial would end sooner.

"Oh, you are no fun, little Pure. I do so enjoy our sparring matches."

"Why are you here?" I asked, reminding myself that the Sacred Servants were watching me, and I could *not* take this man's bait.

"I was curious."

"About?"

"You." He stated simply, as if this were answer enough — as if I would know what to do with an answer like that.

I stared at him, unable to form words as the flames swirled inside me, responding automatically to the smoke behind him.

"Why would you be curious about me?"

"Did you get my letter?" He asked instead, changing the conversation as he strolled past me, moving further into the meadow. Somehow this felt more like an intrusion on me than anything, my hackles rising with each step he took — my fire testing the walls of my mind in case it had to escape.

Not yet, I tried soothingly as I reinforced the walls around them.

When I didn't answer him, he turned back to me, and his piercing gaze told me he knew exactly what I was doing.

"I thought when I asked Rem to deliver it before your trial, he would catch you at home before you departed to the palace. Not wait for you right *before* your trial. Though I suppose I should expect nothing less from him. He has a way of both following and ignoring orders at the same time."

So that was my messenger's name, Rem – like the deepest part of sleep that held you captive each night. I thought that the name fitted him, as I was sure he had fuelled many a fantasy in the Ladies he kept and nightmares in the men who'd crossed his path. I couldn't help the smile that crossed my face as I thought this, though I tried to hide it as I looked back at the man whose name I still did not know.

"I'm not sure that would have made a difference. After would have been preferable, or never if it were entirely up to me." I stated, walking towards where he was standing in my meadow as if I could shield him from its beauty and keep him from tarnishing it.

Even if this place weren't real, my memories of him in here would be.

"You wish you did not know the author of your letters? Or is it that you did not wish them to be from me?" He asked as he moved his hand in front of me to stop me from walking any further. I turned and gazed up at him but could not read his face as he looked at me expectantly, no glimpse of emotion showing.

"As I do not know who *you* are, I cannot answer that question. Rem, I understand could not tell me as his duty was to you, but why will you not tell me?"

"You are not ready for it." He said, simply.

"For your name?" I asked, not able to hold in the irritation in my tone. He smiled as if he were a cat chasing a mouse and had just won. Further igniting my irritation.

"For all of it."

I rolled my eyes in reply and walked away from him again. None of this made sense – not his words and not the trial. He could not be my test, I had no temptations over this man, though if I was stuck here with him for much longer, I may be tempted to commit the sin of murder. Though I had shown no inclination towards it before.

I could feel him following me as I walked towards the centre of the meadow. I wanted to tell him to leave me and this place alone but knew that it was pointless if I wanted to let this trial run its course. So instead, I waited for him to speak again. It did not take long.

"I was impressed with your judgement before, though I must admit; I was uncomfortable seeing Rem being sentenced to die. They know I would never condemn him myself – though that does not stop them from trying." At this I stopped.

"You were in the courtroom? Before?" I asked, willing my voice into a calm I did not feel inside. Emotions banged at my walls, demanding to be felt at the reminder of what I'd just done.

"Oh yes, though I can understand why you did not see me. You were otherwise distracted by more... important matters." He finished off carefully. I could not tell if he meant my condemning of Imogen and Sebastian or my breaking out of this trial.

"You saw what I did then."

"Yes, I did. Do not think on it too much – the judgement is designed that you would never have known who you were to condemn before the call is made. And once it is, there is no taking it back. That is the beauty of judgements, one box fits all no matter how close we are to them."

My flames burned through its containment in an instant at his words – and it took everything in me to hold them in, so much so that I did not recognise the anger in my voice as I said, "*Do not think on it?*" the words hissed through my teeth as if they were flame itself. "I condemned my own siblings in that room, and your advice is to *not think on it?*"

He shrugged in answer, watching me closely with those swirling eyes of his, as if he could see the heat emanating from me as my fire tore through my body, looking for a way out.

Out of the corner of my eyes I saw the smoke inch closer to us, trapping us in more and my breathing picked up at the thought of being under their control again.

"I merely meant that —" He tried when he saw that I was not calming down.

"That what?" I interrupted him. "That they deserved to die no matter who they were? That I shouldn't let the thought that I condemned two of my own family members consume me? I may not care about many things, but my family is all I have — and I do not care how many sins they have, or how many sins I must commit, I will *always* protect them."

My flames escaped as I spoke, licking down my arms, lifting through my hair as if it would protect me the same as I'd declared I would my family. Power coursed through my veins as fire rushed through me, seeking more of my emotions so that they may find reason to do my bidding. Though my anger at his words was enough to illicit such a response that I was afraid what I could do if my emotions were ever fully unleashed.

I glared at the man before me as panic washed over his features, his eyes widening as he took in my flames. So fast I barely registered it, he dove at me. Slamming into me with his body as the smoke encased us completely — shielding out all light but the illumination of my flames. With them I could still see his face as he looked me over, as if searching for injury – though I could have told him there were none.

My flames did not hurt me. They protected me.

"I need you to breathe, little Pure." He whispered calmly in my ear, his breath like a cool wind on my searing body – but they were words I did not want to hear as I thrashed against him in an attempt to free myself from his grip, knowing that if I could reach the smoke billowing around us, I could burn through them and escape like I'd done with the meadow. But his grip on me only tightened, one arm wrapping tightly around my waist, the other weaving through my hair to cradle the back of my head as we connected with the ground beneath us.

I hadn't even realised we were falling.

My flames dove at the smoke around us now, trying to find a means of escape for me – leaving me to fight the man who was now balanced precariously on top of me, though I felt none of his weight.

A thought in the back of my mind told me that I had never been in such a compromised position with a man before – I could feel the length of his legs on mine, the hard lines of his torso moving as he repositioned himself so that he was lifted slightly off me, arms still wrapped tightly around me in such a way that I felt both protected and contained by him.

The face that I refused to think of was now mere inches from my own. His stormy eyes swirled fast and dangerous as he gazed into my own, and I fought the urge to get lost in their power, to drown in the intensity in which he looked at me – because that is not what I wanted, what I deserved.

I needed to feel this anger, let it burn me whole for I could not take it out on those who really deserved it. The

Sacred Servants, the Gods, the Saviour himself – they were the ones that put me in this position, forced me to live this way of life, and they were all the reason that I'd had to stand there and condemn my siblings today.

If not for them and their games of sins and society I would be free, *they* would be alive, and I would not feel like I was crumbling to pieces.

"Rae, sweetheart, I need you to breathe. It wasn't real. *This isn't real.*" He tried again. But I was beyond listening to him as I thrashed against him uselessly.

"Don't you see? This is the real me. This is what I must become for them, but I cannot – *I refuse.*" I hissed back in his face, clawing at him as I tried to break free from his grip, but he did not budge.

"Don't." His voice dropped to a growl as his face hardened, and I couldn't tell if he meant I shouldn't fight him or them.

"I sentenced my family to die, for what? For the God's amusement? For the Saviour's grand plan? Well, *fuck them, and fuck you.*" His teeth ground together at my words, and I knew I'd said the most damning thing of all. Dishonouring the Gods is punishable by death, and I'd just yelled it into the void they'd thrown me into.

"*I am trying to help you.*"

"No, you are trying to make me confess, what is hidden in my soul. Well, here it is, I condemn all the Gods and our precious Saviour to their own false truths. To the finality that this world is far worse than the one from before – because we are *not* free. We are merely chained closer to the ground so they can control us more effectively. I cannot *move* without fear that it may be wrong, I cannot think without being told that I am coveting something more and I cannot *love* without being told I am no better than a sinning whore. I am sold for breeding – and unless fate has granted me contentment with a man, I will hate him." The fire within me roared as every truth inside my soul was finally set free, encouraging me to continue as I willed them to find me a way out of this nightmare of a trial.

"But this is what you created. According to you, this is who I was destined to be from birth – someone who kills her own sister because it is needed of me. Someone who sits above and judges those below. Pure is not how I feel, but it is what I must become, and I hate that I was chosen for it." I growled out the last part, hatred consuming me as I lost my most guarded truth. If I was going to die, I may as well show them who I really am.

My flames sharpened to knives as they fought with the smoke that was swirling fast and heavy now, that it was a wonder that there was still air left in our little bubble. I watched as my flames danced with it, entwining itself so effortlessly, but never penetrating it enough to make a crack.

Uselessly I tried pushing against the giant on top of me, but he just moved to grip both my wrists – pinning them above my head to stop my struggles. I glared at him, willing him to tell me I was wrong – that our lives were better off because of the Saviour, but he did not. His face twitched with emotions as they flitted over his face, shock, anger, sadness, and last of all, understanding. But I did not want to see what he was thinking, did not want false sympathy from this conjured man, so I tried turning my head to the side – choosing to will my flames into penetrating the smoke around us. Pulling my arms tighter above me, he trapped my head between our arms, making it so I had to look at him. Eyes storming, face hard and controlled as his breathing heaved in time with my own racing heart.

"You cannot run from who you are." He murmured, sadness enveloping his features.

And my fire sputtered as I realised…

He was right.

I was trapped.

This was the end.

I had shown them too much, given them too much of myself and there was no going back now. He watched me as resignation filled my features, the defeat that I could now feel coming as I became limp in his arms.

I watched him as his eyes moved to follow my flames, disentangling themselves with the swirls of smoke, as if they too felt that there was no point in carrying on – I would only give them more in which they could punish me for. We watched them crawl back to me, licking up my arms once again until they rested above my heart, the one place that they would still protect until my dying breath.

There held all the secrets they would never know, and they would never get from me. This slip had been enough for them, I would give no more of myself.

With the fight of my anger suddenly gone, I felt exhausted. Spent in a way that I never had been before, and I was ready for this trial to end. But as I lay there, still vividly aware that this man – whose name I would never get now – was laying above me I couldn't help but wonder about the God of the Citadel.

Would I meet him before my demise? Surely, he would want to see the girl that had given his Sacred Servants a run for their money. Maybe then I could ask him what I thought that day in the town square. If he was content with his life up there. If ascending truly did make him an evolved creature, and if so, why he didn't help those in need achieve the same?

As my eyes drifted closed, I waited for this trial to close in on itself. Soon I would be back in that beige room full of Servants who would condemn me for ever thinking such atrocious things, and I was ready for it.

I was ready for it all to end.

My mind drifted, quietened until all I could hear was the steady breathing of the man above me, feel his assessing gaze on me as he watched me give up completely.

We stayed that way for a while longer, and I almost opened my eyes once more to ask him why the trial hadn't ended yet, ask him what more they could possibly want from me – but then I felt him lean closer, his breath tickling my nose in a cool burst that I couldn't help the sigh that escaped me instead.

"Quieten your thoughts, little Pure. Before they hear them." He whispered calmly, as lips touched my forehead, the same place the Servants had lain their fingers.

I drifted off into a peaceful darkness.

CHAPTER 16

I felt as though I was lying in a sea of warmth and contentment. My mind drifting lazily in and out with its currents. For the first time in my life my mind was blissfully silent – my thoughts and emotions that usually swirled and fought for release seeming to have drifted away in this sea of warmth, leaving me with only one train of thought.

I never want this to end.

I heard voices speak in the distance, directing questions into the space around me, but I could not gather the energy to focus on them – or move my thoughts from their lazy swimming to care enough about them.

It wasn't until the warmth beneath me rumbled low and commanding in answer to those voices that I realised that my sea was not at sea at all.

It was a person.

Jerking myself into a sitting position I groaned as all my thoughts and emotions slammed back into me all at once. Angry that they had been disturbed, jumbled as they all scrambled into one incoherent ball of emotion, causing me to feel dizzy as they all began fighting for dominance once more – alerting me to the fact that my walls had once again been shattered in the trial.

Fighting through the dizziness I quickly erected new walls and shoved everything behind them. Praying that they would hold until I had time to sort out something stronger to bind them behind. I had never had this much trouble controlling myself and part of me longed for that fleeting moment of floating again – but as I remembered this, I also realised that it had not come from me, but from the person who was still seated behind me.

Ignoring the fact that the room was still spinning, I turned slowly – taking stock of my new surroundings. I was surprised to see that I had been moved from the beige, sterile room of the Citadels palace. Now, I spied walls and walls of dark aged wood, stocked to the brim with what looked to be small, word sprawled spines.

A library. I realised as I took in the various lounging chaises and lampshades around us as they filled floor in sporadic intervals. The room looked to be as tall as my own home, though still just as cosy as our own small library at home. My eyes met with the three Sacred Servants across the room, each one still hooded, though now keeping their distance – as though they thought me dangerous after my performance in the trials.

I heaved in a breath, knowing they were limited now that they were here in front of me. There could be no plausible excuse that would get me out punishment. They had heard me condemn the Gods and the Saviour in my fit of rage and speak of the 'old world'. Something that was unforgivable in the eyes of the Sacred Servants, as this world was the only one we knew and needed – the *old* world was broken, and savage and it was a blessing from the Saviour himself for hauling us up and out of that mess.

Or so they told us.

My heart pounded in my throat as I remembered what I had done, and my breathing grew shallow. I had failed my final test – no, I had obliterated their test and threw down all my thoughts, all my self-righteous and sinful thoughts into their world and left them there for all to see. I would be lucky to be branded Unworthy and thrown into the Eastern Paradise at this point. No, they would much rather kill me and make a lesson out of me.

Even those we think Pure can turn into the Devil we hide from, they would say.

"Give her space, you are scaring the poor girl." A low rumbling voice commanded from beside me and I remembered the reason I had awoken.

I was sleeping on another person. No, I was *laying* on a man in front of the Sacred Servants.

Turning much too fast for my head to handle, I came face to face with the source of that warmth and peace, my cheeks burning instantly as I recognised him.

"Hello again, little Pure." He smirked as he lounged against the other end of the chaise we were sitting on, his long legs parted enough to remind me that I had lain there moments ago.

In any other setting, this would have looked intimate – two lovers reclining on a chaise in the library. I may even admit that I liked the idea of spending more time in that sea of warmth that I woke to, and more time amongst the walls of this place, seeking out its stories and worlds as if I could sink into them both and be away from this place.

But this was not the time for either of those – so I fought back the embarrassment creeping up my neck, fought the lingering feeling of his warmth surrounding me as I slept and the knowledge that I would never feel so content again as I stared into his eyes. Those deep stormy eyes swirling just like they had in my trial. Power rolled off him as if it were trying to match the ebb and flow of those eyes. My own eyes widened in shock as I felt it for the first time.

In my small encounters with him before I had never felt such power roll off him, never felt such a need to reach out and touch the space between us to see if it were as tangible as it felt. Like invisible tendrils of smoke laying on the wind, I felt it caress me and I shivered at the feeling – my flames that were still nestled inside me purred at the feeling, filling my body with warmth as if it were trying to greet the smoke once more. Though this time as a friend and not its enemy.

Suddenly his eyes tore away from mine, his body becoming rigid, eyes darkening and swirling faster as he glared at the Sacred Servants behind me. I had been so caught up in my own thoughts that I hadn't even heard them speak.

"Did I say you could speak *pawn*?" He growled, low and dangerous and I felt his power flare towards them as if on instinct. I flinched at the deadly feeling of that power moving, even though it was not directed at me.

One of the Servants choked on his breath behind me, but I could not take my eyes off the man in front of me. Though I had spoken to him a few times, and though I now knew he was the author of my letters, I had to remind myself that I knew nothing about him – that he may very well be as dangerous as he felt in this moment.

Though that did not stop me from feeling far safer than I should in his presence.

He must have caught my flinch as his eyes instantly

connected back to mine, softening as his power continued to roll through the room, stifling the air as I still struggled to control my breathing. He looked at me for a second more before he moved, far too lithe and graceful for one who was portraying a relaxed persona and this just added to my thoughts that I did not know him, that he could be a danger to me — especially if he were here with the Servants who were waiting to condemn me.

"How are you feeling?" He asked gently as his face now hovered inches from my own, his eyes scanning me for any sign of injury before meeting my own again in assessment. I was sure if he looked hard enough, he would be able to see the panic rising inside of me — my fire bubbling in time with my fight or flight instinct.

Who am I kidding, I was only ever a flight sort of person.

He sat and watched me a few moments more before I realised that amongst all I had taken in since I had woken, I still hadn't said a word — so I fought my emotions down, caged my simmering flames that had now placed themselves back in their corner and cleared my throat, loudly and un-lady like in the presence of this man.

"W- what are y-you doing here?" My voice cracked as if lingering flames had made its home in my throat, showing my nerves and none of its normal boredom. His eyes still held mine and I wondered what he was searching for in them, and if he found it as he leaned back once again to take up his relaxed position on the other end of the chaise.

"I heard there was trouble with one of the trials, so I came to see what all the commotion was about." He said with a shrug, as if this explained everything.

"Again, I ask. What are you doing *here*?" I repeated, waiving my arm in his direction to further emphasise that I would need more than his riddles right now. My mind was struggling enough with itself, I didn't need him here making things harder. I watched his eyes flicker up to the Servants behind me and I turned to them as I waited for any of them to speak and make sense of all this.

"Your trials were not what we expected." The first Servant spoke in their deep voice that sounded like it came from one of them and all of them at the same time – the only indication they gave was a lifting of their hooded heads as they spoke, quickly lowering it once again one they'd finished.

"We assumed a glitch had happened in the first trial, and so we were unconcerned as you entered the second." The middle one spoke, though his voice was rougher than the first and I guessed he was the one who had been smacked with the power I felt lashing out before.

"But when you held our own power at your command, we knew we were wrong." The final one finished, his last words slamming into me like a brick.

Wrong. They had been wrong, about many things when they entered this trial with me – but none so more wrong than who my family had declared I was. They had thought they were getting the first Pure of the Citadel, and instead they got me.

Defective. Corrupted before her trial.

Wrong.

"What does that mean?" My mouth moved on its own accord, far smoother and calmed than anything I felt inside. My flames slithered out from their corner as my heart pounded so loud, I was sure they could all hear it.

I felt the power shift around me as if in response to the heating of my skin and it curled around me, soft billows of smoke becoming visible as they circled the room, and I clenched my fingers tighter as heat spread to them. As I prepared for them to trap me once more.

I could not fight my way out of this again– though I was not sure if my flames knew that.

"Calm your mind little Pure, we are not going to strike you." The man spoke softly next to me so only I could hear, and I heaved in a breath at his command. Clearing my mind and pushing back against the flames as they travelled back up my arms but lingered at the front of my mind, ready to surge forward the instant they felt threatened

"You threw us out of our own *iter*, we could not gain entrance again." The first one spoke again as if they could not feel the powers swirling in the room before them, as if they were oblivious to the fight going on within me once more.

"*Iter?*" I asked, all their heads whipping up at my rude interruption.

"Think of it as a pathway between their minds and yours. A void of nothingness where worlds and thoughts can be created. The *iter* is the space where they hold the trials. A world created by them and controlled by them so they can measure the outcome." The man behind me explained for me, though I did not turn to face him as he spoke.

"This was something that we had not anticipated." The middle Servant croaked as though we had not interrupted his turn.

"And not something that has *ever* happened before." The third finished and I gulped at the way he spat it like it tasted bad in his mouth.

I had offended them by taking control of their space.

"We were not sure what to make of you at first…"

"Or how you gained control so easily."

"It was not until his—"

"It was not until I came along and saved the day that we were able to stop your trial and pull you out of the *iter*. You lot are taking entirely too long to speak, and we are not all as old and withered as the three of you." My head whipped back to the end of the chaise as he interrupted the Servant's line of speaking.

A grin had spread along his mouth but otherwise he was unmoved. My flames swirled in time with his eyes for a moment, as if they too were caught up in their trance as slithers of smoke danced past me at the same time. Leaving behind a cooling touch on my still heated skin.

I gained enough control to scoff at his arrogance, but my head still spun as I tried to piece together everything they were saying. He must have noticed because he leaned forward slightly, close enough that if I reached out, I could touch him, though still far enough away that I still felt like I had space.

"You manifested, little Pure. Right in the middle of your trial. A first for these old crones and if I hadn't been nearby, I think they'd still be figuring out how to reach in and grab you." He added with another flash of his teeth and my fire froze as I finally caught up.

"*You* pulled me out?" I gulped, realising that he had not been an imagined trial in the world they'd shoved me in, he was a not a conjuring of my temptations.

No, he had *been there*, he had seen me, seen my flames.

Heard my damning words.

My lungs ceased working at this thought. His power caressed me once again as I watched him, searching his face for any inkling of what he was thinking, of what he was going to do with the information he had learnt of me. But he gave away nothing as he continued to grin at me like he held all my secrets, and I suppose he did.

He leaned a little further in and whispered so soft that I strained to hear him over the rushing in my ears. "You may have been strong enough to shove them out of the *iter*, but you could never keep me out."

The way he spoke held no question that his words had little to do with my willingness to let him in to this *iter* and everything to do with the power rolling through the room around me. This man was more powerful than the Sacred Servants if he was able to walk into a world that they had created and pull out the person who had closed it off to them.

"*What the hell are you?*" The words spilled out of me in a hiss as I finally grew tired of his games. I heard the Sacred Servants gasp behind me, but I did not care what their problem was for the moment. The only thing on my mind was getting answers from this man and my flames swirled in agreement within.

"My friends call me Nix." He replied with a wink, as his eyes darted once more to the Sacred Servants.

"I'm not your friend." I retorted, causing his shoulders to shake as a laugh spilled from him. My hackles rose as they always did when someone was laughing at me, and my fire pooled into my fists once more.

"That is no way to speak —" The first Servant began to growl at me but was swiftly cut off as Nix lifted his gaze and glared at him.

"I am just like you, Rae." He said instead and my flames retreated slightly.

Just like me…. He was…

"*You're a Pure.*" I whispered in awe, more to myself than the man in front of me.

That is why I could see no marks on him; I thought as my

eyes instinctively roamed over him once more. No visible marks at all.

"And that is how you were able to enter the *iter?*" I asked, distracting myself and my wandering mind to the more important matters.

"Yes."

"How?"

"Think of the Sacred Servants as false Pures. They are granted some powers for being a Servant of the God, but they are merely standing at the gateway of ascension. True Pures, like yourself, have access to the full rites and powers that come from ascending to a God. In short, anything they can do, I can do with ease." He explained simply, flicking his wrist towards the Sacred Servants as he spoke. My mind spun as it tried to piece together everything I was ever taught about the ascension of the Gods, but we were not taught the process of how one became a God — only that once they passed through the ascension rites, they transcended us in every way.

"So, I Ascended?" I asked as I tried to wrap my mind around it all.

"No, not quite."

"So how did I…?" I tried asking how my flames could have manifested for me in the middle of my trials, *without* ascending — but the words caught in my throat.

"That we are unsure of." The first Sacred Servant murmured behind me, though I could hear the frustration in his voice at having to admit this. Servants were as all-knowing as the Gods after all.

"It has never happened before." The second added.

"*Should* never happen." The third corrected in another snarl.

This one did not like me - that much was clear.

"But you —" The words lodged in my throat, as though speaking them would make them real — as if acknowledging that I was in the presence of a Pure would somehow shatter the already delicate hold I had on my emotions. His gaze narrowed slightly, as though he knew that I could not finish my sentence, though as his eyes flicked from me to the Servants once more, I knew he had understood what I was asking.

"I came from the East." Was all he said in the end. Though I suppose that were enough of an explanation. The Eastern paradise had long since been abandoned after its God was killed in a war with the Unworthy long ago.

Even if Nix wanted to ascend, he could not return to become God of the East. There was nothing left for him to rule and a death sentence if he tried.

Here he was, stuck as a Pure with no land and no people.

"You're…. Uh… My…. Pure Phoenix…" The first Servant stuttered, and Nix's brow twitched as his eyes slowly moved back to them.

"If we may finish with Miss Sandoval —"

"The Ceremony has already been missed…"

"And we have much to deliberate before we can announce her results." They finished and I swivelled back to them, my eyes widening as I understood their meaning.

They had yet to judge me on my trials.

"I missed the Ceremony?" I whispered, though their heads bobbed in unison as they heard me.

"You have been asleep for many hours…"

"The Ceremony has come and gone."

"Though we agreed with your parents that we would hold your Ceremony tonight instead."

"But we still need to deliberate…"

"And consider our final decision." Silence hung thick in the room as I nodded, unable to form words.

"You already know your answer." Nix growled as he stood swiftly, stalking towards them like they were his prey. I felt his power thicken as waves of tangible smoke billowed around him. His words were a threat and as the Servants all bowed deep, hoods almost touching the floor – a sign of utmost loyalty and servitude, something the Sacred Servants reserved only for those above them – and I knew they'd received the instruction loud and clear.

Without another word, I watched as Nix stormed out of the library and the Servants turned their hooded attentions back on me.

CHAPTER 17

The Sacred Servants said nothing further as they ushered me out of the library we had been occupying and down the many halls of the Citadel's palace. I wanted to ask them more than once if they knew where they were going, but wisely kept my mouth shut – if they hadn't yet decided my fate, anything I said now would just make it worse.

As we rounded the final corner, I spied my parents waiting in a foyer – father pacing back and forth in a fast stride. I knew that stride, it meant he was worried about something but would never dare speak it in case it came true. I had seen it often when he was about to preside over a judgement or more frequently whenever Imogen lost track of time and was not found in her bedroom before breakfast.

He was worried I was going to fail.

My mother spotted us first and leapt out of her seat across the room, reaching the Sacred Servants before my father turned in his stride and noticed she had moved. She swept me up in a hug and I struggled to remember the last time this had happened. My mother was a loving and thoughtful woman – but she had taught me long ago that Ladies suppressed their emotions in the eyes of society, least we want everyone to know what is written in our hearts. Another lesson I had taken and twisted as my own as I threw more shields around my heart. My emotions were holding behind their walls for now, but this unexpected gesture was sure to get a rise out of them if I let it.

So, I tightened my hold on them and ensured it didn't.

"We have been *beside* ourselves with worry, Raewyn!" She sobbed into my shoulder as the Servants made way for my father. I had been walking behind them and was shocked my mother had not bowled them down in her dash towards me.

"What on earth happened in there?" My father demanded, although his voice was not aimed at me. His voice had gone cold and smooth – his Judge voice. It was the one I had tried to mimic in my trial… and failed.

Can't think of that right now. I scolded myself as I pulled out my mother's embrace, giving her a small smile instead. She nodded her head in understanding before brushing the front of her dress down, as if she could sweep her emotions away like dust.

"We cannot discuss anything…"

"Until we have deliberated."

"We will reveal all at her Ceremony tonight."

The Sacred Servants all spoke as one again and my father's spine straightened under the authority they spoke with. He may be a high member of society and the father of the Commanding Lord of the Citadel, but he was not above the Sacred Servants of the God.

The command in his tone earlier had left completely

as he bowed low to them in response. "Of course, we will await word of your arrival tonight."

They ignored him of course, turning their hooded gazes on me once more before they departed. No bow, no acknowledgement, just a swish of their cloaks as they turned the corner. I swallowed thickly as unsaid words passed through the air they left. I was not to speak a word of what I'd learnt about myself. Not until they had thought more on what my manifestation meant to them.

Though to me that went without saying. I was not telling a soul about my trials, my flames heating my skin at the thought of everything that I had done.

We piled into our carriage, both mother and father refusing to look at my way once — even though I could feel their questions swirling through the air in the carriage, we rode the whole way home in silence. They knew I would not speak of the things I had been subjected to in my trial, and even if I wanted to share, I would not know where to start.

Those trials — while they were meant to test me in the eyes of the Saviour and his Gods, they had done so much more to me than I could ever describe. The mark they had left on my soul would forever be there, and I was not sure a day would pass where I would not think of the look on my siblings faces as I condemned them to death — the words of my mother ringing through my mind on an endless loop. And then there were my newly manifested flames, my control over their created *iter...*

Even now, safely out of the trial, this manifestation seemed to enhance the world around me. Everything around me seemed to thrum as if the wind itself had a heartbeat — as if I could *feel* the power of the earth as it moved through each and every living thing.

It felt different from the power I had felt from Nix — his was dense and primal, lethal. Slithering through the air with precision as it continuously sought out its next victim. His was a power that was honed and perfected.

This power swirling around me now, felt uncorrupted, despite the devastation the human population had waged on it for thousands of years. It felt untapped, ancient, and wild in its ways. Untamed and untouched by even the original Gods themselves. It thickened the air around me until I could almost taste its potential to *be* — though as hard as I tried, I could not see it rolling through the air like I had with my own flames or Nix's coiling smoke.

Instead, it pulsed against me gently, my own flames rolling through me in response to its beating — as though greeting an old friend, and I suppose that wasn't far from the truth.

A God's power, while coming inherently from within themselves, was gifted to them by the earth, from these doorways. From the map drawn by whatever deities came before the Saviour. I wondered silently if they had ever been able to touch the power that I felt around me now.

Something told me that very few had been able to tap into its true potential — if anyone at all.

CHAPTER 18

As we pulled up to the house, the sun had already begun to set, and I realised that I had spent the entire day in the palace.

Better than planning the party, I thought to myself with a smile as we climbed up the steps into the foyer and stopped in my tracks. The house had been completely transformed while I had been away — vases of carnations and lilies lined the polished wood floor of our foyer, spaced between with golden candelabras that let off an ethereal glow as the sun began setting behind the house — the theme a marking of purity in itself that my family was so certain I possessed. I looked on in horror as a maid came bustling out of the side room that we rarely used unless we were entertaining. Rows upon rows of white pressed linen lined long tables and chairs, white and gold silks threading themselves through the rafters of the ballroom, linking with the ceiling high windows that peered out onto the street — so that those who were not so fortunate as to gain an invite would be able to watch on and covet what we so clearly had more of.

This was… a lot.

"Imogen and Analise prepared for the celebration while we were away. We know you don't like all the fuss, so we kept things simple. I only hope with the Sacred Servants now coming that it is elegant enough for them." My mother fussed as she straightened candelabras as we passed – giving her last-minute instructions to any maid that came close enough.

I would never tell my mother that I thought this far more elaborate than simplistic. That this entire show of nobility was wasted on me. My idea of simplistic would be not to decorate at all, a small gathering in the gardens outside – or nothing at all.

This, this was extravagant, and all the Ladies of society would see it for what it really was, a display of superiority over every other family – the Sandoval's now had a *Pure* in their household.

Or so they expected.

My stomach twisted harshly as nerves swam through me, a weight heavier than anything I'd ever felt settling low on my shoulders. It didn't matter what I thought about this celebration, or the society my family surrounded us in – none of that would matter once the Servants came to deliver their verdict of me. Soon, everyone would find out that I wasn't what they all thought I was, and shame fought for dominance in my mind as I finally realised how much my family had riding on this, on me.

I didn't voice any of my thoughts though as I took to the stairs, which hadn't escaped my mother's planning as they too had been carefully woven with ivory silks – entwined at intervals with daisies and gold painted roses.

Even though I was running late for my own celebration, I walked at a leisurely pace, knowing that once

I was inside, they would swarm me once more. I took the moment of peace to check on the defences I had hastily thrown up inside me — stumbling slightly on a step as I felt thick, stone walls encasing the corner of my mind where I held everything I had ever felt. Inspecting it closer I found, what was once an imaged armour that stood guard in front of my walls, was now a tangible force field — what once was imagined steel made of will and desperation, was now a swirling force field of energy and strength.

Prodding gently at my new shield, I felt it bend to my will with ease — knowing instinctively that if threatened it would coil itself stronger than any shield I'd had in place before this.

I guess my flames weren't the only thing I manifested in the trials.

Pondering this as I climbed the rest of the stairs, I was so lost in thought that I almost dismissed the group of people that had gathered themselves outside of my rooms. Stopping just before them, I spied Analise smiling encouragingly at me, while the other two stared at me with impatience. I instantly knew I was not going to like this.

"Is there something I can help you all with?" I asked when none of them uttered a sound, though all of them were admittedly too busy eyeing every inch of me assessing. Everyone except Analise that is, who took the chance to step in front of all of them, towards me as she held a long gown bag in her hands. I gulped at the sight of it, realising why they were all waiting for me.

"We are here to prepare you for your Ceremonial Celebration, Miss." The tall girl beside my door spoke. She looked to be the leader, as she was the only one of the three not holding a thing. Her eyes bore into mine in distaste and I could tell that she found me lacking. It was a good thing I had been surrounded by Imogen and her friends my whole life or I may have found her gaze hurtful.

Now, I just found it annoying.

"Though we are dreadfully behind schedule now," The other girl said. She was shorter than the other, though they both had the same dyed blonde hair that Imogen had, both their faces caked in powders and creams — though that didn't stop either of their marks from being fully concealed as I noted the dark swirls on both their faces.

The sin of Vanity, of course. Nothing less for the stylists who pride beauty above all else.

"I am sure there is a good reason for it, Miss Sandoval does not keep people waiting for the sake of it." Analise scolded the two girls behind her, though her tone suggested that this was not the first time she had told them so.

"I- I yes," I started, opening the doors to my rooms, and letting them in before I followed behind them. The two women dove for my vanity and began unpacking their boxes of powders and creams while Analise moved to my bed to lay the gown flat on it.

"My trials took longer than we thought. It even caused me to miss the Ceremony. The Sacred Servants are now coming here to deliver my verdict." I explained and all three of them froze in place at the mention of the Sacred Servants. The tall one glared at me in a huff like I had done this to her on purpose.

"You expect me to make you presentable in less than an hour before you are to go before the Servants of our God?" She shrieked, her voice raising two octaves.

"I had honestly not thought of that. But yes, though surely it will not take an hour to get ready. Usually, I just go as I am."

"*Go as you are?!*" She hissed, and Analise shot her a

warning to remember her place – which she wholly ignored as she grabbed me by the arm and shoved my in the seat before my vanity – facing me away from the mirror so I could not watch what they were doing to my face.

"There is a reason we were hired to style you Miss Sandoval, and from first impressions you desperately need our help. If only you had more foresight to give us enough time to work on you properly. Now, I am not so sure there is much we can do for you in the time we have. As it is, your hairstylist has already left, so we will need to allot time to take care of that for you too." She finished as she began tugging on my face, analysing it at different angles as if I were a canvas waiting to give inspiration to.

I yanked my head back, out of her pinching claws and looked at Analise to save me, though she was too busy stifling a laugh to do much. She inched towards the other two girls and gently pushed them away, making room for me to breathe and offered them a hand. The tall one looked her over and nodded once, satisfied that she had another minion to order around no doubt. She gave Analise the task of my hair before she began barking orders at the shorter one, who I was certain was one of her sisters. Family business in styling wouldn't be too bad if it didn't cause you to instantly fall victim to the sins that plagued the obsessiveness they placed on beauty.

With everyone in their places, the tall one walked over to my bed, unzipping the gown from its cover, and gazing at it. I still hadn't seen the final design, and if I was being honest – I couldn't remember the style of dress we'd decided on.

The lead stylist seemed to approve of the gown though, as I watched one eyebrow rise in appreciation before she stormed back over and continued pulling and prodding my face. With a final nod, she seemed happy with her decision and began barking orders at Analise and the shorter, much less temperamental stylist, whose name I learnt was Sylvie when the tall one hissed it in her direction.

Quickly they got to work, moving in sync as each of them took up residence around me. It was hard not to feel self-conscious with the three of them constantly staring at me, pulling me this way and that as they all positioned me into where they needed me to be, only to have another person pull me in another direction moments later. When Sylvie asked me to close my eyes – much more polite than anything her sister had barked at me – I took the opportunity to sink back into myself and drown out their voices.

Breathing deep I found that it was not so hard to tune them out once I'd reached the part of myself that they would never see. Focusing instead on the whirling energy that now encased the corner of my mind where my emotions lay, I prodded it once more. Noting that in the presence of others, it was indeed wound tighter and harsher as it whipped past me in defence of itself.

I recalled faintly the time I had asked a boy in my class what his mind looked like – if he too were able to walk into his mind like an extra room in his home, and what he filled his room with. The look he gave me in return answered my question as he turned and ran to the other children, telling them all that Raewyn had an imaginary world in her head, laughing at me as they followed his lead.

I knew at that moment that I was not like the others around me – that walking through your own mind was not something that everyone could do, and though the only thing I could do at that time was cage my emotions in and build walls around them to keep prying eyes out, it was not normal.

I was not normal.

I wondered idly as I watched the shield weave through the bricks I'd constructed if this were a Pure thing. Could Nix walk through his mind as well? Was this how we Pures survived in a world that was still built to tear us down with temptation to sin everywhere we turned?

My flames wove their way out of the corner of my mind as panic spiked through me, wrapping around me as I imagined Nix reacting as that boy from school had. They slid over me in a warm embrace, protecting me as the energy from my shield whipped out towards me, like a gust of air, noting my fire and protecting the wall from it. I watched in awe as they collided in a mass of fire and energy, whipping my hair as they danced around me inside my mind.

Taking deep breaths, I tried to calm myself, tried to control the flames that thrummed against my skin as they fought to get through my walls – the force of that shielding energy my first defence against them. I threw a command out into my mind for that fire to calm, as I whispered to my new shield that my flames would not hurt us, that they were a part of us now. Slowly, they settled themselves, weaving around one another in acceptance. I would have to learn to control these two new forces of myself if I had any hope of surviving.

"The guests are starting to arrive, how much longer are you going to be?" Imogen's voice echoed through my mind, pulling me back to reality. Behind her, the sounds of announcers and mingling could be heard. It seemed I was late for my own party.

I opened my eyes and watched Imogen eye the transformation they'd given me, her eyes widening slightly in shock as she looked at my face. I wished at that moment that I had been seated facing the mirror as worry filled me.

"Almost." Sylvie responded without looking back at Imogen, swiping more product onto my cheekbones.

"Maybe if we had started at the arranged time, we would have been able to create something truly worthy of the Sacred Servants." The older sister added, brush sticking out of the corner of her mouth as if she were assessing a masterpiece and not my face.

"I've already told you – I had no control over that." I explained again with a sigh as she tapped my mouth, effectively scolding me for moving her art before it was done.

"Your hair is done, Miss Sandoval." Analise spoke as she made her way into my line of sight. The warm smile that lit up her face as she took in what they'd done to me relaxed me a bit more. Analise had always shown her emotions clearly on her face, if she did not like something, it showed.

"This is the finished dress?" I heard Imogen ask in the distance, having moved further into my room.

"No, that is just the material shaped to look like a dress." I replied sarcastically, grinning at Analise as she stifled her laugh behind a cough. My sister tsked and whirled towards me, her face pinched as she tried to contain her anger in front of the stylists.

"Sarcasm is not an admirable trait of a Pure, Sister, or is there something you should tell us before the Servants arrive?" Her voice sounded sickly sweet, and I groaned inwardly at her tone. It was the one she used around her minions, inferring words for the gossipers to hang on while being able to deny spreading a thing.

It was a talent, her cunning. And I knew she'd succeeded as the stylists froze around me, eyeing me as though the confession would be written on my painted-on face.

Though with my new walls and shield protecting me, I didn't have to school anything as I eyed my sister, ignoring the stylists completely.

"I know not what they have decided yet Imogen, though I can assure you that my trials were not as simple as the temptation you seem to fall into time and time again." Images of the courtroom flitted behind my eyes, and I clenched my fists in an attempt to control the shame that tried to slither through my walls.

That was not real, this is. Imogen is safe.

The real Imogen went red in the face at my dig, turning swiftly on her heels and storming out of the room, slamming my door on her way out. I breathed deep as the stylists resumed their ministrations without another word, and I was thankful that they didn't press it further.

Once they were done, they departed with a bow, instructing me not to cry, least I want to ruin their work. I assured them that I would refrain from doing so and made my way into the bathing room to undress with Analise trailing close behind me – the dress draped gently over her arms. She helped me undress without messing the arrangement she'd put my hair in or smudging the paint on my face and then instructed me to step into my gown.

I refused to look down at it as she tied the back, cinching it tighter until I could barely breathe. How Ladies wandered around in these dresses all day was beyond me, I would be lucky if I lasted the night with the way Analise was violently tugging at the strings. Once she was done adjusting my gown, she lifted the hem gently so that I could strap the heels my sister had chosen for me on one of our trips into the town square and I immediately frowned at them. How was anyone meant to walk in these things?

I tested my balance on them, Analise giggling as my arms flailed about before landing on her for support. At least one thing was certain, I would not be escaping the hordes of society tonight. Not in these death traps.

Finally ready, I held on to Analise's arm as she led me from my room and down the hall to the top of the stairs. From there I was told to wait until I was announced so that I could make my first grand entrance into society.

Leaving me to hide, I cautiously made my way back down the hall to the full-length mirror we had placed in between all the rooms, the heels making the walk twice as long, as I fought for balance.

The hall mirror was the only place one could check their entire ensemble — as we did not promote vanity in this house. I was certain Imogen was the one that got the most use out of it considering her marks and would have it placed inside her room if given the chance.

Though I did not care too much about my appearance in general, curiosity was driving me to see the final product of everything they'd done to me over the last hour. Turning to face the mirror head on, my breath lodged in my throat as I stared back at the girl who was meant to be me, but most definitely was not.

The gown shimmered in thin layers of gold and cream — the bodice tight against my skin, low and constricting. Delicate gold threads embroidered in floating foliage swirled over the material in intricate patterns — on closer inspection it seemed to be both a nod to both our home in the Wooded Village of the Citadel, and the markings gifted to us by the Saviour. Full ballooning golden sleeves that cinched at my wrists, sheer enough that it gave my pale complexion a golden hue — while also displaying enough of my skin so that they might know if I had been marked with any sins of Lust or Greed. The skirt flared out at my waist, emphasising my small frame, and adding a femininity that none of my gowns had ever done before. It was a beautiful gown, that I could not deny – but I had never felt so suffocated and confined to society than I did in that moment.

The necklace my sister had picked out for me in spite, clung to the base of my throat, threading around in its layers of garnet and onyx – restricting air to my lungs as my eyes finally rose to see what they had done to my face. At the way they had added gold to my eyelids, darkening the outer corners making my normally lifeless blue eyes look alluring under the powdered shadow.

I looked like I was trying to imitate Imogen, like I was trying to fit in with all the women downstairs, and while they would all be pleased at this attempt – I couldn't help but feel like I'd been trapped into this.

I watched my chest heave as my breathing became shallow, tendrils of neatly draped curls Analise had pulled out of the high bun she'd pinned on top of my head, tickled the bare skin of my shoulder as I tried to shake myself out of the panic. My flames unfurled themselves on instinct and a sweat broke out on my skin from their heat.

This was not going to end well.

CHAPTER 19

"You look absolutely breath-taking, Dear." My mother's voice broke through a moment later as she and my father stepped into my line of sight. I exhaled once more before plastering a smile on my face as I turned to them, internally checking that my walls hadn't budged at my slip before they reached me.

"My little girl, all grown up." My father appraised as he held his arm out for me to take.

"It's the shoes, which I am certain were not made for walking." I replied as I wobbled my way over to him, grabbing his arm for stability. My father let out a loud hoot of laughter as we began to walk towards the staircase, my mother taking up the other side of me.

"Remember everything I taught you Raewyn, this night is as much for them as it is for you." My mother whispered as we appeared at the top of the stairs, every voice stopping on instinct, as if they could sense me above them.

All eyes turned to us at once, and I swallowed as my

tongue turned to ash in my mouth.

I can do this. I thought desperately as my nails dug into the arm of my father's Lord's jacket — but the trials, the dress, the stares. It was all too much, and I felt it all tighten around me like I noose I would never break free from.

I was just about to turn to my father and tell him I needed a second, a minute, a lifetime before I would be ready for this moment when his voice filled the space around us. That booming voice of an official Judge leaving no room for interruptions.

"Welcome everyone, we have gathered you all to our home to celebrate the Ceremony of our youngest child, Raewyn Sandoval." He announced, patting the hand that had gripped him tightly in reassurance as he did so. It was his way of telling me that he believed I could do this; that I *had* to get through this.

I breathed deep at his faith in me, lifting my head higher above the crowd in response, taking on everything I had ever been taught by my mother — and I saw her nod of approval out of the corner of my eye.

My father continued his welcome speech, thanking certain Lords and families for making the journey from their own Villages to be here tonight — to speaking on behalf of our family. I tuned it all out as I focused on a spot in the distance above all their heads, refusing to make eye contact with any of them.

I spent the time wisely, effectively shoving down my flames as panic reigned front and centre in my mind. The urge to unleash them and run flowing through me with such strength, that I didn't hear my father's final words until I spotted movement directly below us.

"Now most of you will have heard by now that the Sacred Servants conducted a test so rigorous for my dear child, that she could not make it to the official Ceremony held at the Citadel today. It is for that reason that I welcome them here now, to give their verdict in front of the whole of society, so that you all may bear witness to what I believe will be the proudest moment in my life."

I froze as three hooded figures stepped onto the staircase as my father finished his speech, gliding their way up to the landing, halfway between us and the people gathered below.

I didn't have to see their faces to know they were the same Sacred Servants who had put me through my trials, who had forced me to condemn my family. Heat pooled in my palms as fire slithered down my veins. My breaths came in short bursts as my father tugged on my arm, steering me down the stairs and closer to the Sacred Servants.

I cursed myself for not preparing for the sight of them again. I had been too caught up in seeing Nix and finally gaining answers from him in the library that I'd blanked when said they would be attending my celebration to deliver their verdict to me.

Now, I would be outed in front of the entire society.

Unlike the Ceremony that was held in the Citadel where your shames were only announced in front of the families of those being put on trial that day – this would be public.

I kept my eyes on the hooded cloaks before us, refusing to look at anyone else, refusing to even glance at my parents on either side of me – knowing that once the Servants spoke, they would be heart broken.

I was meant to be the redemption of this family, after Sebastian's betrayal, and Imogen's selfishness. Orion had been the Saviour back then – but this family's reputation, *my families* standing in society depended all on me, on whether more than one of the Sandoval children could be worthy of the lives we were given. On the lives that society let us continue to keep as a favour to the Commanding Lord of the Citadel.

They would not be so kind after tonight, after the Sacred Servants announced all the infamous ways I'd slandered the Saviour and proved my impurity.

I should have tried harder, I scolded myself, guilt rising through me as my eyes blurred. This would ruin my family – they could not make it back from a verdict such as the one they were about to give me. I would be sentenced to death for defiling the name of the Saviour and they would be stripped of their ranking in society. They would be outcasts, and there was nothing I could do about it.

My emotions slammed against me under the weight of my reality. If this just affected me, I would not feel so panicked – I would not be so worried about the outcome of my trials. In fact, I would have been inclined to show them *more* of my true thoughts and feelings.

I felt a vibration rumble within me as my emotions pummelled against the stone, fighting to be freed before they existed no more. My newly formed shield dove its way around my mind, securing everything it could, coiling so tight that I could feel the force of it turning harder than the stones it stood guard for. It became impenetrable as my emotions locked themselves back in – muting the rising hysteria.

I breathed deep as everything receded behind my shield, my thoughts quietening until all I could hear inside me was the soft crackle of my flames, who had woven themselves into my bloodstream, flowing through me as though they readied themselves for war.

My eyes levelled to where I felt the Sacred Servants

watching me from beneath their hoods and I knew instinctively that my eyes would show my lack of emotion as my flames fed me bravery that I'd never felt before.

Strengthening my resolve and straightening my spine as we stopped beside them, perfectly aligned so that everyone could see them deliver my judgement.

I'm ready my flames whispered, and I was.

My father nudged me forward, stepping so that I was between the Servants and my parents. It was symbolic in Ceremonies for the parents to stand behind the subject, signalling that they were the past and the Servants before us were delivering us to our future.

A maid rushed forward and placed a large cushion before me and held my arm as I knelt onto it before the Servants – my eyes never leaving their faceless hoods as I did so.

Somewhere behind my walls I was freaking out, I felt the vibrations within me as they slammed against the stone, fighting to be freed. My shield wove its way through the stone of my walls once more, strengthening it so that it could not crumble.

Thankfully my face remained impassive and blank as my shield locked me out of my own mind, my flames beating gently in time with my steady heartbeat.

I felt blessedly calm as the middle servant stepped forward once again.

"Earlier today we held Miss Sandoval's trials." The first one spoke, their eerie voices echoing throughout the room with ease.

"As is customary – her trials consisted of everything we have learnt from watching her since her sixteenth year." The second one spoke, stepping forward. Without their movement it would have been impossible to follow which one of them was speaking as their voices joined together to create one.

"As a potential Pure, she received a total of three trials, testing her faith and loyalty to the Saviour and her temptations to sin." At this a gasp rung up from the guests below us. It was normal for trials to consist of only one or two tests, the Servants knowing exactly what your weaknesses were before you entered the room with them.

For me to have three trials signalled to everyone here that they indeed considered me as a candidate for the Pure of the Citadel. *Too bad I ruined any chances of that happening.* I thought humourlessly.

The Servants then asked that everyone lower their heads in prayer to the Saviour and my mouth opened automatically as I lead the prayer — each word feeling like lead in my mouth as they rang through the crowd before me — my flames flaring in response to how opposed to them I was. It was customary for each Ceremonial candidate to speak the words, to beg the Saviour for a forgiveness we didn't yet know we needed — though after the way I declared my true feelings towards the Saviour and his Gods, the words that I used to recite every night before bed like a mantra felt heavy and wrong on my tongue.

"Oh Saviour, you who tore the world from the sea for me to be born. You who sacrificed so much so that I may flourish under your care. Grant me my benevolent Saviour, the strength to learn from my weaknesses; the wisdom to know what is right and what is wrong and the acceptance that I am tainted by sin. That I am impure. Saviour, forgive me for everything I have done and everything I will do. For I do not know better, and my will is not as strong as yours. Saviour my sins are heavy, my temptations many, but under your infinite power and guidance I pray for the hope to one day be worthy of you."

I raised my head as I finished, noting that the Sacred Servants had moved closer so that they were right in front of me, and a feeling of panic zipped through me at the memory of what they'd put me through the last time they stood this close. The feeling didn't last long though as it was carried away behind the walls in my mind, by the shield that I was fast becoming to love.

"Raewyn Sandoval, we have assessed you today and we now stand here to deliver the judgement of the Saviour." They said in unison, their already multi-voice synchronising with each other until it sounded as though each person standing below us had spoken along with them.

Each of the Sacred Servants raised a long bony finger towards me as I felt their power stir around them. White fog encased the space between us, slinking closer until it wrapped itself around me.

I clenched my fists as my flames began to manifest, dancing along my knuckles in retaliation to the power of the Servants that was trying to weave its way inside me once more. Focusing on the sharp sting of my nails digging into the flesh of my palm, I willed my flames to recede, to let the Sacred Servants power into me as they needed to gain entrance in order to mark me.

Slowly I felt my power retreat to its corner in my mind, obeying my command as the Sacred Servants fog completely enveloped me now. It didn't swirl like Nix's smoke, but rather rolled into me like a tidal wave. My body jolted as it entered me, sliding down my arms and up my neck as I struggled to breathe through the intrusion.

This didn't feel natural, it didn't feel right – but I fought against that instinct too as I felt it flow down to my toes.

After what felt like an eternity, the fog lifted, its power receding out of me until it was gone. I slowly opened my eyes, not realising I had clenched them shut as I gazed up at the Servants once more – refusing to look down at the markings I was certain now covered my body.

I heard my father shush my mother behind me as a cry escaped her mouth, and the entire floor of guests below us went silent as death as the Sacred Servants withdrew their hands and spoke as one again.

"Rise, Lady Raewyn Sandoval. First Pure of the Citadel."

CHAPTER 20

There had to be a mistake.

My mouth dropped open in shock. Had they not heard me condemn the Saviour, the Gods and everything the Ise of Salvatorem stood for?

I had thrown them out of their own *iter*, yes, but Nix had opened a door for them — for them to all see how irrevocably unlike them I was on the inside.

I glanced down at myself, my pale skin peeking out through my gown — my hands turning themselves over as I sought out marks that I was so sure I would have on me, but there was nothing. The only marks found on me that I could see were small crescent shaped slits lining each palm that were slowly pooling with blood from where I'd broken skin with my own nails.

I felt my shield inside me rattle as my emotions threw themselves around restlessly, not understanding and not willing to submit in this moment — my shock causing a crack in the walls, slipping emotions through that I didn't have time to deal with.

Fighting to keep them off my face, I rose as the Sacred Servants spoke once more.

"Tell no one of your abilities, Pure Sandoval." They whispered in my mind as I looked back up to their hooded faces. A shiver ran through me at the intrusive feeling of them in my head and my shield slammed down, pushing them out before they could say more.

As one, they took an instinctive step back in shock – a small shake of the third Servants hood as he raised his hooded glare in my direction, a low hiss echoing through the space between us, but I stared them down defiantly; they would never come near my mind again.

My parents chose that moment to swoop me up into their arms, oblivious to the power struggle between the Sacred Servants and I as they sang praises of how proud they were of me. As though being crowned the Pure of the Citadel was an achievement, and not the life sentence I was beginning to feel like it was – and perhaps it was to them.

After all, it was the highest achievement our society had to offer.

I should be thankful, but all I could think about was how my life as I knew it was over. Even if they hadn't judged me on my complete breakdown in the *iter*, I would never again be able to go unnoticed, never be able to hide away from the spotlight the society would surely now keep posted directly on me. If I didn't know any better, I would swear the Sacred Servants were playing a cruel joke on me.

Even if they were, I was the *Pure of the Citadel* now, and I needed to become her before the rest of society saw through me.

My parents lead me the rest of the way down the stairs and into the waiting mass of people who tugged and touched me as they congratulated me. Introducing themselves like it was my first time in the Citadel, like I hadn't played with their children on the streets. I suppose in a sense they were right. The Raewyn that they knew, the Raewyn who shied away from people because she was shy or because she didn't understand them and their motives, that Raewyn had died in the trials when she was forced to condemn her siblings. She'd died when she realised that she was trapped in this life no matter the outcome.

My newly crafted shield may protect me from feeling the overwhelming force of my emotions, but it also hid me from the rest of the world, and for that I was grateful.

I slipped into the role of Pure like a defence mechanism, all the years of training my mother had put me through finally paying off as I smiled as though I were happy to be here. My emotions stilling as it realised the motion was anything but genuine.

Come get me, my flames whispered as it layered itself inside me like a second skin, my cheeks flushing from its heat, though for all the crowd knew it was another testament to my innocence of being the centre of attention. The old Raewyn may have hated the attention, and the crowds with all their touching – but the Raewyn who stood before them now, the *Pure of the Citadel* had power coursing through her veins, echoing through her blood.

This Raewyn didn't have emotions waging war inside her mind – she had a shield, protecting herself from the world because she knew there was no alternative.

To save my family, save them from the disgrace of who I really was – who the Sacred Servants had seen in that trial, I would stay this Raewyn. Graceful, regal, happy to be touched by these people who only sought me out so that they may gain favour with the new royalty of the Citadel.

I continued smiling although it hurt, I stayed myself

from flinching away from their touches as they swarmed me in crowds, welcoming invitations to their homes echoing throughout the house. They were invitations I had no intention of keeping, but for the sake of tonight, I would make them think I had nothing better to do than drink tea with them all while they gathered gossip and sharpened their talons against me.

The Ladies of the society gushed over me, and I held in the irony that these were the same Ladies that had whispered behind my back a month ago at Orion's celebration.

"Your gown is absolutely stunning…"

"But not as stunning as the woman wearing it. You are a beauty, Pure Sandoval."

So now they think me beautiful, I thought as I hid my laugher behind another smile as we made our way into the dining hall, my parents having left me to the horde when they were unapologetically shoved away from me by these Ladies.

"I just have to have the name of your silk merchant…"

"Is there a particular diet you use?"

"Oh, and your necklace!"

"Such a statement piece, if only we had your style, Pure Sandoval."

I couldn't stop the laugh that left me at that, I was certain they were aware that the necklace was last season's fashion in their eyes — though that didn't stop them from attempting to butter me up anyways.

They'd all have one by the morning, I'll have to remember to warn the craftsman.

"I guess a congratulations are in order, little sister" Imogen piped up once I'd finally made my way to our dining table. The swarming groups of people seeming to be never ending as they all made to congratulate me on my way to the room where dinner was waiting to be served. Our normally empty ballroom was now lined with rows upon rows of tables, ready to accommodate all our guests, crisp white linens, lined with the same gold, carnation, and lily blend along their lengths – the silks that I had spied from the foyer on my return stopping a foot above the men's heads, so that they may still be seen and tied into the room, but not a nuisance to our guests.

"I did nothing of note to be congratulated on, Sister, I am still the same person I was yesterday."

"Albeit more popular now." Orion smirked, as he took a seat across from me. If he were closer, I would have swatted him on the arm. As it was, I settled for sticking my tongue at him in defiance, causing him to choke on the drink he was throwing back in laughter. That will teach him.

"We all knew you could do it." Alyssa said from beside Orion, and I smiled at the kindness in her voice. She always believed the best in everyone, no matter what marks they received.

It was her naivety that got her stuck in the binding to the blacksmith before my brother met her and was also the reason for all three of her markings. Dark lines running the length of her right arm and leg respectively from lusting after my brother while she'd been contracted to another, which had in turn led to the mark of coveting what was not meant to be hers.

She had been open to me one afternoon about her trials, and how they tested her ability to see through the person they were and judge them as the Saviour had intended us to – from their sins. She had failed that test and gained the mark of the sloth, a long dark whorl across her torso marking her with the sin of failing to uphold the laws of the Saviour.

It wasn't a broken law, but the inability to act as she should was shame enough in the Servants eyes. Though if you asked Alyssa, she wasn't ashamed of it at all. While she couldn't openly admit that she disagreed with the way society was laid out and judged, she would happily fail that trial time and time again.

My father and brother stood to give toasts about my new status once everyone was seated. Father congratulating me in front of the entire room on something they'd guessed from the moment I'd been old enough to understand the concept of sins.

Orion filled his toast with anecdotes from our childhood that left our guests in fits of laughter and my cheeks redder than the wine in front of me in embarrassment. They'd tried to make me stand and give my own speech, but one look at my emotionless mask and my father knew he would not succeed.

It did not matter how renowned a Judge he was; my stubbornness would not budge me from my seat. And though normally he would have pressed me harder, knowing that in the eyes of society disobedience towards the head of the house would not be tolerated, he'd relented.

I wasn't sure if it was because tonight was to be a celebratory occasion or if it was my new status as a Pure — in which I now technically outranked both him and my brother, but he did not press my quiet objection. Instead, he laughed it off and praised me some more and the guests were right behind him as though I didn't just disrespect him and everyone there.

Dinner was brought out after that and thankfully, it meant a moment of respite from all the congratulations and falsities as everyone was too busy eating and speaking amongst themselves to approach me. My family laughed and joked around me, and I almost felt normal, like this was any other day. I savoured the moment between bites of succulent meats and roasted vegetables – laughing as my brother leapt across the table for his third plate, the maids rushing around us, ensuring that no table was going without in this lavish display of wealth.

I had the Sacred Servants to thank for this.

If they had revealed the true outcome of my trials, I would not be sitting here, watching my family like this. I wondered idly what their end game was – though to be honest it did not matter. To keep my family together like this I would do anything they asked of me, and I knew they could ask anything with the leverage they held.

I peered inside my mind, my shield still up in full force, blocking me from my emotions and allowing me to play the part I needed to tonight. I would have time to sift through them later, but for now I was constantly aware of peoples' eyes on me.

If I concentrated hard enough, I could also feel the pulsing energy swirling around everyone like auras converging into one massive ball in the room. It overwhelmed me and made the room feel thick and stifling, causing my flames to stay just under my skin in case I needed them. My earlier manifestation was most likely the reason for the Sacred Servants verdict on me tonight, I'd decided as I shook off that uneasy feeling. Especially when they warned me against telling anyone about them.

I just needed to find out why I was important enough to let slide through the system like that after I had condemned everything this world holds dear.

After dinner was done, Orion paraded me around the room, escorting me to every Lord who had expressed interest in a Binding contract with me once I was proclaimed a Pure.

Thankfully, my brother did most of the talking as he questioned them about their businesses and family history. The only time I spoke was to accept congratulations on my Ceremony, though that did not stop more than one of them from eyeing me like they had already decided I'd make a pretty trophy wife. The more time I spent trailing after Orion, the more and more frustrated I became with the whole process.

I was not impressed with any of them, though I knew my thoughts on the matter did not bear any weight in the final decision. Finally, we were done, and I retreated to a corner – willing the people to leave me be for a moment as they wandered idly between the dining room and the foyer discussing politics of their villages and trade over the freely flowing wine. All things I had no interest to weigh in on.

Just as I settled into my hiding spot, Imogen grabbed my arm and dragged me through the house, demanding that she needed me. I stumbled along behind her in my heels, not used to moving as fast as her in them, grumbling as we went.

As we neared her destination, I realised I was being tugged towards my father's office; where three men stood waiting for us to enter. Two of them I recognised as Orion and my father as they stood behind my father's desk as they faced us, chatting with drinks in their hands, but the third I did not know.

He was faced away from us as he spoke to my father and brother, in such a low, commanding timbre that it demanded he be heard. I angled my head out from behind

Imogen more as she continued her march towards them and noted that the man was very tall – broader than both Orion and my father, his uniform straining against his muscles as he lifted his glass to his lips. His boots were more for combat than they were for status, though they looked like they'd recently been shined clean.

Imogen squeaked out a greeting as her eyes fell on him, halting her steps in the doorway so suddenly that I bumped into the back of her. He turned at the noise and smiled widely, the sun-kissed tan of his skin stretching and crinkling in the corner of eyes so pale blue they were like glass as he ran them down the length of my sister. His hair was cropped close to his scalp on the sides, blonde that had been soaked from the sun so much that it might as well be white. It was the natural colour that all the Ladies of Society coveted to achieve, Imogen included.

Once he was done perusing my sister, his eyes turned to me, and immediately fell as he bowed low at the waist.

"Pure Sandoval, it is an honour to meet you," he said by way of greeting as he rose again, and my cheeks flushed in embarrassment. No one had ever bowed to me before. "And you must be the Imogen that I have heard so much about." He transitioned back to my sister, moving forward to kiss the hand that she was already offering him, giggling away as he did. I looked to my father in confusion.

"Imogen, Raewyn, this is Lord Ruskin. Lieutenant of the Northern Radical army and Imogen's soon-to-be husband." He filled in for me as I side-stepped the Lord and Imogen, who used the opportunity to step even closer to him.

"He has come to meet Imogen before he finalises the Binding contract, though we should have expected she would drag you into this, Wynnie." Orion finished for my father, and I swatted his arm at the use of my childhood nickname as I reached their side.

"You promised not to call me that once I became a Pure." I commented dryly.

"I promised no such thing, Pure *Wynnie*." He replied with a laugh. Lord Ruskin watched our family squabble from the other side of the desk with amusement as his arm wound around Imogen. I had to admit that together they looked like a match, and it was obvious that my sister was smitten with the man at first glance.

"Orion, your description of your sister did not do her justice. She is absolutely stunning." Lord Ruskin declared once Orion and I had settled, though as my sister erupted into another fit of giggles, I noted that his eyes were on me instead of Imogen.

Eyes that I noted held no emotion.

A chill ran down my spine at the look of emptiness in them — emptiness and darkness, as though he had seen far too much darkness in his life. I suppose being a Lieutenant of a Radical army would cause him to see some things that I couldn't even dream of. I wondered briefly if that's what my eyes looked like now that my emotions were firmly locked away, though minus the darkness that held him captive.

My thoughts travelled back to my first trial, and panic gripped me as it slithered out from behind my walls as I thought of Ruskin cancelling their Binding contract in the *iter*, leaving my sister alone and me as the blame for the end of her potential binding to a Lord. Surely this could not be happening in real life. That was only a trial to determine if I could turn my own sister in and keep my loyalties to the Saviour and the Gods.

But the more I watched Lord Ruskin interact with my

family stealing glances my way when he thought no one was looking and having effectively ignored my sister even though she clung to his arm, my panic turned into fear. I could not let this happen in real life. I would not let my sister suffer because of something I could change.

"Lord Ruskin, what is it you require from a wife?" the words spilled from my mouth before I had a chance to stop them, interrupting something my father was saying. I ignored the look of disapproval from him as I fixed my gaze on the Lord who would not break my sister.

"The same as any man looking for a wife, Pure Sandoval."

"And that would be?"

"Companionship, loyalty. The chance to produce an heir." He listed off casually as he sipped from his drink.

"And you believe you can find all these things in my sister?"

"I do." He spoke confidently as he gazed down at her for only the second time since we'd walked into my father's office. I was still not convinced.

"You are not disappointed in her lack of power? In her markings?" I prodded further. He laughed at this, a deep cackle that sent more shivers down my spine.

"No, Pure Sandoval. I am not. I am powerful enough that I do not require a wife whose power exceeds my own. Had I wanted that, I would have slaughtered all your suitors in order to secure a Binding with you." His eyes held mine and I saw a shift in them that was gone before I could decipher its meaning. One thing I did know for certain though was that he was done playing my games. He turned back towards my father, who seemed pleased enough by his answers that he signalled Ruskin closer to his desk as they poured over the contract.

I had never seen first-hand, how much detail went into a Binding contract, but it seemed as though they were agreeing on land movements and money distribution as part of the settlement for my sister's eternal servitude.

Once they were done, my father filled the men's glasses and raised his own in a toast. Imogen still plastered to the side of her new husband-to-be, seeming to have no issues coming to terms with her departure back to the Northern Paradise. The Binding Ceremony was set a few months away, as Lord Ruskin had things to prepare before he was able to take a leave of absence.

Imogen would make her way down to him in a few weeks, once she'd packed up her things and then I wouldn't see her again until it was time for her to be bound to Lord Ruskin. The thought that I was losing my sister made me sad, although I was sure she wouldn't see it that way. She was getting what she wanted, a handsome husband who had the social standing to fulfil all her needs.

I should be happy for her, but there was something I couldn't put my finger on that made me weary of Lord Ruskin.

I made to leave the office after the toast, needing some space to collect all my thoughts. Lord Ruskin gripped my arm as I passed him, squeezing just hard enough to halt me in my steps, but not hard enough that anyone would notice should they look our way.

My eyes shot up to his as he spoke, voice still cheery even as his eyes darkened in warning. "I look forward to getting to know you more, Pure Sandoval. We are family now after all."

CHAPTER 21

Turns out I was not able to back out of any of the invitations I'd accepted at my celebration as the next few weeks were filled with teas and luncheons with all the Ladies of Society. They all surrounded me with never-ending offers of style and company.

Luckily, news of Imogen's impending Binding Ceremony had also spread so I was able to drag her along to all my engagements with me, making the most of sister time while also using her to divert the attention to whenever their questions got too much for me — and it didn't take long for that to happen.

During every outing I made sure my emotions were tucked back behind my walls, bringing forth the Raewyn who had emerged from her trials. The Pure Raewyn, the girl with grace and patience for all things society related.

It was no surprise that every day when I finally returned home, I was exhausted from having to keep those mental shields up and alert — my fire all but accepting that its new home was coursing through my blood as if it needed to protect me from the gossip and nagging of the Ladies that I'd been forced to surround myself with.

Mother told me it was a necessary evil to build relationships and connections through these women, as one day I would be head of a household and in need of their acceptance if I wanted to secure a place in this world. I disagreed, of course. If I had my way, and I was sure that I now could, seeing as I was now that I was the second highest-ranked person in the Citadel – I would remain unbound and live out my days in solitude. Only ever travelling into society when the needs called for it.

Which I would make certain were rare.

I hadn't broached this topic with my parents yet, as I was certain they would have much to say in attempt to change my mind, but I did not want to be swayed. Keeping everything at bay, was already too much, and I while my new shield helped me stay in control of my thoughts and my newly developed fire, I knew I could not keep it up forever. Which meant I could never be bound to another.

Unfortunately, the Saviour had other ideas. The day before Imogen was set to leave for the Northern Territory, I was called into my father's office as I returned from yet another luncheon with the Ladies of the Citadel. These ones had not accepted my diverted attentions to Imogen, and the hunk of raw stone that Lord Ruskin had fashioned into some sort of binding ring that Ladies demanded as a sign that she was contracted to someone of wealth and status. Instead, they'd fixated their attentions on me, and who hand thrown their hat into the ring for the chance to bind themselves to me. According to these Ladies, I had the pick of every eligible man across the entire Isle, and they quickly got to work ranking and discussing each man in far more detail than I needed – as if I had any say in the matter

It was safe to say that I did not eat much and thus was on my way to the kitchen to find a something before I was called in.

"I have some matters to discuss with you, Raewyn, dear." My father spoke by way of greeting, as I sat in the visitor's chair across from him. I couldn't help but recall the last time I had sat here as Father and Orion poured over my Binding prospects.

After the day I'd just had with the Ladies of society, a lump of dread formed in my throat.

"I have just received word from the Citadel, and they would like to meet with you as soon as possible. They would finally like to discuss what role you shall play in society now that you are the second highest ranked member of our Paradise."

Well, that was not what I was expecting.

"Am I meeting the God of the Citadel?" I asked as curiosity mounted inside of me. Though no one had seen him in over a century, surely the new crowning of a Pure would be enough to draw even him out of hiding.

"From what I received, no. You will only be meeting with the Sacred Servants who administered your tests. They already have an idea of where they would like you to sit in society, though that knowledge was not given to me."

"Okay, I can organise the carriage to take me there this evening."

"Already done, dear. You will depart as soon as I have finished speaking with you." My father replied.

Well, there goes my chance of eating first. I thought as my stomach growled in protest.

"Does that mean there was something else you wished to speak with me about?" I asked cautiously, and the look on my father's face told me that I would not like the next words that would come out of his mouth.

"Yes, there is. I have been looking over your Binding prospects, and while I have whittled it down since your Ceremony, the four left are all good men with good lineage options. I thought, as you are now Pure of the Citadel, and effectively can override any decision I make for you, that I would ask for your opinion on them. I have set up meetings with each of the respective men for you to meet before we make any decisions."

"You mean I get to choose my own husband?"

"No, the final decision will still go to Orion and myself— as we must factor in things that you will have no understanding of, despite your new status. But I think your input on who will compliment you most in your new role will help us narrow down our options."

My fire pushed forward, filling my veins with courage as I hedged my next words carefully. "What if…. What if I don't like any of my suitors?" I asked him as I willed myself to sit up straighter. It was not how I had planned to broach the subject to him — but if it saved me what I imagined would be some painful meetings with men I had no interest in, then I would swallow my awkwardness and try.

"What do you mean?" he asked clearly confused by my question, so I tried again.

"What if I decide that I do not want to be bound to any of the suitors you bring before me? What if I was to remain unbound? That could be an option I would be happy with." Silence entered the room as my father's face scrunched up in disapproval.

"No." He finally said after what felt like an eternity. His gaze moved from me down to the files sat on his desk, signalling that he would not elaborate further.

But I was not accepting that.

"What do you mean, no? If this is my choice, if I can overrule your decisions, shouldn't I be able to make the decision that I simply do not wish to bind myself to anyone?"

"It is not your choice. I was simply giving you the decency of seeing who you would prefer, Raewyn. Pure or not, I am the head of this household, and it is my job to secure a husband for you. Not binding you to someone at all is not an option, and I will not hear any more of this."

"But I do not desire a husband, Father, you know I never have." I pushed as desperation clawed at my insides.

"*That is enough.*" He bellowed, looking up from his documents at me, anger lining his face. It is the first time that I had seen that look directed at me and my flames flared to life in response, raising my temperature as I fought to keep them down.

"You will be bound to a Lord, just like every other Lady in this society. If you do not wish to have input, then I will choose for you. But you *will* have a Binding Ceremony. You are a Pure, and your lineage must carry on." I nodded in acceptance as I pushed my flames back, the heat searing my hands as my nails dug into my palms. I knew I'd drawn blood once again, but the pain was small in comparison to the waves of pulsing heat that threatened to escape me.

"Good. Now, I have put together a schedule for you to meet with these Lords, it may have to be adjusted slightly once we find out what the Scared Servants wish of you, but tomorrow you will have breakfast with Lord Carron, and we will go from there." I nodded once more, knowing a dismissal from my father when it was spoken, and with the way my flames were spiking through me, I grabbed the chance to leave his office.

Making my way back out the door, I stepped into the

waiting carriage and focused on calming myself as the wind blew through the open windows. That ancient thrumming power surrounding me instantly now that I was out in the open. I'd noticed it every time I stepped out of the house since I left the trials, and it was beginning to become a constant soothing balm on my powers whenever they got too much. Which seemed to be a constant with my flames as they fought for control within me.

My arrival at the Citadel Palace was not as daunting this time around in my newfound role as Pure of the Citadel – something I was glad for as I'd just managed to calm the fire inside me on the ride over here, thanks to the pulsing ancient energy surrounding us.

Though instead of being greeted by the Sacred Servants, this time I was greeted by an ordinary doorman. He led me through the corridors with silent confidence and I had to resist the urge to ask him if he'd ever gotten lost in this place – I know I certainly would have by now without him. All the walls looked the same as the first time I had walked through here, the wood and stone bending and twisting away from the direction we were heading as if in warning. I itched to open each door we passed, curious as to what secrets each room held. I knew one of these rooms would be that same non-descript beige room the Servants had conducted my trials in – and I wouldn't be surprised if the doorman were leading me to that very room.

To my surprise, we approached a set of wide arching oak doors at the end of the final corridor he led me down. It looked as though this section of the palace was rarely used, and well away from the main wing of the palace. As he produced a set of keys to unlock said doors, nerves began to fight their way through my internal walls. Surely if this was a matter of where I stood in society I would be led to the more main part of the palace, where all matters of society were conducted – but the further we walked the more I was convinced that where he was taking me was a place that not many people ventured.

I could not tell if that was a good thing or not.

I tried to tell myself that because I was a Pure, I might have more rights, more access to the parts of the palace that were hidden to the commoners, but the panic in me that never fully left – even when reinforced with shields that numbed the rest of my emotions – overrode every logical thought I could have.

That irrational part of me, told me that the Sacred Servants had called me here to discuss my outburst in the final trial. That they were going to punish me for condemning the Saviour and their Gods. I cursed myself for being so stupid in thinking opening my mouth would do me any good. I'd been in the house of the most powerful God, and I'd condemned him in my anger and panic of the trials.

I'd deserve whatever punishment they sought fitting for me.

As I followed the doorman down the new section of the palace, I took note of the way the walls grew lighter, as air around us became fresh, that thrumming outside pulse of energy slithering in through the walls.

It calmed any panic that had slithered through the cracks in my internal walls, and I embraced its assistance. Breathing deep I swore I could smell the earth, and just as my curiosity overrode any part of me that was screaming to keep my mouth shut, we emerged in front of a garden – halting anything I might have been about to say.

The space was wide enough that I couldn't see the walls surrounding us, and I stopped in my tracks, shocked as I took in the secret garden within the palace walls. Massive, jagged stone pillars arched above my head in welcoming, as if they'd been ripped from the earth beneath us. A breeze swept my hair back from its normal resting spot on either side of my shoulders – despite being crowned a Pure, I was still opposed to caring about how I looked. Grass met the concrete floor I was still situated on, and I felt warmth seep into me as I took in the high, dome-shaped glass ceiling that let in the natural sunlight, making the room feel as though we were outside in the woods.

If I were the God of the Citadel, I would never leave this place.

The doorman had stopped beside me, not daring to go any further and I glanced at him in question. He still hadn't said a word to me, and at this point, I wasn't sure he was allowed to. In society, the help was seen as less – especially since our sins designated our positions, so he had to be decidedly marked – and he worked for the God who oversaw the entire Citadel. Just because he worked in the home of our God, did not mean he would be treated any differently than the maids in my household – one would even wager that he would be punished more severely for simple infractions.

Our God was a temperamental one after all.

Maybe he had been punished before for speaking.

He extended his arm into the garden, indicating that I should go in without him, and with a nod of understanding from me he turned and walked back the way we came. Without any more prompting I moved further into this garden inside the palace, relishing the feeling of the soft grass beneath my flat shoes.

It had been days since I'd been able to go to my meadow, and I'd craved it — the peace that surrounded those grassy fields calling to me every time one of the Ladies tried to pry into my life, which was constantly now that I was considered top tier society.

I walked through the room, noting the way the sun seeped into the flowers that dotted throughout the room, not lined in neat rows like the gardens you'd see behind every family home in the Citadel. But naturally, as if they grew wherever they felt like the place needed more colour. The space felt free, like my meadow — able to grow and flourish in ways that only nature could decide.

Noise caught my attention to the middle of the room, behind the growing bushes and trees, and I followed the sound instinctively. There in the centre of the room was a clearing and on it sat two men at a long table, reclining like they had no care in the world, though I would wager that it was the world that had to watch out for them — both men looking far too lethal for this peaceful space, even in their resting positions.

"If it isn't the Pure of the Citadel." Rem drawled as their heads swivelled in my direction. He was in his usual vest and leather pants, long legs stretched out to the side as he nursed his glass on the edge of the table.

"I'm uh, I'm looking for the Sacred Servants… I was told they wanted to speak with me." I fumbled, startled by the sight of them in the garden. My internal shields loosening their grip slightly as relief flooded through me, the combining action confusing me somewhat.

I had tightened the reigns on my shield enough over the last few weeks that it had become almost automatic to throw them up in the presence of anyone — to clear my mind and school my face into the impassive Pure they were expecting them to be. For my shields to go against me for the first time since they had arrived almost two weeks ago was…. disconcerting.

"They're around." Nix replied, as I shook off my own problems and looked towards him. He had one leg hooked over the other, arm thrown over the back of his chair – more buttons on his tunic undone as if he hadn't expected company, and here they were – waiting for me.

I felt Nix's power flowing through the room then, seemingly unaware that its Master was at ease lounging on the chair as it moved through the space searching for any signs of danger. It mingled with the constant power I felt moving through the world and I was momentarily stunned at the way they interacted – seamlessly, as if it couldn't exist without the other but so opposite that they shouldn't be able to co-exist at all.

"Can one of you please tell them that I am here, then? Or better yet - take me to see them? I would like to get this over and done with." I finally asked, taking my attention off that power and back onto the men sat before me.

Apparently, that was a mistake.

"Somewhere better to be?" Nix questioned with one brow raised.

My hackles rose in response to him as they always did and I glared at him, heat filling my palms as those shields loosened a little more against my will. Anger was seeping through my walls now that they weren't air-tight and it fuelled my flames instantly as they travelled further through me, spurred by my irritation of the man in front of me and that smirk that seemed to be permanently attached to his face. If I were any closer to the table, I think my flames would have shot forward to wipe it from his stupidly beautiful arrogant face.

"The Servants didn't summon you, Nix here did." Rem eventually admitted, breaking the staring contest Nix and I were engaged in. I pulled my eyes from him and glanced down at my hands, noticing that they weren't just filled with heat, they were covered in flames.

I sucked in a deep breath as I fought them to go back inside of me, shaking slightly with both effort and rage as I willed them to climb back up my arms and return to their home in my mind.

Once they'd retreated, I retightened my hold on my shields, forcing them to close and lock away my emotions. When I was satisfied with my effort, I looked back up at the two men to find they were also staring at my hands. Rem's eyebrows had shot up in surprise, while Nix just looked deep in thought.

"To tea?" I asked sceptically once I was certain I was emotionless again.

"Do I look like a man who drinks tea?" Rem coughed out as he choked on his drink. I withheld a laugh at his reaction as Nix just shook his head at his companion.

"Is that an answer you want?" I replied sarcastically. Okay, maybe not every emotion was on lockdown...

"This one is mean, Nix." Rem replied instead, ignoring me with a hand on his heart as if I'd wounded him. I smirked at the thought that such a big man was so easily wounded, though his marks should have been indication enough that a blow to his ego would be enough to put him down.

"I did warn you."

"Warn him of what? You know nothing of me." I scoffed.

"Of that bite of yours." His eyes locked with mine as I felt his power swirl in time with his eyes, though instead of feeling dangerous it felt almost as if it were calling me to play. My shield unravelled itself slightly in response, and I had to tear my gaze from his before I got lost in them once more and let more power slip out.

Stupid smirk, stupid eyes.

"Right, well, if you invited me here just to insult me some more, then I will be taking my leave now. I have better things to occupy my time with." I spoke in the politest tone I could muster, thinking of how my mother would handle the situation when all I wanted to do was smack Nix on the head for his blatant rudeness towards me.

I was the Pure of the Citadel though — I could not act how I wished. I turned on my heel without waiting for their response and made it to the bushes on the edge of the clearing before I heard Nix speak again.

"I still need to speak with you." Nix called, stopping me in my tracks. I debated how much I needed to hear the words he wished to say to me, how effectively I could control myself in the presence of such an arrogant man — but in the end my curiosity got the better of me and I turned to face them.

"Why?"

"We have things to discuss." He said shrugging, as if it explained everything.

"*We* don't. I came here to speak to the Scared Servants."

"And I am here in their place."

"I don't —"

"If you just sat and listened, you'd find out little Pure." His voice smooth as silk, taunting me some more. Huffing in protest, I made my way over to their table and sat at the far end of it, away from both enormous men, while still able to keep an eye on each of them.

"I'm listening."

"We need to talk about your trials." He stated calmly, eyeing me as panic shot through my walls, but I schooled my face into the impassive mask of Pure Raewyn before it could make its way out.

"What about them?" I tried for nonchalant, but it came out as more of a squeak.

"The Sacred Servants are trying to find out how it is that you were able to manifest the powers of a God without having gone through all the ascension rites. But while they investigate it, they would appreciate if you kept that knowledge to yourself."

"I wasn't planning on telling anyone. I don't need people swarming me more than they already are." I replied with a scoff.

"But can you control it?" he pressed further, glancing at my hands again as if my fire would still be there.

"Well enough."

"You are the Pure of the Citadel now. They require you to uphold the expectations you now hold in society. If you are struggling, we need to know so we can help you."

"I don't know what it is I'm meant to be struggling with when I don't know anything aside from the tale spun in my childhood classes."

"Then I will teach you and train you."

"*What?*" I blurted, loudly and what my mother would call 'rather un-lady like'. Rem laughed as he watched the conversation unfold, leaning further back in his seat as though this was the highest form of entertainment for him. I turned my glare on him and his mouth shut instantly, though his shoulders were still shaking from amusement.

Nix opened his mouth to repeat what he'd just said but I beat him to it. "I don't need you to teach me anything.

I will be fine on my own."

"I disagree."

"Why would the Sacred Servants ask *you*, why not the God, or literally anyone else across the Isle —."

"They want to make sure you don't accidentally expose yourself or harm someone because you don't know how to keep it under control. If that means I must train you, and maybe throw in some history lessons then yes, I suppose they did ask that of me." He interrupted, leaning back casually as he spoke, his smirk telling me he knew he'd won our battle.

I forced myself into a calmness as I willed myself not to be riled by his arrogance. How he wasn't marked with sin was beyond me. He was the most annoying person I'd ever met.

"And it *has* to be you?" I tried again, hoping my voice held at least some semblance of polite, respectful etiquette… but all that came out was unbridled sarcasm.

"Why not? I am the only one in this Paradise, aside from the God himself, who has the knowledge you need to be able to control it." He grinned wide, despite my irritation. I couldn't argue with that, although the quiet laugh coming from Rem told me he thought this idea as ridiculous as I did.

"We will begin tomorrow. Meet me back here first thing tomorrow morning and I can assess where we should begin." Nix added when I didn't respond to him, too busy trying to tell myself that I could not shoot flames at this man's face.

It is impolite, it is rude, it was an abuse of these….

Wait, when?

"Uh, can we make it mid-morning? I have a prior engagement." I asked, my cheeks reddening in a way that had nothing to do with the fire burning inside of me.

"More Ladies to impress?" He teased and my irritation of him rose a little higher, not helping my internal monologue at all.

"More like suitors to choose from." I spat back, and both Nix and Rem stared at me as their mouths dropped open and I grinned in victory.

I was a Lady of society now, what did they expect?

"Mid-morning it is then. I will see you then." Nix replied once his mouth had closed, a thin line where his lips were meant to be, and I felt a wave of his power flare again, though this was different from the playfulness from before. It was almost as if he were angry.

I moved to stand, assuming I'd been dismissed when I saw his mouth open again and I paused, waiting for him to speak – but he snapped it closed a moment later without a sound, and I took that as my cue to leave.

CHAPTER 22

Imogen set off early the next day – all her friends gathered outside to wish her farewell, each of them showing various stages of jealousy, clearly untrained in the art of restraint, as they watched their ex-leader set off with such a highly ranked Lord.

Lord Ruskin had returned two days ago to see his new acquisition over the border and into the North. Though while everyone saw it as the romantically protective move he probably intended it to be, I still couldn't shake the feeling that something about him was off. I'd noticed more than once when he was sat at our dinner table that his eyes would cloud over when he thought no one was looking, and a darkness would envelop him – as if he had his own energy.

It had caused me to feel on edge, and I was constantly having to focus my efforts on withdrawing my flames.

I watched in amusement as one of the girls of Imogen's little band, Stacia I think her name was, trying to assert herself as the next dominant leader of their group, pushing her way to the front and speaking for the lot of them. It would be interesting to see how they survived without my sister as she was always the bold one. She was the one who inserted herself into places to find out all the gossip and mayhem they spread.

Maybe if we were lucky, they'd disband, and the Citadel nobility would be left in peace for a little bit.

My mind had focused completely on the scene before me, that I hadn't even noticed my father approaching me until he was standing right next to me.

"This will be you soon Dear, Saviour willing."

"Saviour willing indeed." was all I replied. I hadn't spoken much to my father last night at dinner, he knew I was still upset at the dismissal he'd given me in his office. His refusal to even think about the possibility of me not Binding myself to someone had hurt me more than I could admit, and when I'd returned home from my visit to the Citadel, he hadn't asked how it went which told me that he was angry at me for even thinking it was a possibility.

So, we chose to ignore the subject altogether…until now it seemed.

"Raewyn, I know you do not wish to be bound to someone. But my Binding Ceremony with your mother is the best thing I have ever done in my life – I just want the same for all my children." He tried and I continued looking at the scene before me as I replied.

"*You* got to choose mother. I do not."

"You get more than Imogen did. I thought you'd at least be happy about that." He sighed as he spoke, and my emotions flared at the concept of my father yet again being disappointed in me. This is not why I had fought so hard to keep myself under control. I did all of this so that my family would be safe, happy. This was just another one of those things I would have to sacrifice to achieve that, but that didn't mean I would be happy about it.

"I understand that Father, but it is not what I wanted. Ever."

"Given your new status in society, I thought you'd understand more than ever the importance of you securing a good husband. I only wish to give you the opportunity to help find someone who is complimentary to you, and hope that it blossoms into more. Just like it did with your mother and I, like Orion and Alyssa."

"Like Imogen and Lord Ruskin?" I countered. My father chuckled in response, taking my tone as a jest rather than the sarcasm I thought I was emitting. Maybe I needed to lower my shield a little to input more emotion into my words.

"It is too early to tell, but yes, I do hope so. She is smitten with him, and he seems to be enjoying her company. Things could be worse."

I didn't have anything to say to that, so I kept quiet, and we watched together as Lord Ruskin helped my sister into the reddish-sand hued carriage of the North, the black Ruskin crest of an armoured soldier sitting upon his stead, a stark contrast to the sunset tones surrounding it. My fire squirmed restlessly, as it too could sense more beneath the man who was taking my sister away. Imogen's tears streaming down her face as she looked back at us through the window, her face contorted in a way that meant she was genuinely upset, and that it wasn't just for show.

We'd said our goodbyes last night as we huddled together in my room until our eyes had grown so heavy, they would not stay open. I had said all I needed to then – but even still a lump formed in my throat, and I couldn't shake the feeling that this would be the last time I ever saw her again. Which was silly considering she was just across the border. I could venture out to visit her in the Northers Paradise if I wanted to, and even if I didn't, she would be back for her Binding Ceremony in a few months' time anyways.

I would see her again. I would make sure of it.

My father waited until the carriage was out of sight before he spoke again, turning me to look at him this time so the full impact of his words could hit me. "All I ask is that you work with me, Dear. Your Binding Ceremony is just as important to the family as it will be to you. All I ask is that you get to know these men and help me find the one you disagree with least. It may save both of you some headaches in the future if I can get this right." He said with a slight smile that lit his eyes up with hope. I could feel the weight of his words like cement in my soul and so I nodded in agreement, knowing that for my family, I would do anything.

"Good. Lord Carron will be here shortly for breakfast, so why don't you head into the garden and wait for him there. Analise will keep an eye on the two of you if you need anything." With that, he walked me back inside and pushed me towards the garden doors.

I moved towards them as the weight grew inside of me and I tried to convince myself that at least I was going to know the man I would be bound to. I was not as naive as my sister to think that a titled man meant a good man — though I questioned why she would still believe that after all the bound men that had fallen at her feet before her future husband came into the picture.

Regardless though she still held onto the hope that the man she would bind herself to would dote on her and love her for all he was worth, and I hoped for her sake that it was the case with Lord Ruskin.

I, however, held a more cynical view of the Binding Ceremony. I saw the contract and payment as a transaction and my own Binding to a man as the selling of myself for his satisfaction. I knew it was possible to fall in love from these contracted Bindings – my mother and father were the best example of love born from a contract, but my mother had not had a choice in the matter.

Imogen did not choose Lord Ruskin.

If I were to ever choose to be bound, I would want what Orion and Alyssa had.

Father was wrong in grouping my brother's Binding with his own – for although Orion had chosen Alyssa, she had also chosen him in return. They had fought for each other and even accepted more markings of sin in order to be with one another. There was no other Binding in all of the Seven Paradises that came close to the kind of bond those two had, and there never would be. What those two did was risky and selfish enough that the sacrifice of societal reprimand for their love appeared selfless enough to appease the Saviour himself.

That is what I would want, if I got the choice. Love that transcends the notions of proprietary and society, though I would be equally as satisfied just being left alone.

Analise came along and poured me some coffee, setting out another cup and saucer along with my favourite pastries and fruit and I knew that meant Lord Carron must have arrived.

She nodded towards me in encouragement before she left and I took a moment to shove everything I had just been thinking about behind my walls, tightening my shields just enough that I would not leak emotion, but I could still hold a proper conversation.

It had been trial and error these past few weeks

learning just how much of myself I could shut off before I came off as cold and indifferent. The Ladies who had met that Pure of the Citadel, had not spread particularly nice words about me. Calling me rude and self-absorbed and I'd received an earful from my mother about proper manners and etiquette. Honestly, they should have been happy I hadn't burnt them all to a crisp by accident.

Crap, not what I should be thinking about right now. I thought hurriedly as my flames spurred forward as though the thought of them were invitation enough to come out. Heat pooled my palms as licks of fire danced along my knuckles. I inhaled deep as I willed them to retreat, but they did not listen. Instead, they crawled higher up my wrists, warming my skin in welcome as they soaked in the earth's ever flowing energy surrounding me since I was sitting outside.

"I was told I would find you out here."

Shit.

My flames had covered my forearms, and panic surged through me as the voice of who I assumed would be Lord Carron floated through the air from the direction of the house.

I couldn't see him yet, but I knew the table I sat at was visible from the doorway. Stuffing my hands in between my legs in an attempt to hide them, I prayed the material from my dress would douse the flames as I scrunched my eyes closed and tried to imagine the flames retreating under my skin.

"I am extremely humbled to be here this morning. However unorthodox it is to meet with the woman like an interview." He ended his words with a high-pitched chuckle, and I opened my eyes to find him standing before me. He was an ordinary looking man with plain brown hair and brown eyes. He would still be taller than me if I stood, though he was by no means a tall man, his slouching posture eating up inches he desperately needed back. His Lords jacket was crumpled as if he hadn't thought to press it before coming to meet with me.

The only interesting thing about him were the books he held in one arm, and I eyed them curiously as I willed my mind to focus on the words I could see scrawling soothingly down the spines of his books…

On the fact that he looked anything but a threat to me…

That I was calm and safe and *not on fire.*

"I bought these for you, as a gift." He tried again and I realised that I had not yet spoken a word to him. I smiled in response, certain that my voice would entice my flames more, though he took that as sign enough to sit down with me, grinning in what I assume he thought was a charming manner.

Analise came out at that moment and asked him for his drink preference, and I raised an eyebrow at his choice in tea. He chuckled in response to my obvious distaste, as he eyed my untouched cup of coffee.

"I find that caffeine heightens the mind a little too much for my comfort. I prefer to be clear minded at all times. But I do not judge you for liking the stuff." Uninteresting man indeed.

"I find that my mind does not function properly without it." I said as I tested my voice, steady and calm and I smiled more to myself than him at the victory.

"Ah! That is the addict in you speaking. I am surprised the Servants did not pick up on the dependency." He laughed at his own joke, and I felt my flames climb higher up my arms in mention of the Sacred Servants.

"They had more important things to test me on." I responded through gritted teeth, hunching over further so that he could not see my arms on fire. I strained against the power of my flames as I fought them from travelling any further and cursed them for deciding that *now* was the time to disobey me.

Maybe I did need that lesson in control after all.

"Of course, forgive me I was only trying to lighten the mood." He apologised, bowing his head slightly in deference to me, who was technically above him in station. I blinked at the gesture and attempted another smile when his eyes raised back to mine. I had to be nice to this man, get to know him. For my family's sake.

My flames retreated slightly at that thought, knowing that I would be risking it all to show this man what I was capable of. I breathed a sigh of relief as they began to listen to me.

"I thought we could use this breakfast to get to know one another, Pure Sandoval." He tried when I hadn't responded to him in over a minute. I nodded my agreement as I continued focusing on my retreating flames. I knew I was being rude, but I hoped it came off as the shy Pure they had all claimed me to be.

His answering smile told me that is exactly what he was thinking.

"Okay, well, a little bit about me…" he soldiered on as my flames slid back down my arms, covering only my hands once again as I felt sweat drip down my back at the effort it was taking to control them. The first thing I would ask Nix to teach me was how to command these powers more effortlessly. He didn't even look like he acknowledged his power and yet it flowed constantly around him, seeking out threats without him having to exert any effort.

Keeping mine at bay was a constant struggle and it was only held within me.

Lord Carron rattled on about things he liked to do while he wasn't working as a historian in the Citadel's archives, preserving anything they found from the old world, categorising it, and rebinding texts and books so that they could be kept and passed on to the next generation. The whole thing sounded rather boring and dull, though I did find his monotony rather soothing as my fire acknowledged that they weren't needed at all and retreated fully, finally giving me back use of my hands.

I smiled happily as I lifted my hands to the handle of my cup and took a grateful sip. It wasn't until I placed my cup back on the table that I noticed something was wrong. Looking down at my gown, I gasped in horror as I realised, I was looking at bare skin. Heat crept up my neck as I quickly folded my legs over each other, tucking my dress over itself to cover the arm sized hole I had burnt into the fabric when I hid them from Lord Carron. I cringed in embarrassment.

Note to self, only you are inflammable.

"…and even the Sacred Servants thanked me for my work on preserving what appeared to be the first ever text from the Saviour himself." Lord Carron finished, too engrossed in his own story about himself to notice anything else.

Thank the Saviour for egotistical sinners, I thought as I made a noise of what I hoped was wonder as I took another sip of my coffee.

"Sounds like you really love what you do." I added when I realised, he'd paused for me to do more than make noises at him.

"I really do. Not many people can say they gather

knowledge as important as I, or know the proper methods required to preserve them. I am the best binder in all seven Paradises." At this I glanced at his hands and noticed without surprise the swirls of ink that crawled along the back of his hand and along his fingers. Sins of Coveting.

"What about you, Pure Sandoval?"

"What about me?" I repeated blandly.

"What are you passionate about, what would you like to do with your time?" His enthusiasm towards my interests made me uneasy and I used Goddess Patricia's stalling method of taking another sip of my drink as I thought of the correct response, of anything but the truth.

"I am passionate about anything the Saviour deems me worthy of." There, that was the answer expected of a Pure.

"Any interests?"

"Not really. I enjoy the peace nature offers, but other than that I am rather boring." A small portion of truth for the man. The accompanying smile he gave me told me he liked my admission as well.

"I also love the outdoors, the endless things I find in the Wanderer's Wood astound me to no end."

"You venture into the Wanderer's Wood?" I asked, finally interested in something he said, though he took the shocked tone in my voice to mean I was worried for him.

"Oh, don't worry about me, Pure Sandoval. Rest assured I am well armed with guards when I do. But in answer to your question, yes. We have excavating sites all throughout the woods to find as many artifacts as we can. How can one learn about the ruin of the old world if we do not know anything about them after all?"

"And you write about these things that you find?"

"Oh yes of course, I even give presentations in the

Citadel sometimes. If you were my wife, you'd be able to attend them anytime you pleased if it interested you." His chest puffed out as he said the words 'my wife' and any interest I had in the subject faded as I remembered why he was here. I'd give anything to learn more about the old world and everything they've found in the Wanderer's Wood – ancient pieces of discarded life that had been lying silently in the depths of the ocean, before the Saviour rose it to life. But I would not bind myself to this man just to satisfy that curiosity.

He talked a bit more about his findings and his daily life in the Village of Steel, needing very little prodding from me as I found he really did like to ramble on about himself and his accomplishments. Another thing I should have assumed from him as I spotted markings crawling up the side of his neck, curling over his right ear. The sin of Ego.

I was tempted to ask him how many sins total he had, but that was rude etiquette in society and so I refrained from doing so. Eventually he'd had enough of talking about himself, or maybe he had just run out of stories to tell, but he quietened for a second and I looked up at him as he appeared deep in thought.

"I must say, this is rather unorthodox in terms of Binding proposals. I have never gone to such lengths to impress someone I intend to bind myself to." I cringed openly at the admission that I was not the first woman he'd tried to contract into a Binding Ceremony and resisted the urge to ask him just how many times he'd been rejected. If I had to wager a guess though, I'd say quite a few.

And they hadn't even had the pleasure of eating breakfast with him.

"My father thought it prudent that I meet the men who wish to be bound to the first Pure of the Citadel. In case I see something that he does not." I replied instead. Injecting some more honesty into my words in case he thought I was joking.

"And your verdict?" He asked hopefully.

"I have enjoyed your stories." *And we are back to lying again.* Though the grin he gave me in response told me he bought it.

I bid him farewell after that, calling for Analise to escort him out as I remained sitting. I was not about to stand and show him the mayhem of my skirts and what lay beneath them. That would be improper in all respects and give him the absolute wrong idea.

In any case I would have to sneak back up my room to change before I departed for the palace.

Waiting long enough for them to make it to the other side of the house, I gathered my skirts, folding them upwards so that they were lifted off the ground, ensuring they covered all the indecent parts of me that you'd be able to see through the gaping hole I had created. I sprinted for the staircase just inside the doors. Climbing them two at a time in case my parents were close by to ask me what I thought of Lord Carron.

I would tell them my thoughts — a resounding no unless they wished for me to die of boredom from the sound of his voice — but first, a change of clothes.

"Sweetheart?" my father's voice called from the bottom of the staircase, and I cursed at my luck.

"Yes?" I replied, turning my head towards him while keeping my skirts clutched in my hands. If he wondered why they were lifted so high up my legs, he did not ask.

"How was breakfast with Lord Carron?"

"It was fine."

"I need more than that, Raewyn." He chastised.

"And I need more than one breakfast to decide if I like a man. At the very least ask me to rate them once I have met them all." I called as I continued walking up the staircase, and then threw in, "I have a meeting at the palace to attend, so I am going to prepare for that now."

That ought to keep him from following me up the stairs. I didn't need anyone asking me how I managed to burn a hole through my dress – it was not something I was certain I could explain without showing them what I could do, but I was forbidden from revealing anything.

I really needed to learn how to control this thing.

CHAPTER 23

"You're late."

I knew I was, though that didn't stop me from taking time to hide my ruined dress from the likes of Analise and mother before I left. Though the tone Nix threw at me as I entered the garden room we'd met in yesterday, made any apology I might have had ready, fly out the window.

"Did you have something else you needed to do today?"

"Not the point. You said mid-morning, it is almost noon." He replied in a dark tone, his power flaring out around him, and I could see wafts of smoke escaping him. The sight should have terrified me, I still knew next to nothing about this man — but instead I found I was mesmerised by the way his power moved through the air. My flames unfurled themselves from where I'd shoved them at breakfast in answer, though they made no move to come out this time.

"How do you do that?" I asked suddenly, changing the subject in hopes to distract him from his foul mood. He tilted his head to one side at my question, as he watched me approach the table he sat at again today. For training, this looked remarkably like another invitation to tea.

"Do what?"

"That," I emphasised my question by pointing at one of the swirls of smoke emanating off him. "You control it so easily, like you're not even aware that it's reacting to your every move." He stared at the spot I'd pointed to, and his eyes widened in realisation as he turned back to me.

"You can see that?"

"Why wouldn't I be able to?"

"Interesting. What else can you do?" he queried, as he finally stood from his reclined position. I had forgotten how impossibly tall Nix was, struggling to tilt my head back far enough just to look up at him.

"You didn't answer my question."

"I have had far longer to learn control than you have, little Pure. My manifested powers are now a part of me and me of it."

Huh? "That's not an answer." I frowned.

"Yes, it is, now answer my question. What else can you do?"

"I don't know. I thought that's why I was here."

"Not an answer." He repeated mimicking me and a grimaced more at the tone. My flames slid through my blood at my irritation of him and I welcomed the extra armour against him.

"I can make flames appear, as you have seen. I feel them running through me all day long and it is exhausting trying to control them." I admitted with a sigh, choosing to leave out any mention of my new and improved internal shield. "I need you to teach me to control them like you do with your smoky thing you have floating around here to avoid another accident."

He stared at me with furrowed brows as he considered something. It was a look that unnerved me, as if he were seeing straight into my soul and I could only hold his eyes for a minute before the feeling overwhelmed me, shields tightening in reflex.

He shook his head after another minute, his face giving away nothing of what he was thinking. I opened my mouth to ask him what he thought he was doing, but he spoke before I could.

"What accident?" He asked finally, although I could tell it was not the question he really wanted the answer to.

"I uh – had a fumble with my control this morning and almost revealed my fire to Lord Carron."

"Almost?" His eyes darkened at my words, and I could tell he was not happy that I'd almost gone back on the only order I'd been given from the Sacred Servants.

"I was able to get them under control eventually. He didn't even notice the hole I'd burnt in my dress. Would have made for more interesting conversation though if I'm being honest." I muttered the end of my words, more to myself than him. Though he snorted in response, his eyes relaxing in their swirl as his powers calmed slightly as they moved through the air around us.

"Today we will focus on where your power comes from or meant to anyway. In order for you to understand how to control it, you need to know how the ascension rite works." He said suddenly, changing the subject from my doomed morning meeting with a suitor.

"Today is just a history lesson?" I asked, pouting in disappointment. I needed to learn how to *not* shoot flames out of me at inappropriate times – not a schooling lesson on how our Saviour created the Gods. Nix merely nodded his answer as he gestured for me to sit at the table he'd just occupied. Frustrated, I marched over and claimed the spot Rem had been in the day before as I looked at him expectantly.

"Well?" I probed when he didn't speak straight away. If he was looking to annoy me further, he certainly didn't have to work very hard — my flames were still sitting just under my skin, readying themselves to come forth at the slightest raising of emotions. *I'll just do it my way then*, I scoffed to myself as I breathed deep, attempting to calm myself as I tightened my shields a little more. Once I was as in control as I could be, I glanced at Nix, whose brows were drawn low in disapproval — but he said nothing as he settled back into his seat before he began my history lesson.

Truth be told, I'd always enjoyed my tutoring — I loved the feeling of growing through knowledge; my mind seeking to understand anything new and questioning those who did not agree with it.

Though those questions got me into a lot of trouble when I was younger, meaning I learnt to listen more than speak…learnt that people only liked teaching those that would follow.

"The first thing you need to understand is the power of the Sacred Servants. They draw on the power of ascension, although they are not Pure enough to go through themselves. It is only because of their devotion to the Gods and the Saviour that they are able to harness it, able to create the *iter* they use to administer tests, and mark people accordingly. Think of them as a conduit to the power that creates a God." He glanced at me to see if I was still following along and I nodded eagerly, so he continued.

"When someone pure enough does go through the ascension rites, there are four gateways that we must pass through, each increasingly more difficult than the last. We call these the *Anima Fores*, or the doors to the soul. The first door is called *Veritas* – it is the door of reality. It breaks down everything that you ever knew, every tangible and intangible spec of self that you had ever considered to be real and rebuilds it – opening your mind to the divine power of the universe. Our sense of self becomes so entwined with the power of the universe that we are able to crawl between it, merge into each fibre and create spaces that aren't meant to exist. Though because it is not natural, the *iter* is only ever created as a temporary space."

"Has anyone ever tried making it permanent?" I blurted, interrupting him, though it did not look as if he minded as his head shook in response.

"It's not something that can be done. It needs a host to become tangible, a mind to hold onto, and because it essentially becomes a new reality it would shatter the mind of anyone who holds it too long. There are even those in history who did not survive the *iter* created in the trials and so the Servants had to separate each test in order to let the mind reset itself." I nodded once more in understanding, recalling the way the Sacred Servants had ended my first trial before starting the next one – and I suppose they were trying to pull me from the second one before I kicked them out. He waited patiently for my mind to come to terms with the first doorway and I nodded once more for him to carry on with the rest, my mind craving the knowledge he was offering.

"The second door is *Natura* – the earthen door. This one connects those who are worthy enough to the earth. It is where the elemental connection to our powers comes from as our life's energy is forever entwined with that of the earth's natural power. It is that bond that ensures we do not harm the earth like our forefathers did — for its pain becomes our own." I thought of that ancient energy I felt drifting through the world and wondered if that was the natural power he was talking about — but I did not want to interrupt him once more, so I waited as he carried on the lesson.

"Then there is the third door. This is called *Tentatio*. The door of temptation. This separates the willing from the unwilling, as all your temptations are tested and judged on whether they are truly Pure. This is different from the trials, as those tests only the base of your desires. This door deconstructs every thought, every feeling and throws them back at you like knives to see how strong minded you are. I have known Pures from long ago to fail this door solely because they were not strong enough to resist their natural instincts."

"How can someone be both Pure of soul and still fail the ascension?"

"Some things, little Pure, are not worth giving up. No matter the cost." He stated, his eyes darkening slightly as they swirled faster — gaze locked on mine. I felt his power swell around us as I lost myself to the pooling storms — wishing I could dive deeper into them to see what lay beneath.

"Finally, the last door is named *Anima* — the door to the soul." He continued, clearing his throat as he turned his eyes away from mine, breaking through my thoughts. "Only the Original Gods have managed to pass through this door. It is not clear what exactly happens in this door, it is different for everyone. The only thing known for certain is that if you are worthy enough to pass through, the gift you are given is the greatest honour you could ever receive from the universe. Originally, one had to pass through all four doorways, in order to be crowned God of a Paradise – but now, any Pure may ascend if they pass through at least the first one."

My mind froze as his words sunk in, the possibility that I'd already passed through at least two of the four gates unknowingly – without the rituals and doorways terrifying me more than I'd anticipated. Who was I to forego all these tests and claim that I was just as good, just as pure as all the people that came before me? I wasn't broken down, I wasn't thrown through these gruelling tests and commitments to the earth just to be reconstructed to be this all-knowing, all-Pure being.

I was just me. Not worthy of the powers I'd created in my trials.

I was a fraud. A fraud who just happened to be lucky enough to unlock something that didn't belong to her.

The air around me grew hot and I struggled to inhale as my flames twisted inside me as if they knew the truth too. They didn't belong to me. It was why they constantly fought to be freed. Why I had to contain every other thing about me, as if a thought, a feeling, would give away what I really was.

Saviour be, I even admitted it to the Sacred Servants in my trial.

Yet they'd ignored that damning bit of treason on the basis of my early manifestation, and now they were looking into exactly what that meant. Panic surged as flames licked over my fingers, and I felt a power press into me from outside of myself. I looked up into the bottomless whirl of Nix's eyes as he appeared directly in front of me. Closer than the seats were arranged, as his smoke became corporeal, slithering closer to us cautiously as though it might frighten me more.

I wasn't afraid of him, but if he came any closer, I was would not be able to control my flames if that lashed out in defence.

"Why do people want to ascend if it sounds painful?" I asked in an attempt at distraction, breathing in the hot air I'd created around me. Each breath burning its way down my throat, choking me. His chest heaved through the heat I'd created, though he made no move to escape its radius as his gaze flicked down to my hands. I knew what he would find. My fire was still dancing along my fingertips as I clenched them into fists.

"I'm not sure. Selflessness I suppose, or a chance to declare yourself as an elite."

"And you?"

"I wasn't given the choice." He replied, his eyes darkening as they churned faster in response. I saw smoke curl closer towards us. *Wrong thing to ask,* I thought hurriedly as I racked my brain for anything else to ask while I was trying to get myself under control. Sweat beaded on my brow from the effort, my flames not moving up my hands, but not leaving either.

"And me?" I croaked. Apparently, it was a struggle for me to blurt out more complex words now. He laughed at my attempt either way so at least I was distracting someone.

"We are not sure why you manifested the way you did. Those who do pass through all four doors though are granted these gifts on the notion that they are used in order to help the rest of humanity to become the same, so that they may also ascend. Or so the original scriptures say, maybe that is your purpose."

"So why aren't we putting everyone through this if we are created to encourage them towards it?" I blurted in a half shout.

Good. More words, more distraction.

I can do this.

"Why not indeed, but that is not what the Saviour commanded of us. Perhaps those with sin are not able to pass through the first gate and so it is not worth the risk of failure. There is a reason the Sacred Servants are only a conduit of the Anima Fores, and not ascended themselves." I nodded in acceptance of his answer, even as every part of me was screaming that it did not make sense.

With that logic alone, I was the wrong person to bestow gifts upon with the idea that I would help people to do better, to *be better.* I wanted very little to do with the people I knew and giving me these uncontrollable flames did not help – if anything it made it all worse.

If someone was going to sin, there was nothing that I could do to change their minds. I was not strong, and I did not have a voice in our society – something I did not see changing no matter how long I lasted as the Pure of the Citadel. Their temptation to sin would be there regardless of whether a Pure commanded them or not.

Especially a defective one who shouldn't be a Pure at all.

Oh no, maybe I can't do this.

I needed to find a way out of being a Pure before they all realised that I wasn't meant to be this person. That I was not meant to have all these things that made me who they thought I was.

Before they saw exactly who I was inside.

"I know this is a lot to take in. Ascension is not an easy thing to grasp, so I say we leave it there for today. Tomorrow we will focus on what you can do with those flames of yours." Nix's tone was light, teasing, meant for a turn in conversation but I had already lost myself in my thoughts again.

I wasn't sure my voice would be able to work anyway at this point, even if I had something to say – the fire that had burned itself down my throat only growing hotter the longer I sat here. I stood suddenly, needing the space it created between us as I moved to leave.

Though before I could take another step, Nix placed a hand on my arm, stopping me. His face serious as he looked up at me. "I cut them out of the *iter* the moment I touched you, Raewyn. The only people that know how you really feel are you and me. You are *safe*." His tone was softer than any I'd ever heard from him, even when he was trying to calm me down in the *iter*. It almost reminded me of those whispered words he's spoken as he took me out of the trial. I faltered slightly as I continued walking past him refusing to even acknowledge that he'd spoken, knowing that doing so would break open these shields I was struggling to maintain.

Fire roared through my blood and thinking about anything other than the next step I was taking would collapse me. I needed to get outside, to feel the full force of that power that surrounded us so it could help calm me. I stumbled out of the magical courtyard that I hadn't yet been able to fully enjoy – and all but ran for the arching wood of the double doors that signalled my first step to freedom. I spied the doorman waiting on the other side of them to escort me back out the way I came, but he merely nodded to me as I approached, and as I exited the doorway, he closed and locked them up behind me. I felt the exact moment the lock clicked home as that ancient power that had been flowing gently within those walls cut off – leaving me instantly and I realised that it had also been feeding my resolve.

Panic rose in me as my shield swirled like a storm, catching each emotion that escaped from behind my crumbling walls, my flames burning their way through me as they anticipated a threat.

But I was the threat. I'd held them all in for too long.

And now I was going to explode.

I navigated the palace walls in a daze, relying purely on memory as I half ran through the hallways, leaving the doorman behind me as I fought to keep myself under control. The irony was not lost on me that I'd *just* told Nix that I could control myself less than a day ago, and now I was anything but in control.

Though I completely blamed him for the crumbling of my mental state now. Who in their right mind would casually mention something as important as that? We both knew that what I'd said in my trials was treason, so what did he have to gain from keeping the truth from the Sacred Servants? Why would he kick them out of the *iter* again, just to protect me? We weren't friends, and we certainly did not get along – yes, he was the author to my letters, and yes, I wished to dive deeper into that side of him. But I did not know him, nor him me.

None of it made sense, and I was spiralling deeper into those thoughts with every step I took. I could feel the effort it took for my shields to catch each thought, each emotion as they slammed around inside me. Each one feeling like a punch to the gut. Even my flames had realised the fight was inside me rather than out and had moved to try and piece my walls back together.

When I finally made it out of the palace, I ran straight past my waiting carriage, the driver yelling for me to stop. But I carried on running, pumping my legs as fast as they would take me down the winding hillside — needing to feel the push of the wind against my face, the pulse of the earth's energy as it surged around me. It felt frenzied, wilder than its normal calm caresses, as if it could sense my inner turmoil now that it wasn't diluted by the walls of the palace.

I ran until I could see the Town Square and a memory surged through me of the time Nix had caught me staring up at the palace, wondering if the God of the Citadel was lonely. I could honestly answer now that he would have to be. I barely had half the power and expectation he did in society, and I was crumbling under the weight of having to keep everything inside. To act how they expected me to act, to think how they think a Pure should think.

Not that I was a shining example of what a God should be, as I was still convinced this was all some big mistake; but I could understand why he would seclude himself for centuries at a time. It was exhausting, and I had been a Pure for only a few weeks. I couldn't imagine centuries of this isolation I felt now.

I veered right as I closed in on the square and slipped down a winding pathway that I knew would lead me straight to the centre of the Wanderer's Wood. The strength of that ancient energy surged as soon as I entered the woods — and as the wind whipped my hair around my face and tangled my dress between my legs, I dove between the trees in a way I never had before. I instinctively found my way to the middle of the woods, my meadow, my peace, my sanctuary.

I'm a mistake.

I'm a lie.

I'm not meant to be here.

My thoughts pounded against me as I continued running, circling back again and again as I refused to accept their meanings.

Crowning me the Pure of the Citadel had been a mistake, something they never would have done had Nix not interfered in my trials and closed them out before I confessed my true feelings towards him.

I hated that he had taken that moment from me — remembering how good it felt to finally be honest, to speak what lay in my soul.

I hated that the Servants of our ever-loving Saviour missed out on the opportunity to end me from this existence that wasn't worth living if it was all a lie. That my turmoil over whether or not they would punish me was for nothing.

I cursed Nix that he hadn't confessed that to me sooner, and that he'd protected me at all.

Most of all, I hated that some part of me savoured the feel of being saved by him.

Collapsing in the middle of my meadow, I felt my walls breach and shatter as both my shield and flames pushed outwards, a scream tearing its way from my lips as everything I'd been holding in left me.

Every emotion I had ever felt poured out of their confines as my flames singed the ground beneath me. Waves of heat pulsed around me as pure energy kept it contained.

I struggled to breathe as pain and sorrow washed over me — the feeling old and angry as they demanded to be felt. Fragments of me passed behind my eyelids, me as a child, me on my knees, crying, begging… me lost and desperate for someone, *anyone*… and the pain, when had I experienced so much pain?

I couldn't understand any of it as the images faded too fast for me to latch on to. More emotions shoved their way to the forefront of my mind, and I felt them all.

Watched the fragments as they flew past me — all stronger than the last as I felt every moment of my life in such agony that I wished my flames had the ability to burn me from the inside out.

Desperate, and panting — I willed them to sear out the pain and clear them all away.

But my flames were no longer inside of me. I could still feel my connection to them as they whipped around the space I had created, but now they moved in a protective dance as they circled me — as if they knew I needed to be kept safe from the outside world.

As if they knew I'd reached my limit.

I tried to reach out to my shield, begging them to pull my emotions back inside, to build a wall higher and stronger between them and me so I didn't have to feel *everything*, but they did not listen.

Somewhere in the distance, behind all the flashes of memory, stabs of guilt and heartbreak, I heard someone calling my name. At first, it felt like a whisper in my mind, and then a pounding — but it was quickly drowned out as I felt another wall crack inside of me, the pain overriding every sense as my vision blurred.

If this was death, then at least it would be over soon.

I was unaware how much time passed as I screamed myself raw within my own bubble of fire and power — the images increasing in intensity along with the pain as soul wrenching sobs fought through the screams. I could no longer feel my own body as floated through my now fragmented mind, the images whipping past me so fast that each blow felt like a slice to my soul. The pounding continued outside of me, a calling of what I could only assume was meant to be my name — but in the pain I couldn't remember what it was, couldn't remember who I was outside of this feeling of pain and sorrow.

When that pounding entered my mind for the tenth time, my fire froze for a moment, sensing something I could not. The images halted in their assault as curiosity rose up through them. Without hesitating, I forced myself to move through my mind, crawling over to the space they'd created around the intrusion. Gripping onto the fine thread of power that was struggling to penetrate my mind, I tugged it hard, a plea for it to take me away from this insanity – and sighed as it catapulted me into nothingness.

CHAPTER 24

"Raewyn."

I opened my eyes as a feeling of being disoriented filled me. I couldn't remember how I got here, and as I sat up from my position on the ground, I felt the coolness of the grass surrounding me — but something felt off. I just couldn't place it.

"I fell asleep?" I mumbled the question to myself rather than whoever had just called my name. The last thing I remembered was being at the table a few meters away from me, not lounging on the grassy floor of the palace's secret garden. I must have drifted off during Nix's story — he would not be happy with me.

The thought made me grin anyway.

"No."

I whipped my head around to the other side of me where Nix sat back on his haunches, staring down at me with a frown on his face so deep it set off alarm bells inside of me.

"What do you mean no?"

"I need you to focus. What is the last thing you remember?" He asked, running his hands through his hair, pushing the dark curls up just to fall back into a messier disarray. I blinked up at him confused.

"You were training me. You explained the Anima Fores to me."

"And after that?" He prodded.

"I woke up here, so I can attest to your terrible teaching ability if I was able to doze off during a lesson." I smirked, crossing my legs as I faced him fully now. I still had to tilt my head back slightly to look up at him, but at least now I didn't feel like I was *under* him.

I felt my face heat at the thought, and I immediately shoved it away.

"Does this look like a time to joke around, Raewyn?" His sternness caught me off guard and that feeling of something being off came rushing back. I looked around the courtyard, but nothing seemed to be different, though I couldn't tell for sure since I'd only been here twice.

I looked back at Nix and saw the concentration on his brow, the serious look in his eye and I paused.

"What's wrong?" I asked and he laughed, loud and humourless as he leaned forward until our noses almost touched, his eyes sucking me deep into their stormy depths, and I had no choice but to drown in their power.

"What's wrong is that you ran from me instead of telling me you were losing control. What's wrong is I had to follow you into the middle of *fucking nowhere*, just to watch you explode and then lock me out with an energy shield so powerful that even *I* cannot breach it. I have been throwing *iter*'s at you for the past half hour without luck. Saviour's grace, I still don't know how I got through to you." His head shook as he leaned back, giving me room as his words sunk in. As reality sunk in.

My walls had broken.

I had exploded.

Shit, this was not good.

And then I realised what was missing.

"I can't feel anything." I murmured numbly as I stood and looked around the courtyard. The now familiar feel of that ancient power had disappeared, so had Nix's overwhelming power.

Saviour, I couldn't even feel my flames – my whole body feeling empty without that feeling of power running through me. I hadn't realised just how used to them I had become.

How dependant.

"I had to create an *iter* in my mind and lock it tight so your powers wouldn't follow you in. It is taking everything in me to keep them out right now."

"That's why I can't feel you, or anything really –" I replied absentmindedly, more to myself than Nix, but he responded, nonetheless.

"What are you talking about?"

"You – the earth. I can't see or feel any of the power coming from either of you that I normally do. I feel hollow without it. I don't like it."

He blinked once, twice, as if my words weren't making sense. Slowly, he mulled over his next words, as though they would send me into another spiral if he were not careful.

"No one else can see that, Raewyn. I can see and feel my powers moving through the room because they are *mine*, but you are the first that I've met who can see another person's energy move. Unless manifested to life, like your fire for instance, it is just invisible energy."

"But I can normally feel it too, even when it is invisible. Like it's moving through the air around me. Yours is very different to the earth's energy so I'm able to separate the two– though somehow it seems to compliment it like it was made from it."

"You've lost me." His brows furrowed in confusion.

"The earth's energy? You know that ancient pulsing feeling that literally surrounds everything? It's usually just outside but I normally feel it in here, though it is muted. I assume that is because this is an indoor garden and not directly connected to the earth outside." I was rambling now, but the look on Nix's face was making me feel more and more crazy, that I felt the need to continue explaining myself.

When he didn't answer right away, I panicked that maybe I'd said too much.

"I thought every Pure felt that?" I whispered, embarrassed that I was yet again different from the rest.

"No, Rae. Just you."

Well, that sucks.

"Every Pure is different. Once ascended, we manifest in ways that enhance our own selves and connect us with the earth. While we all have innate abilities that remain the same, our primary sources of energy that separate us from the rest of humanity differ. I have never heard of someone other than the Saviour being able to physically feel the earth's energy moving, though I am not surprised it manifested in the one person who doesn't have to ascend to achieve manifestation." He added when I didn't speak, and my cheeks reddened in response to his awe before my stomach dropped at the thought that this whole mess had been created by the realisation that I was *not* meant to be a Pure – and yet now he was telling me I had the one power that only the *Saviour* had accomplished.

I was screwed.

"What do you do?" I asked, in attempt to move the attention off me and my stolen abilities.

"I control the elements of fire and wind. I also have the ability to feel the truth in a person's soul." That explained the smoke-like tendrils I saw around him.

"Like a lie detector?"

"It's a bit more complicated than that, but yes. Essentially, I am a lie detector, so never try to lie to me and we will get along just fine." He chuckled.

"We don't get along to begin with." I blurted and his laugh grew genuine and contagious as small bursts of laughter erupted from me.

I liked his laugh, it felt warm.

"Why did you do it?" I asked when he made no more to reply. I wasn't sure if I was asking why he'd condemned me to this lie that I was Pure, or if I was asking why he bothered to save me at all, so I didn't elaborate.

But I didn't need to. He knew.

"It wouldn't have made a difference." Was all he said, his eyes refusing to meet mine as his brows furrowed further in concentration – he was struggling to maintain the *iter* for me.

He was saving me. Again.

"It would have made *everything* different." I challenged, refusing to acknowledge the feelings that tried to break through at the thought that he was protecting me. Instead, feelings of betrayal came rushing in, fuelled by an overwhelming anger as it took control – admitting truths it knew I would never get another chance to speak.

"You took the ability to set my truth free from me, took my confessions from the Sacred Servants. You have *no idea* how hard this has been for me. To pretend that I am what they declared me to be. To feel everything and not be able to do a damned thing about it! Who are you to take that decision from me? To make a choice about *my life* when I know I would be better off if you hadn't?"

"You manifested right in front of the Sacred Servants – they would not have harmed you." He tried and I laughed at the absurdity that they would have kept me alive after the offense of my truths.

"*Liar.* We both know what they would have done. Tell me why you really saved me from treason!"

His eyes darkened and swirled faster as they finally met mine and I looked around, anticipating the tell-tale swirl of his smoke as his anger flared.

But it was absent inside his *iter.*

"You would be dead if I didn't." He finally growled as he leaned in so close that our noses were almost touching once more. Despite the lack of his powers, I could still feel the anger seeping out of him and it fuelled my own.

"Would that be such a bad thing? You know nothing of me, you owe nothing to me." I yelled even though he was a breath away from me – glaring straight into his eyes as I dared him to lie to me again.

"I couldn't let you kill yourself. Not when it wouldn't have made a lick of difference in the long run, even if you were speaking your truth. Not when you manifested powers that we haven't seen develop in anyone before they go through the *Anima Fores*." His chest heaved as he accepted my challenge, eyes not leaving mine as he spoke – but then he as he took one final breath he whispered. "Not when you haven't yet found what true happiness feels like."

My anger choked and fizzled out instantly at his honesty, at the rawness in his tone. My mind whirred at his confession, evoking feelings that I didn't have strength to pick through right now. I needed to not feel – not think. To shut everything down until I could get back to the real world and deal with them.

Nix's eyes widened the moment I locked everything down and I knew that if he looked close enough, he'd see the emptiness in my eyes. Pain speared through me suddenly, but it was distant. As if it was happening to my body outside of the *iter*.

"How long can we stay here?" I asked, breathing through the pain that was growing more and more insistent as I ignored everything Nix had just unloaded on me.

"As long as you need to gather your thoughts and control. With your soul in the *iter*, your powers should have extinguished themselves, but I can't have you going back and exploding again."

I nodded in agreement - I definitely didn't want that either. Though I was feeling a little of its effects still, the initial pain I'd felt consume me was something I never wanted to relive.

"I think I'll be okay. It was just a little lapse in control." I tried, rising as I squared my shoulders, readying myself. He scoffed at my answer, and I glared down at him as he stayed crouching where I'd found him when I'd woken.

"*That* was a complete loss of control."

"Was not." I shot back, petulantly. That smirk I constantly wanted to wipe from his face reappeared and I narrowed my glare at him as if it would satisfy the urge.

"I have Rem guarding our bodies because *someone* lost control in the Wanderer's Woods. A place I might add is not safe for people to be wandering in—"

"Okay, okay you made your point. You don't need to

rub it in, it was painful enough without your self-righteous speech."

"What made you lose control like that?" He asked suddenly, switching back to the serious face

"I don't know." The pain flared again, and I winced in response.

"Raewyn." He growled loudly. I looked back up at him as he rose to his full height, gulping. Right, *lie detector.* "It was painful enough that you are still feeling it, so what was the cause?"

"It was everything and nothing, okay?" I growled right back, my voice rising to match his. I was tired of this back and forth. Tired of having to hide it all.

"My walls shattered themselves. *Everything* I'd repressed came out with a vengeance – and apparently my flames are just as attached to my emotions as they are to me, so I exploded. It was as if I'd wronged it by locking it away." I shuddered at the thought, of what was happening to me out there in the real world, of the pain I'd felt as they released themselves. I hadn't realised I'd repressed so much until it was too late.

Nix's gaze pierced me as his lip curled back in anger, curses leaving his throat as if they'd shoved their way up without him knowing and I lifted a brow in challenge.

"*They are one in the same!* Your emotions, your thoughts, and feelings. They. Are. *You.* By locking them away, by ignoring them you are ignoring a fundamental part of you. And in separating your powers from them makes not only the power unhinged, but yourself." He yelled at me, and I flinched at the pure rage in his voice.

"Are you calling me unhinged?"

"Anyone who locks their soul away is bound to become unhinged eventually." He threw his hands in the air in frustration as he turned and walked away from me, needing a moment to calm himself, I suppose.

My thoughts moved through me as he left me alone and I realised that the coping mechanism I'd used for years was slowly tearing me apart from my soul. My breathing became ragged as I realised that I'd have to keep my walls down. Keep my emotions under control. I wasn't sure it was something I could do. I'd relied on those walls for far too long, my mind instinctually pulling them up whenever I felt something.

I thought of the energy shield I'd created after the trials and wondered if that was another part of my being Pure, or if I'd created it out of desperation to protect myself from the trials. I thought I'd created them to protect myself, but really, I had been feeding my own downfall.

I didn't know how I was going to cope without them, but if I had any hope in controlling the flames that now inhabited me — if I was going keep me from shattering my own damned soul, I had to.

"I've been locking my emotions away for years, why is it suddenly an issue now?"

"Because you have ascended, little pure. The universe demands connection, and one way or another it will get it from you - shattered soul or not." Nix answered, glancing back at me, though he still kept his distance.

"Will you teach me to control all of this? So I don't destroy whatever is remaining of my soul?" I asked quietly, knowing that I was going to need all the help I could get to navigate being the Pure of the Citadel. Whether I liked it or not, I was a Pure, and until I found a way out of it, I would need to learn to survive.

"Of course, but first we need to get back to the real world. Are you ready?" He asked, closing in on me as he did. I swallowed the fear that arose in me at the thought of going back to that pain but nodded as I drowned that emotion in resolve.

I would do this. I could do this.

"I'm ready."

CHAPTER 25

I woke on the grass for the second time today, and I almost cursed Nix for not taking me back to the real world. But as I reorientated myself, I felt it.

The earth's ancient power. It caressed me in welcome and I breathed deep as I let it soak into my bones, letting it calm the flames I could now feel swirling within me, and I'd never been more thankful to feel their movements.

As I opened my eyes this time, all I saw was clear blue skies above me. No domed glass ceiling, no moody Nix beside me, and I knew he'd taken me out of the *iter* he'd created.

I took a second to feel around inside my mind and found all my thoughts and feelings calm – as if the explosion had settled them into submission. They'd all but beaten me in demand to be felt before, but now they lay happily amongst the space of my mind, no wall in sight to keep them behind. It felt odd, wandering through my feelings instead of the blank space I normally held within, though I still felt that shield of energy surrounding them, each one tethered to the other like thread and I knew it would be ready to pull them back if I ever needed it to.

Voices broke through my concentration, and I peered over in the direction of them, just in time to see Rem throw a punch.

Right at Nix's face.

"Your carelessness almost shattered this girl's soul. *You stupid fool!*" He spat at Nix, who just stood there and took everything Rem was giving him, not even flinching as his fist collided with his cheek once more. I gasped at the impact and both heads swivelled my way, eyes narrowing as they took me in.

"Are you okay?" Nix asked, his voice rough.

"I'm fine. Why are you punching Nix? I thought I was the only one who wanted to do that." I directed my answer to Rem, who just barked out a laugh as he moved towards me, arm extended in a gesture to help me up. I placed my hand in his large one and he hauled me up so fast I thought I was going to go flying off the ground, but he steadied me with a hand to my waist. A movement I promptly moved away from once I was stable.

"If you ever get the nerve, make sure I'm watching. I'd pay to see you deck him one."

"Noted." I replied, brushing the grass from my skirts. Though as I glanced down, I noticed that the only grass remaining was a small patch where I'd been lying down. Burnt ground surrounded me in a large circle, embers flickering in the breeze as they were carried away. Guilt crawled up my spine as I realised, I'd ruined the one place I'd felt at peace in, and I mourned the loss of the earth beneath it. Tears slipped down my face as my emotions poured through me freely, my lack of wall already damning me as I struggled to breathe.

With sobs racking my body, I kneeled in the smouldering earth and laid my palms on it, feeling the damage that I'd caused it like a knife in my heart.

"I'm so sorry" I whispered into the dirt, and the earth's energy poured into me in sympathy, threading itself through my flames as the wind around me threw Rem back a step.

I wasn't sure what was happening, but I felt a calmness in me that I never had before, and I willed that energy to help me make everything right again. In an instant, my flames whipped out of me, blue where they were normally red as they slithered over the destroyed earth, gently at first and then wildly, as if it had a mind of its own.

I heard them shouting behind me, but I threw my shield out of me on instinct, keeping them away from me until I was sure it was safe. I didn't want to hurt them, not when I wasn't in full control of these powers.

Eventually, my flames returned to me, the earth's energy unravelling itself from my fire as I watched them turn back to their natural reddish hue, though this time as they made their way back to me, they destroyed nothing. Once they were safely back inside my mind, my shield dropped and I heaved in a breath, sweat coating my skin as the effort I'd expended slammed into me all at once.

I raised my head slowly and smiled at the long tendrils of grass and wildflowers surrounding me like a wall of nature, so full and alive that I could barely see Rem's shocked face above the height of them.

"Raewyn!" Nix's voice blasted through the meadow, and I stood so that he could find me, wobbling slightly on unsteady feet. I was too drained.

I felt his power rush at me, as if it were seeking out an enemy and when it found none, washed over me, inspecting me for injuries. I watched the way it moved through the air, soft waves of smoke snaking its way around me until it seemed satisfied with its assessment.

"I was fixing my mistake." I stated as they continued to stand there and stare at me like they'd never seen me before.

"*Saviour help us.*" Rem cursed under his breath and Nix nodded in agreement.

"Saviour indeed." Nix finally replied, as they watched me beam at the control I'd shown, at the emotions I'd let pass through me instead of locking them up.

I was proud of my efforts, and they should be too.

Things could have gone much, much worse.

"Again." Nix called from the table he seemed to love sitting at. If I had any energy left, I would burn it to ashes just to spite him.

Rem occupied the same chair he had when I first met them here, the same one I'd sat in the day Nix had told me about the ascension doorways, and I wondered how we'd come so far in such a short amount of time.

Around these two men, I felt like I could be myself — though I had no choice as I was often growled at by Nix if I was anything other than completely honest with him. It helped me more than I would ever admit to either of them though. I had to constantly fight my innate urges to throw up walls while I was around others, my emotions struggling against their new freedoms in my mind — that it was refreshing to come here once a day and not have to worry about what people thought of me. To not worry that I would say or do the wrong thing.

According to Nix, nothing is wrong if it is the truth.

It had reminded me so much of the letters he wrote me before I became a Pure that I didn't fight him on it. Even if I still believed him wrong.

Since that day in the meadow, almost a week ago now, it had been a constant struggle to keep my flames inside of me. Especially with my emotions running rampant without walls to shove them behind; and though we hadn't discussed it since, that stunt I'd pulled regrowing the grass was not something that *anyone* should be able to do. I could tell by the way they had looked at me after I'd done it, and though the fact that I was able to control both my flames *and* the earth's energy was not lost on me, I tried not to think too much on it.

I was an anomaly, I knew that already and until the Sacred Servants came back with answers, I'd pretend that I wasn't.

My flames flared slightly in retaliation to my denial, and I focused on willing them where I wanted. I'd lost control of them a few times in the days after, my energy too depleted, emotions too raw and demanding that I could not effectively manage both it my flames.

Especially whenever I'd gotten angry at Nix, which seemed to be often.

I'd postponed our training a few days after the incident to attend breakfast with another Lord my father thought worthy enough to be bound to. When I'd arrived in the courtyard, he'd been in a foul mood - commenting that I was more concerned in becoming a breeding housewife than the Pure of the Citadel. I'd singed a hole in that too-white shirt he always seemed to wear, flames shooting out of my hand before I could think to stop them — though he merely wiped them away with a flick of his wrist, seemingly unbothered by my outburst.

It seemed I still had a lot to learn.

I took another breath and concentrated on moving my flames through my body, sweeping down one arm and up the other, each time I did so, lighting the tip of one finger to show that I'd made it to the other side. Sweat was forming on my brow from concentrating for so long, and I hoped we were almost done for the day.

"Is that all she can do?" I heard Rem ask as I made it to the other arm. Lifting my hand so that they could see better, I raised the finger I'd conjured flames on in a vulgar gesture meant just for him. The laugh that came out of him sounded more like a bark and I smirked in satisfaction as I continued my training.

"She is learning control, maybe you should try it sometime?" Nix replied in a drawl and my flames stuttered as a laugh tore from me. Rem joined us when he wasn't out doing whatever it was he did for a living – though annoying me would be his full-time job if he had any say in the matter. Those two seemed to enjoy sitting and watching me fail far too much.

"She looks like a candlestick."

My flames lit up my hands at his comment and Nix's power flared around me in an instant, smoke dancing on the wind.

"What are you thinking about?" He asked me calmly, his power caressing my hands as I tried to focus on bringing the flames back inside me. I breathed in deep once, twice, three times before I felt the lingering emotion fade.

"I'm thinking about what it would feel like to be completely alone right now."

"And your emotions?" He prodded, though he didn't move from his spot at the table as my flames started receding.

"You don't what to know what I feel right now." I responded honestly, though the growl I received told me it wasn't honest enough, so I tried again.

"I *feel* like I want to turn Rem into a candlestick. Happy?" Rem threw himself back with a roar of laughter almost knocking himself out of his own chair. Nix smirked at me before he turned to shove Rem the rest of the way out.

"Very." He replied with a laugh, as he watched his friend's face turn from amusement to shock as he landed on his back, cushioned only by the grass that surrounded us.

I continued with my technique for a while longer, pausing only to tell them they had to leave if they kept distracting me as their constant bickering broke my focus more than once. I longed to ask Nix how it was he became friends with Rem, but we weren't anywhere near small, personal talk. He was training me on behalf of the Sacred Servants, and despite the freedom I felt to express myself while I was around them, I'd meant what I said in the *iter*.

We weren't friends.

"If I am not welcome, all you had to do was say." Rem grumbled as he dusted himself off.

"You're not welcome." both of us replied in unison, causing Rem to scowl further though he made no attempt to leave.

"I think I'm done for the day anyways. I'll see you both tomorrow."

"It's barely noon. I thought we could do some more history today." Nix offered as he stood from the table and headed towards me. We hadn't done any more history since he taught me about the Ascension process. I think he was afraid I'd have another melt down.... I suppose in my current state I couldn't guarantee that I wouldn't.

"I am required at home. Commanding Lord Westward is visiting, and my mother thinks now is a good time for me to showcase my decorating skills." I couldn't hold in the grimace as I said the last part. I'd been fighting with her all week, trying to convince her that I would not do a good job; but without Imogen home to take the load from my mother, it fell to me.

Even though I was the Pure of the Citadel, I was still a woman – and that meant house presentation was non-negotiable.

"Why is Grayson visiting?" Rem asked as I collected my things. I suppose I should have assumed they'd be on a first name basis with the Commanding Lords of the other Paradises. They were high up in society, no matter how immature they may act at times.

"He has business with my brother.... And he is on the list." I shrugged in response.

"Your suitor list?" Nix inquired and Rem's eyebrows shot upward as he fought to contain whatever remark he wanted to throw at me.

"It is not *mine*, but yes. That list." Both men looked at each other, exchanging words without speaking.

"How does one choose a suitor?" Rem asked eventually, a smirk playing on his lips as he tried to remain serious, apparently deciding that he couldn't hold in all of his comments.

"You'd have to ask my father that. He is the one who decides who I will bind my life with." I sighed as I tried not to let that thought bother me as it always did when I discussed my impending Binding Ceremony, but I'd just spent two hours moving my flames through my body. I was exhausted, and it showed as the air heated around me. Nix's power flared around me again as I breathed deeply trying to will my flames to stay where they were.

I didn't need him to come to my rescue, I could do it myself.

"But you are a Pure?" Rem's tone was saturated with disbelief that I; a high-ranking member of society didn't get to choose who she was bound to. The laugh that escaped me was sharp and harsh.

"I am aware of what I am, Rem. But if you hadn't noticed I am also a woman, and so I have no say in the matter."

"That is the biggest load of shit I have ever heard." He growled, and I agreed. Wholeheartedly. Though it would change nothing.

"Yes, well the rules of society are as binding as the Saviour's Covenant. I have no more say in my husband than I did in becoming a Pure." My gaze locked with Nix as I said this. I was still convinced that the Sacred Servants would have ruled differently had they heard my confession in my trials, but I would never know because that choice was once again taken from me.

I closed my eyes as I felt anger rising in me, the air around me growing almost unbearably hot – my breathing harsher as the heat invaded my senses. I needed to calm myself down and this wasn't the way to do it. Focusing, I imagined my anger flowing through me like my flames - each sweep through my body pulling it higher and higher until it was rising out of me - being absorbed and merging with the ancient energy of the earth surrounding me.

I was certain that this was not the way most people dealt with their emotions – but I was not most people, and I could not handle my emotions the way others could.

I'd locked them away for too long to be able to.

When my eyes opened once more, I noticed that Nix's power still flowed around me, darkening until it was corporeal smoke as his gaze lingered on mine – though he'd remained silent as he watched our exchange.

I glanced over to Rem, who was now watching Nix with a worried expression as his power rolled out through the courtyard, shifting the room into shadows. It felt swift and deadly as waves washed over me, whipping my hair around me as wind that didn't belong here enveloped the space. A tug pulled at my gut, and I realised that my comment angered him more than I'd intended it to, but I shoved it to the side – I didn't have the strength to deal with the guilt of a brooding Pure right now.

Rem motioned for me to leave with a jerk of his head, and I nodded in acceptance. He didn't want me to be here for this either. If I couldn't control myself when I was upset, I couldn't imagine what would happen if a controlled Pure lost their cool.

Death and destruction probably. I shivered at the thought, walking through the archway that would lead me back through the palace before I did something stupid, like stay and help.

I couldn't help him – I couldn't even help myself.

I didn't need the doorman to lead me back through the palace halls as I made my way from the courtyard anymore, in fact I had begun to walk through the palace like I was welcome there. I wondered, not for the first time, where the God resided, and if he would mind that we had taken over a wing of his home for my training. I had no doubts that he knew why I was there, but I hadn't seen a thing that indicated he lived there. I suppose the rumours of him being a recluse now had more truth to any other gossip I'd heard.

I rode the whole way home in the carriage focused on my breathing, on my emotions, clearing everything that did not need to be in my mind out — letting it drift away on the wind I'd let flow through the opened windows as I did so.

I let go of my morning with Nix and Rem, of the way I'd left him in turmoil over my comment that I'd had no say in becoming what I was now. It was not a lie, I didn't. But that did not mean the blame was solely on him either. The world that was created by the Saviour, by the centuries of Covenant and societal laws that dictated I had no choice but to go through with the trial.

The alternative was leaving everyone I loved and joining the Unworthy in the Eastern Paradise, but that would also shame my family and I could never do that to them. I'd made my choice to stay and hide in plain sight, hoping that one day I'd live a life that was peaceful enough to at least grant me some sort of happiness.

No, it wasn't entirely his fault — but that didn't make my statement any less true, and he would have felt my truth through his lie detector power. I huffed as I closed my mind off, willing it to cooperate for at least one night before it decided to lose control on me again.

One night, that is all I am asking for. I begged my fire and my emotions squirmed in response, thought I could not tell if they were agreeing with me, or rebelling against my request.

By the time I made it home, my mind was clear, and my flames rested comfortably in the corner they'd inhabited inside my mind's room. Strolling in through the doors, the house was teaming with life as maids ran this way and that

— no doubt as per my mother's orders as they began to prepare for tonight's dinner. I found my mother in the drawing room and I stopped in the doorway, contemplating turning and walking back out the door.

She did not look at all pleased with me as her eyes caught sight of me.

"Lord Westward is arriving earlier than planned, Orion wanted to include your father in the business they need to discuss. And since I couldn't find your plans for the theme you decided on, I had to make do without you." Her tone was tight, and I knew if she had time, she would scold me for not being more organised. I would definitely not be admitting to her that I had not designed any theme for tonight, hoping that I would just be able to make do with whatever I found.

"Thank you for helping Mother, I do appreciate it. I can take over from here if there is something else you need to do." *There, that sounds like something I'm supposed to say.* I smiled politely as I sat across from her, noting the way she relaxed at my words.

She'd been expecting me to push back again, and part of me did. All of me did. But I understood where my mother was coming from, and now that we had no Imogen, I needed to step up more and be the Lady my mother had tried to train me to become.

Or appear to be at the very least.

My mother ran me through her design plans, and I baulked at exactly how much planning when into something as simple as a dinner guest. The flowers, the drapes, everything was changed and altered to suit the occasion. This would take me hours to organise. When she was satisfied that I could hold my own, she left to attend to the cooks and no doubt the gardeners would be called in to do last minute touch ups that I am sure weren't needed.

My mother was nothing if not a perfectionist when it came to hosting in her home.

I got to work, utilising Analise as she directed me to the right rooms and storage closets that held the supplies I needed. I stopped two more maids on our way to the third closet to help carry everything and asked for their help in changing the drapes. Their eyes bulged out of their heads at the way I'd thanked them, and I wondered if my mother had ever said a nice word to the staff in our home – my guess was no, as they fell over themselves to help me in my pleas and I wondered just how much I'd ignored in my time growing up.

It was not the first sign I'd seen growing up that my mother – as kind and loving as she was to her children, and husband – was just as ingrained in the ways of society as the other Ladies I'd visited. Nevertheless, it always seemed to surprise me that she had no issues with the ways we are raised to be. A feeling of heaviness settled in my mind, as a wave of loneliness washed through me, and I struggled to breathe through it.

Gritting my teeth as I forced my emotions to run through me and then out – releasing them through the open doorway that led to the gardens outside, a trickle of that earthy power sweeping in to take it away as I did. There was no use dwelling on the things that I could not change, and I was certain that if I ever broached the subject with my mother, she would reply with something akin to; 'Our sins decide how we are to be treated, it is not up to me to change the course of our Saviours will'. Not that I would ever tell my mother my thoughts on what society has done to the Saviour's original vision – it would be a losing battle neither of us would ever win.

Focusing back on the upcoming dinner, we set about fixing up the dining room first, and then the foyer, before finally entering the parlour to match the new drapes we'd hung so that the house would match. Mother had indicated that the theme be neutral but classy, but also in taste to the Commanding Lords village and so as I hung the last of the cream embroidered drapes, I walked back to the dining room and assessed my work. The deep green napkins nodding to the Western Paradise rested amongst the crisp white plates, golden cutlery emphasising the wealth and stature of our household.

It was simple, but it worked.

I directed the last of the maids to place the green and white vases overflowing in ferns and lilies around the rooms and thanked them all for their efforts before dismissing them for a brief reprieve. The sun was well and truly setting now as its golden rays streamed in through the open doorway of the dining room and I stood in its warmth for a moment, soaking in the earth's energy I felt moving towards me, energising me as it did. My mind had been so wrapped up in the setting of drapes and tablecloths that I hadn't realised that apart from the one incident in the beginning of it all, I had been blissfully distracted from my own thoughts and emotions.

If this is what decorating a home did for me, maybe I could do this after all; be someone's wife, lead their household.

It was worth a shot, especially if the end result meant that I'd be distracted enough to keep my powers at bay. My flames flared slightly at that thought and I loosed a breath, turning towards the stairs as I did.

They felt the lie in my thoughts, even if I didn't want to admit it.

Being someone's wife would not make me truly happy, no matter how hard I tried.

CHAPTER 26

Commanding Lord Westward and my brother had arrived hours before I was done decorating the house, though they kept to my father's study, so I hadn't yet seen either of them.

Orion had told me that Lord Westward had sent his apologies for his absence at my Ceremony celebration almost a month ago, that he'd had urgent business to take care of in one of the Western Villages. Though I couldn't say I had noticed his absence – I'd had bigger things to deal with than an absent Commander.

Though now that his business was resolved in the West, he had travelled up to stay in the Citadel for a while – and Orion teased me mercilessly as he delivered the news that Westward was coming only to spend some more time with me.

The thought did nothing but plague me with dread that I would not get a moment to myself until he left. Between training with Nix, the luncheon gossip sessions with the Ladies and all the meetings my father had lined up for me in regard to possible suitors, I hadn't had a moment to myself.

Though I had my emotions and my powers slightly more under control – now that they weren't caged in and shattering my soul slowly, it also meant that I craved to be alone more than ever as I needed the time and space to gather myself. An urge that was harder to ignore now that I was willingly feeling things.

Tonight, was no exception, and as I climbed the stairs to my room, the door to my father's study opened and all three men stepped out into the freshly decorated foyer.

"Lady Sandoval, what a pleasant surprise, I was just coming to find you." Lord Westward called, and I cursed silently that I hadn't run straight for my room instead of spending those precious moments soaking in the energy of the earth.

Turning back towards them, I placed a smile on my face, polite as my mother taught me. The Commanding Lord was dressed like any other Commanding Lord, his boots spotless as if he didn't dare travel anywhere he may dirty them – his hair perfectly styled back

"Commanding Lord Westward, it is nice to see you again. Though if you are going to use titles, it would be Pure Sandoval now." I tried for a light teasing, but my father's scowl told me it had come out with more bite than it should have. Orion laughed beside my father and Lord Westward joined him after a moment.

"Oh, how I have missed your honesty, *Pure Sandoval!*" He crooned, emphasising my new title as he flashed his teeth in a wide grin. I'd forgotten how green his eyes were in the weeks since I'd seen him last at the luncheon - how warm and handsome his face really was.

"Though, I'd prefer if we dropped the titles

altogether. You may call me Grayson."

Charm, that is what leaked from him in waves, and I almost wondered if it was a power he had, though I didn't think that was something someone could receive. The energy was all him.

"As you wish." I nodded in acceptance, though I gave no indication that he should drop my title. I didn't know how I felt being so informal with the Commanding Lord just yet.

"Why don't you join us in the parlour, Wynnie. We were just going to go and relax while we waited for dinner. I'm sure Lord Westward would love to hear about all this time you have been spending at the Citadel's Palace in your new role." At this, Lord Westward's eyebrows rose in surprise, and I wondered if it was from the fact that I was invited into the palace itself or if it was because I was carrying out my role as a Pure.

I made my way down the staircase reluctantly and followed them into the parlour, my mother having already taken up her spot in the highbacked chair my father had gotten her as a Binding Ceremony gift. It was cosy enough that she could sit and relax in, but regal enough that she would always look like a Lady of the house as she did so. It was her favourite spot in the house.

My father took his seat next to my mother, pressing a kiss to her temple as he did so and she beamed up at him in response, her cheeks reddening slightly at the display of affection in front of a guest. Orion sat next and he took the last remaining chair in the room, leaving Lord Westward – Grayson, and I to fit on the two-seater couch. I had no doubts Orion had planned this as I narrowed my eyes at him in silent accusation.

His answering grin admitted his guilt.

"What is this I hear about your new role in the palace?" Westward asked after we had all settled in.

"It is nothing special, I assure you. I am mainly there to learn more about what it means to be a Pure, and I suppose figure out what it is I am going to do, seeing as we have a God in the Citadel."

"And have you seen him? The God of the Citadel?" He inquired, leaning forward to rest his forearms on his knees, head bent in my direction as he did so, ensuring we were sitting closer than I would have liked, but there was nowhere for me to go.

"I have not. I'm not even sure what part of the palace he would be in, as I have stayed in the lower level only. Aside from the trial room, I have only ever been into the gardens where we conduct all my training."

"You make it sound like it is more than mere lessons."

"Not at all, they are rather boring if I am being honest. The only reason I attend them is because it was requested of me from the Sacred Servants before they left." Not a total lie, but an omission of the real reason I attend.

"The Servants have left?" Orion spoke up this time and I whipped my head towards him in panic. Was I not supposed to reveal that?

"Uh, I believe so, although I do not know where or why." I lied, dread crawling up my chest and constricting my lungs. I would have to ask Nix tomorrow if people were allowed to know about the Sacred Servants leaving on their research trip for me, though if it were a secret, surely, he would have told me sooner.

"They never leave their palace, not without good reason. I wonder why they decided that now was a good time to go." Orion mused as he and Westward exchanged theories on why they could possibly want to leave their God alone and unprotected. I wanted to tell them that the palace was guarded enough to be safe without Servants in it – that Nix was there, and he was powerful enough to stop any threat without blinking, and Rem too I suppose with the build he walked around in. But I refrained from speaking any of that, worried that I'd reveal too much of how I really spent my time in those palace walls.

Eventually the conversation turned back to me though, and I narrowed my eyes at the subtle way Mother nudged Father in her attempt to do so.

"Raewyn, you still have not given me an answer on the two Lords you spent time with this past week. Are we to assume you think them suitable enough to consider a proposal from?" I glanced at Lord Westward as my father spoke, watching for his reaction. I was not attached enough to consider his feelings in my answer, but I was a decent enough person to feel embarrassed that my father would choose this moment to announce I was considering other men in front of him.

Though his answering laugh as he caught me watching him told me he did not see the others as a threat.

"I am well aware of the way things are done in our society, Darling, you do not need to worry about me. My only wish is that the man who wins your hand is able to bring you happiness."

"How very noble of you." I murmured, but inside my stomach was twisting in flutters at his words. Neither Lord Carron nor Lord Huntly had spoken of my happiness in my meetings with them, and I wondered if Lord Westward could be the one to give me the life I wanted. He bowed in response, flourishing his hand as he did so while he still sat beside me. Grinning at me and causing a laugh to spill from my lips at his mockery.

"Is that a blush I see, little sister?" Orion teased and I moved my attention back to my family. My mother was looking at the two of us with a dreamy look in her eyes and I could tell that she was already planning our Binding Ceremony.

I squirmed in my seat, refusing to meet my brother's stare.

"Neither of the Lords I've met so far have been particularly captivating. But I told Father I would wait until I had met them all before I made my decision, and I believe there is one more on the list for me to meet." I replied instead, ignoring the smirk that appeared on my brother's face at my deference to another topic.

"Lord Morozov has officially withdrawn his proposal, so the only one left to decide on is Lord Westward here." Father explained, and my eyes widened in surprise. I had been dreading meeting with Lord Morozov later this week, as every time I thought of him, flashes of my first trial raced behind my eyelids. Images of Imogen begging me to help her escape his Binding contract, her informing me that he had somehow made himself into a God, despite his sins and his wives' mysterious deaths.

I'd also heard nothing good about the man from the gossip columns and luncheons I'd attended since I found out about his interest in claiming me as his wife, but what terrified me more was the possibility that my trial could become a reality as we barrelled down the same path.

Relief swam through me at the change in course and I openly acknowledged the emotion.

"Guess I need to make a better impression than Lord Huntly and Carron then." Lord Westward joked, and my father and Orion laughed alongside him.

Dinner was served shortly after my binding prospects were discussed, and I faded blissfully into the background during the entire meal. Preferring to listen to the men in the room as they discussed business over their plates of roast meat and vegetables.

If this was the alternative to them talking to me about who I would be bound to, then I would take it – even if I did not understand a word of what they were speaking of. I hadn't come around to the idea of my father selling me off to someone yet, even though he'd granted me the ability to have some sort of input. If it really were my own choice, Lord Westward would not be here right now trying to woo me.

Though I could admit that out of the three men I'd met, he would be my preferred person. His one comment about my happiness making its way through my mind, not for the first time – and I wondered if he indeed could be that person to create some sort of happiness in my life. I knew it would never be the true happiness that I was seeking, but it would be better than nothing.

Lord Carron, while he'd piqued my interest in his profession for learning more about the old world, had not impressed me at all and Lord Huntly had spent the entire breakfast meeting talking of himself, that I found myself becoming more and more irritated with him and found an excuse to leave early.

Neither were men I could see myself with – but could I see myself as Commanding Lord Westward's wife? Living in the Western Paradise, holding galas and luncheons as the wife of an influential Commanding Lord as he oversaw the village around us. I'd valued his goals the last time we met, and I was always intrigued at the way the West had kept mainly to itself all these years.

If I were any other woman, I would be flattered that Lord Westward was even travelling out of his Paradise borders to consider me.

My mother had spared no thought to the meal as every inch of the table was laden with food before us. Even as we all stuffed our faces. I noted in the back of my mind to ask her where all the leftover food went, as we never ate leftovers – it was a sign of a struggling family to save food for the next day after all.

She'd smiled proudly as we entered the dining room earlier, approving of my decorative skills and colour palate. I wanted to tell her that the maids had done most of the work and provide ideas to help me tie everything together – but I didn't think she'd appreciate that, so I kept quiet.

Once dinner was done, and desert had been served, I thought of ways to excuse myself from the rest of the night. With my training that morning and setting up for Lord Westward's visit, I was having trouble keeping my eyes open, and now the less focused I became, the less control I possessed. But just as I was about to voice my desire to retreat to my room, Lord Westward looked my way as he stood.

"Would you care to join me for an evening stroll through the garden before I depart?" All eyes turned towards me, and I knew I would never hear the end of it if I declined. So, I nodded and placed my hand in his, letting him guide me from the chair and towards the open doorway that led outside.

Once we were out of the eyes of my family, I withdrew my hand from his, resisting the urge to shiver at the contact. I'd been able to feel the energy running through him, like his lifeforce was tethered to a power I could not identify – and it spurred something inside of me.

Taking a deep breath, I turned my face towards the moon as a cool breeze swept across us. Summer in the Isle was ending, and the air was growing colder with each passing day. The air chilled me but also woke me at the same time – carrying that ancient power along with it as it caressed me in greeting.

"You love the outdoors." Lord Westward commented as he watched me. We'd walked in far enough that we were now surrounded by the floral gardens my mother adored attending to. Or at least directing the gardeners to attend to.

"It affords a feeling of peace I have not found anywhere else." I admitted truthfully, lowering my head from the sky so that I could look at him. In the shadowed evening light, he looked more mysterious than I'd ever seen him, though his too green eyes blazed brightly as they regarded me with a look I'd never seen before. I wanted to look away from it, to ignore the feeling of shivers against my skin that had nothing to do with the cold breeze, but I found that I could not.

"There is a waterfall nestled in the woods near my home in the Western Paradise, and in the rare moments that I have some time for myself, I find myself there…watching the water flow through the earth as if it has a will of its own."

My heart beat faster at his admission, at his willingness to share a part of himself that sounded so honest and so *like me* that I couldn't help but be a little more drawn to him in that moment. I wasn't the only one who craved the peace and seclusion that nature offered.

We walked in silence a little further, and like the luncheon it was not awkward, it was peaceful. Natural. A feeling of contentment washed over me as we wandered through the gardens and I felt myself accepting more and more that if I had to be bound to anyone, Commanding Lord Grayson Westward would not be a terrible option.

We spoke occasionally, mostly about the villages and Paradises he had travelled to during his position as Commanding Lord of the Western Paradise. We spoke of his aunt, the Goddess and how she still wished to see me especially now that I had become a Pure like her. I made a mental note to travel there one day and tell her my story, all of it, and ask her how she managed her powers.

"I have a meadow." I found myself admitting as we made our way back to the house. The night sky twinkling above us indicating that we had been out here far longer than I'd realised. Not once had I told someone about the meadow I loved to hide in. Even Nix and Rem had found out about it purely because they'd followed me there that day my walls crumbled – though I still had not come to tell them the significance of the place. No doubt they thought I'd just happened upon the field in my delirium.

"I would love to see it while I am here, maybe I could pack a picnic. We could make a day of it. If you wouldn't mind sharing it, that is." Lord Westward suggested and I could not stop the smile that took over my face at his suggestion.

"I would be happy to show it to you."

"Then it is a date." He smiled genuinely and I couldn't help but think again how handsome he was.

CHAPTER 27

Rae,
I have business to attend to, so your training is on hold for the rest of
the week.
Keep practising.
I will call for you when I return.

Nix.

The letter was sitting on my bedside table when I awoke the next morning, and I wondered why Analise didn't wake me as she delivered it. Disappointment moved through me at the words written so elegantly on the paper before me, and I found myself re-reading it more than once.

His previous letters had expressed more, so much more and even though this was just a message to inform me that I was not needed, I longed for the emotional words that used to invoke feeling in me.

Sighing, I readied myself for the day anyways, though I now had no reason to be up so early. I was free to do as I pleased for the first time in weeks, and here I was wishing that I still had my morning sessions at the palace with Nix. I'd even take Rem's barbs if it meant I was there. Seeing them. Feeling freely without consequence.

Dressed and ready for the day, I ate my breakfast in the gardens, recalling the ease of which I had spoken to Lord Westward last night. The last time I'd spoken with him I'd been too caught up in finding out if he were the author of my mysterious letters to focus too much on his words, needing him to be that person for me. And while he wasn't, never could be, I found myself now thinking whether he could instead be the person I needed to be with.

He was simple, kind, pure enough though I hadn't seen any inclination of markings on him to know exactly what sins he had fallen too. He may not invoke feeling and thought in me like Nix had in his letters to me, but I had difficulty controlling my powers around him because of it.

Not once did my powers flare last night though, and I liked that.

Which meant that I could grow to like Lord Westward. He certainly was easier to look at than my other two options, that much was certain.

Done with breakfast, I wandered out the front doors of my family home, intending to find a space as quiet and secluded as the garden room at the palace for some training. Nix had told me to keep practising, and although he wasn't here to instruct me, I was sure I could carry on the lessons without him by my side. I didn't dare do it in the back garden of my family's home for fear that a maid would find me and alert my parents that there was something wrong with me.

Though as I descended the steps onto the street, I felt eyes on me.

Looking around, it didn't take long to spot him. He didn't exactly make an effort to hide. Leaning up against the same tree I found him on the first time I'd met him, same smirk on his face – I felt myself relax at the familiar face.

"What are you doing here?"

"Did you not read the letter he left you?" the way he asked made it sound like Nix had delivered the letter himself, snuck into my room and placed it beside where I slept. I shook the absurd thought from my mind instantly.

"It told me nothing." Rem cursed under his breath as he kicked off from the tree, making his way towards me.

"Nix has to deal with something outside of the Citadel, so he sent me to make sure you stay out of trouble while he's away." My flames instantly ignited my blood at his words, and I grit my teeth in effort to keep them down. We were in public. I could *not* burn Rem to a crisp here.

"I don't need a babysitter." I snarled.

"I'm not here to babysit."

"Then leave."

"I can't do that either." I threw my hands in the air in exasperation.

"Fine, then at least find me somewhere private so I can train before I burn you where you stand." I growled instead, the need for me to release all this sudden emotion and fire outweighing any thought I had about having an overgrown man following me around for the next few days.

"That, I can do. This way, milady." Rem smirked, flourishing his arm towards a waiting non-descript black carriage that I hadn't noticed was waiting outside my home. I climbed in before anyone could see me with Rem following along, the smirk still playing on his mouth. I resisted the urge to wipe it off his face as I opened all the windows, my flames building rapidly inside me.

It was as if the brief reprieve I'd experienced last night was coming back with a vengeance and I shook from the effort it took to keep them contained. I needed help from the earth's energy if I was going to make it wherever we were going.

Rem seemed to understand my need for silence as he remained quiet for the duration of our trip. My eyes were closed as I focused on the winding energy that flowed into the carriage through the exposed windows. I let all my emotions rise slowly, one at a time as they were carried away with each wave of energy that swept through me. It seemed that the more I connected to that ancient power, the bolder I got – bringing it inside of me now, to aid in the sweeping away of emotions that I did not need stoking my fire.

The carriage suddenly stopped, and my eyes opened, just in time to see Rem opening the door. We were at the palace. Why were we at the palace?

"I thought Nix wasn't here." I asked as we climbed out of the carriage.

"He's not. But that doesn't mean you can't use the courtyard. It's the most private place in the Citadel. No one will bother you there." He replied as we climbed the steps and entered the massive building. I would call it a home, but it was so much more than that – and with the way the Sacred Servants used this place to conduct business, I would never want to associate this place with the image of warm fires and cosy nights that I had of my own home.

"What about the God? Won't he mind that I came here without an invitation?" I asked as my thoughts once again turned to the man no one had seen in years. He was the most powerful person left on the earth, if he were to find out I'd come here without Nix, I shuddered at what he could do to me.

"He's holed up sulking somewhere, he won't find out." Rem commented and I bulked at the nerve he had to speak about the God of the Citadel like that. I looked around to make sure no one had heard him, but we were all alone.

We walked through the halls until we reached the double doors that had been locked again for the first time since I'd started my training. Rem pulled a key from an invisible pocket in his vest and unlocked the doors before holding one open for me. I passed through and walked down the corridor towards the courtyard, moving on instinct as I felt the energy of it calling me. I'd learnt fast that the energy in the courtyard, while part of the outside world's power, was very muted in comparison to the real thing. Though it still called to me regardless as my fire swirled through my veins.

I walked through the archway and immediately froze.

We were not alone.

Bustling around the courtyard were what looked like gardeners as they pruned the flower beds and bushes. A gasp left my throat in surprise and one by one they turned their eyes on me. I'd never seen them before, didn't even know this place was open for the staff to tend to. An older man straightened upon seeing me, anger covering his face as he began to storm towards me, seeing me as an intruder. Though as he neared, Rem appeared at my side, and he stumbled to a stop. Eyes instantly dropping to the floor in the presence of the hulking beast beside me.

"Leave." Rem demanded, the word coming out low and gravelly – so different from the laid-back man I'd come to know that even I wanted to obey him. Danger rolled off him in waves so strong I took a step back instinctively. The gardeners scattered instantly at the sound of Rem's voice, all except the man who had been closing in on me.

"My Lord, no one is meant to know of this place, especially not your newest consort." He stuttered, his eyes refusing to leave the grassy spot he'd situated them on when Rem entered. I suppressed the laugh that threatened to escape at his calling me Rem's consort.

"Did you not hear me?" Rem repeated, his voice dropping another octave. The man had guts; I would give him that. He was stupid, but he had guts.

"They will hear of this." Was all he replied before gathering his things and making his way out the same as the others had done, sneaking through a side door I didn't know existed. Rem relaxed as soon as they were gone and strolled right into the middle of what I now knew was called the courtyard, acting as though nothing had happened.

"Are we going to get in trouble for this?" I asked once he had put enough distance between us that I no longer felt the power coming off him. Even in his relaxed state now I couldn't shake the feeling of lethal danger that had come from him seconds before.

"You, no. Do not worry though, I can handle myself."

I did not doubt that.

Moving further into the courtyard, I glanced towards the secret door the gardeners had gone through and ensured it was closed – Rem sounded like he would be in enough trouble without us having to explain my God like powers to the palace staff. Rem had already settled himself at the table the boys seemed to live at when my eyes swung back to him, and I took that as a sign of encouragement to begin.

Shaking my arms out, I opened my mind up and breathed deep. My flames instantly filled up every corner of my mind, lining my blood with heat as it surged through me. I'd released enough of my emotions on the ride over here that I didn't have much in the way for the flames to latch onto, though the panic that the gardeners had seen me, that Rem would be in trouble for bringing me here was still in the front of my mind – my flames consumed it like food, washing over me as it flooded me with more power, more emotion as it ripped through me with enough strength to protect myself if I ever needed it. That thought was comforting as I walked into the middle of the grassy area that surrounded the table, aware that Rem was watching my every move.

Closing my eyes once again I focused on converging all my fire in the palm of my hand, commanding it to pool at the tip of my finger as Nix had taught me. My flames followed my will, bursting through me with such ferocity that I stumbled slightly. It hadn't been this restless in a while, and I struggled to control the path. When the heat finally reached the palm of my hand, I opened my eyes and groaned. My flames had covered my entire hand like a glove of fire.

That wasn't what I wanted… I cursed inwardly as I stared at my flaming hand. How was it I was able to move the earth's energy through me with only a few tries, and yet I couldn't control the power that came from *inside* me? I tried to think of what Nix had told me at the beginning of every lesson as I stepped into my mind once again.

Clear your thoughts – check.

Control your emotions – as controlled as they ever will be.

Envision it as an extension of yourself – I could do that.

Willing them back, I tried again. Moving them through me, narrowing their path slightly so they had no choice but to obey, and directing them down my left arm, imagining a ball of fire extending from the tip of my finger as if it was always meant to belong there. Sweat coated my brow as I concentrated on the movement of my fire, feeling them slither through me, flaring slightly as they tested the restraints I'd placed on them. They were restless, and unless I figured out why, I would never keep them under my control.

Sinking deeper, I willed the shield of energy out of my mind, pulling it far enough away from my emotions that they all floated to the front of my mind, crashing into my barriers with such force that I gasped at the impact.

"What are you thinking?" Rem called out in front of me, and my head whipped up at the sound of his voice rumbling through the space.

"I'm trying to figure out why my flames feel so restless this morning. It isn't normally this hard to control them."

"And your emotions?" he added once I had responded, and I almost laughed at the way he mimicked Nix's words exactly. My fire flared at the thought of Nix's name, my emotions rumbling against the corners of my mind.

"Powerless."

"Why?"

"I don't know."

"Yes, you do." He pressed, and my eyes narrowed in his direction as my flames slithered down the outside of my arm, breaking free of their restraints.

Damnit, I'd been so close too.

"Because I can't control something that lives *inside* of me. Because I can't figure out how to properly feel anything without it completely consuming me to the point that it becomes unbearable. Because Nix left without warning, and

I need his power to navigate my instability. Because I am mere days away from leaving the Citadel with whichever man I do not know, and probably do not care for in order to make my family happy and I *need to know how to control it all, so I don't burn the world down because all* I feel *is anger!*" My chest was heaving by the time I was done, my voice having risen to a shout. My flames flooded back through my body, protecting me from the pain of too many admissions, but it was too late, I'd already spoken it out loud and there was no taking it back.

Rem rose from his reclined position, covering the distance between us in three great strides, gripping my arms so tight that I had no chance of retreating from his touch. His eyes locked onto mine as he did so, and when he spoke his voice was calm and serious, as if he were talking down a deranged person.

"I may not be able to help you with the fucked-up way society deals with its women, but I can tell you this; you are the furthest thing from powerless that I have ever seen. Feeling is a strength more than it is a weakness. Without emotions we are no better than the Servants that crawl between the God's feet. Hate, love, desperation, they are all the same. They. Are. Strength. Use it. Be the emotion that runs through you, for that is what keeps you alive." I felt my emotions halt at his words, pausing in their relentless hounding as if he were speaking directly to them. But he was not done with his speech yet and he carried on, though he'd released his grip on me, taking a step back as he breathed in. "You don't need Nix's powers to control your own. They are yours, and they respond only to you. Now go again and try not to burn anything down." He stepped back once more, granting me more space and nodded his head for me to try again.

His command gave me no room to unpack his words, or the emotions that swirled because of them, and for that I was thankful. Had Nix been here, he'd want me to unpack everything – something that I was not comfortable doing in front of anyone. But Rem knew that, knew that I needed to vent my thoughts, let them out and then move on as if they never happened. Maybe he even felt the same as I did and in that I felt like we were kindred spirits.

I wondered again how it was he came to know Nix, they seemed so different, and that had nothing to do with the markings of sin that covered Rem's arms.

Moving my fire through me once more, I let them wash over the emotions that filled my mind, letting them acknowledge one another but not consume. They calmed slightly once they realised, they would no longer have to fight to feed on my emotions and followed my will – travelling down my right arm again and pooling in the palm of my hand perfectly. I refused to look up at Rem to see his reaction, as I moved that fire back through me to the other arm. I felt in sync with myself in a way I never had before, and I had to resist the joy that ran through me.

I could do this. I was powerful. I was in control.

I moved my flames through me for another hour before I was satisfied with my progress enough to call it a day. With Nix absent, I wasn't sure how long I was meant to stay here practising, but Rem assured me that I could stay here for as long as I wished.

He didn't speak much after his pep talk, and I was thankful that he left me to my own devices. Though he didn't move from the spot he'd taken up right in front of me, as if he was prepared to jump in again if I lost control.

When we left the courtyard and made our way back to my home, the silence between us more companionable than it had been before. But with that companionship I now felt towards Rem, also came a flurry of questions that I could no longer ignore.

"Ask what you need to." Rem smirked as I looked his way for the fourth time in as many minutes.

"What do you do? For Nix that is."

"Whatever he asks of me." He shrugged in answer, but that wasn't enough for me. Not this time.

"But you two seem more like friends than anything." I prodded.

"Yes, well, when you spend as long as I have beside that arrogant ass, you learn to get along with him."

"How did you come to work for him? I thought someone…. Like you couldn't work in the palace." I stumbled over the end of my words, my face flushing with such a sensitive topic as someone else's sins. It was not proper etiquette asking someone about their markings, but I was learning that Rem at least sat himself outside the rules of society.

"Someone like me?" He asked as he raised one eyebrow in challenge. He was going to make me say the words.

"Your markings."

"Ah. Things are not always as they appear little Pure. I loathe the Citadel and its minions, but I am loyal to Nix and neither society nor the Servants will tell me otherwise. No matter how much they try to." I wasn't sure how I felt about his use of Nix's nickname for me, but I ignored that for now in favour of information.

"I don't understand."

"I'll tell you my story one day Rae, but for now, we have arrived. I will stick around, though you won't see me unless you call for me. If you need anything just ask and I'll be there." He opened the door to the carriage as he did so, though he made no move to leave.

"You really don't need to stick around. I will be fine on my own, I always have been." I tried once more. It was not a lie, I had lived my entire life without the help of Rem or Nix, and I didn't know how I felt about being watched constantly.

"Sorry, orders are orders. Though if you need someone to warm your bed for you, I would be more than happy to oblige." His eyebrows moved suggestively, and I snorted in disgust, smiling as I did so. His answering laugh eased the vulgar comment into a jest, and I thought for a moment that I could have a friend in Rem – and that made me feel not so alone for a moment.

CHAPTER 28

With nothing to do, the days merged into one another.

I hadn't gone for another training session with Rem, although I often saw him stalking between the shadows of the gardens as he watched me. He made no move to approach me again though and I didn't seek him out. I had taken to practising my control in the sanctuary of my own room, opening the windows to let in the earth's power as I did so, just in case I needed some help controlling my own, but ever since Rem's words of wisdom in the courtyard, I hadn't felt as unstable in my ability to manage both my flames and my emotions.

It was if I was finally in sync with every part of myself, and that gave me the courage I needed to push my powers a little more than normal. By day three of Nix's absence, I had managed to trail my fire along the outside of my body with ease, wisps of flame snaking wherever I commanded it to. I could also extend them slightly – fashioning something that looked like a butter knife in the palm of my hand. That trick had cost me a lot of energy and control though and so

I refrained from doing it again.

I'd had to sleep with the windows open that night as my flames refused to retreat into my mind after training — as if the weapon had spurred them into attack mode, and in my drained state I found that I could not force them back in like I normally could. The only consolation I had was that they kept me warm throughout the night as the impending winter breeze filled the room, causing a chill to settle over everything inside of it.

Analise though, had not been pleased the next morning when she came to wake me and found my room colder than an icebox.

"What has gotten into you lately, Miss Raewyn?" She scolded as she closed the windows and lit the fire in the corner of my room. I did not tell her that I was practically sweltering from the fire inside of me, and she hadn't noticed that I slept with none of my usual blankets surrounding me.

"I forgot to close them before bed." I tried, and the motherly disapproval that set on her face as she turned to me told me that she did not buy my lie one bit.

"I need to get you ready for the day. Your mother insisted on your company in town today to pick out the final arrangements for the upcoming Saviour's Feast." I nodded in agreement and let Analise guide me through our usual morning routine. She had been serving my family my entire life making her often feel like a second mother — one I could open up to a bit more though as she seemed to have more insight than judgement. Though I supposed being a maid, she would be thrown out of the house without a second thought if she judged the actions of a noble family.

I was more excited than normal about Saviour's Feast Day this year, though I couldn't figure out why as I dressed in my usual dress and coat. It had always been my favourite night of the year growing up as a child. The Saviour's Feast was a celebration of the creator of the Isle of Salvatorem, yes, but it was also the one night where everyone in the villages came together to dance and drink as one, no matter their title. I had heard tales of how every Paradise celebrated Saviour's Feast, and though they all differed, the one thing that remained the same was that everyone celebrated together. As one people – not as Lords or maids, but as one collective human race.

As a child I had asked my father every year why every day wasn't like Saviour's Feast Day, why we would all return to the normal noble hierarchy as soon as the sun rose the next day – and every year, I would get the same answer; *That's not how things are done here, Raewyn.*

Now that I was older, I understood more that it wasn't that it couldn't be done, but that the people of society just didn't want to let go of the pedestal they all situated themselves upon.

Analise combed through my hair as I sat at my table, and as she did, I took the time to make sure my flames were going to cooperate with me. They seemed appeased for the moment, having blended with the earth's energy all night. Surprisingly I felt more invigorated this morning than I had in a long time, so much so that I did not mind one bit that I would be shopping all day with my mother.

Once I was ready, I ventured downstairs where my mother was waiting, carriage ready and waiting to leave. I suppose I woke a little later than I had meant to.

"We have a morning appointment with the drapery, and we are now running dreadfully behind schedule thanks to your sleep in." While her scolded greeting held no notes of welcoming, I didn't let that ruin my mood. I felt good today, more so than I had in a while, and I was determined to keep it that way.

"I apologise Mother, but I am here now, and I am ready to go shopping." I replied, rushing my way down the remainder of the stairs. Her answering huff as she strode out the door told me she had been expecting more pushback from me on our shopping trip. Had I been in any other mood I would have, I detested shopping - especially if it required having to parade around town where all the Ladies mingled and gossiped.

But the energy humming joyfully inside me would not let me feel anything other than positive thoughts.

I climbed into our family carriage after Mother and together we made our way to the centre of town. I had ridden through here too many times now on my way to the Palace that it almost felt as if that were our destination. I wondered idly where Rem was, if he had kept that carriage by our house in case he needed to follow me on outings. I hadn't seen any other carriages surrounding our house, so I did not think so. Maybe I should have informed him of our trip? Though as I thought this, I reminded myself that it was not my job to inform him of anything.

He was the one who wanted to follow me around, he could come and find me if he wanted to keep his orders.

I followed my mother through the shops for the remainder of the morning, as she asked my opinion on multiple themes and colours, and I realised that this was the first time since my Ceremony that I'd spent any quality time with her — and even before then, if we did it was filled with lessons on Ladies etiquettes, or my celebration planning.

Imogen had always been her go to daughter for this type of thing, but I found that I was enjoying it more than I thought I would. I savoured that feeling throughout it all, not knowing when I would get the chance to do something so mundane with my mother again.

We were getting one of her dresses fitted in the silk merchants store when a group of Ladies entered, and I recognised them instantly as the group of girls who used to wander behind Imogen.

"Pure Sandoval, what a pleasant surprise." The new leader, Stacia crooned as they filled the small waiting room where I was sitting, enjoying the rays of sun that shone through the storefront windows.

"Ladies, always a pleasure." I kept my tone light, polite, and not sarcastic at all. Though I had not seen any of them since my sister left for the Northern Paradise, I had heard the rumours they'd been spreading about her.

As they told it, Imogen had gotten pregnant with Lord Ruskin's illegitimate child and so he was forced to bind himself to her or face the shame of society. Or the one about how Imogen was making her way through the Lieutenant's men because he did not pay her enough attention. That one had made my blood boil when one of the other Ladies I'd met for tea asked me to confirm if such things were true.

It had taken all I had in me to keep my fire from lashing out across the table, and even then, the tone of my voice when I'd told her not to believe in such vile things had been less polite than I'd intended.

She had not invited me over since.

"We have been trying to invite you over for weeks, but every time I request a date, you are always busy. We must remedy that soon." Stacia spoke again, her high-pitched voice going straight through my good mood. I refrained from telling them I'd been intentionally avoiding them so I didn't say something I would regret. I did not like these women one bit.

"I have not had much leisure time, I am afraid. The duties of a Pure do keep me quite occupied." I tried as an excuse, but her polite smile turned into a scowl, and I knew she did not buy it.

"Though you have had time to meet with all the other Ladies of society."

"Good timing on their part, I suppose."

"Are you free now? Maybe we could find a nice tea store and make an afternoon of it." She tried again, and I knew the feeling of being left out of the graces of the Pure was the only thing spurring her on to act this desperate towards me.

The lot of them had mocked me relentlessly before the trial and I saw no reason for that to change now. I opened my mouth to tell her as much, my good mood entirely ruined now by their presence, but before I could my mother stepped out and spoke for me.

"She is with me today, Ladies. You will have to make an appointment to luncheon with the Pure of the Citadel like everyone else in society. Though I must warn you, she is fully booked for the remainder of her life." If my mouth could fall any lower, it would have hit the floor of the merchant's store. As it was, I gaped like a fish out of water at my mother's polite dismissal of these Ladies. I had never seen her act anything other than the demure lady of the Sandoval household.

Grabbing my arm, my mother hauled me out of the store before her words had time to sink into the Ladies who were also standing there, stunned as I was. We made it back into the carriage before my mother burst out laughing, and my eyes widened further.

Never in my life had I heard her act like this.

"I've heard the rumours, Raewyn, and - while I don't

condone what your sister has done in the past - I know my daughter and she is none of the vile words they are using to describe her. It was time someone put that jealous pack of sinful cretins in their places." She finally explained once she'd calmed herself enough to speak, though she was still clutching her chest as her body shook with silent chuckles.

"It's like I don't even know you." I replied as I joined in with her laughter, my mood skyrocketing as the wind wove through the carriage, the earth's power threading through the open windows and sinking under my skin.

"Oh sweetie, where did you think you got your spark from? Your father?" She said as if that explained it all, and I laughed harder.

If every shopping trip ended this way, I would volunteer for them all.

CHAPTER 29

There was a carriage in front of our home when we arrived back. Dark forest green and trimmed in gold – and I knew instantly that it belonged to Lord Westward. Though that wasn't the only thing I spied as I exited our carriage.

I told my mother to go ahead without me and she gave me a small smile, thinking that I just needed to collect my thoughts before I saw Lord Westward again. I didn't move to correct her.

Once she was within the walls of the house, I turned and headed to the side of the house, where I'd noticed Rem waiting patiently for me.

He looked as he always did, dressed in his vest and dark pants – though his hair was more wild than normal, and I wondered when the last time he'd gone home to rest was, or if he'd spent all his nights out here watching over me like he was ordered to.

"Enjoy your shopping trip?" he said by way of greeting, and I noticed the tightness of his jaw, the narrowness of his eyes. He was not happy.

"Is something wrong?" I asked instead of replying to his question.

"Why is Grayson here again?"

"I wouldn't have a clue, if you hadn't noticed I have not yet been inside to see him." My fire moved through me at the tone in his voice – if he thought, he could speak to me like this he had another thing coming.

"I heard them speak of a date. Is the contract signed then?" Disapproval dripped from his voice, and I wondered what was between the two men to have Rem lose his cool at the mere mention of the Commanding Lord.

"Several men are currently courting me. It is what happens when one is interested in a Binding Ceremony. Westward is just more ambitious than most." I hissed, making sure that I did not raise my voice high enough for others to hear.

His answering stare chilled me to the bone, and caused my flames to rush faster, rising to meet my skin but not breaking surface just yet. Thoughts of threatening to turn him into a candlestick ran through my head and I was not opposed to them. We faced off against one another, holding our gazes in a game of who was more stubborn than the other.

I refused to speak first, and he seemed quite content in not speaking at all.

"Remember my words. Call out if you need anything, and do not tell him anything." He said after what felt like an eternity, turning his back on me as he did so. I resisted the urge to scream out in frustration at the mass of a man I'd slowly started to consider a friend in the past few days.

Maybe friend had been a stretch, after all – he was only here doing his duty.

I turned and stalked back to the front of the house,

slamming the door as I entered, and taking in a deep breath. I needed to calm myself, needed to will my flames back into their corner and away from my skin before anyone came to find me.

Just as my flames began moving back through me though, voices sounded on the other side of the foyer, and I opened my eyes to see the man Rem had been so upset about.

"Pure Sandoval, I have come for that picnic we spoke about the other night. I do hope this is a good time." Lord Westward called out as he neared me, my father on his heels as they exited his office. Images of the meadow flew through my mind and the urge to be outside, to be out in my sanctuary were too strong to pass up.

"Now is wonderful timing, Commanding Lord Westward. I am ready when you are." The smile that broke through my face was genuine, though my flames hadn't yet retreated fully. Silently they lingered, as if watching the interaction and I paused where I was as he continued walking towards me.

I have control. I have control. I repeated in my mind as he held his arm out for me to take. I took a breath, and then another as my flames slithered inwards a little more, listening to my command and my smile grew, though I declined the offer of his arm as he led us back out the front door.

"I'm not too sure on where to go from here, as it is your meadow. Do we require a carriage?" He asked as we descended the steps.

"There aren't any roads that lead there. Do you mind walking? It won't take too long." I replied automatically as I scanned the area for any sign of Rem. I had no doubts that his duty would mean he was about to follow along after us wherever we went, though I couldn't see him like I normally could

"And spend more time in your presence? I do not mind one bit." His grin lit up his eyes, and I couldn't help the blush that rose onto my cheeks at his flattery. He gathered the picnic basket he had made from his carriage before we took off down the road towards the town, and then into the woods beside it — weaving over roots and debris before we came out onto the trail.

Walking next to Lord Westward was easy, the silence just as comfortable as talking with him was. As we weaved along the path, I felt my flames slowly retreat into their corner, understanding that there was no danger surrounding us.

"What is the Western Paradise like?" I asked as he helped me over a fallen log in the trail. He'd grabbed my hand before I could say anything, and I blurted the first thing I could think of as I fought the urge to flinch and pull away from him.

"It is much like these woods, in most parts of the West. Though my main village, the Coastal Village is situated on the furthest boarder of the Western Paradise. It is built into the side of a cliff, merging down until you get to the sea that surrounds us. It is quite a beautiful view and I miss it often when I am called away on work."

"I couldn't imagine being away from my home for too long. Or even my parents. I would miss them all too much." The words were out before I could think of their meaning, and I looked to Lord Westward as my words fully sank in.

"It is quite alright to feel that way, Darling. You know nothing else. Though I hope if today goes well that you will at least consider the possibility of visiting my village sometime. I still need to show you my waterfall."

"You don't plan on whisking me away anytime soon?" I teased.

"Oh, have no doubts Miss Raewyn, if given the chance I would bind myself to you the minute your father permits it. But politics takes time and I do not mind spending more time getting to know you in the interim." He winked before he lifted me over another fallen branch and I blushed at the ease in with which he touched me, at the honesty in his words. As if he had already declared that I was his. I refused to look at him the rest of the walk, which only lasted a few minutes more as we entered my meadow.

Suddenly shy that I was sharing my most private place with someone, I walked ahead of Lord Westward, the meadow swaying gently in the breeze, and I sucked in a breath before I turned towards him.

"This is my meadow." I mumbled, so quietly that I thought he hadn't heard me at first.

"I can see why you like it here. It is a beautiful place." He replied as he sat the basket on the ground, the long strands of wildflowers and grass instantly swallowing it whole.

"I come here when I need to be alone. It calms me. Reminds me that the world is beautiful, even if sometimes it doesn't feel that way." That ancient power swelled up next to me as I spoke, acknowledging my compliment towards its owner and I smiled slowly as I felt it fill me, mingling with my fire and keeping them docile.

Lord Westward said nothing as he watched me, and I didn't feel the need to fill the silence as peace washed over me. Images of the last time I'd been here flooded my mind and I glanced around the clearing, trying to find the spot of grass I'd had to regrow as images of Nix racing towards a crumbling me flashed behind my eyelids.

Clearing my throat, I settled my gaze on the man who was here with me now.

"Where would you like to sit?"

"Where is your favourite place to sit when you come here?" He questioned back at me, and I instantly turned and walked a little farther in until I found the centre, the combination of the earth's energy and my own flowing fire giving me a confidence I'd never had in front of another person before. Raising my hands above my head as I glanced over my shoulder to make sure he was following behind me. With a grin I fell backwards, my back hitting the long tendrils of grass, cushioning my fall.

A deep chuckle echoed throughout the meadow at my move and that, mixed with the sun and the earth's purring energy surrounding me, made me feel fuzzy.

This was nice, this sharing a little of my soul.

"You are something entirely unexpected, Pure Sandoval." He whispered and I tilted my head back so that I was staring directly up at him, his frame covered in shadow as the sun hit his back. A niggling in the back of my mind reminded me of a dream I'd once had very similar to this and I wondered if it was a sign that Lord Westward was the man I was meant to bind myself to.

Surely, if every moment felt like this with him then I would be content enough in life.
I watched him as he unfurled a blanket from inside the basket he'd carried the entire way here, and laid it out next to me, making sure that no grass was covering our view of one another as he began to take out various items, spreading them before me as he did so.

"You asked my brother what I liked to eat, didn't you?" I questioned accusingly as I watched him unwrap the best pastries the Citadel had to offer. Light and creamy, the pastries melted happiness onto your tongue with every bite. It was all I wanted to eat whenever I stayed in town long enough to become hungry. I'd begged Orion to stop at the bakery enough times in my life that he now brought them to me whenever he was in town.

The sheepish look on the Lord's face as he pulled out freshly cut fruit and a jug of apple juice confirmed my suspicions.

"I am man enough to admit that I did. I didn't know what you would like to eat, and also, I wanted to impress you."

"Call me impressed, Lord Westward."

"I must insist you call me Grayson."

"Okay then, Grayson." I tested the name out, and his answering grin made me feel as though he liked the sound of his name on my lips.

"And I won't, imagine you are impressed by me — not yet. If it were that easy with you, I would have suggested this a long time ago, Darling. No, this is just the beginning." He added as he held the bowl of fruit towards me, and I blushed again as I held his gaze, fire burning in his too-green irises.

"Well, I can honestly tell you that no one has put this much thought into anything they did for me. So, thank you." It was my turn to act all embarrassed, though I covered it by grabbing some pieces of fruit and popping them in my mouth.

We ate in companionable silence, making small talk about the wildflowers that grew here, or what it was like in the Coastal Village he grew up in.

I found that the more I spoke with Grayson, the more I found myself relaxing in his presence — opening up more and more until I wasn't just a Lady of society, or the Pure of the Citadel, but me. Plain old Raewyn Sandoval.

I couldn't remember the last time I felt like I was anything other than myself and I didn't want the feeling to ever end.

Once we were done with the picnic, and Grayson had packed it all away, he moved over on his blanket and motioned for me join him on the space beside him. I hesitated for a second, feeling like it was too close to laying in a bed with someone, and his body shook with silent laughter as he watched me closely. As though he could see what I was thinking.

"I am not going to pressure you into anything, Darling. I only wish for you to be comfortable."

"The grass is comfortable." I challenged back, laying down again where I'd fallen before. His laugh echoed through the space between us before I heard him moving around. I turned my head to the side just in time to see him stuff the blanket back in the basket as he stretched out on the long grass next to me.

"I think you may be right there. It's as if a bed of hay is beneath me." He joked and the laugh that came out of me was loud and joyful.

A noise that sounded odd in my own ears.

"No one asked you to put the blanket away, Grayson." I chided as he squirmed around trying to get comfortable.

"I wish to see life the way you do, to feel it the way you do."

"Why?" I asked, my tone more disbelieving than anything. All my life people pretended I didn't exist, and then when I reached my sixteenth year thought me too egotistical to be counted as one of them. I'd never had someone wonder why I live my life the way I do. I guess one needed friends for that, and in those, I was severely lacking.

"So that I may truly learn who you are. You intrigue me like no one else has and I find myself more drawn to you with each encounter." Out of the corner of my eye, I saw him turn on his side as he spoke. Facing me so that he could look at me fully, one arm bent so he could prop his head up. I kept my eyes on the sky above us, on the clouds moving slowly as they travelled to wherever it was they went, as I fought down another blush from heating my skin.

"I've told you before, I am not that interesting to know."

"I disagree wholeheartedly." He replied, chuckling. I didn't know what to say to that, so I said nothing. Choosing instead to ignore the feel of his eyes on me as I let the energy around me sink underneath my skin, willing it to rid my body of this fuzzy feeling I could not yet identify.

"Tell me something no one else knows." He asked eventually. It was the same question he'd asked me back at the estate, and back then I had skirted the question I didn't want to answer.

This time though, I found myself thinking of everything within me. No one truly knew a thing about me.

"I almost failed my trials." I finally settled on, letting him in a little more.

"I don't believe you." He scoffed and I turned to look at him so he could read the honesty on my face.

"It's true. My second trial was a test of my loyalty to the Covenant and my position as a Pure in society. I almost threw it all in when I realised what I'd done." I watched his eyes widen as I told him the story of my second trial. Of how I'd had to condemn my sister who in that world, had attempted to flee a binding to a God, and how the moment I'd realised what I'd done – I wanted to take it all back and save her instead.

"What stopped you?" He pressed once I was done speaking.

"I'm not sure. I think I realised that it didn't matter – that no matter my decision, the law was the law and so it had to be that way. Doesn't mean I don't still feel guilt over it though." I shrugged causally through the lie. I knew exactly why I'd stopped – but I couldn't tell him that without going against the Sacred Servants. My gut twisted at the thought of concealing the truth from him and I didn't like the feeling one bit.

"The trials play on our worst fears and our greatest desires. They are so real that it is impossible to separate them from reality. I still have nightmares over my trials, and mine were a long, long time ago." He replied and I watched his eyes darken, as if even thinking of his trials brought back dark memories.

"Can I ask?"

"Are you asking to see my markings, your Pureness?" He teased and the blush I was fighting moments ago rushed forward.

"I do not need to see them. It's just, I have not been able to see any markings on you and I was merely curious."

"You have been looking at me?" He questioned, shocked though the tease did not leave his voice and I scowled in response.

"I will stop if that is what you desire." I scoffed back, the fuzzy feeling I felt returning in the pit of my stomach. Guess the energy didn't make it go away after all.

"Don't you dare." His voice dropped and almost sounded like a growl as he leaned closer towards me, his breath brushing along my face as he spoke. My heart slammed against my chest at his proximity.

He was too close.

"I received two markings on the year of my Ceremony, and I have worked hard to ensure that I do not receive any more."

"Oh." Was all that came out of my mouth, my eyes glued to the way his lips moved as he spoke. He was still too close, far too close but I couldn't for the life of me move away.

"Would you like to see them?" He inquired as he raised one perfectly handsome eyebrow. My voice had stopped working by this point, so I simply nodded. He chuckled low, quiet, only for me to hear before he sat up suddenly. Lifting his pant leg up to his knee, I finally found black whorls of ink covering his skin.

Glancing back at me he raised his arm as he pulled the sleeve up and I found more lining his wrist like a bracelet.

"Envy and Greed." I breathed as I took his markings in. He nodded as he covered himself back up.

"I was an ambitious fool when I was younger."

"And now?" I couldn't help but ask.

"A much more sensible fool."

CHAPTER 30

We stayed in the meadow a while longer, watching the clouds move across the sky together until the sun began to sink lower in the sky – talking about everything and nothing as I got to know the Commanding Lord of the Western Paradise more in depth than I had anyone in my life. Even Nix, although our relationship was more anger and mentorship than anything else.

Grayson was company I did not expect to enjoy, and I found on returning to my family's home, that I did not want the day to end. I did not want to go back to feeling like I had to hide that piece of myself I'd opened for him.

"What are your plans for the Saviour's Feast?" He asked me as we climbed the steps of my home.

"I'm not sure. Usually, Imogen drags me along to the town square for the festivities, and we often have a family dinner beforehand. I hadn't decided yet what I was going to do without her here this year." I'd given Grayson more truths in one day than I ever had in my life, and this was no exception. Had he been anyone else, my response would have consisted of one simple word. *Nothing.*

He nodded as if he were considering something, and I found my eyes following the movement of his actions. "I have been asked to attend your family's dinner, though I was hoping you'd invite me personally." He winked at me, and I blushed once more. "Shall I instead ask you to do me the honour of escorting me to the town square afterwards? I have never celebrated the Saviour's Feast in the Citadel and I would very much like to see how you celebrate the eve."

"I can show you, though my celebration style is less celebrating with the nobility of the Citadel and more people watching from the corner as everyone drinks themselves into a stupor. So maybe Orion could escort you instead? I've seen him engage in the festivities a time or two." My reply was more teasing than anything, though I was still speaking my truths. I had never engaged myself in the festivities in town. Even though it was my favourite day of the year, watching everyone come together like we all belonged, I still felt as though I was the exception.

Especially since Imogen often abandoned me early in the night. I supposed this year would be no different now that I was the Pure of the Citadel. But perhaps if I had someone with me, someone who would stick with me the entire night as I showed them around, I wouldn't feel so alone. That feeling in my stomach returned and this time I embraced the warm fuzziness as Grayson's gaze lingered on me.

"There is no one else I would rather spend the eve with, than you my dear Raewyn." He declared as he locked his gaze onto mine, and I felt that fuzziness expand within me. It felt like a mixture of nerves and excitement — it was the first time he'd dropped my title, and it caused another round of fuzziness to invade me. I was beginning to realise that the feeling was caused by the attention Grayson was giving me.

That I had never felt this before simply because I had never allowed myself to be courted by someone. It was an odd sensation, but it was also one that I couldn't deny I did not mind.

So, I didn't correct him on the use of my name.

"Then it is a date." I said instead, mimicking the words he'd used on me the other night.

"One I cannot wait for." He replied as he lifted my hand and pressed a kiss to the back of it. The sensation felt odd, and I resisted the urge to yank it out of his grip – but the look of pure delight in his eyes as he lowered my hand once more told me I'd done the right thing in letting him provide even the smallest amount of affection.

Before my mind could scramble itself back into coherency, I entered the house and closed the doors on him without another word.

My parents were out for the evening, at one of my father's work functions no doubt, and so I was able to stand in the dark, emptiness of our foyer while I worked through my thoughts from all that had happened today.

I'd let myself open up to someone, wholly, for the first time in forever. And while the thought terrified me that Grayson may find me lacking in everything he expected of a Pure, I also felt free and content in a way I never had before. It was invigorating, that feeling that someone may truly know you and still accept you, and yet it was the single most terrifying concept to me that I almost walked back out the door and begged him to forget everything I had exposed to him.

Choosing to let him decide for himself what he thought of that side of me, I grabbed one of the candles at the base of the stairs and climbed up before I could think too hard on it and chase him down the street. I hadn't felt the swirling of my unruly emotions or power in the last few hours as they slumbered in peace, and though I was riddled with anxiety now, they stayed silent.

I took it as a good sign and whispered a thanks to the combination of the earth's energy and my openness with Grayson. I was almost tempted not to rouse that power in me just to practice my control – though I knew that I would be closing myself off soon enough and I needed to make sure I could handle it when that inevitably did happen.

Shutting the bedroom door behind me, I opened the windows once again, letting in the night breeze along with the tendrils of the earth's energy. I felt more connected to it now that I'd spent an afternoon basking in its warmth, and I felt it move throughout the room as if it were an extension of my own soul. It twisted lazily as it scanned its surroundings, turning back in on me as if it was happy to see me again and I smiled as though it could see.

Pulling my fire out of its corner in my mind, I let it fill me- sliding down my arms, all the way to my toes until the night air no longer bothered me. Focusing on that power, I moved it through me like a wave, rising and falling through me as it swirled from one hand to the next on command.

Maybe I was getting the hang of this after all.

I moved those flames through me a few more times, each time lighting a different finger as they followed my command like they were an extension of my own mind –

and I knew that they were, but they didn't often cooperate enough to feel like it.

Deciding to step my training up a notch, I opened both my palms, willing balls of flame to appear in both at the same time. My fire accepted the challenge, igniting its way through my blood, shooting straight for its target. My control slipped and my teeth clenched as I fought to maintain it. I knew the effort I was expending on focusing my powers into two places at once would mean that I would have to sleep with the windows open once more as I pushed more energy into the move than I ever had the nerve to use before.

Call it recklessness, but I was hopeful that my slumbering fire would be more amenable with all the truth's I had confessed today. Knowing that the key to controlling my powers lay in being in sync with all of myself., something I thought I was getting better at.

Turns out, I was wrong.

A cry slipped past my grinding teeth as flames shot out of me, whipping through the air around me as if they were finally freed from their cages and I willed that part of me that shielded my emotions to claw them back in. Groaning under the pressure building inside me, I pushed further, knowing that if I couldn't control them together, I would never be able to control them at all.

I am the one in control. You are merely an extension of me. I groaned to the flames around me as I drew them back inside of me, slowly.

So painstakingly slow.

Each second I pulled them further inside of me felt like a lifetime, but eventually I was left alone in the darkness of my room once more, my flames instead raging throughout me like they were not pleased at being caged once more. I was momentarily stunned by the strength with which my flames held as they resisted my commands. They felt more powerful as they coiled themselves inside of me, as if they had a life of their own.

I pushed harder, shoving them back under my control, commanding them with more force than I'd ever needed to use – and as they moved, I felt that ancient power swell around me, encouraging me as it lent me some of its strength. Seeping in through the tips of my fingers and guiding my flames where they were needed. I gasped at the sensation, of my flames concaving under the weight of the earth's power as they bent to its command with ease, swelling in my palms until I could feel the balls of power weaving through my fingertips. Dripping in not only my own power, but also that external earthly power that I could now feel thrumming through me.

Opening my eyes, my mouth dropped open as I stared wide-eyed at the blue flames that were now swirling in the palms of both my hands. Flickering calmly in the darkness as they danced between hues so fast, it appeared to be every colour at once. I'd never seen anything so beautiful – it was like my own personal, shimmering rainbow.

They were beautiful, and I wondered briefly if my flames in the meadow had looked like this too, and I'd just been too preoccupied to see their magnificence. I'd once again merged my powers with that of the earth's mysterious energy, though I still had no idea how I'd done it.

It wasn't like the many times that I'd swept the energy through me in an effort to weed out unwanted emotions – my flames had always made certain to keep themselves well away from that ancient power when I did so. No, this was like the meadow once more, the earth's power threading itself through mine like we were one.

With my focus drawn inward to my leaping thoughts and away from keeping those balls of fire in the palms of my hand, my fire slowly crawled their way back under my skin – sensing that they were no longer needed as the earth's energy withdrew from me.

I felt the exact moment the earth's power left me as my knees buckled, exhaustion hitting me like a tidal wave as I collapsed to the floor in a heap of limbs, my body too tired to support any part of itself. I willed my eyes to stay open, for my limbs to move me to the bed before I gave in – though try as I might, they did not budge.

Two things registered in my mind as unconsciousness claimed me. The first, was the soft but undeniable feeling of someone else's power drifting through the room, dark like night and as strong as its owner as it wove itself under my limbs and caressed my cheeks as if in greeting.

The second was a medley of confusion and peace as a set of arms wrapped themselves under me, replacing those tendrils of power and I became weightless, lifted off the ground like I was nothing more than a feather. I tried to fight my exhaustion once more, open my eyes and see who was in my room where I was meant to be alone – but they wouldn't budge.

My fire purred as it settled into a peaceful slumber once more, humming quietly in my mind as this power surrounded me in a cooling embrace.

I mumbled incoherently as my mouth struggled to work – trying to call out to the person who felt like safety and contentment, washing away any other thought in my mind as it rode the wave of exhaustion happily before shutting down completely.

The Saviour's Feast Day was here, and I'd been so busy helping my mother plan the Saviour's Feast dinner that I hadn't been able to see Commanding Lord Westward – I mean, Grayson - since our picnic two days ago.

Though that did not stop him from trying to impress me. Each morning as I descended the stairs, there would be another delivery of flowers, and jewels waiting for me in the dining room, Grayson's way of persuading me to choose him I suppose.

If I were any other girl, I would be keeling over with all the swoon worthy gifts and flattery. But I was not, and it hindered my thoughts of him a little that he did not see that. My mother tried to convince me that I should be grateful of the gifts, regardless of how I felt about them – that a Lord baring gifts to a girl he was not yet contracted to, was the highest honour I could receive, and was a sign of his true affection for me.

I'd shrugged her words off like it did not matter, though I could not deny the warmth that spread to my cheeks every time I thought of the way he'd placed a kiss to my hand as we stood at the door on our return from the meadow the other night.

My father had been pestering me relentlessly to give him my opinion of all the men I'd met, so that he may confer with Orion and decide on a course for my life; but every time he asked, something held me back.

My powers had also been strangely erratic ever since my lapse in control a few nights ago. It was harder to keep my flames down and I'd taken more and more to sleeping with the windows open so that earthly power could help me soothe them. It probably didn't help that I'd been so exhausted by the time I climbed the stairs to my bed each night that all I'd managed to do was move my flames through me a few times before collapsing onto my bed.

I needed to ask Rem to take me back to the courtyard soon to let me release my powers before they built up too much for me to handle.

I'd awoken the day after my attempt at pushing my control to its limits, to find my windows closed and myself nestled snugly underneath my blankets. I knew I had not been the one to put myself there, and the vague memory of someone lifting me had not helped one bit. I decided that my father must have come to check on me once they returned home and placed me in bed...that it couldn't possibly have been Nix like my brain willed it to be. He was out of town after all, right?

However, my father had not questioned me the next morning at breakfast, as I was sure he would have if he had indeed been the one to find his daughter passed out on the bedroom floor, surrounded by the chill of the outside weather.

"Enjoy the Feast, you two." My brother called with a wink to me, as Grayson led me out of the dining room and through the house. Alyssa's responding giggle pulling me entirely from my thoughts as I once again tried to focus on where I was and what I was doing.

The whole night, my family had made little insinuations that I had chosen Grayson as my choice for a husband – all the other Lords forgotten behind him and although I still hadn't confirmed anything, I couldn't help but realise, that maybe subconsciously, I had chosen Grayson as my most preferred husband... but that did not mean I was ready to be bound to the man.

Perhaps that is why I refused to give father my answer

— I simply was not ready to give up my life for someone else. I was not ready to move so far away from everything I knew in the Citadel — every*one* I knew in the Citadel.

I still hadn't heard from Nix, which meant he still had not yet returned. It had been a week since he'd left me that note, and although I'd continued to see Rem stalking around my family's grounds, I hadn't interacted with him since that day he accosted me about Grayson being in my home. I missed the connections I was forming with the two men - the only two people I had managed to become anything close to genuine friends with, and I hoped that Nix would return home soon so that we could resume the strange dynamic that had somehow become so normal to me.

"You seem terribly lost in your thoughts tonight, darling. Though I do hope they are all of me." Grayson's low voice wove into my mind as he placed my hand in the crook of his arm. We had made it into the carriage without me realising it and were already halfway to the town square.

"I do apologise, I have just had a lot to deal with lately." I lied, my gut twisting once again at the thought of having to hide myself from this man as I pulled my hand back into my lap. I couldn't admit to a potential suitor that my thoughts in fact were filled with another set of eyes — that part of me missed my mentor, no matter how much I wanted to punch him in the face whenever he was near.

No, that would not be an appropriate admission at all. So, I settled on a smile I could only assume he would interpret as embarrassment.

"Is everything alright? I may not be a Pure of soul, but I am a good listener."

"It's nothing, it has just all been an adjustment and every time I think I am used to something, it changes." I admitted, weaving as much truth into the words as I could.

"Does this have anything to do with those meetings in the palace your father told me about?"

I had no answer to that.

I turned my head to look out the window instead, watching as the sun began setting behind the woods surrounding us, casting the entire town in a golden glow that I adored.

The carriage windows were closed, and I longed to open them to feel the power weaving its way through me.

"Or is this perhaps to do with the fact that you have not yet told your father who you'd prefer he make a contract with?"

At this my head whipped back to Grayson, shock lining my face that my father would divulge such information to him.

"Do not be angry at your father, I was merely curious. It is not often a woman gets a say in who her father binds her off to. Though I was a little hurt that the choice for you is not yet clear."

"Is it meant to be?" I couldn't help but tease in an effort to distract him from the hurt I could hear lying in his words. I hadn't meant to insult him with my refusal to choose.

"There are only so many ways I can show you how badly I want you by my side, as my wife, before I begin to look desperate here, Darling." His wink was meant to disarm his words, but I could still hear the truth in them.

He had been trying — I could see that, and despite the fact that the fuzzy feelings returned each time he did I still had reservations about signing my life away so soon. Not when I had just started moving somewhere in my life, controlling it how I had always wanted to.

"Let's forget about all of that for the moment. Tonight, I want you to shut off that pretty mind of yours and just enjoy what surrounds you. Show me why you love the Saviour's Feast."

CHAPTER 31

The town square was already teeming with life when we arrived – the festivities mixing with the swirling power of the earth, creating such a heady concoction that it almost swept me off my feet as I stepped out of the carriage. Music pounded off the cobblestones, reverberating through each step I took as we made our way through the throngs of people who were eating and drinking to their hearts content – basking in the full glory of the Saviour's deeds. The lanterns were lit at intervals around the square, illuminating the space in golden light as the shadows danced across our faces as I felt the earth move through each and every person surrounding me. If I concentrated hard enough, I could feel the tethers it created in each of us – tying us all together as one people. Almost as if tonight's Feast was not just a celebration of the Saviour who created this land for us, but also a chance for that ancient energy to feed off of our combined energy. My fire hummed in response to that connected energy, pooling lacily in my limbs as a feeling of being light and airy washed through me – as though my power had become drunk off the feeling.

Momentarily lightheaded, I watched as people approached stalls of food and drink that various people in the Village had prepared for tonight's Feast, lining them outside of each store so that they were free for all. Ensuring that no one had to work the evening away. It was a way for everyone to enjoy the freedom that the Saviour had granted us.

It was the reason we celebrated after all.

Stories circulated throughout the square every year about how the God of the Citadel used to join in on the celebrations, coming down from his palace to mingle with all his people. This was of course well before even my father was born — before the God locked himself away, and became nothing but a bedtime story, though every year we all held out hope that this would be the year that he came down from his dark tower and joined us once again.

Grayson confirmed that this was the same in the Western Paradise. His aunt, the Pure Goddess Patricia participating every year in the festivities they held, and everyone loved that she was able to switch off Goddess mode and drink with the rest of them.

He also spoke of something called the 'Saviour's Dive' where everyone would come together at the end of the night and dive into the oceans below the Coastal Village as one. It was tradition to mark the end of the year and begin the new one fresh and cleansed by the waters that surround them. The concept intrigued me, and part of me thought of how I may be in the Western Paradise for the next Saviour's Feast — how I may be diving with Grayson and the Goddess off the coast and into the freezing oceans in order to cleanse myself for the new year.

Shaking those thoughts away, I wove through the

crowd and bee-lined straight for the baker's table, snagging a few of my beloved pastries before nestling myself down on the edge of the fountain that took up the middle of the square. It was where I sat myself every year. The perfect spot to watch everyone and everything around me as I basked in the energy of the night. This year would be no different, I would just have company for it.

So far, I'd listened to Grayson and pushed everything out of my mind that did not have to do with the Saviour's Feast and my date with the Lord who was trying so hard to impress me, but I couldn't help the memories that swam up to the surface at being back in the square.

It was the first time I had been back since Nix had walked up behind me and asked me what I was thinking about, and I couldn't help but miss him a little more, but more than that I missed how simple my life used to be before my trials, before the Ceremony and my crowned title of Pure of the Citadel.

"You are thinking again, Darling." Grayson teased, when he noticed that I still hadn't touched the pastry in my hand. I blushed at how easily he'd begun to read me and pushed everything out of my mind once more.

Stop thinking about Nix, stop thinking period.

"I was actually thinking it's been a while since I've been in the town square. I haven't had much time to wander these days." There, that ought to get us back on track.

"Ahh, the perks of being a Pure — no time for fun anymore." He winked as he said this though and I caught myself laughing at his dig.

"Hey, I still have plenty of fun. I believe it is *you* who is all work and no play."

"Is that a challenge, *Pure Sandoval?*" His eyes gleamed with mischief, and I couldn't help but take the bait.

"Always."

"Come then, Darling. Let me show you how the Commanding Lord of the West celebrates the Saviour's Feast." He grabbed my hand as he said this, hoisting me to my feet and dragging me towards the drinks table we hadn't yet visited. This time I did not pull away from his touch, instead choosing to embrace this small freedom with a man I was becoming quite fond of.

As we neared the table, I watched the patrons around it, tipping sideways as they fought to stand upright, screaming nonsense at one another, and enjoying themselves like they had no worries in the world tonight.

I wanted to feel what they did.

Grinning up at Grayson as he handed me a cup of cold amber liquid, I downed it all in one go and coughed at the burning sensation as it slid down the back of my throat. Grayson merely laughed and followed suit, grabbing two more cups before tugging me back into the throng of people dancing in the middle of the square. I could see merchants mingling with the nobles of society, laughing, patting each other on the back like they weren't living on opposite sides of the Citadel.

Come tomorrow they would be strangers again, but for just tonight they were friends.

This was why I loved the Saviour's Feast.

I danced with Grayson for hours, the music pounding through my limbs as the energy surrounding me grew, sweeping through me in waves as it did so. I felt drunk on the power of the earth's energy as it weaved through the fire inside of me – though Grayson teased me that those two drinks I'd consumed were the reason for my giggling state. I'd had to refrain from telling him more than once that I wasn't drunk on the alcohol, but on the earth itself.

Instead, I found myself moving closer to him as he watched me dance around him, laughing every time he tried to grab hold of me and failed. I didn't want to be tethered down to his embrace, and so I skipped away from him, basking instead in the feel of the wind caressing the exposed skin my dress did not cover, cooling the sweat that coated me as my hair whipped around me in time to the beats pounding through me like a heartbeat.

I danced with people I had never met before, laughing with them as we became one in a crowd that never seemed to lighten up as the hours passed on, drinks flowing continuously throughout the night. I had people offering me food and drinks as the night went on, but I declined them all as I twirled around Grayson, full on the swirling energy of the earth as it consumed every fibre of my being. I even waved at Stacia and her new flock of minions as they passed by me, unbothered by her scowl for once.

I felt happy – free in a way that I never had before, and I didn't want whatever was happening to me in this moment to ever end.

"You absolutely astound me." Grayson whispered in my ear as I felt his hands grip my hips, pulling my back to his front as he finally caught hold of me. My head had been thrown back to watch the stars, arms in the air as I swayed to the music, and I hadn't noticed how close he got.

"I am not what everyone thinks I am." My mind admitted before I could think to keep that truth inside.

"I am starting to see that, Darling." He was closer now, his breath brushing against my ear as he spoke, the heat of his body pressing up behind me as he closed the distance between us. I was coherent enough to realise that he was far too close to me, closer than I'd let anyone get to me – though at the same time, I felt so high on the energy

I was absorbing into me that I found myself leaning back into him rather than away.

"What do you see?" I asked as I turned around to face him, his eyes bright in the darkness that surrounded the square. Candles flickering at intervals were the only thing keeping us all from stumbling in blackness. My heightened mind itched to reach out and touch the golden strands of hair that fell over his eyes, his normally perfectly styled hair mussed by hours of dancing in the wind.

More than anything I longed to reach out and touch someone to see what that would feel like.

"I see someone who is so Pure and innocent that she can't help but be the most infatuating person in the room. Someone who is drawn to the beauty of the earth just as I am. Someone I can't help but already think of as mine even though I will wait as long as you wish to make that so." His words were so sweet, so flattering that I should have been swooning at his feet with the energy sweeping me into submission the way it was tonight.

I watched as his head dipped towards mine, his intent clear as his eyes found mine and held. He was going to kiss me. I was going to have my first kiss with the only man I'd let come close to me. I felt that ancient energy swell around us, as I stood rooted to the spot, frozen in my decision.

Did I want Grayson to kiss me? I hadn't planned on it, but I supposed if he were going to become my husband it would happen eventually.

Slowly, as though even my body were fighting the decision, I tilted my head back, and his lips curved up at the permission I was giving him, his eyes shining a brighter green in approval. I felt his hands tighten on my hips as he secured me in place, his head lowering more. He was so close now that I could feel his breath on my face, and it felt like fire – snapping me out of the stupor I'd been drowning in.

No, this isn't what I wanted. Not at all.

Snapping my head down, I placed both palms on Grayson's chest and pushed off, breaking the connection as his lips hit the top of my head. Stepping back out of his arms, I breathed deep, inhaling the energy of the earth as it strengthened my resolve. I was not any other girl he could flatter, and watch melt into his arms. I was the Pure of the Citadel, and I did not wish to be kissed for the first time in the middle of a drunken crowd of people.

Meeting his eyes again, I watched as anger flashed through his eyes, quickly masked by an apology as his mouth opened.

"I apologise if I stepped out of line, Raewyn. I thought you were enjoying yourself." He explained, attempting to move closer once more.

"I was. I mean, I am. But I am not ready for that. I'm sorry if I gave you the impression that I was."

"Do not apologise. I told you; I am willing to wait as long as it takes for you to choose me. Though I will admit I have never been rejected, so it may take a second to get over my wounds. But you are worth it." His words melted some of my panic and a laugh escaped me. He smiled in response, offering to gather us more drinks. I nodded in acceptance as my mind spun, attempting to work through everything I was feeling.

Just as Grayson returned with our drinks, I felt my flames suddenly coil tighter, right as the power that had gathered around us slammed into me and I gasped at its impact.

Grayson immediately ran to my side, drinks forgotten as he gripped my arms to steady me. I felt ready to explode with the amount of energy that now coursed through me. It was overwhelming all my senses, my eyes blurring slightly as I struggled to maintain my footing.

I vaguely heard Grayson saying my name, pleading with me to tell him what was wrong with me as I staggered back from him, the roar inside of me drowning out everything around me.

Suddenly, it was all too much.

Too many people.

Too much energy.

"*Rem!*" I called into the crowd as I clutched my chest, panting through the pain. I couldn't breathe, couldn't move, couldn't think. "Rem, I need you!" I screamed louder as I doubled over in pain, the power from the earth fighting with my fire as they attempted to push one another out of me. I couldn't let either of them loose, not in the middle of a crowd.

Not in front of Grayson.

"You know Rem?" Grayson's shocked words filtered into me, and I heard the anger in his tone just as I looked up to see a hulking mass barrelling through the crowd towards me.

He was still here, still watching me.

Thank the Saviour.

"What did you do to her?" Rem growled as he approached us, his tone deep and threatening.

"I did nothing." Grayson threw back, stepping in front of me in an attempt to block Rem's path – but he moved him aside in a shove so hard I was surprised Grayson kept his footing.

"If you even thought about touching a hair on her, I will not hesitate to put you down, *cousin.*" People had now gathered around us at the scene that was unfolding in front of them. No doubt, we would be the talk of all Seven Paradises tomorrow – The Pure of the Citadel being fought over by a Commanding Lord and a man who appeared more like a Radical Soldier, than the right-hand man of a Pure.

The Ladies would all be swarming in their gossip circles at the sight of us, but I fought away the thoughts as the earth's power slammed into me once more.

"Rem." I gasped, grabbing his pant leg as I fought to keep the scream that begged to be set free. I needed to get out of here before I lost control of the energy inside of me.

I felt him turn in my grip, lifting me effortlessly as he carried me out of the town square without another word to Grayson. I heard him shout after us, after me – but I was too far gone to focus on his words. I wasn't sure how I was going to explain this to him when I next saw him, not without telling him everything.

But that was something I would have to figure out when I didn't feel like there was a war going on inside of me.

My fire pushed against the hold Rem had on me – heating my skin until I was certain it would burn through my dress, attempting to get to Rem as it considered him a threat to my wellbeing. I tried to will it calm, to retreat into my mind because Rem was only trying to help – but it didn't listen, and from what I could tell, it didn't seem to bother him, though I felt him pick up his pace as my temperature skyrocketed.

"Where is that prick?" I heard him mutter over the roaring in my ears.

"What the hell is happening to me?" I growled as another wave of the earth's energy passed through me, hitting my wall of flames, and barrelling straight through it.

That scream finally broke free from my throat, and I dug my nails into Rem's shoulder as his grip on me tightened.

"I don't know, but Nix will, just hold on a little longer."

I wasn't sure I could promise him anything at the moment, so I kept my mouth shut, eyes clenched tight as I concentrated on keeping everything inside of me.

I just needed to get to an open space where no one will see me – and then I could let all this out.

CHAPTER 32

"*Phoenix, we have a problem.*" Rem boomed as we burst through a doorway, his voice echoing throughout the open space.

My scream followed his words a second later as another wave of energy whipped through me, my flames turning to knives in my soul as they fought off the earth's energy. I couldn't feel the energy surrounding me now, which meant that we'd gone indoors. I wasn't sure yet if that was a good thing or a bad thing, as I willed the remaining power inside of me to merge together so they could stop fighting.

But neither listened.

"What happened?" A voice called to our left and I writhed against Rem's hold on me as sweat poured down my face — or maybe they were tears, I wasn't sure at this point.

"I don't know. One minute she was dancing with him and the next she was on the ground."

"I'll kill him." His voice dropped to a low growl,

sounding lethal as it rang through the room around us, his power exploding outwards in a wave so intense, my eyes snapped open at the feeling of danger, and I watched as thick smoke rolled around us – hunting.

"You'll have to get in line. I have first – *Saviour's sins*, I can't hold her any longer she's burning up. Literally burning."

"Why did you bring her here, Rem? You know my power is as unstable right now."

"*Put me down before I burn you.*" I ground out between breaths, my lungs burning with the heat of my own skin. I felt like I was melting, and these two idiots thought now was a good time to argue over who was going to kill Grayson, who hadn't even done anything?

Why did I ever think these men were helpful? I thought as Rem's grip loosened at my threat, and I tumbled to the ground at his feet – the marble flooring so cold against my skin that I sighed in relief.

Nix's power instantly enveloped me, and I felt its cooling caresses as it covered me whole. My flames hummed gently as the earth's powers backed down slightly, clearing the pain enough for me to focus on their words as they continued to bicker above me.

"This shouldn't be happening to her – she hasn't even gone through the Anima Fores."

"Yeah, well, I think we can both agree that she hasn't done anything the way they were meant to be done. You should have anticipated this – you should have warned her."

"I didn't know, and I can't risk her being near."

"Risk my ass." Rem snarled, and Nix's power flared tighter around me as though it were protecting me from an impending fight.

"What on earth are you two talking about?" I panted

out between heaving breaths, breaking up their glaring as both sets of eyes landed on me.

"*The Restituo.*" They both replied at the same time, and my fire flared at the name, causing me to cry out once more.

"That sounds about as good as it feels."

"It's meant to be relaxing. The universe restores the earth's energy and in turn our energy is restored. It makes us more powerful, more in control." Nix offered, and if I could, I would have laughed at him.

If being ripped in half was meant to be 'restoring', I didn't want any part of it.

"I feel none of those things. What I do *feel* is a war inside of me, and I'm about two seconds away from letting it tear me to pieces." I hissed, and curses spit from Nix's mouth at my admission.

In the next moment, he was right in front of me, stopping mere inches away from my curled-up position — anguish furrowing his brow as he tried to think of his next words.

"I can't touch you." He ground out slowly, teeth clenched as though the words were painful for him to speak.

"I don't need you to touch me, I just need you to *make it stop.*" I screamed out as my fire flared against the earth's energy that rolled through me violently.

"Get her to the courtyard." Nix finally ordered, and Rem's arms once again tried to pick me up — but recoiled instantly as my skin made contact with his.

"*Don't touch me.*" I cried, his touch feeling like lava on my skin.

"I don't think I can lift her again; she feels like she's on fire."

"I-I can't…. My powers… I don't want to hurt her." Nix replied, hands tugging at the strands in his hair as though he was warring with himself as much as my power was inside of me.

"You won't."

"You don't know that." He growled towards Rem, glaring at him a moment more, before crouching down to meet my gaze, hands slowly reaching for me. "I'm so sorry, this might hurt." He whispered soothingly, and I braced for the heat that would burn me at his touch.

My flames had never felt like this before, never felt like they were attacking me directly — but as they fought for dominance against the ancient power that was forcing its way into me, the separation between what was me and what was an enemy blurred so fine I was terrified I'd combust into ashes at any second.

Slowly, Nix inched forward, the lines of his mouth tight as if he were too scared to even breathe in my direction. His eyes were swirling whirlpools of mesmerising storms as they moved in time to the power flaring out behind him.

He said his powers were unstable as well.

Pain flared in me just as his arms braced under me, and I screamed loud, writhing on the ground as I felt myself being cleaved in two. The powers had turned to knives, lashing out at one another inside me. I heard Nix curse as I tried to move further away from him, terrified that my powers would no longer stay contained within me — but I felt his hands pull at me a second later, crashing me to his chest, the contact causing a moan to escape me as everything inside me froze.

His touch felt like ice, and I climbed into his embrace without thinking, curling my limbs around him as I tried to touch every part of myself to that icy feeling of bliss. My flames silenced their battle as the earth's energy settled into my bones, thrumming through me as I began to feel its drunken affects once more. Stunned, Nix sat there for a moment more, his head tilted backwards, barely even breathing as he let me wrap myself around him.

"Maybe all she needed was you." Rem murmured after a moment of silence, though my mind was far too focused on that feeling of cool peace, that none of his words registered.

I turned towards him anyway, the sound of his voice echoing through the palace foyer, and immediately laughed at the way his mouth stayed open like a fish. Nix's hand began stroking my hair and I nuzzled into the crook of his neck, finally content as my skin began to cool off.

"Let's get you to the courtyard, little Pure." Nix finally replied, standing in one fluid motion as he lifted me with him. Some part of me realised that I was too close to him, that I shouldn't be clinging onto a man like this, especially one who was not destined to be my husband – but every other part of me that flowed with power pushed that thought away as I nestled my head further into his chest, relishing in the feel of his cool touch on every part of me that made contact with him.

He moved swiftly through the palace, not even stopping to unlock those double doors I had come to know so well, which told me they had locked the entire palace down for the night if we were able to roam so freely.

As it was, I hadn't spied another person, another worker as we walked the halls and usually there were a few scurrying about.

"Why is this place so empty?" I wondered out loud, my mind hazing over as the earth's energy entwined itself through my mind once again.

"It is the Saviour's Feast. You think we'd make

people work?" Nix replied and I felt the vibrations of it along my skin.

"I think the God could make anyone do anything. Especially when he hides away like a coward on the one day we all come together as one." I responded in a whisper, so as to not let the God himself overhear me. I still hadn't figured out exactly where he resided in the palace, and I didn't want to take my chances. Rem's laughter in front of us though told me that my whisper was perhaps not as quiet as I'd intended it to be.

"I'll be sure to let him know your thoughts, little Pure." Nix murmured into my ear, and I withheld the purr that tried to escape me as his power wound itself around us, cooling every part of my skin that was not yet touching Nix.

"You wouldn't dare." I screeched, my voice rising two octaves in a sound that reminded me too much of Imogen's whine.

"Oh, he would." Rem joined in, laughing still as he entered the courtyard. I thought the place beautiful in the daylight, but as I twisted myself in Nix's arms, I gasped at the sight before me.

Light lit up the walls, pale like moonlight as it encased the courtyard in an ethereal glow, making it seem more magical than anything I'd ever seen before.

"They are called solar lanterns. They harness the power of the sun and light up once it has set. The God had them installed years ago when he found them – technically they are a forbidden item. From the old world." Nix explained as his arms tightened on me to stop me from tumbling out of his arms as I twisted around further.

"It's the most beautiful thing I have ever seen in my life." I breathed.

"I thought you might like it."

I more than liked it, I loved it. I couldn't understand why the God didn't spend every second of the day in a place like this, why he let us use it so freely when I would never want to share this place with another living soul.

"Yes, open them. She needs to filter the energy out before it consumes her again." Nix called in response to something Rem had asked while I was taking in the scene before me.

He had already walked to the other side of the clearing, over by the door I'd seen the gardeners walk through. I was about to ask him what he was doing, but the answer came a second later as he pulled on a lever in the wall, and I heard a noise above me.

Looking up, I watched as the glass domed ceiling peeled itself back like a flower blooming in the morning light – opening to the world outside. A breeze wandered down first, cooling me further, followed by that ancient power as it found me again. Though, instead of slamming into me once more, it seemed to dance around us, weaving through me gently as it joined in on the power it had left in me.

"When did you arrive home?" I asked once Nix had finally set me on my feet, and I resisted the urge to climb back up into his cooling embrace – the hand pressing into the small of my back the only thing stopping me.

"A few days ago."

"You didn't call for me." I pouted, knowing that if I hadn't been drunk on the power that flowed through me, I would not have spoken with such a whine in my voice. Nix just laughed at the tone as he led me further into the clearing.

"I am sorry, little Pure, I had things to take care of. Though from what I hear you were too busy courting a certain Commanding Lord to train."

"I was not." I argued and Rem's resounding scoff sounded through the room. "You were watching me! Tell him I was training." I commanded, stamping my foot like a child.

"I know you were training, Rae, I am only teasing you." the way he said it made me think that maybe he was there that night when I pushed myself too hard, maybe I wasn't losing my mind imagining him putting me to bed.

"You weren't losing your mind, little Pure."

"You're reading my thoughts?"

"No, you spoke them aloud for all of us to hear." He chuckled gently, and the power drunk part of me thrummed as it longed to hear the sound again.

"Oh. I hadn't meant to."

"Clearly." Rem drawled as he settled into his regular seat at the table, content to just input his own commentary.

I moved towards him, deciding that sitting looked like a really good idea, now that I wasn't in pain — though as soon as I stepped out of Nix's touch, the earth's power slammed into me like a wall. I cursed and fell to the ground, groaning at the impact as my fire flew through my body — attacking the intruder viciously.

"*What the hell is this?*" I screamed as the power faded from me just as fast as it had come. I craned my head back to see Nix leaning over me, his hand on my shoulder as his power swirled out behind him.

"This isn't meant to be happening."

"Explain. Now." I commanded, my mind sobering just enough to need answers.

"Restituo is a regeneration of our powers, just as the earth regenerates itself each year. It's how the crops regrow themselves each year, how the world keeps turning after everything we have done to it. It affects us all differently, depending on our level of ascension. In most, it is merely a feeling of drunkenness, a happiness akin to drinking too much. In some, it can cause your powers to flare and become slightly unstable, especially tonight when the earth's powers have hit its peak – but it is not meant to be painful. More intoxicating and uncontrollable, but never painful."

"It's why he can't touch anyone. His powers are too unstable to be around others." Rem chimed in once more from his seat.

"Does that mean you are more powerful than the Western Goddess?" I asked, sitting up to face Nix.

"Tris only has one power related to the earth itself. It helps her more to be outside with the people – and by the time the earth reaches its Restituo she is safely back in her home." My fire coiled tighter inside me at the use of nickname Nix had used for the Goddess, but I ignored the feeling – I had more important things to figure out than the history behind the two of them.

"One year he literally stole the air from a room of people. Undeserving scum, yes, but I was also in the room, and I can tell you I did not enjoy it." Rem chided, shivering as though the mere mention of the memory brought back nightmares he'd rather forget. My eyes widened at this, and I looked back at Nix for more – but his eyes had darkened as his powers flared around the room and I knew now was not the time to press him on his past.

"This isn't about me," Nix growled.

"So why is this affecting me so much? I feel like there is a war inside me. Like my fire is pushing out the earth's energy just as much as the earth's energy is trying to stay.

"I want to try something." Nix said suddenly, standing as his hand grabbed onto mine. Refusing to break contact with me as he hauled me to my feet.

"Will it hurt?" I asked, as I watched his mind whirl behind those eyes of his.

"Honestly? Probably. But I think the problem with you is not that you haven't gone through the Anima Fores, I think it is that you have access to another energy source that is not your own – but it has chosen you to harness it regardless."

"What do you want me to do?"

"I want you to accept it." He spoke simply, shrugging as if it really were easy.

"How?"

"That, I am unsure of. No one has ever had to. But it is worth a try if it means you stop hurting." He'd spoken the last part as if he felt my pain too, and perhaps he did with the way he could feel the truth in a person's soul.

Maybe I was hurting him just as much as it was hurting me.

"Okay." I breathed, nodding as I did so in order to convince myself more than Nix that I could do this. Nix hesitated a second longer before unlinking his fingers from mine, and I felt the moment I lost contact with him.

Pain shot through me instantly. Igniting me in white hot fire.

I accept you...

I whispered as that ancient power swelled inside of me. As soon as I gave it permission – it began filling every inch of my being. My mind and soul feeling like it was brimming with excess energy that still wasn't mine.

I am you...

That power hummed in acknowledgment, settling themselves down just as my flames bristled shooting inwards at the takeover, trying to regain control of my limbs, my mind — but they had been locked out by the earth's energy. Content to keep me all to itself. I screamed as I forced myself inside, tearing open a door to my mind for my flames to pass through as pressure built inside my mind.

But I am also fire!

I cried into the doorway as I pushed my flames through. They circled each other around the internal me that had formed in my mind space — my own personal *iter* I suppose, and I threw my arms out wide as I willed them to calm in opposite sides of my mind. They whipped out across me, desperate to destroy one another, throwing me across the room as I was hit with a blast so powerful it was a surprise I wasn't kicked out of my own mind.

My shielding power threw up walls around me, protecting me as the war raged on — and I begged it to stop, the pain building in my skull until all I could see was white hot light. Another scream tore through me as I threw my shield out, a blast of pure energy towards them as I commanded them to submit.

And you cannot take all of me.

Infusing my shield into my words as they rang throughout the void in front of me, I watched the walls tremble at the power my words held. I felt my flames halt in their attack, the earthly power doing the same as they finally recognised who was speaking.

I sucked in a breath, opening my arms once more as I called to them both, commanding them to kneel before me. Slowly, I watched as my reddish flames slithered over to me, trickling in until it lay in a swirling ball beside me. The earth's power took a little longer, flaring out once more before I could wrap my shield around it like a leash, pulling it towards me and I commanded it to bend to my will. It whimpered slightly, not used to having to obey an owner before it wrapped a tendril around my ankle, the mass of power bowing in half as if it were grovelling at my feet.

Now that it was stationary, I could see that it wasn't wind at all, but pure energy, glittery in its translucence, as if it wanted to be every colour it could think of.

"I do not know how this is going to work, but if you both want to be here, you need to work together. Is that clear?" I told the two masses of energy in front of me, and I felt them hum in agreeance. I sucked in a breath as the pain dispersed from me — the air around me cooling slowly as I watched the powers inside of me mix together, testing one another as they found a way to work together permanently.

I did not know how much time I spent inside my mind, watching these two powers merge as my skin cooled to its regular temperature — but I could feel the smile pulling at my lips before I even opened my eyes.

"What?" I asked nervously when my eyes landed on a stunned Nix before me, Rem now standing from his seat as though he couldn't believe what he was seeing. If I were still as power drunk as I had been five minutes before, I might have laughed when Rem's jaw hit the floor for the second time tonight — though his words did nothing but fill me with dread.

"Saviour, it's *her*."

CHAPTER 33

"How much have you had to drink Rem? I've been here the whole time." I tried for humour, uncomfortable as their stares refused to leave my face.

"Rae, your eyes." Nix breathed as he stepped closer, cupping my cheek in his large hand before I could think to step back. His power moved around him, whispers of smoke twirling through his fingers, tickling my cheek as if it too needed to touch me.

"What did I do to them?"

"Come." Was all he said before turning and leading me to a side of the courtyard I'd never been to before, hidden by a row of trees that I'd always assumed covered the back of the room.

Though as we walked through them, the space opened up to a large pond that sparkled under the moonlight floating above, not even the solar lanterns came this far. Nix stopped just in front of the water, nodding towards its clear surface and I moved towards it — needing to know what it was he saw.

Gazing down into the crystal-clear water in front of me, fish unlike any I'd ever seen before, swam lazily through the shrubs, undisturbed by our sudden appearance. They gleamed shades of gold and orange as their scales moved around them, and I almost lost myself in the beauty of their movements. Shaking my head slightly, I focused my eyes, watching slowly as my reflection ebbed and flowed along the water's edge – and then leapt back with a yelp when I finally saw what they'd been looking at.

My eyes.

They *were* different. They were....

"Like yours." I gasped, spinning towards Nix as if he might be able to confirm it. His eyes swirled faster at my words – his power slithering closer.

"So much more beautiful than mine." He replied, and a blush spread up my neck at his words. My eyes, which were once a dull, lifeless, Sandoval blue – were now a glittering, iridescent, swirling storm. So pale in colour that they would be clear if not for the undercurrent of blue that swam through them. The only sign now that I'd come from the Sandoval line.

I felt my powers move at the panic that swelled in me, along with the thought that I would not be able to hide this anymore.

That everyone would see that I was not normal.

I felt both my newly submitted powers climb into my veins, strengthening me, encouraging me. Whatever I had to face now, this power would be here to help guide me. Testing, I moved them through me like I'd been taught, focusing on pulling them down my arm to rest in a ball in my palm. Raising a hand, I turned it over as flames danced along my fingertips, pooling until it became the ball I'd called for.

The only difference? They were now that magnificent rainbow blue.

"I knew you could do it." Nix whispered as he closed the distance once more, reaching out a hand towards my flames. I watched in fascination as his own flames erupted on his skin, drenching his hand in red hot fire as they moved to fall from his index finger, dripping into my own. The powers swirled together, red mixing into my blue as they became one.

My eyes shot back up to Nix, wanting him to explain this to me, but his were fixed on the way our powers mixed together, on the way they cohabitated in my hand – as if they were always meant to be one. My heart began to pound in my chest.

"What do you see?" I blurted into the silence that had stretched out between us. I'd noted a while ago that Rem hadn't followed us over to the pond, and a part of me was grateful that he wasn't here to witness such an intimate moment between us.

"What do you mean?" His head cocked to the side as his eyes slowly moved up to meet mine, lingering longer than they should as they travelled upwards.

"I mean, what do you see in me?"

"More than you let me. I see the girl who fought for years to be what her family told her she was. The girl who was willing to risk her life to speak her truth in the face of the Sacred Servants, because that was more important than any status in society. And then when that failed, I saw her commit to the role, to the powers she never asked for – all to save her family from the shame of yet another child who defected for *feeling*. Even if it meant shattering your soul to achieve it. I see you fight every day to become the thing you cursed, I see everything you feel, and every little ounce you let through to the surface." My breathing stopped as he spoke, as he saw straight to my soul. I shouldn't have asked him. I should have known he'd seen too much of me.

Of course he had.

But he wasn't done, as he moved his hand to my waist pulling me against him, and his eyes held mine as he confessed his own soul. "If I were a better man, I would refrain from telling you that every truth you let slip is more intoxicating than the last to me, that your soul has become the air I need — and I would do anything, give anything to free you from the constraints you struggle against. But I have been told that I am not a better man, so I will not lie to you if you ask me for the truth."

I stood there stunned, feeling his truth thrum through me as though I were the one who had the ability to hear the truth in a person's soul. Or maybe it was simply because I was pressed up against him that I was able to feel his own power seeping into me, overpowering my own senses.

Without thinking I leapt, slamming my lips up onto Nix's as my arms wrapped around his neck, holding me closer to him. He froze as we collided, motionless as I pressed further into him — uncertain in my move, or perhaps he was giving me time to rethink my actions, but when I didn't pull away from him, he melted. Moving in such fluid grace, his lips moulded against mine, hungry, commanding, coaxing, as a growl of approval rumbled through him. His arms circled my waist completely, crushing me to him, and I felt as though I was finally sinking into his depths — breathing him in, as though he were the air I needed to breathe, just like he'd confessed to me. My fire purred as his smoked enveloped us, encasing us in our own little world where nothing else mattered, and as his tongue swiped along the seam of my lips, begging me to open, I gave in completely. I whimpered at the way his tongue commanded mine to give in and I sighed as my mind calmed, knowing that this was a battle I was not willing to fight if it felt this good – my hands weaving up into the nape of his hair as I held on tighter.

But he had other plans.

Just as fast as I'd thrown myself at him, he pulled away, broken from my spell. Chest heaving in time to mine as we stared into each other's eyes, his powers moved in time to the swirling I saw as I drowned in the depths of them. For a second, I swore I was staring straight into his soul. His beautiful, powerful soul – and then I watched him close off from me, slowing in their movements as his power dispersed, opening us up to the world again.

"I'm sorry, I didn't mean for that to happen." I rushed out, heat climbing higher up my face, my voice hoarse as I untangled myself from him, dropping to the ground.

I can't believe I jumped him. Shared my first kiss with him. Though I couldn't say I regretted it.

"Don't ever apologise for that. I won't." He spoke breathlessly, as though he was still just as affected as I was from the kiss.

"Thank you for helping me." I tried again.

"Of course."

"I, uh, should go. Grayson will be wondering where I went." Guilt swam up with the mention of his name and I watched Nix's eyes darken in response.

"Be careful around him. He is not the man he appears to be."

"None of us are who we appear to be, Nix. But I must bind myself to someone, and he seems to be the only one worth the effort of trying."

"Just… don't let him in. Don't show him who you really are."

A laugh escaped me humourlessly. "Bit late for that isn't it? If he is my husband, I should not keep anything from him." I motioned to my new eyes as I said this, knowing they would emphasise why I couldn't hide this from anyone anymore.

"I know. I am not telling you to, I –"

"You encourage me to be truthful, but now you want me to lie?"

"Yes." His voice dropped to a growl, as though he disagreed with the word himself.

"Why?"

"I cannot tell you."

"Of course not." I scoffed. Anger rising in me, sweeping away any feeling I might have had towards him a moment ago. My voice raising to match the heat flooding through me as I pressed on. "Do not worry, I will not go back on my word to the Sacred Servants. Although if I cannot share anything with anyone, I may as well be bound to you. At least then I would not have to lie to my husband every day for the rest of my life."

"I do not want a contract with you, Raewyn." He snarled, as though even the thought repelled him, his power swirling around him as the air filled with anger. His and now mine.

"Oh." Was all that came out of me as I diverted my gaze from his – my power coiling tighter at the feel of rejection that rose in me.

The earth's energy pooled around me in defence, creating a barrier as it spurred the new energy inside of me back to life – but Nix's power dove inside before it could close me in, wrapping arms of smoke around me as he stalked closer, gripping my chin in his hand so I couldn't avoid his intense stare any longer.

"I do not want a contract because I need so much more from you than your obedience to society. Though I would gladly take more disobedience, if it always felt like that." His words were so raw, so honest that my mind blanked, taking me back to that first night when he asked me if I wished to choose with my heart.

My heart hammered in my chest as my powers swarmed to it, protecting the organ like it might protect me from my own traitorous memories.

"Th-That is not something…. I don't – I can't." I stuttered in reply to all his requests, spoken and unspoken as I ripped myself from his grip. Breaking the connection.

His stare was too much, those words were too much, the touch too much for me. Though as I moved away, I heard his sigh echo throughout the courtyard as he watched me close myself off once more.

As if he knew he'd pushed me too far.

"I know. That is why I haven't asked."

CHAPTER 34

The carriage had been waiting for me outside of the palace as I left, Rem waiting at the helm to drive me back as all the men were busy partying in the square. Luckily, he had nothing to say once he took in my appearance and so the ride remained silent as I delved into my own thoughts.

What I was not expecting though was for Grayson to be pacing the foyer of my home when I returned. It was almost sunrise – the festivities still going strong in the square on my way past. His head whipped towards me as the sound of the door echoed throughout the empty house and he closed the space between us in an instant.

"How do you know Rem?" He demanded, eyes wild as he stepped far too close for comfort, boxing me in. My newly merged powers slipped through me in warning that they would not stand for this man to speak to me this way, though I held them back with a simple command.

"He was ordered to watch over me, since I am the Pure of the Citadel. Apparently, the role comes with unseen dangers." I responded simply, a statement that was not a complete lie.

"Why wasn't I aware of this?"

"I wasn't aware you needed to know."

"Of course, I do, Raewyn. If I am to be your husband, I need to know the people you keep company with. If I had of known you spent your time with the likes of him, I would not have bothered."

"Not even my parents know. It is not something I announce to the world."

"Clearly. It would not look good for the Pure of the Citadel to have a bastard as a lover. I am such a fool to think that you actually cared for me." He scoffed, and I baulked at the accusation, disbelief coursing through me as I wondered how the night had gone from one of the best in my life, to one of the most infuriating.

"Lover? What are you talking about? He is my guard. Or was. The assignment is over now – there has never been anything between Rem and I. Saviours, I barely even spoke to the guy!" I screamed at him as my anger dove through me.

"But his markings…. I thought…"

I laughed at him, cutting of whatever explanation he thought I needed. "Wrong. You thought wrong. And clearly think as little of me as the rest of the people in society if you think I would jump the first man who came near me."

"But you called his name, *his!* What else was I to think?"

"I was in *pain* Commanding Lord Westward. Or perhaps your judgement has made you forget the fact that I was bent over in the middle of the square with pain I did not understand. Rem was helping me."

I watched him flinch as I reverted back to his title, all progress he had made with me ruined by his accusations. I was huffing with anger now, shaking with the effort it took to keep my powers from erupting from me – from attacking him, that at this very moment, I did not care what he thought. "Now, if we are done here, it has been a long and trying night and I would like to go to bed." I moved my way past him, but he gripped my arm, spinning me so I was pressed up against him as he brought his other hand up to cup my face, the movement so similar to Nix's that my breathing faltered.

"I apologise. I was overcome with jealousy. Something I must admit I have not experienced before and did not manage well. Of course, you are Pure. You are the Pure of the Citadel after all. I should have known you would experience the restituo as my aunt does every year – and your eyes. Saviour, they are mesmerising. It is like stars floating in a sea of beauty. I have never seen anything like them." His words of flattery moved straight over me, my anger still swirling through me, refusing to listen to a word he was saying.

"I would like to make it up to you." he tried when I did not respond to him, my eyes choosing to say everything I was feeling with one look. I felt his thumb brush gently against my lip, a move no doubt meant to placate an angry woman – it took all I had not to wrench my jaw from his hand at the thought that he still considered me as easily charmed.

"I do not need your apology. I need your trust. If I do not have that then we have nothing."

"Of course. And you have it, of course you do. There is just bad blood between my cousin and I – I will not bore you with the details. I simply do not like the thought of him being around you. He is not good."

"What did he do?" I could not help but ask. I had

seen nothing in Rem to indicate he was a bad person, and Nix trusted him with watching me so that had to count for something.

"Nothing you need to concern yourself with, Darling, now go on to bed. I have some things to take care of, but I will see you when I can."

Well, that answered nothing. I thought as I turned and strode up the stairs before he could call me back down.

Exhaustion seeped into me the higher I climbed, and I only just made it to my bed before collapsing in a heap on top of it, not even bothering to remove my shoes before I was succumbed to sleep.

I awoke the next morning with a pounding head, and a stiffness in my bones that told me I had overdone things last night. I hoped Nix was right in saying that the Restituo was normally calming and intoxicating – because I never wanted to experience it again if I had to go through all that pain.

But as I moved through my morning routine – Analise having not yet come to rouse me like she normally did, I felt different. Stronger. More in control than I ever had as the two powers that now resided in me hummed in contentment.

I watched my reflection as I brushed my hair, my new eyes swirling white masses of glittering starlight and I was entranced by the way they moved so fluidly. The difference in how I looked now that my eyes had changed startled me. I could see a glow on my skin that normally looked too pale, the humming in my veins strengthening my spine so that I sat a little taller than I did before.

I looked like a different person.

A woman born of grace and power – someone I never was and never aspired to be.

Finished with my preparations, I took a deep breath and moved towards the door, knowing that I would not be able to stay in my room and hide from my family forever. Grayson may have been too caught up in his anger to notice the differences in me last night, but my parents would not be so blind. Regardless, I took my time on my way to the dining room where breakfast was already being served and noted the way my body moved now. I felt lighter, more connected as I all but glided down the staircase. I was not opposed to the changes – I knew they meant that my powers had fully merged inside of me.

This feeling would take some getting used to though.

My mother was the first to look up at me as I entered the room, my father engrossed in his paperwork as usual – though her yelp of surprise alerted him a second later.

"What happened to your eyes?" She screeched, her voice rising two octaves as her hands came up to cover her mouth in shock.

"Perks of being a Pure?" I tried, smiling slightly as I shrugged, hoping if I did not make a big deal out of it that neither would they.

I was mistaken.

"How on earth does that even happen?" My father queried as he leaned forward in his seat, inspecting my eyes as if they were an alchemic discovery.

"I am not sure. It began during the Saviour's Feast last night."

"They move." He murmured, his fingers twitching as though he were trying not to reach out and touch my eyes. My powers stirred inside at his acknowledgment, and I knew my eyes were swirling faster at its response as I watched my fathers widen in shock.

"You look just like a God."

"But I am not."

"Y-yes, of course." My father stumbled, coughing loudly as though he could rid his throat of the accusation that could be seen as disrespectful in the eyes of society. Fluffing his papers about on the table, he tried again. "I suppose it has been a while since the Paradise has had a Pure who is not immediately made God – so it is hard to know what changes your Purity will bring you, and which are reserved solely for the Gods. They suit you though dearest." My father reasoned and I smiled at the compliment. I would not admit it to myself in the vanity, but I thought they suited me too.

"Is that why you left Lord Westward alone and wondering where you were all night?" My mother questioned and I turned my attention back to her as I took my seat at the table between them. Of course, she would not pass up an opportunity to scold me for my lack of manners.

"A mistake I will not make again, I assure you." I appeased her, just as Analise entered to bring me my breakfast – and promptly dropped it on the floor in shock as I smiled my greeting to her.

"For Saviour's sake, Analise, have you never seen a Pure before?" My mother immediately turned her scolding look on the head of house as more maids rushed to help clean up the mess. Clicking her tongue at them, my mother dismissed them – each of them stumbling to a stop as they noticed my eyes.

"Be sure you apologise to Lord Westward, Sweetheart. We do not want him thinking I raised a brute."

She stated as she returned to her breakfast, my father nodding alongside her as he looked down at his papers once more.

Maybe it was not as big of an adjustment as I thought.

CHAPTER 35

Grayson had not come to see me since the night of the Saviour's Feast almost two weeks ago, and I could not help but embrace the doubt that had creeped inside me at our last encounter. I was still unhappy with the accusations he threw at me. My parents however could not stop singing his praises whenever I was around them long enough – begging me for an answer on whether I found him a suitable husband or not.

Still, I gave them nothing.

I'd also taken to avoiding them more and more as their constant stares towards my newly acquired eyes began to grate on my nerves – though they had not asked more details on what had happened to make them change, and I had not offered the information.

I was not sure how to explain it anyway.

I filled my days with training as Nix once again resumed his place in my morning routines. We had silently agreed to never speak about the moment that occurred between us, a lapse in judgement and excess energy heightening our senses. That is all it was, all it could ever be.

I was to bind myself another man after all. One who did want a contract with me, though I could not help the thoughts that floated through me when he was near — thoughts about the way his lips felt against mine, how the hard planes of his body lined up perfectly to mine, holding me to him as if I would disappear.

And his words — his words still echoed throughout my mind, making my heart race every time I failed to *not* think about them.

"Why didn't you tell me Grayson was your cousin?" I called to Rem as he entered the courtyard one morning. I had not seen him since he returned me home from the palace the other night, and I was beginning to miss his company — and I needed answers.

"It is not something I chose, Rae. If I had it my way, he would not be breathing." I sucked in a breath at the venom in his words, knowing that only one person had the power to stop Rem from whatever it was he had planned for Grayson Westward.

"Rem's mother is Goddess Patricia." Nix explained and my eyes almost popped out of my mind in shock.

"*You* are the son of a God?" Maybe lineage had nothing to do with inclinations to sin. If his mother were a Pure, and now a God — I would have thought the sins lining his arms would be fewer.

"Such shock, Pure Sandoval. One would think you are judging me." Rem mocked and I could not help the blush that heated my skin. He was not wrong. "I've told you before, things are not always as they seem."

"Rem's father was not the man who eventually bound himself to Tris. Before the contract was finalised though, she attempted to overrule the Binding Ceremony, and conceived Rem as proof that her choice was not the Lord that her family wished her to bind her eternally long life to." Nix added as he motioned for me to continue moving my now blue flames through me towards each hand.

"Except the Lord had more than enough influence in the West to overrule a Pure's command. Though he was not happy to have a tainted wife – he craved her power. So, he kept her bastard-born son and tried to dispose of me when dear old mother Goddess wasn't watching – but I am not so easily put down."

"And what of him now?" I asked without thinking – it was not common knowledge that the Goddess Patricia has a husband and my own curiosity beat out any form of politeness my mother might have taught me.

"I killed him." Nix answered simply, his eyes boring into mine as he watched for my reaction, and I had to remind myself that he was a lethal weapon, that his powers were seen as terrifying to those who were without them – something I kept forgetting in his presence. Regardless, I thought none of those things.

Instead, my mind produced one word: *Good.*

I let the word was over me, as I felt the truth of it in my soul. I had no doubt that Nix was fearsome and powerful, and perhaps rivalled a God with his honed skills – but I would be lying if I said I didn't think this Lord deserved what he got in the end. The act of murder is a sin, after all.

Nix watched me closely as I thought of all this, a smile playing on his lips as though he were reading my mind – and I made a mental note to ask him if that is something God's could do.

"My mother's family never accepted me, and

ignorance runs in our lineage so it's only natural that Grayson dislikes me for the sins of our fathers alone – but since Nix took me into his personal keep, they cannot touch me." Rem finished off, bringing my mind back to the present conversation at the mention of my absent suitor.

"Have you spoken to him since he became Commanding Lord?"

"I make it my mission to stay away from the West." Was all Rem said in response and I refrained from telling him that I had met his mother, that Grayson felt just as strongly against him too – but I did not think any of those would be welcomed now.

"He thought we were sleeping together." I threw in instead, and Rem's bark sounded through the courtyard, so loud that it was impossible not to join in on the absurdity of those words.

"He would."

"I think it may have ruined my chance to have a contract him." I added between breaths, and this caused Rem to laugh even harder.

"Well, you wouldn't be the first woman he has had after me, arrogant prick still thinks he is better than me." I snorted in response, though before I could throw my sarcastic response back at Rem, Nix's voice injected itself into the space between us, cutting our banter off immediately.

"I want you to make that weapon you told me about."

Rem winked at me as I scowled at the tone, but it was Nix's lethal stare at Rem that shut us both up completely.

Someone is in a grump today. I thought as I turned to the man with the deep scowl set on his face.

"It was less a weapon and more a butter knife. A move that exhausted my energy might I add." I said, bringing his attention back to me and away from his friend who was still silently laughing, though I felt as if it was for an entirely different reason now.

"Yes, but that was before the Restituo. Have you tried since then?" He asked as one eyebrow arched in question. I watched his eyes darken slightly, swirling faster as if the memory of what we had done after I merged my powers was playing on a loop behind his eyes.

My checks flushed as it did behind mine.

"No." I finally admitted, squaring my feet as I anticipated his next words.

"Go ahead, try it." I was already moving my energy through me as he said this, revelling in the way they moved so smoothly together now that they had accepted me as their master. Sliding down my arm, I imagined a knife, the sharp planes of folded steel – the hilt just big enough to fit snug in my palm. I pictured one of the small throwing knives my father kept as decoration in his home office – detailing the slight curve of the cross-guard as I flattened my palm out in front of me. I felt the energy inside the courtyard swirl around me in response to its kin that was now linked with my fire – as if I now had a permanent tether to that ancient alchemy. I felt it brush over me, encouragingly, begging me to harness it too.

I did not dare take any of it – I needed to learn to control my own portion flawlessly before I took on more of the earth's wild power – but it comforted me that I had something surrounding me that would help if I ever did lose control.

Moments passed as my power flowed through me, pooling in my palm before it shaped itself into the knife I had been imagining. It looked just like the ones my father kept, albeit made entirely of blue shimmering flames. I grinned at the ease of which I had been able to conjure it, the lack of effort it took to control the powers – and for the first time in my life I felt as though I was completely in control, and it felt good.

"Raewyn, could I speak with you a moment?" My father called as I returned home from the palace. Once again, I had been heading towards the kitchen, starving from having missed breakfast to get extra training in.

I really needed to begin demanding Nix fed me if we were to continue these sessions.

"Of course, Father."

"I have just been to see Lord Westward, and I have news." He began as I took my seat on the other side of his desk, and my heart froze at his words. Had Grayson finally pulled his name from the list of my suitors?

"Father, I –" I began, but he continued speaking before I could get the words out.

"Your Binding contract has been finalised. You will be bound to the Commanding Lord of the Western Paradise. Congratulations Dear, this is a proud moment for the entire family."

What? When did this happen?

"But I had not given you my recommendation yet. I had not decided."

"And I told you it would not be the end decision. Besides, I ascertained that you continuing to see him was sign enough. Clearly you are fond of the man, and that is all I needed to know before I made my decision."

"So, I have no say in the matter?" I threw back, but I already knew the answer. Of course, I had no say in the matter – why would I think that my father would ever have given me a say beyond who was nicest to me?

"Had you said something, I may have chosen different. Though because I know how you feel about being bound to anyone, I assumed this stall was a tactic of yours to remain free for as long as you could – something I might add may have worked for a while more had Lord Westward not pressed the issue."

He did what?

"He pressed the contract with me?"

"Oh yes, he was quite persistent. He has been hounding me all week to decide, and I could not hold off any longer. He is quite taken by you dearest, and I think he will make you incredibly happy." My father smiled brightly, as if he had done something brilliant in securing me a husband.

Grayson had not called for me like he told me he would, yet he had been speaking to my father all week about me. I was not sure if I should be flattered or offended that he had gone to such lengths to secure me behind my back. Though I suppose in matters of society, this was considered normal procedure – he did not need to come to me with a proposal before seeking out my father.

He no longer needed my permission.

He had my contract and now I would be his wife.

"He is anxious to return to the Western Paradise, there is much that needs to be done there. Though he was adamant on one point before you departed...." My father continued as if my mind were not raging inside at the injustice of it all.

"And what point would that be?"

"He would like you to have the Binding Ceremony before you leave. He was insistent that he could not wait any longer for you." My father's voice dropped as he said this, knowing I how I would feel at the fast turn of events. *I was to be bound with Grayson before we departed…*

My powers circled through me, waiting for the command to be set free and I pushed them down with a gentle tug. This was not something I could escape. I knew this, though my powers would try if I willed it.

"When do I leave?" I asked when I felt like I could keep my voice steady.

"The end of the week."

"That is in *four days* father. I cannot get married in four days' time."

"And why ever not?"

"Nothing is ready!" *I am not ready!* I screamed internally.

"Oh hush, your mother has been planning your Binding Ceremony since before your trials. She has already started preparations. Besides, he thought it kinder on you to keep this a minimal affair, family only. Seems your soon-to-be husband already knows you well." *Or he needs a way to keep people out.* I thought instantly as I thought of his cousin. Clearly, he was threatened enough to be worried about who might attend the Binding Ceremony if it were made a public affair.

"Is this not something the nobility would want to celebrate publicly?" I tried, pulling at the string that held my family by their boots. They would never want to disappoint society by withholding such a prestigious event such as the Binding Ceremony for the Pure of the Citadel. But as I watched my father's shoulders move upwards in a shrug, I knew I had not pulled hard enough.

"Since when have you ever thought about what the nobility wants, Raewyn? This will be good for you! You will be able to work under the Goddess herself, create a home for you and your husband, perhaps provide me with a few grandchildren before I become too old to enjoy them…" he rattled on, but I had stopped listening.

I could not believe this was happening. I was going to be married by week's end. My flames flickered slightly, pushing against the command I gave them, and I knew I could not hold them at bay much longer with the amount of energy I had expended in training today.

I needed air.

I needed my meadow.

I needed out.

CHAPTER 36

I am beginning to think you are avoiding me little Pure.
You have until sundown,
or I will be forced to come looking for you.
N.

I had been avoiding him — but I would not tell him that.

It had been two days since I had gone to training.

Two days since I had been told I was contracted to bind myself to Grayson before I left the Citadel — and I did not have time to process any of it. My father had let me leave his office and have my moment alone, but on my return my mother had begun to hound me with Binding Ceremony details and plans that I needed to finalise.

I did not have time for Nix's incessant need for me to feel and speak my feelings. I was firmly set on ignoring them — my own power reminding me that constantly, as I felt them roaming through me restlessly every moment of the day.

Father was right about one thing though – my mother had been planning this since long before I had a contract. Luckily, it required me to do extraordinarily little as she took over all the decorating and catering details, running through the house at all hours of the day as she commanded the maids, bending them to her will as if she had powers of her own.

I had tried to stay clear of her line of vision, though I had been seen a few times as I snuck back from the kitchen, or the garden – and consequently been cornered into making decisions that I had no concern over. It may be my Binding Ceremony, but I was just as uninterested and clueless as I was about any other function. The one thing I did put my foot down on though was my ceremonial gown. I would not rope some poor, stressed-out silk merchant into this event with only four days until the deadline. I would wear the gown my mother had made for her Ceremony, and we would alter it to my slimmer frame.

It seemed to please her as tears gathered in her eyes at the thought of her Pure daughter declaring the dress good enough for her to wear. Really it was my way of showing them that I did not care too much for any of this, especially when the groom-to-be still had not come to visit me. All pretences of affection and attention seemingly gone now that he had gotten what he wanted from me.

A binding to the first Pure of the Citadel, a lineage that would surely rival anyone around him – even his aunt's, as we both knew her son was less than ideal in the eyes of the world we lived in.

"I bring good news." My father announced as he walked into the dining room.

"The Binding Ceremony has been postponed?" I mused as my eyes tracked him across the room. My father scoffed and gave me a look as if to say, *do not be ridiculous.*

"Sweetheart, what is it you have against the Commanding Lord Westward? You have been nothing but sarcastic since he proposed this Binding Ceremony. Unless something has happened that we need to know about, this attitude of yours is not becoming of a Lady, let alone a Pure." My mother scolded. She was right, I had nothing against Grayson himself.

The times we had spent together had proved that I could let my guard down a little around him, that I could one day be as close as I could with someone. But the demand that we have our ceremony before the end of the week, alongside the crazed look he had given me on my return from the Saviour's Feast had halted any progress we were making, and I no longer knew how to feel about him, other than that he was forcing me into something I never wanted – even after he told me he would wait for me.

"The Sacred Servants have returned." My father's words broke through my thoughts and my fork dropped to the table in a clang.

They had returned from their search into why I was the way that I was.

They must have found something.

"Oh, how wonderful! I was beginning to think we were going to have to get the Western Paradises Sacred Servants over. The Saviour must be watching over this binding. Isn't that a sign of good things, Raewyn dear?"

"Saviour's grace indeed." I mumbled as I felt my powers move in anticipation to learning what answers they had found. I had to resist the urge to march over there this instant and demand it from them, but I knew they would call for me when they were ready.

My parents proceeded to talk about the final

preparations of the Binding Ceremony now that the Sacred Servants would most definitely be Binding my life to another under the power of the Gods and the Saviour. I slipped out once I was done with breakfast, knowing that I was not really needed for this.

It may be my Ceremony but at this point all I had to do was turn up.

With nothing planned for the reast of the day, and determined to continue ignoring Nix, despite the note he left by my bed this morning, I walked out the front door, determined to get as much time as I could in my meadow before I had to leave it.

Though that plan was gone as soon as I walked out the door.

"This looks oddly familiar." I drawled as once again Rem was waiting by the tree he seemed to like leaning against.

"Morning Rae, I am here to escort you to the palace."

"And here I thought I had until sundown before you came looking for me." I joked and Rem quirked his eyebrow in question. I just shook my head at him, he must not have read the note Nix had him deliver. He motioned for the black carriage waiting for us and I moved towards it, knowing that I would not be seeing my meadow today.

"Have you heard the news?" He asked once we were firmly seated inside.

"About the Servants coming back in time for my Binding Ceremony? Yes, I had heard."

"Binding Ceremony?" Rem repeated, confusion furrowing his brow.

"Surely it is all over the Citadel by now. I am to bind myself to your cousin in two days' time. He was adamant it be done before we left the Citadel."

"Well, this changes things." Rem mumbled, so low that I knew he had not meant it for me, but I strained to hear him over the rumbling of the carriage as it passed over the cobblestoned road of the village.

"What does it change?" I asked, gulping at the look of unease that passed over his face.

"Nothing." He said quickly and I narrowed my eyes at the way he brushed it off.

"I know I will not be able to train with my leaving for the West, but I am sure we will be back often. Grayson seems to do a lot of business in the Citadel."

"Oh, quite the opposite. Grayson has never spent this much time in the Citadel, if any. Often if the West has business, he sends an emissary on his behalf, or more often than not, life your brother, they go to him. He only came to the Citadel for you, Rae."

Oh. That fuzzy feeling grew inside the pit of my stomach once more at his words and I could not help but feel special knowing that the Commanding Lord of the Western Paradise would spend all this time here for me.

"But no, that is not why I came for you. The Sacred Servants found something on their travels."

"Do you know what it is?" I asked, impatient to know my fate. Rem scoffed a laugh as the carriage began slowing, we were here.

"They would never tell me if their lives depended on it." With that he climbed out, holding his arm up to assist me, and I wondered once more what Rem had done to deserve such scorn from everyone around him.

We climbed the stairs of the palace, comfort sinking into me as it always did as we entered its halls. This place had become a second sanctuary for me, a place where I was able to be myself in front of people I would have never expected to befriend, and I would miss it when I was gone. We made our way down the corridors I had come to learn off by heart, although as we passed by the double doors that always stayed locked when we were not using it, I scrunched my nose up in confusion. I had never been this far before.

Climbing up a set of stairs in a corner I had never seen, we began ascending to the second floor. And then the third. Nerves twisted in my gut, worried that the higher we went, the closer we would get to the God who presided in these halls. Tales of his terror and power flitting through my mind as we walked further in.

He was just a man, just a man who had been around for hundreds of years.

"Where are you taking me?" I asked when I could not handle it anymore.

"To the Servants, don't worry they are just ahead in the office."

I nodded, checking that my powers were safely nestled inside that space of my mind that stayed open now, my emotions flitting around like they were taunting my powers to come and get them. Breathing deep, I sent a command in that they were not to move, not to react, no matter what happened – and I felt them stir slightly as they heard me.

Rounding another bend in the hall, the walls turning from its pristine blandness to a deep mahogany colour as a sense of seriousness encased the air, we came upon one last set of double doors. Pushing them open, Rem stepped inside without hesitating. I on the other hand halted at the door.

The office was like any other: deep wooden desk, walls lined with books and trinkets that every office seemed to possess – though one wall was cleared entirely for a window that stretched as high as the ceiling, making the room feel as though it was carved into the sky. But that still was not what froze me in place.

No, what stopped me was the man sitting behind the desk, poised as if he commanded the entire room without effort, his tunic now buttoned completely, sleeves rolled down in a move that made him look far more serious than I had ever seen him.

The sight was more damning than if he had worn his Lords jacket, especially accompanied by his power sweeping through the room as if it were daring someone to challenge him.

"Good morning, Raewyn." He spoke as his eyes locked onto mine, my powers humming in time with his as they moved closer to me — and I whispered my command again, worried they would not obey me now.

"What are you doing here, Nix? I thought I was meeting the Sacred Servants?"

"They will be here momentarily. I hear that a congratulations are in order though. No wonder you have not been training, you have a Binding Ceremony to plan."

Rem's eyes widened in surprise at Nix's words, and that knot of nerves in my stomach twisted painfully at the disjointed sound of his voice.

I had never seen Nix so cold, so emotionless.

I did not like it.

"The contract was signed before I knew of its stipulations." I admitted, injecting as much truth in those words as I could. As if that could make it any better.

"Of course, you are but a Lady in society. One must do as we are expected." His words were simple, but I could not help but feel the dig in them. The anger swelling in me in response also did not appreciate them.

"If I am here to be judged, I would like to leave. I still have much to plan before I leave the Citadel with my almost-husband." At this his eyes darkened, swirling faster as his powers became visible smoke.

There, that got a rise out of him.

Rem cleared his throat, amusement clear as he drew our attention off one another; "As much as I would love to watch this play out, the Sacred Servants will be here momentarily. Perhaps we could save this until they disclose what they have found?" He offered, dispelling the anger flowing through the room instantly.

Yes, I was here for a reason.

As if they were waiting for their moment to enter, three shadows appeared at my back and I stepped aside, moving closer to Rem. The Servants were here. They looked as they always did beige hooded cloaks flowing to the ground, covering every inch of them as if they were not to be looked upon. They glided into the middle of the room, ignoring me completely as they stood before Nix and bowed low.

His head nodded in recognition, though his eyes never left mine.

"We apologise for taking so long." The first one spoke in his monosyllable tone.

"We have found something most interesting in our travels."

"And we think we now know the reason for Miss Sandoval's early manifestations." The third finished.

It is Pure Sandoval. I thought sarcastically, but since none of them had acknowledged me yet, I did not think it would benefit me in any way to remind them.

"Go on." Nix commanded, and they obeyed.

"There is a prophecy."

"It is very old."

"We had to go back to the beginning of Paradise to find it. Back to the original landing of the Saviour."

"We almost came back with nothing."

"Will *one* of you just speak, this is tiresome." Rem piped up and three cloaked heads turned in unison at the sound of his voice. I swore I heard a hiss from the third one — the same one that I assumed did not like me. Although he made no move to indicate it was him.

"*You cannot be here.*" The first one voiced, extending a finger towards Rem who now stood slightly in front of me as if he were protecting me from these Servants.

"You do not belong."

"You —"

"*Enough.*" Nix's voice boomed through the office and their heads whipped back immediately, bowing slightly in submission as they did so. "He stays and you will not waste any more of my time." As if to emphasise his threat, his powers circled them, becoming more corporeal as it did so. I shrunk back slightly, feeling the deadliness of his power thrumming through me.

His eyes flicked back to me at my move.

"We are sorry, Your Highness."

"As you command, Your Highness."

"Forgive us, Your Highness." They all spoke at once, and my nose crinkled at the way they addressed him - so formal, almost as if...

"*Speak.*" He ground out once more, dislodging my thoughts as I took in his tone — harsh, demanding, as though it was taking everything in him to control himself.

"The Prophecy states that an individual will emerge, the perfect match to the Saviour himself. They will wield powers no one has seen since the beginning of time. This person shall destroy the world as we know it and rebuild one where Gods and men are no more. In this new world, the Saviour shall emerge, and true freedom shall be achieved." They spoke as one, their eerie voices echoing through the room and chills crawled up my skin.

They could not be talking about me.

I was not... I... no.

"So, it's true, she is the prophecy." Nix stated as his eyes once again watched me, standing behind Rem, trying not to freak out as my mind spiralled downwards.

Wait...He knew?

"It seems so."

"She could be a blessing from the Saviour."

"Or she is a warning."

"And will be the downfall of us all."

I am the downfall of us all. My mind repeated as I spiralled further.

"But you don't know that." Nix demanded, his tone dropping lower as his powers flared towards me, assessing me. My lungs constricted as I struggled to draw in a breath.

"No, we do not."

"This is ridiculous, you cannot seriously be thinking that Rae, *this Rae*, will be the downfall of us all." Rem scoffed and my mind clung to his last words.

Downfall of us all, downfall of us all.

"The prophecy was clear, Your Highness."

"*God and men will be no more.*" The second Servant recited once more. "We must protect you."

"As God, you —"

"What?" My voice rang through the room, cutting the third Sacred Servant off, and I felt his eyes narrow in my direction even if I could not see them behind his hood.

"Pure Sandoval, we do not mean to offend you, but

the scrolls —"

"I don't care about that right now." I spat, cutting him off once more. I was doing myself no favours when it came to the third Servant, but I was past worrying about him now.

"When were you going to tell me?" I demanded, my eyes narrowing in on Nix as I watched his already cold features harden to stone — grey eyes swirling like storm clouds as they whipped towards the Sacred Servants.

But he made no move to answer me.

"How long have you known what I was?" I tried instead, my voice rising to shouting level as my powers thrashed through me, demanding to be heard, to be answered — the Sacred Servants whipped around, facing me fully as they addressed me in a hiss at the tone in my voice.

"Watch how you address the God of the Citadel little one..."

"You are speaking to God Phoenix Ansaldo. Last Original God and God of the Citadel."

"And you are not above being reprimanded for disrespecting a God."

So, it was true...he was...

No, *no, no, no.*

All his words slammed into me at once; every moment we had spent together, every second since I had met him. He had been able to enter the *iter* in my trials, been in the palace at the *exact* moment I needed him — the place the God himself lived. He knew so much about the ascension process because he had gone through the Anima Fores himself.... How did I not see this sooner? I had been so blind to my own problems, my own struggles with this new power inside of me, that I let myself believe that he was just another Pure — one no one had ever heard of or seen before.

Everything suddenly made sense, every piece clicking together as though the answer was there all along, waiting for me to glance at it.

Nix was the God of the Citadel.

CHAPTER 37

"Get out."

"Your Highness, we must discuss —" The first servant stepped forward, but Nix cut them off, his eyes never leaving mine as he watched the realisation pass through me.

Oh Saviours, I was going to be sick.

"OUT. NOW." Nix bellowed once more, his power filling the room as I heard the Scared Servants scramble away from it, fearful for their lives — the door clicking shut behind them.

"Rae, are you okay?" His voice had switched so suddenly that a choked laugh bubbled up inside me. Great, now I was hysterical.

"They bowed to you like a God." I stated instead of answering his question. I could feel that he had moved to be right in front of me, my powers humming once more at his nearness, but I refused to look at him.

I refused to see on their faces what I knew deep down.

I was so stupid.

"They do no such thing." Nix tried but Rem cut him

off with a click of his tongue.

"I told you she would find out eventually." Disapproval dripping from his voice, and I lifted my head as I realised, they had both been hiding this from me.

"You are not helping here," Nix sighed deeply before turning back to me "I didn't want to hide this from you, but I didn't see any other way –"

"How did I not see it before?" I murmured to myself.

"I honestly thought you'd figure it out." Rem chimed in and my eyes narrowed towards him as my power swirled inside of me.

"Leave, Rem." Nix growled, and Rem's hands went up in surrender as he left the room, closing us in as he did so, leaving us alone.

Leaving me alone with the God of the Citadel.

Oh Saviour, *I threw myself at the God of the Citadel!*

I hid behind my hands, embarrassment crowding in the rage in a confusing mix of emotions that I could not handle. I felt my power flow down my arms, warming my palms as they waited for my command. I threw a thought inside my mind that they were to stay where they were, there was no way I could attack the God of the Citadel.

I'd die for sure.

"What are you thinking?" Nix asked when I didn't speak, I spread my fingers so I could see him, and was startled at how close he was to me – at the swirling storm in those dark eyes as he focused only on me.

"Nothing." I lied and he bared his teeth at me – as he felt the lie seep into my soul.

"Liar." One simple word. That was all it took to ignite the anger that had been hiding between all my thought and emotions, all it took to pull the thread to my powers and fuel them into action.

Blue flames licked down my arms as they pooled in my hands – which were now fisted at my sides as I tried to keep them from swinging at Nix's face. His eyes tracked the movement of my powers cautiously, assessing me as though I were the threat, which only fuelled my anger more.

He is a God. He is the *God. You cannot attack him.* My mind tried to reason, but we were past listening to that part of myself as the air around me grew hotter.

"You have no right to call me that. Not when you've been keeping things from me."

"I did not lie." His powers dove straight for us with the force of his words, blocking my path from him and blurring his form. But that did not deter me as my veins turned to lava, strengthening me.

"No, you **did** something worse. You withheld the truth from me, made me believe that you were my friend, that you were helping me – when all this time you were just monitoring a problem in your Paradise."

"That is not what I –"

"That is exactly what you were doing!" I shot back, and my flames lashed out on instinct, shooting towards that wall of smoke, straight at Nix – but before they could make contact, he shot an arm out and threw his own fire out in a whip. His power slammed into mine as he threw it against the door, and I gasped as I felt the impact of the attack.

My eyes followed the movement and I stood there stunned at what I had done, my gaze zeroing in on the hole my flames had created in the door. An equally stunned Rem staring back at me as blue flames still licking around the edges of the damage.

"When you condemned the Gods in your trial – *when you condemned me* – I felt it. Your soul shouted it louder than your words did. You hated everything we had made you into and I knew you would want nothing to do with me if you knew who I really was." Nix snarled as though I hadn't just attacked him, as though I hadn't just broken the Covenant and attacked a God.

My knees buckled and gave out under me as I locked my powers back inside of me, throwing my shield up around my mind like I used to, locking everything down. Locking it all out. I'd deal with the consequences of a shattered soul later – when I wasn't overflowing with thoughts that I should be dead, how everything I'd done since my trials was worthy of death, of banishment.

I wasn't the prophesized Saviour reincarnated.

I was a fraud, and I was only alive because this God had taken pity on me.

"Oh Saviour, I condemned you to your face and you still saved me. Why? Because you think I'm this almighty prophecy come to life?"

"I didn't –" Nix began as he knelt down to my level, placing a finger under my chin so he could look into my eyes. I was sure he could see that I'd shut myself off, feel the coldness seeping out of my eyes as they locked onto his. I jerked out of his grip and moved away, refusing to be touched by him, refusing to let him break down my shields once again.

"*You did.* Had they known I'd condemned a God to his face, they *never* would have let me live – you should have never let me live! There is no other way to look at it Nix. I. Condemned. You. The last original God ascended by the Saviour. I'd just gone through a trial where I sentenced death to others who had done exactly what I had. So do not tell me I would have been fine if they had heard. Do *not* lie to me."

"Fine. But it still does not change anything. You are

the prophesized one, the one destined to bring the Saviour back." He growled low and my powers struggled against their confines inside me. But I had more control than before, I was not the helpless Raewyn who had no idea what awaited her in that trial. I was no longer the girl who screamed at the Servants for hopes of a reprieve from this world.

He'd taken that away from me and made me into his puppet.

Made me into Pure Raewyn of the Citadel – this supposed girl from the Prophecy. I squared my shoulders and rose, all the while feeling Nix's eyes following me.

"You have no idea how long I have been waiting for you." He tried again when I didn't answer him – eyes pleading in all their swirling depths, but I would not be pulled under this time. Rem stepped into the room at that moment, moving towards us – the God of the Citadel still on his knees before me and I would have laughed at the imagery if I had access to my emotions.

Assessing the situation, Rem moved closer to Nix and a sharp pain caught in my chest at the sight. I shouldn't have been surprised though, he was the right hand of the God of the Citadel, and I had already tried to attack him once today.

The pain grew as realisation hit – I thought they were my friends. Turns out I was just a plaything for them to pass the time.

"You're wrong." I declared with a tone of finality that had them both watching me with weary eyes. I would not be what they wanted, what they claimed I was. I was Raewyn Sandoval, Pure of the Citadel – and it was about time I embraced her.

"This changes everything."

CHAPTER 38

The next two days were a whirlwind of finalising decorations and food choices as my mother pulled me around the house while I dove into her mind as a distraction from my own.

I still hadn't let my walls down, and I was content to keep it that way until I was well out of the Citadel. In this state I did not care if I never saw Nix or Rem again, I did not care that I was being contracted off to a man I barely knew, that I was prophesized to bring down the world as we knew it.

None of those things mattered to me here.

I felt my powers strain against my hold constantly, but I did not budge – they would not shatter me while they were contained along with my emotions, and I needed it to be this way until I had space and time to deal with all of it.

I just couldn't do that now.

Grayson had been here constantly for the last two days, finalising things with my father and stealing me away from my mother whenever she would permit it – and it was as if the Saviour's Feast had never happened. He was back to his playful self, not that he noticed, and I was disconnected enough to not bother asking what had changed. Likely I knew the answer.

He had won, he had my contract. Despite the pestering thoughts of doubt, every moment with him was as comfortable as it always was and a part of me wished that I had some semblance of feeling to at least bring back the fuzziness that I was beginning to feel around him. He on the other hand, thought I was just being me, aloof and distracted with preparations like all women would be, and I had no energy to correct him. He even went as far as to present me with a ring, as a sign of our upcoming binding. To anyone else, the ring would have been beautiful – a single refined diamond the centre of attention, as tiny, delicate, pear-shaped emerald stones perched along the band in sporadic intervals that they almost looked like leaves. Even in my emotionless state, I could not deny that it was a beautiful design – even if I did think it another useless trinket.

"Your brother will be here within the hour, the Sacred Servants within the next two, and the gown has just arrived with the stylists." Analise announced as she entered my room. It was the day of my Binding Ceremony and yet I'd spent the better part of it holed up in my room alone and staring at my reflection in the vanity mirror on my dresser. If anyone had checked on me, they would assume that I was exhibiting signs for the sin of pride, of vanity – but they would be wrong. I was moving my face into various expressions, to make it look like I had emotion flowing through me.

Although as much as I moved my face, my eyes gave

me away. They'd ceased their swirling when I locked my powers away and they were now just pale and cold. Even the bursts of colour that I'd gotten used to seeing sparkle through were gone.

Analise snapped her fingers in front of my face, and I turned my head away from the mirror towards her, brows furrowed in concern as she looked me over.

"Did you hear anything I said?"

"My brother, the Servants and the dress are arriving." I tried, wracking my brain for the important notes of her words, she just shook her head at me and lead me to the bathing room to begin preparations.

"It is normal to be nervous, Dear. I had never met my Hugo until my Binding Ceremony, and I was so shaky my father had to hold me up at the altar."

"I am not nervous." I told her, and I meant it.

I felt nothing. Untying my robe, I began washing myself for the Ceremony, unconcerned that Analise was pottering about the bathing room – as she had been bathing me since I was born. Once I was done, I stood and walked out of the room, towards my dressing table, Analise running after me, scolding words flying at me as I dripped water all over the carpeted floor of my room. Wrapping the towel tightly around me, she clicked her tongue and pushed me down into the chair, silence filling the room as she got to work.

"Lord Westward will make a fine husband. I have seen how he watches you when you are not looking, he is smitten." She tried again as she finished drying my hair, and images flitted behind my eyes of a dark-haired man with stormy grey eyes that I immediately pushed out of my mind.

"Grayson is nice." I gave her, curving my lips up in the mirror as my eyes lifted to meet Analise in the reflection.

She beamed at my admission and began humming as she continued with her ministrations. My chest twisted at the thought that one of the closest people to me could not see that I was not completely here, but I guess that was nothing new.

I'd lived my whole life this way after all.

The stylists were let in the room shortly after, and I was surprised to see it was the same sisters who had made me up for my Ceremony. Though this time, the eldest sister didn't even dare to look me in the eye, let alone speak to me like she had the last time we'd met.

Perks of being a Pure, I suppose.

Silently they got to work, utilising Analise once more as they poked and prodded my face, plastering me with make-up that I had never bothered to wear before. I was surprised they let me stay facing the mirror this time, though I was far less interested in what they were doing to me as I watched Sylvie cover my eyelid in glittering white powder.

If they could make me look like I felt something, like I cared to be here, then I would take it.

At some point, they asked me to close my eyes and I drifted off into a peaceful sleep, blocking out all the touching as they continued moving around me.

***

"We cannot let them get away with this. We need to attack, and it needs to be now." A voice flitted through my mind, and I groaned as pain shot through me.

Where am I?

"You are thinking with your heart and not your head. If we attack now, we will be slaughtered, and you know it. He is surrounded by an army of men."

He? Who are they talking about? Whose voice was that? I struggled to fight this feeling of exhaustion as more pain speared through my side. I felt a cold dampness press in on me and I struggled to hear the sounds around me to figure out where I was, why I was here. Panic ran through me as images flitted behind my eyes. Images I could not make sense of.

Suddenly, I felt power move around me, calming me as if it could sense that I was trying to wake up. I breathed deep as my power moved to join it, humming along my veins as if it had been deprived of its other half for far too long.

"You should be thinking *more* with your heart. You are her *Anama Nexum!*"

My what? Who is speaking? I willed my eyes to open, but they would not budge. The power grew thicker around me, as if it were protecting me from its owner as rage filled the space around us.

"I know exactly who I am." The voice growled out. "Do not mistake my calmness for unfeeling – I would love nothing more than to rip the hearts out of each of those men for what they have done to what is mine, but I am not in the mood to go out on a suicide mission just to appease my anger. It would not be fair to her." His words became clearer towards the end, as if he'd moved to be right in front of me, and I felt the power around me release slightly to let its owner in.

Who are you, who are you? My mind screamed as I tried to get my bearings of everything that was happening around me.

"She is going to destroy them all when she wakes." The first voice murmured, and I strained to hear the chuckle in his breath as I felt a cool hand stroke the side of my face, causing a sigh to slip from my lips as the pain eased inside me.

"It is what she was born to do."

***

"Miss, we are done." The younger sister, Sylvie, whispered as she gently shook my shoulder. My eyes opened instantly, startling the poor girl and I curved my lips once more in attempt to smile as my powers thrashed around inside my shield.

It was just a dream. I tried to tell them, but they were not listening to me anymore. Had I not locked them up they may have been more receptive to my words – or it could be the pit in my stomach that told me this was not a normal dream at all.

But I had time for neither of those.

"Thank you both for your service." I nodded at them as I stood from my seat, walking over to Analise in a dismissive move I had seen my mother use on her maids more times than I could count. I heard them pack up quietly and exit out the door behind me.

"The Sacred Servants will be arriving shortly. It is time." Analise whispered to me, as I stood staring at the dress that was laying on the bed before me.

"I am about to be bound to Grayson." I whispered back without thinking. Analise looked at my sympathetically, as she gathered up my dress and held it open for me.

My mother's old gown was a simple design, made from the purest ivory silk, it fit snug against my frame now with lace curving upwards from the bodice up to my neck and then flowed down my back and along the floor like an oversized cape. It had been altered slightly to accommodate my slimmer frame, but otherwise looked completely identical to the many times I'd run into my mother's closest as a child and demanded she tell me her story.

To her, it had been the best day of her life, the happiest she'd ever been the moment my father bound his life with hers — and as a young, naive child, I'd lapped up the story and prayed to the Saviour that I could only be so lucky one day. Now, as I stood here, lifting my arms, I helped Analise drape it over me, and I realised the lie in the story she'd told to keep her child placid.

She had never met my father before he was bound to her, only stolen a glance at him the day he signed her contract. When she stood in my place, the only thing she would have felt was fear.

And yet I still prayed I could only be as lucky as my mother was.

Neither of us spoke as Analise fastened the buttons on the back of the dress, securing me in place as my powers continued thrashing around inside me. I tightened my shield around them, commanding them to stop as I locked my mind up tight.

They could not escape me tonight, I needed to be in control.

"You are ready, Pure Sandoval." Analise said as she spun me around to face her, and I could hear the undercurrent of words in her voice. The confidence she was trying to inject into me with her words. I pulled her into my arms in a hug, something I had never done before, and she froze at the contact.

"Thank you for everything, Analise." I spoke into her hair, and I felt her shoulders move as she sniffed loudly.

"You are more special than you know, Miss Raewyn." She sniffled again as I pulled away and my shield faltered at her words, heat seeping through me as a sliver of my power escaped before I could tighten them again.

"I am just me, nothing more."

"Nonsense, child. You are special, and when you learn to love someone, share that part of you that you don't let anyone see — then, you will see it too." Her words were too raw, too real that I halted my breathing as if I could refuse her words from sinking into my mind.

That slice of power that slipped through heated along my collarbone as it came to rest over my heart, as if they too could see that I was refusing to listen. Analise was like a second mother to me, so astute in every little detail, I should have known she would see through all my falsities.

I swallowed hard at the thought of opening up completely to somebody, of having someone see me truly and still wanting me. Grayson would have no choice soon enough, but that did not mean I would bear my soul to him. Husband or not, he would still have to uphold his duty and report anything or anyone he found breaking the law.

No, I would have to keep some parts guarded at all times.

"Well, let us hope then that Grayson is that man." I said through a forced grin, grabbing Analise by the arm and leading her out the door, silencing any other words of wisdom she might have thought to bear on me.

I walked arm in arm with Analise down the stairs, despite her protests that she wasn't invited to the Binding Ceremony. I shushed her and told her that as the bride, and the Pure of the Citadel, I was personally inviting her. After all, it was only fair that she be there to see one of us off, considering she'd played a major role in our upbringing. She quietened down after that, but quickly disappeared once I'd let go of her at the base of the steps, making herself scarce.

My family was already gathered downstairs, awaiting my arrival and I felt all eyes descend on me as I came to a stop before them. My mother and father swarmed me instantly, showering me in compliments as they hugged me.

"Your sister sends her regrets – Lieutenant Ruskin was not able to get out of his duties in time. But she promises to visit the Western Paradise before her Binding Ceremony." My mother added as they pulled away from me.

"I did not expect them to make the journey on such short notice." I replied and only a small part of me meant it as a slight towards how fast this Binding Ceremony had come together – my mother though saw right through me and the laugh that came out of her was both forced and far too loud to be natural.

"Oh Darling, you are too much sometimes." She chuckled, but I heard the underlying *'Don't start with this now'* as she pulled me towards the others.

Orion and Alyssa were next, joined at the hip as they always were whenever they presented in public, and my brother grinned wide as he pulled me away from our parents and into a crushing bear hug.

"Little Wynnie is getting married, I never thought I would see the day." He joked and Alyssa swatted him in the arm for me, causing a laugh to burst out of me. I would miss these two when I was gone.

"You do not call a woman 'little' anything on her Binding Ceremony Day. It is rude." She scolded him and he even had the decency to look sheepish as I pulled away from him.

"Do not worry, I am not so easily offended by those beneath me, Brother." I shot back and Alyssa gasped as my brother bent in half with laughter, howling in delight.

"Good luck, Westward, she is all yours now." He wheezed between laughs, and I stepped to the side of him to find the man I was here for.

My soon-to-be husband.

His eyes locked onto mine and for a second, I thought I saw the stormy eyes of Nix, causing me to falter in my steps – but when I looked again, they were the same bright green as always. Grayson smiled warmly as he mistook my stumble for nerves and moved towards me instantly.

His golden hair was perfectly styled as always, golden gilded boots glinting of a fresh shine – his dark, Commander's jacket neatly pressed of any wrinkles. The golden domes buttoned right up his neck, as the swirls of his Commanders station shone in the afternoon light.

"You are more beautiful than I could have ever imagined." He breathed, his too-green eyes piercing through me. Words stopped forming in my mind as that sliver of power lit up my veins at the feel of his too warm hands on my shoulders.

"Speechless once again, Wynnie? Maybe you will be good for her." Orion joked and I watched Grayson laugh along with him, but all I could hear was the blood pounding in my ears, the heat spreading through me as that small trickle of power pooled inside my palms. I willed that small piece back in, demanded it to go back behind my walls, but it did not budge.

"It is okay to be nervous, Darling. I am too." Grayson's words floated into my ear as he leaned down to whisper so closely, I could feel his breath on the nape of my neck, the hairs prickling at the sensation. As he pulled away, I looked into his eyes once more and saw the honesty in them. He was nervous? He was the one that wanted to be bound to me. He was the one that demanded we do it before we left the Citadel, why should he be the one to be nervous?

"I am not nervous." I stated and his eyes lit up with

misunderstanding. He took my words to mean that I was more excited than nervous when really, I felt so little of either that I was indifferent to the proceedings around me.

"Good. Neither am I."

"The Sacred Servants should be here any minute, shall we get to our places?" My father called to the rest of us, and Grayson nodded as he began escorting me to the gardens. Mother had informed me that he insisted on holding it outside, in the middle of nature — and if I could, I would have felt pleased that he'd at least thought of me that much to remember that I liked being outside.

As we walked through the side doors of the house, I took in all the decorating my mother had achieved in such a small amount of time — especially with the lack of hep she had from me. White rose petals covered the ground beneath us, the space cleared enough for my little family to gather around us as they bared witness to the Binding Ceremony.

At the end of the opening, sat beneath an archway of more white roses, was an altar and a bowl. That was where I would stand with Grayson before the Scared Servants. That was where I would declare my everlasting servitude and loyalty to the man by my side.

The earth's power rolled around me at the thought, prodding me as it sought out its kin. Clinging to the sliver it found, I felt its question hanging in the air. *Where is the rest?*

I would not give it an answer.

"This is beautiful Lady Sandoval, the perfect setting to bind my life to such a perfect woman." I heard Grayson reply to something my mother had asked him — his words flitting through me as if from a distance. My skin was so hot at this point from the combined power flowing around me that it made my skin red, everyone interpreting it as the blush of a complimented woman.

"Milady, the Servants have arrived, and they bring guests with them." I heard Analise announce from the doorway, panic lacing her voice.

"What guests? This is a private affair." My father boomed in his Judge's voice, and my power threaded through the earth's as it let it inside me. I snapped my walls shut tighter, determined to keep it out as its questions hummed through me. *Why, why, why?*

Analise's voice moved through me again, although I could not make out the words she spoke, but then Grayson's voice echoed next to me.

"Who would dare crash the Binding Ceremony of the Commanding Lord of the Western Paradise?" His voice rising to move throughout the house behind us. My dulled powers hummed in recognition of another's a moment before I turned towards the door, towards the voice that froze me in place as my eyes widened at the sight before me.

"Is that any way to speak to the God of the Citadel, Commander?" Nix drawled as he strolled through the open doorway, hands resting lazily in his pants pockets as he coasted towards us, completely unaffected by the stares he was getting from my family. He was dressed like he had been on that first night I met him, like a Lord – the only difference was his suit jacket, which was now covered wholly in the swirling patterns of gold marks.

The mark of the Gods.

His power saturated the air around us in an instant, and I choked on my breath. It was stronger than anything I'd ever felt come from him – It almost matched the earth's energy as they rolled around one another in sync. Now that it was fully unleashed, I could feel how old it was, how undeniably lethal and dangerous it was. He was pure power in the form of man, and he knew it. I shrank back a step as his power rolled towards me, still invisible to everyone else around us, but I could see it, feel it.

And it scared me.

"Your Highness, we were not expecting you." My father sputtered, bowing low as he did so. The rest of my family followed suit – heads hanging down in submission as they lowered themselves as far to the ground as they possibly could. Grayson hesitated a moment longer, his eyes narrowing at the man standing behind Nix, and Rem grinned wide as Grayson too, bowed before him. I was the only one left standing, too frozen to move a muscle.

"*Raewyn.*" Grayson hissed at me as his eyes cast back up to my stupefied frame. "Darling, you need to bow before a God." I felt all their eyes latch onto me, the pleading on their faces as they feared for my wellbeing if I did not bow to this man – but I stayed where I was, eyes locked onto the swirling grey irises I was just beginning to find comforting, but now found disturbing in its coldness.

Who was this man?

"Raewyn bows to no one, isn't that right *darling?*" Nix's tone was off, and it sent chills down my spine, the ice crawling along my veins – sputtering my lingering flames into nothing.

"You know my daughter?" My father questioned as Nix motioned for them to rise once more, that smirk I'd hated when we first met plastered over his face.

"It is an honour to have you in our home." My mother added hastily, blushing brightly as she took in Nix.

"Of course, who do you think she was visiting in the palace every day?" He taunted, as his eyes moved to take in the man standing next to me and I saw Grayson stiffen slightly.

"What are you doing?" I demanded, my voice steadier

than the rest of my shaken self. My powers thrashed inside of me at his nearness, and I could see the moment he realised I was still shutting everything out as his eyes darkened slightly, his power circling me completely now — whisps of smoke curling off his shoulders.

"I couldn't miss the Binding Ceremony of my favourite little Pure now, could I?" His words rang through me, the tone mocking, and my powers pushed hard enough that I had to grit my teeth in effort to keep them contained.

I was not his anything. He had lied to me, betrayed the one thing I'd never given anyone before. Trust.

"Then where are the Servants? Surely you did not forget to inform them of their importance too." I shot back and the smoke around him rose, my family gasping behind me as they could now see his power too. Grayson moved in front of me in a protective gesture and I almost laughed at his foolishness.

He could not protect me from Nix.

"They are just inside, awaiting my order. I thought I would come and congratulate the happy couple first. Give them my blessing."

"Then give it." I ground out.

"Tsk, tsk, always so impatient. No wonder training has been slow. Although I realise of late you have been distracted with… other things." He clicked his tongue as his eyes darted to Grayson once again whose mouth thinned at the accusation that he'd taken me away from the God.

"What is he talking about?" Grayson asked eventually when it seemed as though neither Nix nor I would elaborate.

"Why she is training up to be my replacement, aren't you Rae?" Nix cooed, and I flinched at the use of the nickname he'd given me. It would not go unnoticed that the

God of the Citadel and I were on friendlier terms than I wanted to admit.

"*She is?*" My family all said in unison, their mouths dropping open in shock and I narrowed my eyes at a smug-looking Nix. I wondered if he would still let me away with my life if I decked him in front of an audience. My fists twitched with the urge to test that theory.

"Why do you think I helped in her trial? She is chosen after all. A useful replacement could not have come at a better time – I was growing rather bored sitting around waiting for something exciting to come along." My heart sank with every word he spoke. Every glint of his teeth as his smirk stayed in place. I willed his eyes to betray his words, to tell me I wasn't just some bored plaything like I had thought to myself when I last saw him. But his eyes remained steady, the humour in them only digging deeper into my soul. He smiled cruelly as my parents gushed around me as he lifted a hand to inspect his nails – as if the thought of conversing more with us now bored him.

"Is that what you really feel?" I whispered, my voice cracking as I strained to contain my thrashing powers, my emotions begging to be set free.

"Darling, I am *the God*. I do not subject myself to simple emotions. I am power, I see what I want, and I take it. Because I can. Because you owe me." A gasp tore from me at his words, at the ice in his voice as his eyes told me everything I needed to know. Fire slammed against my shields so violently they splintered under the force, and I scrambled to reign them back in as that realisation hit.

He was telling the truth.

"What does this mean for Raewyn? What does she owe?" Grayson asked when everyone had calmed down. My eyes had not left Nix as they swarmed me with questions, my mind refusing to form any words to give them.

"It means, Commander, that you can keep your wife. But when I call on her, and I will, she will come to me." His power snaked around Grayson's legs as he spoke this, a darkness slithering up his limbs, daring him to object to the offer Nix was giving.

There was no question that if he refused — there would be consequences.

"But she belongs to the West now." Grayson spat out anyway, straightening himself as he stood up to the last original God.

"She belongs to *me*." Nix growled and Grayson's form began to tremble in front of me. I tried to push him aside, to tell Nix to stop this — but I was not strong enough to make Grayson move and Nix had ceased listening to me. He grinned wider, his power climbing higher until it had weaved its way around Grayson's neck, his throat bobbing as he swallowed his panic.

"M-My au-aunt will not let you —"

"Do not lecture me on what I can and cannot do. Or do you forget what I did to your precious uncle?" Nix taunted as his smoke curled tighter, a choked breath escaped Grayson as he struggled for his life.

"Stop." I pleaded to Nix, but he just laughed as his eyes flicked back to me.

"Is this the man you wish to bind yourself to? He can't even fight his own battles — much prefers cowering behind others, don't you, Westward?"

"*Let. Him. Go.*" I demanded, and the room fell silent at the audacity in my words, words that were worthy of death if the God felt offended enough. Nix glared at me a moment, his eyes hard and lifeless like mine, and then he sighed, waving his hand in a gesture that cleared away his smoke instantly – though I could still feel it moving around us.

"As you wish."

Grayson heaved in a breath, falling to the ground before me, and I sank to my knees to help him – to check on my almost-dead almost-husband as he sputtered air into his lungs. My hands shook as rage slipped through my shield. Rage that Nix could pull something like this, that he could be so different to the man I had thought I was coming to know.

One thing was certain though, I didn't know this man at all.

"You're a monster." I spat, unleashing the rage that pummelled me from the inside.

"I am what the Saviour made me." He stated with a shrug of indifference.

And he was.

He was the last Original God of the Citadel, the most powerful man alive.

And he'd played me for a fool.

CHAPTER 39

My powers slammed against my shield as I helped Grayson to his feet once more, the earth's power twisting around that small sliver of power that remained free inside of me and I gripped it like a lifeline.

Power crackled in the air, as my anger fed it – Nix's power diving towards me as he sensed it, but I swatted his tendrils of power away with a mere thought thrown to the world, I would not let him in again. His eyes widened in shock as his powers were thrown back at him, that ancient energy now pulsing around me as I pulled it in and pushed, forming a barrier between me and him.

Between my family and the dangerous God.

To everyone else, it would like a staring contest between a God and a Pure – but I didn't think about that right now. Instead, I focused on keeping my own energy contained, on entwining the earth's energy into me rather that out of me, so the others would not see the little fire I had pulsing through me. Nix's eyes swirled faster than I'd ever seen, in time with my own as I gathered more of that ancient energy and threw out another thought into the power that surrounded me.

Gathering up every last ounce of it that I could, I fed every emotion that had slithered out into that ball, feeling it grow before me.

I fed it my shame at believing I could trust this man – this God disguised as a friend.

My anger that he could be this cruel of a person, that he could save me and then use me for his own entertainment.

I added the hurt that swelled at the thought that he'd hidden the truth from me – both about who I was and who he was.

And finally, I threw my heart at him.

Splintered and irreparable, betrayed by the one person who I thought would make me feel like I belonged in this world that didn't understand me.

My breathing ragged, I knew I did not have long before I lost control of the mass I'd just created, so I acted – instinct driving me now as I threw everything I had at him. Chest heaving in breaths as I exerted every spare ounce of energy I had to spare, I watched as his head snapped to the side, watched as I slammed an invisible ball of energy right into his face.

I'd just power punched the God of the Citadel.

And it felt *good*.

Slowly, Nix turned back to face me, lip split as blood trickled down the corner of his lip, teeth bared in a grimace so cold I wondered how I had ever seen him as anything different. Rem stepped forward then, intent to protect his God from an enemy he could not see, and it was my turn to smirk in victory.

"Is this really the happiness you choose then?" Nix ground out as he spat his blood onto the ground, seeping into the earth below us and I could almost feel the energy around me lap it up.

"Yes." I kept my voice steady, injecting as much truth in my words as I could as I stared him down, refusing to budge as I coiled that power further into me. Later, I would figure out how I was able to harness the pure energy of the earth while my own was shut off. Later I would mourn the loss of the only person who had made me feel like I truly belonged anywhere.

Now, I would fight to protect my family from the most feared God in existence.

"Remember what I told you." He finally said, a warning that I needed to heed as he turned on his heel. I still could not tell a soul about who I was, what I could do. Hiding his eyes from me – he moved past Rem who stayed standing there a moment longer, confusion etched into his face as he watched his friend and God walk back through the house.

"Welcome to the family, little Rae." He nodded before throwing a daggered look at Grayson who gulped loudly. My eyes followed their retreating forms until I couldn't see them any longer, my lungs refusing to work as I struggled to take in air.

My family stood there speechless, Grayson staring at me like he was trying to figure out an impossible puzzle, but I gave them nothing. I couldn't. I was too afraid that if I spoke, I would open the walls and crumble before them.

I needed space.

I needed solitude.

I needed –

"We are here for the Binding Ceremony of Pure

Sandoval and Commanding Lord of the Western Paradise."
The Servants announced as they entered the garden as one,
breaking my spiral of thoughts.

I needed to complete my Binding Ceremony.

Everyone assumed their places, silent as their
thoughts rang out through the space. They would all have
questions for me after the Ceremony. Questions I was sure
I could not answer without divulging what I really was. Now
that I thought about it, it wouldn't have been the Sacred
Servants that demanded I keep my manifesting powers a
secret, no, that order would have come straight from Nix
himself since he was the highest-ranking person in all Seven
Paradises.

My mind whirled as Grayson placed a hand gently on
my arm, shaking me from my imploding thoughts and led
me to stand in front of the altar, the Servants now situated
behind it.

"We are gathered here today," They began as soon as
we were placed before them, and I breathed deep as I tried
to reign in everything I had just done.

"To witness the sacred binding of these two people."

"Pure Raewyn Sandoval of the Citadel and
Commanding Lord Grayson Westward of the Western
Paradise." I pushed my emotions back in, my heart
pounding as I struggled to contain my fractured shield – as
I begged my powers to stay put.

"As they bind their souls together,"

"Let us remember all that the Saviour sacrificed…"

"All that he rebuilt –"

"So that we might find peace." We all bent our heads
down then, each of us sending up a prayer of thanks to the
Saviour – all except me.

I had no prayers of thanks, only questions.

Why did you choose me? I called into the ether above us – but no one responded.

I didn't expect them to.

Instead, the earth's energy pulsed around me as it tried to find its way in again.

"We will now begin the Binding Ceremony." The first Servant declared once we had all lifted our heads. Grayson moved first, picking up the gold hilted knife that was resting on the altar, gliding it along his right palm in one swift motion. I sucked in a breath as he looked up at me expectantly, and my fists clenched as my power pushed out once again, reaching for that outside source of strength.

Biting the inside of my cheek, I mentally threw a command for them to stop as I raised my left hand, forcing my fingers to flatten as Grayson's came to cup the back of my hand, steadying it. He smiled kindly at me, his eyes warm and welcoming and I nodded once in encouragement. Gently at first, he touched the knife to the skin that rested between my thumb and forefinger, and then it bit down as he sliced – so fast I gasped at the sudden sting, blood blooming instantly along the seam he had made.

Grayson moved our hands over the bowl so that our blood mingled in the base of it and the Sacred Servants nodded in acceptance.

"Please join hands and recite the sacred words." The second Servant spoke, and my throat became dry. I had practiced the words repeatedly, like every good child should, the words ingrained in my mind like a brand – but my mouth refused to form them.

Grayson took in a deep breath, nodding to himself more than me as he clasped my bloody hand in his, swallowing it with the sheer size of his as he began to speak the sacred words of our binding.

"As I bind myself to you in front of the Sacred Servants of the God and Saviour, I vow to always be by your side. May your sins become my sins, your sorrows become my sorrows and your happiness my happiness. As my life withers and is placed back into the earth the Saviour fought to provide us, my loyalty to you will never falter. With my blood, I bind myself to you forever. I, Commanding Lord Grayson Westward of the Western Paradise, am yours." He raised our hands to his lips as he finished, turning them so he could place a kiss on the back on my hand, my blood now coating his lips as his eyes shone with happiness. I swallowed the lump in my throat, turning my head to my family as they watched with tears of happiness flowing down each of their faces.

Every part of me screamed that I did not want to be tied to anyone, that I could not lie to this man for the rest of our lives.

For them though, I would do anything.

And so, I began my vows, each word clinging to my throat as my powers shoved against the doors of my mind in protest.

I have to do this. I have to do this.

"As I bind myself to you in front of the Sacred Servants of the God and Saviour, I vow to always be by your side. May your sins become my sins, your sorrows become my sorrows and your happiness my happiness. As my life withers and is placed back into the earth the Saviour fought to provide us, my loyalty to you will never falter. With my blood, I bind myself to you forever. I, Pure Raewyn Sandoval of the Citadel, am yours." I heaved in a breath as Grayson raised our hands to my lips, and turned them over, providing me with access to his own. My lips touched the back of his hand, the wetness of his blood sticking to my lips now.

I resisted the urge to wipe the back of my other hand across them, to rid them of his blood and looked towards the Sacred Servants for the last part of the Ceremony.

"With this blood, and these vows that have been spoken before the Saviour's chosen disciples,"

"We bind the two of you together as one."

"May your lives be full of the Saviour's love and your souls forever bound together in the earth that he made for our salvation."

With their final words, the Scared Servants tipped our bowl full of blood into the soil beneath us, giving it back to the earth. I felt the power surrounding me pulse once, twice, three times as I watched our blood sink down – the power swelling suddenly as wind whipped around us, my mother grasping hold of my father as though it would sweep her away. I felt an anger in the air that resonated deep within me, and my fire roared in agreeance.

"We present to you, Commanding Lord Grayson Westward and his wife, Pure Raewyn Westward of the Western Paradise. You may now seal this bond with a kiss." The Sacred Servants spoke as one, their voices echoing throughout the world in a declaration to all.

My family cheered as Grayson wrapped his hands around my waist, grinning from ear to ear as my eyes locked onto his too green ones.

I was now a Westward.

No longer a Sandoval.

No longer belonging in the Citadel.

I was now someone's *wife*.

My new husband pulled me against him, my body willingly obliging as my shields shook with the force my powers were slamming against it. I gasped as they finally cracked my mind wide open, and Grayson lowered his lips to mine in the same moment.

Claiming me as his as he had every right to do.

The kiss was soft and gentle, tender as he moved his mouth against mine, and the fuzziness leaked out of me and slunk down into my stomach. My powers tore down my arms and I gripped onto Grayson's arms as I fought against them as a deep sorrow fed their crusade.

Please stay hidden, please listen to me, I begged them, they could not show themselves here, not in front of everyone.

Encouraged by my response, Grayson tightened his grip on my waist, holding me closer to him as his tongue darted inside my mouth, finding mine as he groaned softly. The air around me grew hot, as images flitting behind my eyes of another kiss, of another set of lips, and betrayal burned through me. I pushed away from Grayson then, my chest heaving as I fought for air – as I commanded my powers to get back inside my mind.

To stop betraying me with someone I could never look in the eyes again.

Grayson watched me as I pulled myself back together, our blood still staining his lips as surely as it would be mine. His eyes were a darker shade of green now, hungrier, wilder – the look made nerves shoot up my spine.

"Congratulations!" My family called in unison as they swarmed us in an instant, my father and Orion pulling Grayson away from me as they clapped him on the back and welcomed him to the family.

I relished the distraction as I used the earth's powers around me to calm my breathing, sweeping it through me like I used to, as I willed everything out of me. Slowly, my breathing returned to normal, and I threw my shield up once more around my powers, though this time I left a door open, allowing them a small amount of freedom as I promised them – I wouldn't lock them up if they obeyed me.

I felt them move through me in acceptance and I smiled in relief as they slid down my limbs, strengthening me once more.

CHAPTER 40

"I've already told you – I cannot tell you anything about my time in the palace." I sighed as I repeated the same sentence for the fifth time as we all sat around the tables in my family's garden.

The Sacred Servants left as soon as the Binding Ceremony was completed, and food and drink arrived shortly after. I was sat next to my new husband, Grayson, his arm slung around the back of my chair as his bandaged fingers played with the bare skin of my shoulder.

It was a feeling I was not enjoying, but I felt like I could not deny him.

"You spent a month working with the God of the Citadel, the most powerful and deadly man there is." Orion stated as he downed the contents of his glass.

"Is there a question in there?"

"How are you still alive?" He burst out in a laugh, my father and Grayson following suit as both my mother and Alyssa swatted him on the arm. Orion feigned innocence as he pouted towards both of them which caused me to join in on their laughter.

"Simple, he is more pig headed than I am." I replied

and Orion hooted once more. My mother turned her scolding on me for disrespecting a God and I shrugged my response, knowing that I had called Nix worse to his face. *Like monster,* my thoughts reminded me, and my gut twisted as another thought passed through me.

I would make sure I never had to see him again.

My powers swirled faster inside of me as if they were trying to reject the thought.

"What is the plan from here, Grayson? I expect regular visits to the Citadel now that you are part of this family." Orion asked once we had all calmed down, and I turned to my husband to see his response. He had been nursing his drink for a while, content to stay silent while we all bantered amongst ourselves - though I had felt his eyes on me the entire time we did so.

"First things first, I would like to settle my wife into our estate and show her everything the Western Paradise has to offer. I think I promised her a waterfall upon her first visit." He winked at me as he spoke the last part and a blush crept up my cheeks. So much had happened since that first walk in these gardens that I had forgotten about the waterfall he promised to show me.

Excitement grew in me that we might be able to become those people again, that I might still get some happiness. "After that, I am not too sure. I have some business to attend to in the near future, but I am sure the almighty God will call us back sooner rather than later." He finished, his face twisting into a scowl for a moment, though it left just as quickly that I wondered if it were a trick of the light.

"Let us hope it is after you have given me some grandchildren." My mother added as I choked on my drink, coughing violently as everyone else burst into laughter once more.

The thought of having to bear children into this world drowned out their sounds as my mind spun with the realisation that in order to do so, I would have to have sex.

In all my worries, I had forgotten that being bound to someone meant more than just being tied to someone for the rest of my life, it meant sharing a bed with them.

Would Grayson expect that of me tonight?

Could I give that part of myself to him when I still felt like I didn't know him?

"You are thinking too much again." Grayson murmured as he watched me process this new development. I lifted my cup to my lips once more, quenching the drought that had invaded in my throat.

"It has been a big day." I admitted once I could form words again.

"That it has. Just enjoy the moment, we have the rest of our lives to figure everything else out." I nodded in agreement and turned back to my family as they continued to joke and barb one another, Grayson throwing in his own every so often.

This moment, this was why I fought so hard to become who I was – to hide everything from the world we lived in.

Nix may have taken my choices away from me in the beginning, but from here on out I made my own. Happiness swelled in me at the thought that my family was safe and content, that they weren't shamed and banished as they would have been if I had been condemned to treason in my trials.

This was all I ever wanted, and I was content to leave knowing that they would remain the same.

We stayed in the garden until the sun began to sink behind the trees – my badly hidden yawn a signal for Grayson to begin our goodbyes, guiding me through the house towards our waiting carriage. Analise had ensured that my things had been packed before the Ceremony, and they were all neatly packed atop the Westward's signature forest green carriage. Mother had no doubt handled the placement of each bag to ensure that if the weather turned, my things would not be ruined – not that I had anything of worth to destroy, Pures don't like materialistic things after all.

"Remember everything I taught you." My mother whispered to me as she pulled me in for one last hug. I had never been touched so much in one day – though I supposed I would have to get used to it as I was still acutely aware of Grayson's hand as it rested on the small of my back. He hadn't stopped touching me since our Ceremony had ended, and I was desperately needing some space.

"I won't. I will make you proud." I promised, swallowing the lump in my throat as tears threatened to escape – emotions flowing freely through the open doorway of my mind now. I pulled away from my mother and turned towards my father – whose arms were already spread wide as tears fell freely down his face.

Sniffling loudly, I ran to him and locked my arms around him tightly.

"My dear Raewyn. I have watched you grow into such a beautiful woman. So strong in your belief of how things should be." I nodded into his chest, hiding my tears as they soaked through his jacket, and I clung to him tighter. "Never forget who you are child. Never forget where you belong."

"I won't." I choked out as my father pulled away from me and smiled, eyes crinkling as they let loose more tears. I hadn't expected this moment to be so sad, hadn't expected to feel so much.

Why did it feel as though I was never coming back?

Grayson pulled me into his front, his arms winding themselves around my waist as his head rested on top of mine and I tried not to think too much in this moment as I relished the thought of now having someone help keep me together as I felt myself shattering into pieces – regardless of my inclination for touching. Tears flowed down my face unabated now, and I was a snivelling mess as Orion patted me on the head, no doubt ruining my hairdo as he promised to visit with Alyssa soon.

Slowly, Grayson steered me to the carriage, doors opened and waiting for me to leave the Citadel, to start my new life with my newly bound husband in the Western Paradise. With one last look back at my family, I stole another breath as Grayson entered first, holding his hand out to me and I grasped onto it tightly as he helped me inside.

"Ready to go home, my wife?" He asked as I settled myself in beside him, his hand still clasped in mine as I clung to him like a lifeline – my powers travelling through my blood as it lent me more strength that I did not feel.

I thought I would be ready; thought I would be fine with moving so far away from my family and a village that I had never felt any attachment to – but I was fast accepting that it was not the case. Feelings akin to grief wove through my mind and I choked on a breath as I fought to contain them. They knew what I could never admit to myself, and with the door to my mind open, they were demanding to be felt.

"I'm ready." I finally whispered as the carriage took off through the village – more to myself than Grayson.

We wove through the streets at a leisurely pace, and I watched as people stopped to watch their Pure being carted off to another Paradise – Grayson waving to Lords he recognised with the hand that wasn't held in both of mine as I continued to cling to him. They shouted their congratulations and farewells from their doorways, and I swallowed any trace of sadness and grief as a smile I did not feel curved my lips towards them.

The world will remember what you show them – so show them what they expect, not what you feel. The words floated through my mind as a memory I could not place surrounded me. It was Orion speaking to a much younger version of me – tears streaming down my face as loud wails came out of my small frame. Her grief matched the swirling feelings inside me now – and I longed to reach out and comfort her, but I did not know how.

What would have caused me to feel so much at such a young age?

As the memory faded away, I felt the earth's energy flow into the carriage and I breathed it in greedily as it fed my own powers – the pulse of my own flames building inside of me with each passing second, building my strength and resolve.

Our carriage was nearing the end of the village when I finally felt him – his power so potent, that I wondered how he'd ever been able to hide this much from me. Pain lanced through my chest as an eruption of emotions pushed forward and I scrunched my eyes shut – ignoring the peaks of the palace in front of us, or the gilded gates that now lay closed and opposing as they cast their unwelcome shadow over the town square before it.

Turning inward, I pushed back against those emotions and begged them to silence their cries, but they weren't listening, not matter how much I pleaded. It wasn't just his powers he'd hid from me; it was *everything*. He'd lied to me since the day we met, and I had been a fool to see him as anything but the arrogant self-centred man I had encountered at Orion's celebration.

As if he were sensing my thoughts, I felt his powers glid towards me, slithering into the carriage until all I could feel was him. It overwhelmed my senses as the scent of smoke and woods invaded my mind and I felt a gentle nudging against the room that I had barricaded my thoughts inside. He was seeking entrance, and my powers shoved themselves up against my emotions as they pushed harder against the thin restraint, I was holding on them – trying to accept his *iter* whether I wanted them to or not. Groaning against the weight, I slowed my breathing and cleared a path in my mind, throwing walls up to smother my emotions until I was firmly outside of the Citadel's walls. I didn't need him to sense the lies in my soul – and there was no possible way I could tell him the truth without it ruining me further.

I felt Grayson's eyes on me then, so I tilted my head slightly, to give the illusion that I was falling asleep. Breathing slower, I waited a few more minutes until I was sure he'd bought my ruse – and was rewarded when his other hand came to rest on top of our entwined fingers, gently stroking my skin.

I fought back a wince at the sensation as another, more insistent nudging pressed against my mind. Sighing internally and checking my shield one last time to ensure that my emotions were in check, I felt for the tether of Nix's *iter* and tugged, entering the mouldable space between worlds faster than any other time I had gone into an *iter*.

Dizziness clouded my vision as the room came into view and I immediately regretted my decision, as my eyes focused on the man I'd punched with the earth's power only hours ago.

"I wasn't sure if you would accept." He whispered as I tore my eyes away from him and observed the space around us. We were back in the courtyard of the Palace, the sun glistening down through the open windows and even in this space I could feel the earth's energy as it swam around us through the domed ceiling.

"What do you want, *your Highness?*" I hissed at him, feeling the anger rising in me as I fought every other emotion to stay behind their walls. He narrowed his eyes at my use of his title but made no move to come closer as he replied.

"To clarify some things before you trot off to your happily ever after." He sneered right back – lips pulled back over his teeth.

"I'm still not planning on telling anyone about my powers if that is what you are afraid of." I retorted, narrowing my eyes in his direction as tendrils of smoke flew around him in every direction. Unlike the last time he'd created an *iter* for us, he'd let our powers inside and my own hummed in anticipation as I watched his move. He was angry – his powers lashing wilder than anything I'd ever seen, and I gulped back my fear that I was the reason for his current mood.

Well, you did punch a God in the face, my mind reminded me, and I shut that down too.

"We have more important things to worry about, my little Pure. Your display of pure power before proved that you are in fact the Prophesized one – the one meant to bring back the Saviour and bring about the end of Gods and men.

I just came to tell you that no matter where you go, no matter how much you try to resist what you are, you *are* chosen. We will need to find a way to keep training you, to develop your connection to the earth's energy so that when the time comes you are ready to do what is necessary."

"You're deluded if you think I want anything to do with you after you spent months lying to me, after you almost *strangled* Grayson because he took your toy away." I scoffed in reply.

Nix growled low and dangerous as he disappeared in a puff of his own smoke, reappearing less than a second later right in front of me. A scream tore its way out of my throat before I could stop it and my own power flew to my hands as they ignited in blue flames instantly — but they went no further as smoke circled my wrists, pinning my hands in place and snuffing out my own power, shoving them back underneath my skin with a force so strong it bordered on painful.

"You do not have the luxury of choosing, I saved you from damnation Raewyn Sandoval, and I can just as easily take it back." His words washed over my face that was inches from his now, his smoke pulling me closer until my palms were flush against his chest. Fear prickled in my mind, but I refused to set it free — choosing instead to lock eyes with the God I'd only heard stories about as a child. This man was the stuff of nightmares and bedtime tales meant to keep children in line. This was the man we'd all grown to fear without seeing — merciless and power incarnate.

Gone was any trace of the façade he'd put on for me in the beginning. The secret was out, I guess there was no need for him to pretend anymore.

Pain tore through me as I struggled against his binds,

my own powers thrashing as they fought to free themselves from his hold and I felt my face twisting into a snarl that matched his own. Calling out to the earth's energy that had followed us into the *iter*, I sought for its help, for it to break these binds Nix had placed on me. Nix must have sensed it coming, as his eyes widened slightly, the swirling storm in them deepening a fraction of a second before I sliced that ancient energy between us like a guillotine, cutting me off from his powers.

Now that I was free, my own shot out – and I tore down every wall inside me as I encouraged them to feed on my emotions. In an instant, flames engulfed every inch of me, breathing in everything my heart and soul had to offer as power solidified in my veins. I set the courtyard alight in blue flames, dousing his world in my power until all he could feel was me, *my power.*

"Try that again and I'll burn more than your imaginary world." I growled, but the voice was not my own, it was deeper, gravelly, as the earth's energy shot through me like a conduit – speaking through me as it relayed its threat to the wide-eyed God before me.

"*I do not heel to anyone, least of all a God.*" It declared – so similar to Nix's words at my Binding Ceremony as they rang through the *iter,* my powers flashing in a bright light as ancient energy pooled inside of me – feeding me more and more power as I felt the power of the *iter* around us and pulled at its threads, stealing control from the Almighty Original God before me, and smiled as I watched Nix flinch at the feel of his power being snatched away from him – shock lining his beautifully cruel features.

And the mighty will fall from their tower… the earth whispered to me, as pieces of the prophecy flew to the forefront of my mind – as if they'd been there all along.

With that, my flames flashed once more, burning the *iter* to nothingness in seconds while Nix remained standing there – watching me burn this world between us to the ground. Shock twisted into a painful regret on his face a second before I closed the door between us, and I smothered the part of me that wanted to reopen it, to see what he might have said if I'd given him the time.

Within seconds it was all gone, and I was floating in my own mind once more. That earthy power lingering comfortably inside of me as I thanked it for helping me. Purring gently, it waited another breath before retreating – though I couldn't help but notice that the part of it that I'd embraced during the Saviour's Feast had grown slightly. Deciding not to dwell on it too much, I tucked my powers back into the recesses of my mind and began calming the raging emotions that were still freely roaming through me.

One by one, I acknowledged the feeling, and set it free on the wind that swam through the carriage as the telltale sounds of birds and snapping branches alerted me to the fact that we were now bordering the edge of the Wooded Village – the place I had lived my whole life.

Sadness clouded my mind once again and I bid it goodbye too – knowing that I would have no room for regret or grief in the Western Paradise.

I would be wife to the Commanding Lord of the West, and my duties would have no room for any such emotion.

Once I opened my eyes, I would have to act as if none of this happened – as if I wasn't the prophesized child the Saviour spoke of all those centuries ago. I would have to pretend that I was not doomed to end the world around me in order to bring back the Saviour and whatever plans he might have for us.

And most of all, I knew without a shadow of doubt, that as long as I was alive, as long as that ancient power chose to work through me and no other God — that Nix would never stop coming after me.

I just had to be ready for him when he did.

RANKINGS

<u>Gods</u>
The Ascended Ones.

<u>0 Sins</u>
Pure, next in line to ascend.

<u>1 Sins</u>
An Enlightened. Sacred Servants.

<u>2-5 Sins</u>
Lords and Ladies. The Noble Society.

<u>6-15 Sins</u>
Labor Workers, Commoners

<u>16-19 Sins</u>
The Radical Soldiers.

<u>20+ Sins</u>
The Unworthy.

<u>Covenant Breakers</u>
Instant Death.

MARKINGS OF SIN

Hands and Wrists:
Sins of Greed and Gluttony

Torso:
Sins of the Sloth – Neglect of one's duties

Face:
Sins of Pride, Vanity, and Ego

Legs:
Sins of Envy and Coveting

Arms:
Sins of Lust and Adultery

Back:
Sins of Wrath and Disobedience

ACKNOWLEDGEMENTS

Thank you for reading the first book in the *Isle of Salvatorem Chronicles*!!! I hope you enjoyed it just as much as I did writing it! I would be silly if I didn't take the time to thank those who put up with me while I was writing the beginning of this series.

To Hayden, who believes in me far more than I ever will – words cannot describe how much strength you give me to achieve my dreams…. Or maybe you will if you ever get this far into the book.

To Sam – I would not have gotten through the editing process and made it to printing without you. You are an incredible Alpha reader/Grammar editor – though if you say the word 'comma' in my presence I will not be held accountable for my actions.

And finally, to the rest of the humans around me who encouraged me to follow my imagination and never give up on myself.

You are the real reason this book is complete.

ABOUT THE AUTHOR

K. Violette has been telling stories since she was old enough to know the difference between imagination and reality (though the lines are still a little blurry). Completing a book was always an inevitability and has finally reassured her mother that she is not too 'away with the faeries' to be an adult.

K. Violette lives in New Zealand with her partner and family. When she is not glued to her laptop, or the latest book obsession, she enjoys wandering over hills with a mantra of 'Stubborn not Fit' – a term her partner repeats to her often as she dreams of cushiony cloud-like beds or escalators that could get her to the nearest DOC Hut for a nap.